NENA

Book One of
The Treasure Huntress Series

ANN BOELTER

Published by Trademark Publishing Company, Colorado.

This book contains an excerpt from the forthcoming book *Fiona* by Ann Boelter. This excerpt has been set for this edition only and may not reflect the final content of the forthcoming edition.

Printed in the United States of America
First Printing: September 2018
ISBN: 978-1-7326565-0-5

Cover Design and Interior Design and Formatting by

www.emtippettsbookdesigns.com

Prologue:

The Creation of The Treasure Huntress

Southern Coastal Norway - Circa 900AD

Sigurd eased open the door and swore under his breath as the telltale squeak still announced his arrival.

"You don't have to creep; I'm awake." Leila's quiet voice came from the shadows.

"Sorry to wake you. I'll fix that tomorrow. I swear."

"It's alright, Sigurd. And you didn't wake me. I heard you talking to someone. Did we have a visitor?"

"No." Sigurd closed the door behind him and made his way through the interior of the small cabin to stoke the fire.

"Who was it?" she asked.

"No one." He evaded her question. "Are you cold? Would you like something to eat?" He moved to the bed and bent over to adjust the furs around her. She seemed paler than usual this morning. His heart twisted.

"No one? I recognized his voice, so I know he's been here before."

"It was just a peddler."

"You never could lie to me, Sigurd, so why would you try now?" Leila chided him.

"The healer says you shouldn't waste so much energy being stubborn," he grumbled.

"The healer says it's my stubbornness that's kept me alive this long," she countered, ignoring his gruffness.

He looked at her fondly and shook his head. "A deal then. You drink a cup of broth and I'll tell you who he was."

"Agreed," she conceded.

Sigurd moved quickly to the pot suspended over the fire before she could change her mind. He gave it a cursory stir with the long wooden ladle, then tested the broth with his finger. It was only lukewarm, but she couldn't drink anything too hot anymore. He picked up a large mug, then set it back and chose a smaller one, not wanting to give her any excuse to back out. Getting her to eat was usually a battle.

He returned to the bed and helped her sit up, then propped furs and blankets behind her for support. He tried not to dwell on how light she had become, or how he could feel her delicate, almost birdlike bones just beneath her skin. He held out the cup and waited before removing his fingers to make sure she had a steady grip on it with both of her hands.

Smiling to himself, he shook his head as he watched her resolutely swallow small sips of broth one after another. She wasn't hungry, but she would finish the cup to get the information she sought. In that moment, Sigurd was actually happy that the stranger had returned, though he'd been infuriated at the time by the man's audacity.

Leila finished the last small swallow and handed him the empty cup.

"Satisfied?" she asked.

He took it and pretended to make a full inspection of the inside.

"You are such an oaf," she said affectionately.

He grinned at her.

"So, who was he?" she asked.

"Truly, he is no one you know. No one I knew until he first came here a couple of weeks ago. His name is Jarl."

"A Jarl? Aren't we so important then, to have warranted two visits from a Jarl."

"Not *a* Jarl," he corrected her. "Jarl is his given name, not his title."

"Strange," she murmured. "Why would someone name their boy that?"

"I don't know. Maybe his brothers were already named King and Prince." He smiled at her, and they shared a quiet laugh.

"And he was here before? What does he want?"

"He wanted me to build him a ship."

"And what did you say?"

"I told him no, of course."

"Because of me."

"No. Because I'm too old, and because I prefer to spend my time with you."

"You are not too old, and if I were not here, you would have agreed," she murmured.

"You are here—and I thank the gods for that every day." He took her hand. It felt cold and thin. He rubbed it between his palms, trying to share some of his warmth.

"He had a nice voice," she commented. "Was he nice?"

"He seemed alright."

"You always said you wanted to build one more ship—that you had some grand ideas."

"That was before..."

"Before I got sick," she finished for him.

He nodded and shrugged.

"I would like for you to build one more ship."

"I cannot leave you."

"You won't have to. We shall build it together."

Sigurd frowned at her and shook his head.

"I'm not delusional. I realize I can no longer be of help with saw or hammer or plane, as I was before, but I can still give you direction and supervision—and I know how much you always liked that." She paused and smiled, waiting for him to react to her last words, but Sigurd did not take the bait at her teasing. He only shook his head no.

"Since I cannot help with tools, and you do not seem to appreciate my offer to oversee the project, I could use every day to summon the goodwill and power of the gods to bless each piece of the craft as you build it. Njord to ensure good weather. Frey for prosperity." Leila could see her words were not swaying him. "And it's spring," she continued. "The weather will soon be fair. You could carry me every day to the building site with my furs and blankets so I could watch as you work. That way we would still be together. You can do what you enjoy, and I will be able to see you create something magnificent. You know I always loved that—and to be in the forest in summer." Her voice trailed away as she imagined it. "The fresh air will be better for me than being cooped up here in the dark," she added.

Sigurd stroked her smooth, slightly graying blond hair back away from her face, not seeing the drawn skin or the dark circles under her eyes—seeing only the beautiful strong young woman he had fallen in love with so many years ago. Even in her suffering, she would put his needs and desires above her own. He knew she felt she was a burden to him. How could she not know she was his life?

"I love you so much," he murmured. "But I cannot do what you ask."

"I want you to do it for me. For us." She smiled a weak smile at him. "So there will be some part of us that will live on after I am gone."

He didn't wish to deny her anything, but he could hardly agree. It would be too much for her. He could easily carry her every day as she had asked, and would do it gladly, but the weather would be fair for a healthy person. She was so thin and weak now, that even in the warm cabin she often took a chill. Being exposed to the cool wind that rolled in off the fjord could kill her. Sigurd could not bear to be the reason that they lost even one minute of the time they had left together. He looked at the stubborn set of her jaw and knew he wasn't going to get off so easily. She had clearly prepared further arguments.

"Even if I were to agree, and that is an *if*, I've already told him I would not. Twice now, in fact."

"You could go find him and tell him you changed your mind—tell him you will make him the greatest ship ever built."

Sigurd shook his head. "First, I would have no idea where to look for him, and second, I will not leave you." His tone brooked no argument.

"Another deal then?" she asked.

His eyes narrowed as he cocked his head. "What did you have in mind?"

"If he returns and asks again, you will agree?"

"I've already refused him twice," he reminded her

"Then you should be safe in making the deal. Though I like my odds; the fact that he returned after you refused him once, tells me he is persistent."

Sigurd thought of the two times he had run the man off. The first time his refusal had been rude and clipped, but this second time, the threats if he were ever to return again had been explicit. The man would not be back. He was safe to make this pact with her. "And if I agree, and he does not come back, that will be the end of it?"

She nodded.

"Very well then. To have peace and quiet on the subject—if he returns, I will agree to build his ship, and you can help me. But only if he returns. I will not seek him out."

Leila smiled a genuine smile and leaned her head back in the furs. "Now it is in the gods' hands."

It was the happiest he had seen her in some time. Sigurd felt only a little guilty knowing it would never come about. It was for the best and would still give her something to look forward to—something other than her sickness to dwell upon. Seeing her in such a good mood lifted his own spirits. He returned to the cooking area to pour himself a cup of mead.

"Would you like some?" he asked her. She was still smiling, lost in thought about their deal, but looked up and shocked him by accepting.

"Yes, I think I would. Just a little."

He reached up to the shelf for the oxhorn cup that was her favorite and blew the dust out of the inside. The intricate silver inlay around the rim accented the natural black and gray swirling pattern of the animal horn. He poured only enough to fill the bottom tip, then carried it to her and took a seat next to the bed.

"A toast?" she asked as she took the cup from him.

"A toast," he agreed.

"To our ship," she said, and raised her oxhorn.

He shook his head and raised his own. "To our ship," he said and touched the rim of his cup to hers before lifting it to his lips. In a practiced move, he raised the horn only slightly, and waited for the liquid to make its way over the curve before flooding toward him. He held a mouthful for a few seconds before swallowing. It had been a long time since he'd drunk anything other than water, and he savored the slightly sweet alcohol bite on his tongue. It was good—better than he remembered. He lifted the oxhorn cup once again to his lips.

A bold knock sounded at the door.

Sigurd sat dumbfounded in his chair and stared at the door, then glanced at Leila. She was trying unsuccessfully not to smile.

"Aren't you going to see who it is?" she asked. "It might be another peddler." Her smile widened.

He stood and moved toward the door, his mind racing. It couldn't be. He had threatened the man's very life less than an hour before. It couldn't be him. But who then? Living so far from the village, he could count on one hand the number of visitors they'd had in the past two years. He paused and took a deep breath before lifting the latch and pulling open the door. The hinge squealed in his ear.

"Apologies, for the intrusion," Jarl said before Sigurd could speak. "I could not leave without making another attempt. You say there are plenty of other shipbuilders, and I know that there are, but you are the best. Everyone knows it. Everyone agrees. They say your ships are far advanced beyond anyone else's. That is what I need, and I will do anything to have one. If it is not more gold, then just tell me what it will take to persuade you. I will pay anything you ask. Anything you need or desire, I will secure it."

Sigurd said nothing, only stared at him.

"Don't be rude, Sigurd," Leila prodded and smiled approvingly at the tall young man who stood outside the door. "Invite him inside and offer him a drink."

Sigurd opened the door a little wider and stepped back, still staring at Jarl with a mixture of incredulity, anger, and confusion.

"Please come in," Leila said. "Pay him no mind. He is more than a little shocked to see you, I think, but he'll find his tongue soon enough. We were just talking about you." Her words jolted Sigurd from his stupor.

"Leila, this is Jarl. Jarl, this is my wife, Leila."

"It is my greatest pleasure to meet you, Jarl. Apologies that I do not get up to greet you. I've been ill."

"No apologies required. Gratitude for inviting me into you home," Jarl said, then turned to Sigurd whose stare now held a mixture of consternation and resignation. "Have you reconsidered my offer then? Will you build it?"

Sigurd didn't answer, only glanced to the bed where Leila awaited his response as eagerly as Jarl did. Dammit. He was trapped. Why had he ever agreed? The deal had been safe. What kind of a man came back after being threatened with death? How had she known? And how could the gods play such a cruel trick on him? He could not build a ship and care for her at the same time. Hell, he doubted he could even build a ship alone; she had always helped him in the past. But he had made a deal with her. He looked back at Jarl.

"I will, but there is an additional price to be paid."

"Name it."

"As you can see my wife needs special care."

"I will hire women from the village to tend to her."

"I can tend to my own wife," Sigurd growled. "But I will need fresh meat delivered regularly and firewood cut."

"Done," Jarl agreed and waited for the next.

"And I will require a sturdy horse to drag the cut trees to my work site."

Jarl nodded. "And I am more than willing to help. I'm strong and good with an axe. I know nothing of shipbuilding, but I'm a quick learner."

"Stop right there." Sigurd interrupted him. "I have no need of your assistance, nor do I want it. You will not come to the building site unless invited. That is not negotiable. If you cannot agree, the deal is off. Are we clear?"

Jarl frowned. "Yes, but..."

"Not negotiable," Sigurd repeated.

Jarl nodded. "Understood."

"You can come here to the cabin and hang the meat in the larder, and I'll show you where to stack the firewood. I'll start when you bring the horse."

"I'll be here tomorrow with the horse and the first half of the payment. So the sum I offered before is acceptable?" Jarl asked.

Sigurd scowled and nodded curtly.

With a quick nod to Leila, Jarl hastened to the doorway before Sigurd could change his mind. The hinges squealed their final taunt at Sigurd as Jarl pulled the door closed behind him.

"You should allow him to help, at least with the felling of the trees and the hauling," Leila said after Jarl had gone.

"Woman," Sigurd threatened, his eyebrows raised.

"Only that part. To find the right trees will take you far from the building site, and I will be left alone while you are gone," she reasoned.

He considered her words. "Perhaps you are right. He can help, but only for that."

Leila watch as Jarl unchained the latest log from the horse's harness. He wore only a leather vest, and the muscles of his upper arms bulged, well defined from the labor. He led the animal for a drink before he tied it up, then walked up the hill to check on her, as he had done after each previous load.

"Is there anything I can get you?" he asked.

"No. I'm fine. But maybe sit and rest for a moment."

"I should get back. Sigurd will be..."

"Sigurd will be inspecting and rejecting the next forty trees before he finds one he likes. You have a moment." She smiled.

He smiled back and nodded before stretching out on the ground next to her furs.

"Things are going well. Sigurd seems to be pleased," she said.

"Pleased is not how I would describe him, but you know him better than I."

"He is gruff now, but soon he will not be able to help but be excited."

"Why did he change his mind?" Jarl asked.

"He didn't. When he told me you had come, I wanted him to build it, but he refused, so we made a deal. Only if you returned a third time would he agree."

Jarl smiled and shook his head. "So that is why he stares at me so strangely. You know, I was well on my way back to the village when I felt compelled to turn around. I had to try again. Thank the gods that I did."

"Yes, thank the gods," she murmured. Leila took in the strong cut of his jaw, his thick wavy chestnut hair, and the traces of the dimples still visible from his smile. He was quite handsome. "Are you married, Jarl?" she asked.

"No."

"Someone special then?"

He shook his head.

"Pity."

"It is for the best. When the ship is finished, I intend to sail her to many foreign lands, and amass a great fortune. Having a wife left at home would only be a worry."

"Perhaps."

"I need to get back. If Sigurd were to discover me sitting here with you..." Jarl shook his head as he stood. "Are you sure there is nothing else I can get you? Did you try the apple cobbler? The woman where I'm staying made it especially for you."

"Yes, it was very good," Leila replied, though she had only taken a small bite earlier to appease him. "But it is not necessary for you to bring such things. I do not eat much."

"All the more reason to continue, until I find what you really like." He smiled at her again before he turned to leave, his dimples giving an odd softness to his chiseled face.

"Jarl," she called after him.

"Yes?"

"There is one thing you could bring me."

"What is it?"

"I would have coal and parchment. I have a few ideas for your ship that I would like to share with Sigurd. If I could sketch them during the day when they are fresh in my mind, I could show him at night."

"I'll bring them tomorrow," Jarl agreed.

Leila loved seeing the spark back in Sigurd's eyes. There was a spring in his step as he moved about the cabin—pouring them each a cup of water while he waited for the latest stew Jarl had brought to warm over the fire. True to his word, after the logs were hauled, he had refused any further help from Jarl and had banished him from the work site—though Jarl more than continued to live up to his end of the bargain. Not only was their shed already filled to the eaves with split firewood and their larder full of a variety of fresh and smoked meats, he always brought something extra, some specially prepared food—a loaf of fresh baked bread, a pie, a pouch of soup or stew. She had pointed Jarl's extra efforts out to Sigurd in hopes that he would ease his restriction and accept Jarl's help, but he had not.

After they finished eating and he had cleared away their dishes, Sigurd showed her his crude sketch of a dragon's head and neck. The skeleton frame of the ship was complete, and he was preparing to start on the bow. "What do you think?" he asked.

"It's nice, but..."

"But what?"

"You have made similar before."

"Yes," he said, as he glanced back at his scribble, his brow furrowed as he tried to identify what she didn't like about it.

"This one needs to be different," she challenged. "Special."

"I could use another animal, I suppose, but which would be better than a dragon?"

"Why not all of them?"

He looked at her blankly, and Leila was sure he must be thinking she had lost her mind.

"I have given this a lot of thought, so hear me out before you speak," she continued. "Why not use the dragon's head, but give it scales on its neck, each the size of a man's hand. On each scale you can carve the symbol of another animal. Then the ship can possess and draw from the power of all, rather than just one."

"That would take meticulous carving," he said frowning, but she could tell he was excited by the idea.

"It would, and you can do it."

"Bear, bull, horse." He started to list under his breath.

"Fish, gull, ram," she added. "I can sketch them for you. Not the whole beast, only a symbol of their greatest strength—their essence, if you will. Like this." She picked up the coal and began to sketch an eagle's head and beak, curved to fit into in the shape of a dragon's scale, then a porcupine's spiny back, a panther's paw print. She looked up at him. He nodded.

"And the dragon's head? I suppose you have an idea for that as well?" he asked.

She smiled and nodded before pulling a completed sketch from the middle of the stack of blank parchments.

Sigurd whistled between his teeth.

Her eyes searched his face. "What are your honest thoughts?" she asked.

"Honestly? I think you overestimate my skill as a carver."

"I do not."

"It is stunning and beautiful, but...well, the detail is too fine. It would not hold up to what a ship must—storms, battles."

"I thought of that, too. What if it was made from ironwood?"

"Ironwood?"

"Only the head."

"That's impossible. It would be hard enough to carve this detail from a soft wood, but ironwood? Impossible," he repeated.

"Not impossible," she disagreed. "Difficult, yes, but not impossible. And if it could be done, would it hold up?"

"Aye," he said, nodding and frowning at the same time. "If it could be done, it would probably outlast the rest of the ship."

She smiled and nodded. "Good."

"I didn't say I would do it," he protested. "There are other concerns."

"Like?"

"Like...like the color of the wood would not match, for one." He stammered, struggling to come up with something. He noticed her smug expression. "But I see you have thought of that as well."

"I had thought to save that for another day; I knew you would be concerned about the carving and thought it might be best not to overwhelm you."

"Spill it, woman. What else do you have planned for my ship?"

"Our ship," Leila corrected him before continuing. "You and I have accumulated much gold over the years, have we not?"

"Aye. Our raiding was always successful."

"We have no children left to leave it to, and have more than we can spend. Certainly more than I will ever spend, and even if your next wife enjoys silks and jewels, there should be plenty to accommodate her."

"Do not say such things. Even in jest. You know there will never be another woman for me. So yes, we have plenty of gold."

"Could some of it be melted down and somehow...wiped or dipped on the head and scales? I'm envisioning it thicker on the head—to make it appear as if it were made from solid gold, then becoming less and less down the neck in the scales, until it melds into the natural golden color of the wood at the bottom in the body of the ship."

"You would dip the wood in gold?"

"I don't know how it would be done—dip, pour...burnish it somehow." She was shocked when he did not reject the idea immediately.

"I shall have to give that consideration. I don't know if it can be done. Perhaps I could consult the blacksmith. He might know a way."

Leila smiled again, suddenly very tired. "Good."

Sigurd carried her to the work area every morning. Once he was satisfied that she was snug and warm in her mound of furs and had water and food within her easy reach, he went to work in the vale below. Sometimes she napped. Sometimes she sketched. Sometimes she sat just watching him.

Leila loved seeing him like this. Happy. Productive. Creative. He was in his element. She would not let her failing body take that from him—would not have him reduced back to the sad man who was watching her die. She fought back the nausea, refusing to succumb to it—pooling all of her strength whenever he would come to show her something or ask her advice. She would not let him see how weak she was becoming. How fast it was happening now. When he returned to his work, she would collapse into her furs, exhausted by the effort.

Sigurd worked like a man possessed. He loved what he did. Loved that they were taking on this enormous project together. He wanted desperately for her to see it to completion. He carried her to see each of the dragon scale carvings up close as he completed them—her visions brought to life with his chisel, blade, and rasp.

Jarl was often waiting for them at the cabin at night. Sigurd didn't like it, but he didn't complain, not after seeing Leila eating the special things Jarl brought for her. She seemed stronger to him. Whether it was the fresh air, or the excitement of the shared project, or the extra food she managed to eat so as not to offend Jarl, he didn't know, but he was not about to risk changing anything.

Sigurd held her up to show her the latest scale he had completed, a raven's eye.

Leila nodded. "It is good. It will give the ship the protection of raven's sight."

"That leaves only one," he said. "Will you show me your idea now?"

She nodded again. "I have the last sketch back at my furs. Can you guess it?" she asked as he carried her back up the hill. "I'll give you a hint. It is the most cunning, powerful animal of all."

"Surely we have not missed an animal with such power," he said "And you say the most powerful? More powerful than the dragon?" He could see she was enjoying stumping him so he continued to guess long past when he had tired of the game.

"Do you give up?" she finally asked.

"Aye," he smiled.

"It is man."

He frowned as he gently positioned her back in her nest of furs. "But men will be on the boat. What have you drawn? A sword? A shield? A battle-axe?" He reached for the sheaf of paper, but she pulled it tight against her breast.

"What is the most important power the gods have bestowed upon man?"

He shook his head as she handed him her last sketch. He balked. "This?" he asked.

"It is love. More powerful than a man's battle-axe. More powerful than his sword or shield. More powerful than even his mind. It is so powerful, it can make him do things his mind tells him are impossible or foolish. It can give him resolve or courage when he has none. It is his greatest strength, and it's the true essence of man—like the raven's eye, or the crab's claw, or the scallop's shell. We have added all the great animal powers to make the ship stealthy, fleet, and strong, in order to protect her and to make her invincible in battle. We have ensured all of those things. Now we must ensure that this ship is blessed not only to find the physical riches that her captain seeks, but to make sure he finds the greatest treasure of all."

Sigurd stared at her, shocked by the profoundness of her thoughts. "I would so easily give up everything I ever had and live the poorest pauper, if it meant spending more time with you." His face twisted with the pain that he was normally able to hide.

She smiled as she touched his cheek. "I know. And I you. Which is why this one is the most important. It will capture the essence of that love, our love, and be the most powerful blessing of all."

He nodded and brushed his eyes.

"And the position of the last scale?" she asked. "Where is it?"

"Where you requested—just above the waterline on the starboard side."

"Over the dragon's heart," they said simultaneously, sharing a smile.

"I'm not sure what Jarl will have to say about it." Sigurd frowned.

"If you do not think he will want it, or is ready for it, then don't tell him."

Sigurd glanced back at the sketch of the two figures entwined in a loving embrace. No details, easy to carve, but so clear, as were all her drawings, capturing and expressing the pure essence of whatever it was she had drawn.

"I will do it."

"And if Jarl notices it and complains, then tell him you were only honoring the fancy of a dying woman. He seems very serious. Driven. I don't think he would understand or appreciate the truth. It will be our secret. And Sigurd, I have one last request, if you agree. We did not build this ship for coin. Jarl has paid enough already with his deposit to more than cover any costs. Do not accept the remainder of what is owed. Instead, tell him when he no longer feels the drive to seek riches, he must give the ship to someone else. Someone worthy. No coin or favor is to ever change hands for her. He must swear to that and agree to make subsequent captains swear to it as well. That way she will always end up in the hands of someone deserving."

"I like that," Sigurd agreed. "The idea that something we created will go on forever, enriching the lives of good men."

"And women," she added.

"And women," he agreed, then paused. "I have finally thought of a name for her," he said quietly. "What do you think of The Treasure Huntress?"

Leila smiled and nodded. "It is a good name. May she provide her captain with all the physical riches he desires until she is able to seek out the true desire of his heart."

She was weakening. For the past weeks Sigurd had known and had focused on finishing the ship's bow. She had fought so hard against the coming of the end, as she had fought by his side when they were younger. She was the strongest person he had ever known, but she would not live to see the ship complete—would not take a short cruise around the fjord as he had envisioned. He knew that now. Thankfully, she would at least see the dragon finished.

"I'm very tired today," she murmured after he woke her to tell her it was done.

"We'll go home early," he said as he wrapped her in her favorite fox fur blanket before picking her up. "For a while you were getting better. You seemed stronger. You will again. You just need to eat more," he said as he carried her down the hill for her inspection.

"I felt it, too, but it was not to last. I think it was like the last glorious blaze the suns sends forth every evening before it gives in to the night."

"Don't say such things," Sigurd admonished her.

Leila turned to look at the ship as they approached. "It is perfect." She smiled wanly as her finger traced over the gilded carving of the couple. "Absolutely perfect, Sigurd. I'm so proud of you."

Sigurd lifted her higher for her to view all the symbols, from the golden dragon's head down to the last of the gold-dusted scales. It was not difficult. She weighed nothing anymore; her body had been ravaged from its long fight.

"I am so happy. I just want you to know, you have made me happy my entire life—and now with this.... It is perfect." She wiped a tear from his cheek. "Please don't cry. Do not be saddened when I go. It will be soon now."

"Don't say that." Sigurd shook his head.

"Shush. I must and you know it. Promise me you will not be sad when I am gone—that you will think of our time together with happiness."

"I cannot make that promise."

She smiled again. "Then promise me you will try."

He nodded, unable to speak.

She glanced back at the ship. "Finish her when I am gone. Finish her with all the care you have put into her so far. It will help you through the hardest times. And know that you will not be alone. I will still be here watching and helping you."

"We should get back to the cabin. It's already getting cold." He changed the subject, heartsick at the path it had taken.

She nodded, and he began the trek home.

"Would you like some fish roe?" he asked after he'd gotten her settled into the bed. "I see Jarl caught a fat one in the fish trap today, and there is still some of the fresh butter he brought before." It was one of her favorites—one of the few things she had eaten lately. "I could fry it for you."

"Yes, that would be nice."

He brought her the plate. "Here you go. This will make you feel better. You need to keep up your strength."

"Gratitude, Sigurd. Just set it there. I'll rest a bit and then I'll eat it." Her voice trailed away.

Something in her tone disturbed him—something more than her normal physical weariness. Sigurd pulled his chair closer to the bed and took her hand. She did not awaken. Tears flowed silently down his cheeks as he sat watching her breathe—slow peaceful breaths.

As she drew one longer staggered breath and exhaled, he knew it was her last. The skin and muscles of her face relaxed and her hand went limp in his grasp. Her body was finally free from the fight it had kept up for so long. Sigurd wiped the tears from his face as he stared at the form of the woman he had loved his entire life. He would do his best to honor her wishes. He owed her that and so much more. To fight through his grief to do so would be only a fraction of the fight she had put up to stay with him.

Jarl saw the huge cloud of dark smoke and started to run; that was no cooking fire. Gasping for air, he burst into the small clearing surrounding Sigurd and Leila's cabin. Everything appeared normal. He glanced toward the work-site. No smoke was coming from that direction; the source was somewhere near the fjord. Relieved, he paused briefly to catch his breath, then walked to the cabin and knocked on the door—softly at first, then harder. When there was no response, he opened it and peered inside. The cabin was empty, and while that was not unusual during the day, something was off. Jarl scanned the small space again. The copper pot that always hung over the fire was missing, as was the honey crock he'd brought for Leila when he had discovered her sweet tooth.

Jarl stepped back outside and followed the now-diminished smoke spire to the fjord. There he found Sigurd sitting on a rock staring out over the calm open water. Traces of smoke lingered over its smooth-as-silk surface. Jarl knew only one thing burned on open water. A burial ship. He sat down next to Sigurd without speaking.

"She loved the water on days like this," Sigurd said. "The gods honor her with it today. She had a special connection to the gods—always did. Whatever her desire—other than her health. She thought I hadn't been building any ships since she took ill, but when I realized she would die, I built one for her. I never told her. I didn't want her to think I was ready for her to leave me. I didn't want her to give up." He glanced at the rabbits Jarl had on a tether, then at the pouch that he knew would contain some type of fresh stew. "There will be no need for you to continue to bring food."

"A deal is a deal," Jarl disagreed.

"I will finish your ship, have no fear."

"I do not fear that. I know Leila would haunt you if you did not."

Sigurd looked at him at that and smiled a tired smile. "Aye, that she would."

Jarl nodded. "As she would me if I left you to your own devices to feed yourself."

Sigurd only nodded his acceptance and looked back out over the water.

"I have need of your assistance tomorrow," Sigurd said, his voice surprising Jarl as he arrived at the cabin. Never once during the long winter had he ever found Sigurd at home during the day. "She is ready to launch. I had thought to try to do it myself, but today I could hear Leila's words as clearly as if she'd been standing next to me. 'Don't be such a stubborn oaf,' she said, and I suppose she's right. Be here at dawn."

"I will," Jarl said, barely able to control his excitement.

Sigurd nodded and walked inside the cabin, closing the door behind him.

"I have never seen anything like this," Jarl murmured as he turned to Sigurd in wonder. "The bear, the bull." He turned back to the ship and his fingers traced over the symbols.

Sigurd watched him closely as Jarl continued to examine the scales. He was close to the lovers now. They were right in front of him, over the heart of the dragon as Leila had wanted, but Jarl continued past them, noting the details of all the others—the eagle, the fox, the horse. It was as if the lovers were invisible to him.

Sigurd smiled. Leila had been right. Jarl was not yet ready to see it. But he would in time. Of that Sigurd was certain; Leila would see to it. When she put her mind to something, no man would be able to resist her for long. "She is The Treasure Huntress," he said.

Jarl nodded. "She's perfect, as is her name. I'm only sorry Leila could not see it."

"She saw the most important parts, and I will describe the last to her when I see her again in Valhalla." He noted Jarl's doubtful gaze. "She is in Valhalla," Sigurd said with conviction. "You knew her only as gentle and weak, but when she was younger, she was fierce—a shield-maiden with no equal. Many an opponent fell to her blade." He smiled seeing the memory. "Men were afraid of her, but to me, she was the most perfect woman the gods had ever created. I thought to have no chance with her, of course. I was a decent fighter, but not a great one. My skill lay, well...," he glanced at the ship, "in other forms. But the gods must have taken pity on me, or maybe they knew that by giving me a woman so far beyond my reach that I would cherish her with the proper honor she deserved. That is the only reason I can possibly think of that an average man like me was chosen by a warrior goddess like her. And she was a warrior. Even in the end, she fought as no other could."

Sigurd shook his head. "But I digress. Building this ship made her last days—our last days so much better, and I thank you for that. She thanked you for that. You gave us something far more valuable than your coin, so you owe nothing further. Leila wanted you to..." He paused as he searched for words. "She wanted you to get more than you bargained for," Sigurd finished with a strange enigmatic smile.

"Even at the original sum, I will have already received that. This ship is easily worth ten times what we agreed," Jarl protested. "I do not wish to start off with bad luck from a cheated purchase."

"It is I who have changed the sum so there is no cheating, and it will not be without cost to you. There is an additional stipulation. When you lose the desire to seek further riches, you must gift the ship to someone else. Someone worthy of her. She cannot sit idle and forgotten at a dock, nor can she ever be sold. She must forever serve a captain who is driven to hunt for true enrichment—in whatever form that takes for him." He smiled the strange smile again. "This edict must be passed down to each captain who follows you. You must swear to it, as must they. It is not negotiable."

"I swear. But I would swear it, and still pay you the agreed upon sum."

Sigurd shook his head. "It is what Leila wanted."

Jarl nodded. "Very well, but know that it is only under protest that I accept." Jarl paused, his eyes drawn back to the ship's sleek lines. "What will you do now? Begin another? I must say when people see her, they will flock to your doorstep."

"I will never build another ship."

"You say that now, but when you are over..."

"Jarl, a man hones his craft during his lifetime. Every ship I have ever built was an improvement on the last." He looked at The Treasure Huntress. "I could never build another ship even close to her equal—much less improve upon her. When you realize you have reached your zenith, it is time to quit. There will be no satisfaction and no joy in building something inferior. And The Huntress...." His voice trailed away momentarily. "With Leila, I built something that exceeded my wildest fantasy. Anything else would be a disappointment. I have hung up my tools for good, and there they will stay."

Jarl wanted to argue—to point out that even what Sigurd considered to be his inferior boats were far superior to any others. It was why he had come—why he had refused to take no for an answer. But he could see in Sigurd's eyes there would be no point. His decision was made. Perhaps when his grief had passed, he might change his mind.

"Others will still come...as I did."

Sigurd shrugged. "They will be turned away. Leila was the only reason I accepted your offer. She is gone now, and the next will not be met with such favor or kindness. You can tell that to any man who asks you. They will not be welcome here."

"As you wish. But I fear they will not believe me. They will think I am only trying to discourage them to not have competition."

Sigurd wasn't listening. He was staring at the ship. "I thought it would be impossible for me to see her go," he murmured.

For a moment Jarl wasn't sure which *her* Sigurd was referring to—the ship or his late wife. He realized it was probably both.

"Leila put every last bit of her strength into this ship, and I know she's a part of it. I must admit that after she died, I wasn't sure I could do it—to give up that last piece of her, but...," He smiled a small smile. "It is not so painful as I imagined it would be. I understand now. Her spirit is in there, and she wants to be free. She was trapped in her weak body for so long, but now she's strong again. She'll protect it, you know—and you and the captains who follow you. Of that I have no doubt. She was a ferocious fighter...and an amazing lover." His voice trailed off. "But a word of advice—don't ever cross her. You do not wish to feel her wrath."

Jarl nodded. "I shall return tomorrow with a crew to sail her."

"There's no need. The two of us can take her to Grimstad. I'll return home from there on foot," Sigurd said as he jumped from the dock onto the deck of the boat.

"But we have to pass through the rocks outside the harbor," Jarl protested. "The channel is narrow there, and the winds unpredictable. Two men cannot maneuver a ship this large. I would hate to have her damaged—or worse."

Sigurd only looked at him as if his concerns were foolish. "She's large, but she'll handle nimble like a fox. You'll see. I know the ship, Jarl, and you must learn to trust her."

Jarl was torn. He did not wish to deny Sigurd, but the ship was far too valuable to risk on what seemed like a whim. He glanced up at the golden dragon's eye and swore that it was measuring him. He shook his head and took a deep breath.

"Very well then," he muttered. "Off to Grimstad." As Jarl stepped on board, he had the odd impression that he and Sigurd were, in fact, not alone. He dashed the thoughts from his mind. All that talk of Leila's spirit had gotten inside his head.

"You take the helm," Sigurd said as he moved quickly around the ship, tightening lines, loosening sails. "She's yours now."

Jarl took hold of the rudder. It felt warm to the touch. From the sun, he chastised himself—nothing more. Yet still he could not shake the feeling the ship had a spirit of its own—not necessarily the spirit of Leila as Sigurd had claimed, but a spirit all the same. Jarl shook his head and gripped the handle tighter. It felt good in his hand.

"To our first of many adventures, Huntress," he murmured. "May the gods bless us with good fortune." At his words, the front smaller sail dropped under Sigurd's masterful care, catching a breeze that Jarl swore had not been there before. The great ship glided out into the fjord.

Chapter 1

South of the Caspian Sea - Circa 905 AD

Nena pulled her long thick braid over her bare shoulder, thankful she had insisted on the simple hairstyle and plain leather dress of a Dor female warrior instead of more formal garb. She glanced to the opposite end of the curved dais and the host chief's wife. Though the sun was far from high, the sweat trickling down the woman's fleshy neck was clear indication she was already sweltering under her silk robes and bejeweled, tiered hair.

Her scrutiny of the woman was interrupted by the final arrivals. The host chief, with Nena's father and younger brother, Ruga, close behind, climbed to their positions of honor in the center of the dais. Though younger than her father by several years, the host chief strained to hold in his paunch as he walked. Disturbed, Nena looked away from him. The wife she could possibly understand, but how did a man allow himself to get so soft? Ruga split off from behind the two older men and took the seat next to her without saying a word.

Nena took a deep breath and looked out over the assembled crowd. It seemed as if the entire host tribe was pressed against the colored flags around the tournament area, each anxious to catch a glimpse of her. She tried to ignore them. Their collective tension only added to her own nervous anticipation, and she could not let that show—could not disgrace herself or her family in front of these people by showing emotion. She knew the one question that was on the crowd's singular mind. It was the same question on hers and probably her father's and brother's as well. The question that had prompted their whole journey here to the Eastern Plains. Would she choose today?

It wasn't as if it were really her choice. The gods had already chosen, and through her would reveal their decision when they were ready. It was one of the few responsibilities the gods bestowed upon women. If all today failed to move her, no one in this village would blame her, though they would be disappointed; a marriage alliance with her Teclan tribe, the most powerful of the Dor, would ensure their future prosperity.

Part of her hoped she did choose, that she could choose. That a man here would stand out above all others, and she would finally proceed with the next step in life—becoming a wife and sharing a man's bed. At nineteen summers, she was well past the normal age of choosing, though there were no set rules on age, and no one questioned the gods' will.

An equally large part of her wanted never to choose. If the gods revealed a man for her here today, then she would be forced to say good-bye to the rugged mountains of her birth and take up life here as a migratory flat-lands dweller. She would also say good-bye to her days as a warrior, never again to feel a strong horse beneath her and the wind in her face. This part of her could not imagine being content to languish in these flat grasslands, with a baby on her hip, while the warriors rode away to glory.

That's because the gods have not yet chosen for you. Once they do, you will no longer yearn for such things.

Nena's reassuring inner voice was interrupted by the deep pulsing beat of the tribal drums. Her blood stirred, her bounding heartbeat answering the rumble call on a primal level.

The tournament had begun.

The first warriors to enter were those available to be chosen. Twelve in all, they walked in single file and stood before her, their oiled, bronze bodies glistening in the sun. Nena's eyes took in every detail. These would be the best the village had to offer—the smartest, the strongest, the most successful. Black tattoos, chronicling their victories and achievements, covered their arms. Though she was not close enough to read the specifics in the intricate symbols, the extensiveness of the marks told her who was most accomplished.

She couldn't help but be disappointed. Even the most decorated here paled in comparison to the warriors of her own tribe. Her younger brother's marks already reached his shoulders, and her father's tattoos extended far beyond his arms, covering his entire torso front and back. But that was to be expected, she reminded herself. No other tribe equaled the Teclan in battle.

After a nod from the host chief, an ancient looking man with a hunched back and long white braid that reached almost to the ground, stepped forward from the far side of the dais. His golden robe had no adornments other than a scarlet wheat ear, the symbol of the Eastern Plains tribe, emblazoned across the front. Nena knew the red was not dye, nor paint. The edges were already turning darker. It would be fresh blood from a recent sacrifice to the gods to invite their favor. The meat from the animal would later be shared with the tribe in the great feast at the tournament's conclusion. The elderly herald limped to the center of the line of men, then turned to face the dais before announcing the name and family lineage of the first candidate.

One by one, after their names were called, the warriors approached the dais with a single gift, in hopes of capturing her eye and impressing the gods even before the tournament began. Nena bowed her head respectfully as she accepted each gift, then laid it beside her, trying to show no apparent favor. It was easy to do. She had no interest in the gifts, only the men. She evaluated each one closely, rejecting them in her mind for some reason or another almost immediately. Too short. Too soft. Beady unintelligent eyes. The worst were those who seemed hesitant and approached the dais with trepidation. She understood that her tribe was feared, but still it baffled her. How could a man possibly hope to be chosen if he was intimidated? The gods would never choose a weak man for her mate.

After delivering their gifts, the men returned to the line and stood, legs apart and arms crossed, while the next approached. Most of the gifts were gems—some large, some rare. As a Teclan, Nena already had more jewels than she could ever spend. Generations of successful raiding and hording had seen to that. But as each precious gem was unwrapped and displayed for her, she understood that these people had no such caches, and far different values because of it.

Her mind drifted. Many of the jewels in her tribe could have easily come from these people in earlier raids. She wondered if they ever gave thought to revenge. Now would be the best and probably only opportunity for them to have it. Her group totaled only nine: herself, her father, Ruga and their six escort warriors—and they were far from the fortifications of their mountain stronghold. Even as she thought it, Nena knew their safety was never in doubt.

Her older brother, Lothor, remained at home with the rest of the Teclan tribe. Lothor, whose growing reputation of being even more formidable than their father, Meln, was well-deserved. Should any tragedy befall them on this trip, Lothor wouldn't hesitate to hunt down and kill every person even remotely associated with the deed. Men, women, children—none would be spared. The Eastern Plains tribe would cease to exist. Their vengeance would be brief.

The announcement by the herald of the second to the last candidate, Dorac, pulled Nena's focus back to the present. She recognized the name. He was one of the favorites of the local women who had helped to bathe and prepare her that morning. She could see why. He cut a strong figure. Taller than most by a full hand's width, his muscles bulged and gleamed in the sunlight. Where many of the men had seemed nervous approaching her, Dorac swaggered to the dais with a large bundle. He pulled the ties that bound the outer wrap, then paused before slowly peeling back the cover to reveal the tiger skin.

Murmurs rippled through the crowd at the extravagance of his gift. From the corner of her eye, Nena saw her father stiffen; even he was impressed. They had heard of the tiger skin in their distant mountain home, but none of her people had ever beheld it—the striped hide of the great cat larger than two men. Dorac stood basking in the furor his gift had caused.

It was a bold move, but one Nena found arrogant. The tiger hide was probably the single most valuable possession in this village. She knew no man would give such a gift unless he had every expectation of owning it again. He was staking his claim—giving her the tiger for holding until it was his again by marriage.

She sniffed, annoyed by his presumptuousness, and took the hide, setting it aside with no more care than the carved antler dagger she had received before it. Dorac's eyes narrowed with suppressed fury. Nena dismissed him with a curt nod and looked to the next. Instead of returning to the line of warriors, Dorac took up a position near her, standing on the side of the dais, as if his being chosen were a foregone conclusion. Though Nena's face remained impassive, inside she churned. A great warrior he might very well be, but she prayed the gods had chosen another for her. Thankfully she felt no stirring to choose him—in fact, felt nothing other than irritation toward him.

"I do not care for Dorac, Sister," her younger brother leaned over and whispered in her ear. "Hopefully I can defeat him early in the matches so the gods will not consider him for you." It was a sharp contrast to his earlier boasts of certain tournament victory during their long ride here. His confidence was not near so high after seeing his latest opponent. He leaned closer. "And it would be a terrible thing if your drink were to spill on the tiger." His eyes laughed, though his face remained as expressionless as her own.

Nena fought back a smile; she dare not encourage him. Her brother was irreverent! "You should not speak of such things," Nena whispered, afraid for him, though she knew she should have been angry and disciplined him herself.

Men, even powerful men, were forbidden to interfere with a choosing. To do so risked angering the gods. Thankfully her father had not overheard him.

Rondor was the last to approach. His name was probably the second most mentioned by the local women. He was nearly as tall as Dorac, but his muscles rippled instead of bulged beneath his oiled dark skin. His brown eyes were warm and intelligent, and he moved with a confident, athletic grace that appealed to her—the opposite of Dorac's brash swagger.

His gift was a plush sheepskin warrior saddle trimmed in the black and white hide of the small, striped horses that roamed the distant wild lands far to the south. The animals were too slow and disagreeable to ride, but their uniquely-colored hide and meat were prized. Nena lingered over Rondor's saddle, admiring the craftsmanship in the ivory handhold and the well-placed loops to carry her provisions and weapons. Other than the antler dagger, it was the only gift that recognized her own significant achievements as a warrior.

The extra time she spent on the gift did not go unnoticed. Nena felt the heat of Dorac's baleful glare on her cheek. Rondor must have felt it, too, because he turned and locked eyes with Dorac. The air between the two men seemed to crackle with intensity—neither giving quarter until the chief ended the standoff by signaling for the tournament to begin.

The remaining competitors, including Nena's brother, entered the arena, and dull wooden tournament weapons were distributed among them. As warriors of all ages prepared for their matches, Nena found herself watching and comparing Rondor and Dorac. Rondor could win the tournament, of that she was becoming more confident. The women had said he was the most skilled at horse, and his agility would lend itself to sword and knife. Dorac would dominate in the battle-axe, a heavy weapon, and possibly the spear, but those were only two events.

And what if Rondor did win? Would she choose him? She definitely preferred that he win, but couldn't say she felt any more than that. The women from her village had told her she would know; there would be no uncertainty. Maybe the gods were waiting until after the tournament was over....

Matches were met with shrieks and wails as favored contestants won and lost. Gambling was a favorite past time of all Dor, and the Eastern Plains tribe was no exception. Many gems, furs, and even horses would change hands this day, and they were not quiet in expressing how they felt about it. By mid-afternoon, Nena's brother was still undefeated, as were Dorac and Rondor.

Currently, all attention was focused on a particularly heated battle between Dorac and a wisp of a man who refused to be beaten. The crowd screamed with glee as the lopsided match continued well past all expectations. In his eagerness to dispatch his unworthy opponent, a frustrated and embarrassed Dorac made mistakes, each one only serving to keep the smaller man in it.

Dorac closed on his opponent again, seeming to finally have him cornered. In a bold move, the smaller man rushed forward and scurried beneath Dorac's outstretched arms. He tapped Dorac on the back with his tournament sword, adding insult and gaining a point. The crowd's screams swelled to a roar. Nena laughed out loud and looked to her father. He was smiling, too. The slight man's status would climb considerably this day.

When she looked back, the match had turned to utter confusion. People were spilling into the arena, interfering with the contestants. It was unheard of. No one interrupted a match, no matter who the contestants were, or how well or poorly they were doing. What were they thinking? From her raised seat on the dais, it soon became clear that the front observers were being pushed forward by the surging crowd behind. She assumed people from the rear were trying to gain a better view of the match. Until she saw their faces. The desperate terror in their eyes.

It was then that she saw them.

Northmen! Huge, hairy man-beasts, with pale skin and shaggy beards. Their round, painted shields were unmistakable. They advanced from behind, hacking down the villagers in a great wave of death, forming a nearly impenetrable wall between the unarmed Dor and the weapons they had left in their tents. The dull tournament weapons, though present in abundance, were useless.

Nena pawed through her pile of gifts and grabbed the antler dagger. The gift that had seemed so plain in comparison to all the others, was now by far the most valuable. Slipping it under her sash, she dropped from the back of the dais. After a quick look to verify the path was clear, she crouched and sprinted for the guest tents that fortunately had been set up on the opposite side of the tournament grounds from the attack.

Making it to her tent unnoticed, she slipped inside and grabbed her sword. The thin, curved blade was smaller than a man's and appeared almost delicate by comparison, but in her hands it was every bit as deadly. She ripped through her travel packs, pulled out her spear, then dashed back outside.

Smoke and the unmistakable metallic smell of blood assaulted her nostrils. Screams of the panicked and dying filled the air. The Northmen seemed to be everywhere. Some on horseback, most on foot. The riders had a huge advantage over the terrorized crowd—an advantage they pressed with deadly disregard. Nena palmed her spear—weighing it, balancing it, feeling it; it was the only weapon long enough to overcome their height advantage.

A rider bore down on her, swinging his axe. Nena stood her ground in the horse's path. The man grinned, his teeth barely visible through his thick, matted beard and mustache. At the last second, she dropped and rolled, planting the base of her spear in the ground and aiming its metal tip at the rider's chest. She felt the wooden shaft stiffen upon impact, then flex. She prayed it would hold. The Northman's hardened leather body armor resisted but was no match for the direct strike. As the horse's momentum carried him forward, the razor sharp tip of her spear pierced through the thick leather plate plunging deep into his chest—ultimately driving him from the back of the horse and sending his body crashing to the ground.

Nena was on him in an instant, yanking the spear from his dying body before turning to find the next. She longed for her mare, Nightwing. With a horse, she could kill them by the score, not wait for them to come to her. She glanced toward the corrals. The gate hung open. The Northmen had stampeded their horses to keep them on foot. Nena caught a glimpse of the thundering herd on the edge of the village and whistled in the direction of the swirling flow of horseflesh—a high piercing trill that hung on the wind. For a moment she thought she heard her mare's whinny reply but couldn't be sure. Would it work? Would the horse brave the melee and come to her? She had only taught the animal the simple trick to entertain children in her village, not for anything like this. Nena whistled again and saw the black mare break free of the herd and turn in her direction. Her heart soared.

While she waited for the horse, Nena looked for her father and brother in the smoke and chaos, then reprimanded herself. If her father could have heard her thoughts, his punishment would have been swift and severe. *"Never think about your fellow warriors in battle. It is the surest way to get them killed. All of your focus must be on killing the enemy until there is none left to kill. A single foe you miss while distracted looking for friends or family could be the one who kills them. Never forget that."* Her father's words had been drilled into her from the time she could first hold a sword, but she had never been so pressed to heed them before.

The mare, her eyes wild with fright, slid to a stop next to her. Nena grabbed a handful of mane and swung aboard bareback, guiding the animal forward with her knees. There was no time to soothe her. She had enemy to kill.

The first five Northmen never even saw her. Using Nightwing's speed and agility, she rode them down from behind while they were preoccupied with attacks of their own. She was in pursuit of another now, and leaned low over the mare's neck to better corner around a tent. She never saw the Northern warrior who wielded the great axe—only the flash of bloodied silver. Nena felt as much as heard the sickening solid thunk as the axe head buried deep into the front of her mare. Felt as much as heard Nightwing's bloodcurdling scream.

As the front of the horse collapsed from beneath her, Nena instinctively loosened her grip with her legs so as not to be taken to the ground and crushed beneath the wounded animal. Nightwing cartwheeled. Nena was catapulted through the air. She curled her body and hit the ground in a rolling ball, bouncing to her feet to face her attacker. Her spear lay in two pieces on the ground midway between them. Her sword had landed near her feet, but she could see the blade was broken even as she reached for the hilt. Picking it up with her left hand, she raised the jagged broken blade toward him. He looked at it and smiled.

That was the reaction she had hoped for. Quick as a striking snake, she pulled the antler dagger from her sash with her right hand and sent it winging through the air. Nena watched with satisfaction as the knife buried itself in his left eye socket. He buckled to his knees, swayed, then collapsed on his side in the dirt. She ran to retrieve the dagger, then raced to Nightwing's side. The horse remained on the ground, unable to rise, thrashing and screaming in agony.

A sob caught in Nena's throat at the sight of Nightwing's nearly-severed front leg dangling from her body and the great pool of blood forming beneath her. She covered the mare's eye with her hand, hoping to soothe her one last time. The horse responded to her touch and stilled. "Go and be free with the horses in the sky. I will see you again one day, and we will ride together once more," Nena murmured. With tears streaming down her cheeks, she drew her dagger across the mare's throat.

Her own spear and sword useless, Nena picked up the dead man's sword. It was too big for her to wield for any length of time, but it would have to do until she could find another. She turned toward the sounds of the loudest cries. Channeling her grief and rage, she forced her mind to focus on one directive.

Kill the enemy until there are none left to kill.

The last of the sun had just dipped below the horizon when Jarl reined in his stallion. The mahogany bay tossed his head impatiently, but obeyed. The fighting was all but over; only a few native warriors remained to be subdued. Jarl remained astride to watch one of the final skirmishes playing out before him—his eyes taking in the woman with long bronze legs wielding a sword too big for her. Two of his men circled her warily, while a third—a mountain of a man with flame-colored hair, sat off to one side on a bundle of furs. Jarl easily recognized his second in command, Tryggr, and made a quick concerned assessment of his injuries. Tryggr held one hand pressed tightly against the side of his head. Fresh bright blood seeped from between his fingers and down into his thick red beard.

Jarl dismissed it. The blood was not pulsing, and head wounds always bled worse than others. Far more concerning was the deep battle-axe cleft that had penetrated Tryggr's leather chest plate and another gash on the side of his left thigh. Both of them were ugly wounds, but they hadn't come from the woman. The blood was darker. Older. Jarl took only a second to appreciate the significance. Clearly Tryggr had felt well enough with them to attack her, so maybe they were not as bad as they looked.

"No sense standing there fretting over me like an old woman, Jarl. I'm fine," Tryggr said. "I'm bleeding like a stuck pig, but it's a long way from my heart. And when the day comes that a woman can take me in open battle, then I'll expect you to just put me out of my misery anyway. Today is not that day."

Relief flooded through him, mixing with Jarl's frustration and anger. The battle had already proven far more costly than expected. This was to have been an easy victory according to his scouts. A rich, basically unarmed village preoccupied with some celebration, but from the fighting he'd seen and the earliest casualty tallies, Jarl now knew that was far from the case.

He turned back to the woman. Her hair had come unbraided and cascaded around her shoulders and down her back in a tangled mane of brown so dark it was almost black. She wore the common dress of the Dor female warriors, a supple tan hide tied around her neck, the thigh-length skirt slit on both sides. Her eyes were also typical Dor, large and dark and almond shaped. He glanced at the small black tattoos on her upper arms. He knew each signified something specific to other Dor, but the symbols were foreign to him, and he had no recognition of their meaning. There was blood on her, too, but upon closer inspection, it did not appear to be hers, and there was far too much of it for it all to have come from Tryggr.

"What's going on here?" Jarl asked the other two men, though their intent was clear. They were the victors. They had fought, bled, lost brothers, and now the flame of battle fever would be extinguished with a woman. "Have my men grown so soft that it requires three of them to conquer a single maid?"

The two men stopped and acknowledged him with a salute. They actually seemed to welcome the respite. "She ain't no ordinary wench, sir. She fights like a she-devil," one said.

Jarl shook his head to indicate how foolish he found their words.

"Look at Tryggr." They pointed to his burly, second in command as further proof. "She took his own dagger away from him and cut off his ear."

"Only part of my ear," the red-haired giant protested.

"I thought the intent was for you to do the poking with your other dagger, my friend." Jarl addressed his bloodied second. "Or did you decide to play the woman this time?"

"You're funny," Tryggr responded. The jest, coming from any other man, would have been poorly received, but from Jarl it only brought a tired smile. They had fought many battles together and consumed much bonding wine after. "She's mine by first claim, but I forgo it and offer her to you, if you think you can get the job done." Tryggr slid sideways and patted the spot next to him.

"But I'll save you a place here, where you can rest when she cuts off some part of you. Hopefully it will only be something as unimportant as your ear."

Jarl looked back to the woman. She was stunning in a savage way. A way that very much appealed to him. His own blood ran hot from the battle, though he never participated in the raping. Willing women suited him much better, and he would have plenty of opportunity to work out his tensions when he returned to camp. There was no shortage of women there. But this one...this one was different. Standing there so defiant, so raw, so beautiful. Jarl felt his blood do more than stir as his eyes took in every inch of her. He swung a leg over the neck of his horse and dropped lightly to the ground.

"You should go find the healer and have your wounds tended to, my friend," he said to Tryggr as he passed by.

"There'll be time for that once I'm sure I won't be needing to haul you there as well. My coin is on that we'll soon both be needing to see the healer together," Tryggr retorted.

The two other men hooted, thrilled that their leader was joining the fun. "You're in for it now, sweetheart," one said, as they both withdrew a few paces.

"Careful, Jarl," Tryggr warned. "The boys weren't lying about her, and she still has my dagger somewhere."

From the quality of his horse and the way the others deferred to him, Nena could tell this one was of higher rank. That fact appealed to her. Rank did not affect how they bled or how they died, and better she could kill one of importance than these last two dogs.

She examined him, looking for a weakness to exploit. Unlike the other Northmen with their thick beards and shaggy hair, this one was clean-shaven and his brown wavy hair was cut short on the sides. He was taller than the last two she'd been fighting, but not near so large as the red-haired giant whose ear she had trimmed. Most concerning to her was that, despite his size, he was balanced and sure on his feet. The others, even the smaller ones, were typical Northmen, heavy lumbering movers. Their slow reactions had given her the edge she needed to combat their size advantage. She would have no such luck with this one; he moved like a warrior.

Jarl saw her fingers tighten around the hilt of the sword. Judging from the ample distance his men had given her, he knew she must be able to handle it. He feinted to the right and the blade slashed the air where he should have been. Jarl smiled to himself, impressed. Blade too large or not, she was strong and quick. For many minutes he moved around her, measuring her responses, his weapons remaining sheathed.

Without warning she charged him, her blade whipping through the air in a blur of death. The ferocity and swiftness of her attack caught him off guard. Jarl pulled his own sword, barely managing to withdraw it in time to deflect her first strike. Her blows continued to come with blinding speed, keeping him hard-pressed and off balance. It was all he could do to parry each one as he stumbled backwards.

Ultimately, her earlier battles and the weight of the weapon began to take their toll. Jarl could see her movements, though still fast, were becoming more labored. He went on the offensive. After pushing her back with multiple small strikes, he gripped the hilt of his sword with both hands and brought it down in one crushing blow. Steel clashed against steel. Her body shuddered under the impact. Jarl fully expected to see the blade fly from her hands, but somehow— incredibly—she managed to hold onto it, though the force of the concussion sent her staggering. As she tried to recover and bring the sword back around to face him, Jarl dropped to the ground and kicked her just below one ankle— driving it into her other leg, and knocking her feet out from under her. He lunged for her as she fell, trying to trap her with his body, but she rolled away and jumped to her feet. Jarl did the same. They stood facing each other, both breathing hard.

Jarl caught a glimpse of the outline of Tryggr's dagger under the cloth belt of her waist. He made a grab for her wrist that held the sword. Seizing it with one hand, he squeezed relentlessly. She cried out in pain but still fought to maintain her grip on the hilt. Jarl knew it was only a matter of time and twisted his body around to a position behind her. As she dropped the weapon, he reached around her waist with his other hand and ripped Tryggr's dagger from under her sash. He threw it to the ground, then pulled her in against him in a tight bear hug.

She screamed a guttural scream of rage and twisted in his grasp, her back pressed up against him. When she threw all her weight downwards, Jarl assumed she was trying to reach Tryggr's dagger on the ground with her free hand. He tightened his grip, knowing it was safely out of reach. Too late, he felt her fingers brushing the knife sheath inside his own boot.

"Watch out, Jarl!" Tryggr shouted. "She's got your knife now."

Reacting with instincts honed by years of battle, Jarl released her with a small shove and leaped backwards while maintaining a grip on her one wrist. Air swirled past his throat as her backhanded strike barely missed its mark. She wasn't just strong, she was clever; he had to give her that. While he was evaluating her, she'd apparently been examining him, too. Instead of fighting for either weapon he'd taken from her, she'd located another. His.

A split second later, the dagger slashed toward his wrist to free herself from his grip. Jarl let go. The sudden unexpected release threw her off balance, but his reaction wasn't quite fast enough this time. Searing white hot pain shot up his arm as the blade sliced across the back of his hand. Jarl arched his body and caught her knife-wielding hand in midair as it slashed toward him yet again. He jerked it down against his knee, dislodging the dagger, then twisted her whole arm up behind her back to immobilize her. Holding her arm there and grabbing a handful of her thick hair, Jarl forced her to her knees on the hard-packed dirt in front of him.

"That's it, sir—give it to her good. We'll see how tough she is now. Dor bitch." The two men hooted and called out encouragement as they moved closer.

Jarl ignored them and ripped a strip of leather from her skirt, using the thong to bind her hands together behind her back. Misunderstanding his intentions, the men whistled in anticipation. After hoisting her to her feet, Jarl began to pull her in the direction of his horse. The two men looked confused, then openly disappointed as they realized, not only would there be no male bonding with their leader—worse, there would be no leftovers.

"One of you fetch Tryggr's dagger for him, and the other go find the healer and bring him here immediately," Jarl ordered.

"Yes-sir." The two scurried to do as he commanded.

After dragging her the short distance to the horse, Jarl grabbed the stallion's reins and turned to pick her up. Before he could get a good grip, she bolted past him and kicked the horse in the girth, spooking it and sending it plunging away. Jarl swore out loud but managed to hold onto the reins and her arm as the animal dragged them both several paces. He heard Tryggr chuckle behind him. Jarl gave the horse the battle command to stand and turned back to face her, his jaw set with determination.

After another brief tussle, he was able to lift her onto the saddle, but the conflict was far from over. Screaming in her native tongue, she rained kicks upon the animal, trying to get it to run again. Though the horse quivered under the onslaught, it remained steady this time. Infuriated, Jarl pulled her back down and used his body weight to force her to the ground. "If that's how you want it," he said through clenched teeth as he ripped another strip from her dress and bound her ankles. He hauled her to her feet once more. Satisfied that she was suitably restrained this time, he hoisted her thrashing body over his shoulder, then deposited her face down over the front of the saddle. He mounted behind her and turned back to Tryggr. "Will you be alright?" he asked.

"I already told you. I'm fine. Besides, you seem to have your hands too full to be of any help to me anyway." Tryggr grinned.

Jarl spurred the stallion forward in the fading light—away from the burning village tents and out into the open grasslands.

Chapter 2

"Who goes there?" a man's gruff voice challenged them in the Northman tongue from the darkness.

"It's Jarl." The Northman holding her identified himself as he pulled the horse to a halt.

"Yes sir." The voice changed instantly from challenging to subservient.

Even though it meant more Northmen, Nena was beyond grateful for the reprieve in the pace. Her head was swimming. She'd lost all feeling in her feet and lower legs. At a gallop, her unprotected abdomen had bounced mercilessly against the hard leather saddle, and her muscles burned from remaining tensed to protect her insides from the rough slamming. She struggled to get her bearings and clear her head.

She'd regretted her second attempt to make the horse run almost immediately. Had it not been for that, she would have been sitting astride, hands still bound behind her, but not like this—head down, wedged between the front of the saddle and his hard thighs, with his repulsive meaty hand resting on the small of her back. But how could she have known he held some dark magic over the animal?

She'd been able to see, by twisting her head from side to side, that they'd traveled south and east. Further from her mountain home and deeper into the Great Plains. Where was he taking her? As an offering to his leader? It would explain why he hadn't forced himself upon her there in the village. She'd heard the screams of the other women who were not so fortunate. If that were the case, it would be a long night. Her fight would begin anew when they reached their destination. She needed to conserve what little strength she had left.

The sentry whistled a low warble—a sound that was picked up and repeated multiple times from different locations, some near, some far. It was quiet enough to have been some type of strange night bird, had it not been so repetitive. Clearly it was a warning system, alerting other guards to their arrival. Nena tried to memorize it, wondering if she'd be able to duplicate it and what it actually meant. Were they signaling an all clear, or somehow referring to him specifically?

Jarl had expected to feel her body go limp long before now. Her strength continued to surprise him. He was very aware of every inch of her body where it was pressed against him. Aware of every twitch of her muscles. Even though he knew she was secure, he still didn't trust completely that she could not find some way to free herself. He'd underestimated her before and for that would always bear a mark. He glanced down at the dried blood on the back of his hand, clearly visible in the moonlight. The wound burned, but it was shallow and should heal well. He just needed to be sure to clean it thoroughly when he returned to his tent.

His tent.

Then what? His tent was no place to keep a prisoner. The idea that privacy was going to somehow make her any more willing was laughable, and it wasn't like he needed another woman. What had he been thinking? He hadn't been thinking, was the answer. Even now, the feel of her body pressed against the front of his thighs, the memory of her hair cascading around her shoulders and her sword whistling through the air, made his groin ache. Jarl pushed the stallion forward, keeping him to a walk now. He'd figure it out when he got there.

With the new slower pace, the Northman's big beast-hand remained on the small of her back, but now it was more resting there than holding her in place. Nena smelled smoke and food cooking. They were close to the Northmen's camp. She had to stay alert and pay attention to every detail. She began counting the steps of the animal to know how far out the camp sentries were located for when she made her escape.

———————————————————

Jarl reined in the stallion in front of his tent and nodded silently at the two guards stationed outside the doorway. Ignoring their raised eyebrows at his unusual package, he dismounted and cut the thong that bound her ankles before lowering her feet to the ground. She staggered and fell against the animal, grabbing onto the saddle to keep from collapsing. Jarl gave her only a brief moment to steady herself, then took her by one elbow and dragged her, stumbling behind him, through the tent opening. Her struggles were weaker now, but he knew that would change as soon as she regained the feeling and strength in her limbs—and he did not care to have a repeat performance of what had happened in the village, here in front of his guards. As the heavy hide flap fell silent behind them, Jarl watched her eyes quickly scan the interior. They widened slightly at the low platform and piles of furs that were his bed.

Jarl also made a quick survey of the familiar items in his tent, trying to find something suitable to restrain her to. He hadn't thought of anything appropriate on the ride, but had hoped seeing things would reveal something he had missed. It didn't. His tent was not set up to hold a prisoner. Now what? He knew he should call the guards and have them take her to the prisoner compound; she was just a captive after all. There were a hundred more just like her. He glanced at her profile, partially obscured by her tousled dark hair. Well, maybe not just like her.

The image of his men groping at this proud beauty, bound and unable to defend herself, flashed through his mind. Cursing under his breath, Jarl grabbed a short coil of heavy braided rawhide leather and began dragging her toward his furs. Her struggles increased in earnest now, first jerking away from him, then unexpectedly changing direction and slamming into him with her shoulder, trying to knock him off his feet. She almost succeeded. Using both of his arms, Jarl held her tightly against his chest while he continued toward the bed. She grunted and panted as she fought against his grip and kicked at his shins.

The exertion, the violence of her struggles, and her closeness were exhilarating. He could feel every inch of her body straining against him. Traces of the exotic scented oils in her hair wafted up, teasing his nostrils. So caught up was he in the experience, Jarl almost changed his plan. No one would know. No one would care. And even if they did—no one would dare to interfere with him.

He shook his head and pushed her face down onto the bed, then threw himself on top of her. Her scream of rage was muted in the thick furs. He loosened his grip slightly and waited for her to react. It only took a split second. She pushed up with her whole body, arching her back, trying to turn to face him. Jarl pulled at the same time. Using her momentum, he rolled her in a complete revolution, trapping her legs inside a wrap of heavy deer hide. He sat up, straddling her, then removed his hands to test the results. With her legs and lower body ensnared within the fur, and her hands still tied behind her back, he was able to keep her pinned face down with just his legs and the weight of his body.

Finally able to use his hands for something other than her restraint, he formed two new stronger bindings from the coiled rawhide leather and attached one to each of her wrists. He paused and took a deep breath before cutting the original leather thong. He let go of one of her arms. She squirmed beneath him, using the arm he had released for leverage to twist her body around until she was face up. Her freed hand lashed out to claw his face. Jarl ducked sideways, grabbed it, and tied her wrists together, in front of her this time.

He jumped from the bed platform, dragging her behind him toward the heavy center tent support pole. Her legs were still tangled in the fur, and it took a few seconds for her to kick herself free. That was all the time he needed. Reaching up with one hand, he took the lamp down from its hook on the pole and set it on the floor. As she staggered to her feet, he yanked her arms up over her head and secured the new bindings to the iron loop where the lamp had been.

"There. That should keep you for a while," he said as he grabbed the lamp and stepped back away from her. She jerked against the bonds several times, then stood motionless, breathing hard, looking at him with hate-filled eyes. Safely out of her reach, Jarl stopped to admire her while he caught his breath.

With her arms over her head, her breasts pressed against the thin soft leather of the front of her dress. Her dark hair spilled over her shoulders like a wild beast—a beautiful wild beast with vicious eyes. Her only adornment was a gold arm band clasped above her left elbow below her tattoos. Jarl felt the tightness in his groin growing. Dor women affected him so much more than the fair-colored women of his lands in the North—more than any other women he'd encountered anywhere on his travels, and this one....

"What's your name?" he asked, his voice hoarse from earlier battle cries and now the added thickness of desire. She said nothing. He doubted she understood him, but he didn't speak Dor. He looked back to his furs. He could not believe the power of the temptation, even still, to cut her down and drag her back to them. He shook his head to clear his thoughts, turned on his heel, and went to the tent flap.

"Bring Altene," he commanded one of his guards. "And tell her to hurry."

The guard nodded and raced away. Jarl dropped the flap, filled an oxhorn cup with wine and drained it before unlacing his leather armor. He shrugged the armor over his head into a pile on the floor in the corner, then poured himself another cup. He drained it, too. *Dammit, what was taking her so long?* He'd no sooner thought the words when the tent flap lifted and a lithe Dor woman entered. She had the same bronze skin, the same almond eyes and high cheekbones as his captive, but the similarities ended there. Altene's hair was neatly braided in multiple small braids, and her dress was made from a sheer pale blue gauzy material that swirled around her, accentuating her feminine curves. The biggest difference in the two women, though, by far, was that Altene's eyes were warm and inviting.

She smiled at him and began to undo the dress clasp behind her neck when she spied the other woman bound to the pole. She hesitated, confused, and bowed her head. "Apologies, my lord. I came as soon as I was summoned. Am I too late? Have you chosen another?" she asked.

"No." Jarl covered the distance between them in two strides and pulled the clasp from her fingers. Without waiting for her dress to hit the floor, he scooped her up and carried her to the furs, tossing her to the place where he had wrestled with his captive only moments before. Altene giggled with relief as Jarl stripped out of his bloodied tunic and trousers and joined her. He pulled her head back by her braids and nuzzled her neck, then bit her ear before he turned her away and grabbed her by her hips. Altene moaned with pleasure as he drove deep inside her with one solid thrust.

Nena had been thrilled to see the other Dor woman arrive. She identified her by the olive branch tattoo on her upper arm as Klarta tribe. That was disappointing; Klarta were known to be a weaker tribe, but at least she was Dor. As such, she must also be a prisoner, and her hands were not bound. Even a Klarta should be able to find some weapon, kill him when he was distracted, then free them both. Nena's thrill turned to shock and disgust as they brushed by her on their way to the bed.

Surely they weren't going to…not with her right there—like two animals in rut. How could a Dor woman, even a Klarta, willingly lay with a Northern dog? She couldn't, was the only logical answer. It had to be a ruse. This new woman had no weapon other than her teeth and was simply luring him into a false sense of security until opportunity presented itself. Perhaps she intended to bite out his throat. Yes, that had to be it. Any moment Nena would hear his scream of agony and see his lifeblood staining the furs.

She watched with renewed interest, until it became clear that no such thing was going to happen. The woman had missed multiple opportunities and worse, had even allowed herself to be turned away from him on all fours. As the Northman mounted her from behind, like a stallion would breed a mare, Nena squeezed her eyes closed. She could not watch this—not watch their two bodies grinding against each other. If only she could close her ears as well.

Only when Jarl lay spent beside her did Altene look up at her rival. She draped an arm possessively over his shoulder.

"May I examine your prize, my lord?" she asked him.

Jarl nodded and raised himself to one elbow as Altene slipped naked from the furs and approached his prisoner. As they stood side by side, he could see, though they shared the Dor coloring he found so attractive, Altene was a little shorter, a little softer and a little fuller. He watched as she walked around his prisoner. The hardness of the captive woman's body was nothing compared to the hardness in her eyes as Altene circled her.

"Ask her her name," he instructed Altene from the furs.

"I could, my lord, but you could just as well. She understands your language as I do," Altene responded.

"I don't think so. I've already asked her."

"A Dor trick, my lord. That way they cannot be expected to talk if they are captured. But I assure you, as a warrior, especially a Teclan warrior, she understands your language and many others."

"Teclan? No." Jarl shook his head. "This was a plains tribe."

"I have not seen the other prisoners yet to know about them, but this one is definitely Teclan," Altene reaffirmed.

"How can you be sure? Do you know her?" Jarl asked.

Altene sniffed. "No, but I know of her. See these marks?" Altene pointed to the small black tattoos on Nena's upper arm. "This star indicates she is Teclan. The plains tribes bear different symbols depending on what area they are from: a wheat ear, a bison, a hawk."

"But the Teclan stronghold is in the mountains, many miles from here. We intentionally skirted their lands to avoid them. Though that would explain the casualties," Jarl surmised out loud. He paused, digesting the new information. "They are enemies of your Klarta tribe, are they not?" he asked.

"We've had our disagreements with the Teclan," Altene admitted.

"What else do her tattoos say?"

Altene pointed to another symbol on Nena's arm below the star. "This lightning bolt tells that she's the daughter of Meln, Chief of the Teclan tribe."

"Meln? Are you certain?" Jarl asked.

Altene nodded.

He exhaled. "And a princess, then." Jarl looked back at Nena.

"Of sorts," Altene agreed, clearly unhappy with the new tone in his voice. "She'll command a very high ransom."

Jarl nodded absently.

"I can tell you anything else about them that you want to know," she offered, trying to pull his attention back to her.

"Traitorous Klarta bitch," Nena seethed between her clenched teeth.

Altene's laughter filled the tent. "You see. She understands us plain."

"I understand a traitor who lies with dogs," Nena spat, "But I should expect no more from a Klarta."

Altene's fingers traced the gold bracelet on Nena's arm. "May I have her bracelet, my lord?"

"Maybe later," Jarl dismissed her request.

Altene was quick to hide her disappointment. "My lord asked your name. What is it?"

"He's no lord of mine, whore."

Altene smiled again. Unmoved by Nena's insults, she continued her examination, reading the other tattoos that circled Nena's upper arms. "Tsk, tsk. What is this?" She reached out to touch a small tattoo in the outline of a circle. That drew the first physical response from his captive who had stood unmoving throughout the inspection so far. She jerked her arm away from Altene and pulled again at her restraints. "Shall I tell him what that means?" Altene purred wickedly.

Nena did not respond, regaining her stillness and her silence.

"She is a virgin still, my lord. Unknown by any man. When a Dor woman takes her first man, this circle is filled in. You see," she displayed her own upper arm, "as mine is."

"Lucky for you the circle is not enlarged for every man you take or your body would be blackened," Nena hissed.

A virgin princess. Jarl sat stunned by this most recent turn of events and suspected that had Tryggr and the other two men known that fact, they might have fought a little harder, perhaps even be fighting still.

"Shall we have her together, my lord? Introduce her to the world of great pleasures? You and I sharing her first long moan together." Altene's eyes gleamed at the prospect, but Nena sensed the woman's insecurity, and knew her offer was not motivated by the desire she suggested. The Klarta woman was afraid; she did not want this lord of the Northmen pleasuring himself with another. Not that she had to worry about that, Nena thought with disdain. If he kept her bound, he would be able to force her, but she would make sure his pleasure was minimal—and unlike the Klarta woman, she wouldn't hesitate to bite out his throat.

"I could make her willing for you, my lord. You would not have to force her, as I know that displeases you. I am trained not only in the pleasure of men, but women as well, and I know ways to make even the most unwilling woman beg for your touch. Give me time with her in the furs. You can even watch," she offered suggestively and traced a fingertip down the soft skin on the inside of Nena's upper arm. She glanced at Jarl, happy to see his eyes hungrily following her finger's path. "Many men enjoy that," she murmured. "She will need to be restrained at first, but when she is ready, she will moan for you as I do," Altene continued.

Jarl's eyes moved to his captive's face. She looked at Altene now with even more disgust and a hint of horror. He tried to imagine what Altene was suggesting. Altene, naked and willing. The Teclan woman, hard and passionate. *The three of them?* His heart rate increased. Altene was the most skilled woman in the furs he'd ever encountered, and the prospect of things she might know about another woman was as shocking as it was intriguing. He felt Altene's questioning eyes still upon him.

"I'll keep that in mind," he declined.

"Perhaps later then," Altene murmured, satisfied by the strain in his voice that the decision had been a difficult one. She smiled to herself. The seed of suggestion had been successfully planted and his desire had been clear. He wouldn't be able to help but consider it more later, when he had time to think about it. "In the meantime, I can find out her name for you, if you still want it? The Teclan are known to resist torture, but there are other ways to get information. There will be many among the new captives who will know her. All we have to do is threaten to maim a child and the mother will speak quickly enough."

"My name is Nena."

Altene smirked at her. "You see how easy that was. You'll find things go much easier if you're agreeable."

"Then I foresee things being very difficult for me," Nena responded.

Altene laughed again. "She's a feisty one, my lord."

"I want you to take her to the baths and bring her back clean and dressed. I know it will not be easy, so gather as many other women as you need—and do not untie her hands."

"As you wish, my lord. It will not be a problem." Altene smiled.

Jarl had expected her to complain, but Altene seemed almost to be looking forward to the difficult task. Or was she looking forward to having his captive at her disposal? "And Altene," he added. "She is not to be harmed—not so much as bruised, in fact. Am I clear? Any mark I find on her body will not go well for you."

"Of course, my lord." Altene bowed her head and nodded before slipping back into her dress and leaving the tent.

She returned quickly with four women. Far too few, by Jarl's estimation after his recent experiences with the woman. He was about to say so when Altene produced a long section of thin rope. He watched in silence as the women rigged an unusual loose rope harness around Nena's neck, wrists, waist and ankles, then led her from the tent without so much as even a hint of a scuffle.

With the women gone to bathe, Jarl left to do the same. He returned in a fresh tunic and trousers to an empty tent and stood for a moment contemplating his next move. There was no way he was going to give her to his men, but he could hardly keep her tied with her hands over her head forever. He secured a short length of chain to the ring on the post, enough to allow her to sit or lie down, but not enough to reach him as he slept. Then he cleared out any object that could even be remotely considered a weapon from within the new circle of her reach.

He felt a trickle running between his fingers and glanced at his hand. The wound had reopened and started to bleed again. He dug through one of his packs and found an old torn tunic that had yet to be mended and a vial of salve. He carried them to the table. He cut off two strips of fabric, wet one with water, then wiped away the blood. After a quick check to make sure the wound was clean of any debris, he smeared salve across the top, then wrapped his hand tightly with the remaining dry strip. He had just finished tying the knot in the fabric, using his other hand and his teeth, when the women returned.

Nena stood among them, still wearing the rope harness, her bronze skin gleaming in the candlelight. Her hair was glossy and braided, and she now wore a sheer flowing dress similar to Altene's. The thin material provided Jarl clear view of her silhouette and tantalizingly brief darker shadows of the tips of her breasts and between her thighs. He watched as the women secured her to the new chain on the post.

Altene, who had been inspecting the security of the bonds before waving the other women out of the tent, noticed the path of his gaze and frowned. "I had to give her one of my own dresses, my lord. Hers was too dirty to be re-worn. Once it is cleaned, I will return it for her to wear."

"No hurry. This one is fine," Jarl said, distracted. He finally tore his eyes away, and only then noticed the purple mark on Altene's cheek. "What happened?" He traced his finger lightly along the edge of the bruise. His captive had left the tent willingly enough, but apparently had not remained that way.

"I was instructed to bathe her and make sure no harm came to her, which I did. Your prize was given no such instruction," Altene replied.

"I apologize for that. That was not fair of me. You shall have..."

"Retribution?" Altene glared at Nena.

Jarl shook his head. "Reward. Go to the chest and pick a jewel—any jewel you wish for your trouble." *And for your results.* Without the dirt and sweat and blood, the Teclan woman was even more breathtaking.

Altene's eyes brightened at the prospect, her bruise forgotten. She made her way swiftly to the chest before he could change his mind.

"Any jewel?" she reiterated over her shoulder as she lifted the lid and gazed down on the sparkling array.

"Any," he verified as he moved to stand before Nena. "Now what am I to do with you? I can't be watching you every second, and I can't have you escaping," he murmured.

"Tie her life to another," Altene said from the chest.

"What do you mean?" Jarl asked

Altene returned carrying the biggest ruby Nena had ever seen, so large it filled her palm. "Tie her life to another captive Dor, an innocent—preferably a child. If she escapes, the child will be killed."

"Is this some Dor trick to free her?" Jarl accused. "You speak nonsense. Dor are ruthless. I've seen them kill their own children. Why would the life of a stranger's child keep her grounded?"

"You do not understand Dor law, my lord. Yes, they can be cruel, but no Dor can kill another to save themselves—except in battle, of course. It would bring dishonor and shame to them, and anger the gods. If her escape would directly lead to the death of a Dor child, she will not do it."

"Is this true?" he asked Nena.

"If you trust your whore so much, try it and see." It was the first time she had spoken to him directly, and her thick exotic accent on his words fell pleasantly on his ears. Altene's mastery of his language was far more accurate, with only an occasional hint of her native heritage.

Altene laughed. "She is clever, this one. You see, she cannot admit it and seal her own fate. She cannot deny it because you would most likely see her lie. So she pretends to want it, hoping you will not so bind her."

Jarl surveyed them both. Altene's assessment made sense, and he had nothing to lose. "Bring a child prisoner and do whatever spell it is you need to do to link them." Nena's expression remained impassive as Altene fled to do as he bid, and Jarl wondered again if it were some plot to free her.

Altene returned quickly with a mother and a girl of ten or eleven years. She wasted no time. "Nena, Daughter of Meln, you are hereby bloodsworn to this child, Exanthia, daughter of Relin. If you should try to escape beyond the borders of this camp for any reason, this child will be sacrificed."

The mother fell to her knees before Nena. "I beg of you, please do not let them take my daughter. She is all I have left."

"Have no fear." Nena's voice was gentle as she knelt and took the woman's hands in her own. "I will not risk your daughter's life. You have my word."

"Gratitude. Gratitude," the mother whispered and bowed her head.

"Go with your mother, child, and rest easy. You are safe." Nena smiled a reassuring smile, though she knew the girl's future was uncertain at best. Altene was correct; no harm would come to her as a result of Nena's actions, but what kind of life would it be for a Dor woman-child to be raised as a slave? Is that what had happened to the Klarta woman? Is that how she had forsaken her own people and become such an abomination?

As Jarl watched Nena comforting the mother and child, he was shocked by two things. The first was an almost regal air about her that he chalked up to his own imagination now that he envisioned her as a princess. The second was her tenderness. It was undeniable, and it surprised him the most. Other than Altene, every Dor woman he'd ever met was cold and without emotion. For that matter, so were the Dor men. Kind and caring, she was truly the most beautiful woman he'd ever seen. Though when she stood and met his gaze, no trace of softness remained; her eyes were hard as stone.

"Very good, Altene," Jarl said. "Take the two back to the compound and have a guard put on the girl."

"My lord?" Altene looked confused.

"She's my insurance. I cannot have anything happening to her."

"If the child dies, you can simply swear her to another."

"Altene," he said sharply. "Do as I instructed and arrange for the guard."

"Yes, my lord. But what of her?" She nodded toward Nena.

"I haven't decided yet."

After Altene left the tent with the mother and child, Jarl weighed his options. Judging from the mother's response, Jarl believed it to be true, but was he willing to take the risk? Even if he did trust Nena to remain in the prisoner compound without escaping—which he did not, female prisoners were fair game for his men. No matter what his orders, the only truly safe place for her was here. And if Altene was right about her being the daughter of Meln, what a ransom she would command.

Altene pushed back through the tent flap in a rush. "Shall I release her for you now, my lord?" she asked Jarl, breathless.

Nena wondered if she'd run all the way. Scurrying little mouse. So eager to do her Northern master's bidding.

"I can take her to the compound and make sure she is settled in with the other new prisoners," Altene offered, trying to regain her breath.

"I've decided to keep her here, to better keep an eye on her," Jarl announced. "She's far too valuable to risk something happening to her. And I've seen her with a weapon. Her bond to the child won't stop her from trying to kill my men."

"Keep her here? In your tent? With you?" Altene repeated, not appearing to have heard any words past those.

"Yes," Jarl replied.

"But my lord, her skill with a weapon is all the more reason she cannot stay here. I doubt she would risk her life to kill a foot soldier, but you, on the other hand, would be a different story. For that reason alone, she should be far removed from you. And if you're worried, she can be kept under restraint with the other high risk prisoners."

Jarl cut her off before she could continue. "I did not inform you of my decision to invite debate, Altene. When I want your opinion, I'll ask for it. What I do with her is none of your concern."

"Of course, I only thought...."

"You may go now," Jarl said and turned away.

Altene's disappointment at being so dismissed was palpable. She hesitated, her mouth still open to protest further. Nena wondered with sudden interest if she would refuse him. She'd been so pliable to his every request thus far. Maybe the little mouse had a spine after all.

Altene composed herself and bowed her head again. "As you wish, my lord." Without another word, she turned and left the tent.

Soon after her exit, two thin boards hanging just inside the entrance clattered together. Nena had noticed them earlier, but only now realized their significance. Someone outside was requesting to enter. Nena wondered if it was Altene, returning with some new argument or offering to regain his favor, though she had never used the boards before. Jarl scowled. He must have thought the same.

"Enter," he called out, his tone harsh.

It was not Altene but another Northman who entered, still wearing his blood-streaked battle armor. He was of similar build to Jarl, tall and muscular, and, like Jarl, he moved light on his feet. His face was also clean shaven, though his hair was quite a bit longer and secured with small tight braids against both sides of his head. Nena assumed it was to keep it from his eyes during battle. But it wasn't his form, or the braids, or the length of wavy hair flowing just past his shoulders that held Nena's fixed attention. It was his coloring. His hair was pale as the grass in winter and his eyes the same bright blue as a mid-summer sky. Nena had never seen one colored so strangely.

Jarl approached him and took his outstretched hand before they met in a brief gruff embrace, ending with pats on the back. "You look well for after a battle, Gunnar. I'm glad to see it," Jarl said.

"As do you, my captain. Odin and Thor continue to favor us."

"Come. Sit. Have a drink." Jarl waved him to a chair, filled a heavy fired-clay mug with wine and handed it to the fair-colored newcomer. "And Tryggr? Have you seen him?" Jarl asked.

"Aye. He's fine, or he will be. The wound in his chest was deep, but luckily he's a large man and can take it. And you can rest assured the healer will make sure he mends as quickly as possible. There's already rumor he's a terrible patient."

"Imagine that," Jarl chuckled.

"Though I think it's his pride that will be the longest in healing. Is this the woman who cut off his ear?" Gunnar nodded toward Nena.

"Only part of his ear, if you are to mention it in his presence," Jarl cautioned. "And yes."

Gunnar laughed. "It will be some time, if ever, before I do that. The last thing I want is that great bear out of sorts with me." Gunnar looked back at Nena, his eyes traveling over her with appreciation. "I must say, though, he was a fool to give up so easily. One such as that would be worth at least two ears— maybe even part of a nose."

"Keep your ears and your nose, Gunnar," Jarl warned, his tone friendly, but his meaning clear.

"Of course." Gunnar nodded and laughed as he turned back to Jarl. "Everything is secure. I came to see if you have any other orders before I find myself a hot bath and a hot woman to share my furs. There are many among this new batch of captives, though none so fine as yours." His eyes returned to Nena, despite Jarl's warning, and roved over her once more.

Jarl found himself not at all liking the other man's admiration, though he was confident of Gunnar's loyalty and his obedience on the matter. He was his third in command, behind Tryggr, but now, with Tryggr's injury, he would be acting second. Jarl had originally dismissed Altene's idea of returning Nena to her leather dress when his view with this new one was so much better, but he had not considered the daily traffic in his tent. Seeing Gunnar also appreciating the display made the idea of her being covered suddenly much more appealing.

"You've taken account of the men's injuries?" Jarl asked.

"Aye," Gunnar frowned. "The healer has been far busier than expected and requests at least several days before we move camp."

"I feared it would be so," Jarl said and nodded. "Send out the scouts at first light to verify again this position is safe. Make sure they are aware of how costly the inaccuracy of their last report has proven to be. I would not have that mistake repeated." Jarl's words were laced with underlying threat.

Gunnar nodded.

"Assuming they find nothing new, inform the men that we'll remain here for a week. That should be enough time for the injured to heal and to replenish our stores. These lands are rich. There is plenty of feed for the horses and the game is bountiful. We've pushed hard and made good time; all could use the rest. It serves no purpose to rush an attack on the next village short-handed. It would only jeopardize the healthy. Once the wounded are healed enough to travel, we'll move north to the next target."

Gunnar raised his eyebrows. "A whole week? The men will very much appreciate their leader's warm consideration for their comfort. And I'm sure it has nothing to do with your wanting extra time to explore your new toy." Gunnar grinned, then drained his mug and set it down on the table with a thud. "Though a word of advice." His grin widened as he nodded toward Nena. "With such a beauty occupying your time, you may well need another battle, sooner than later, to get any rest yourself." Gunnar stood and started toward the tent flap.

Jarl shook his head and smiled. "Get the hell out of here before I change my mind and let the men know it was your fault."

"As you command," Gunnar said with a mock bow and a rakish smile.

Nena could still hear the blond man laughing after the tent flap closed behind him. These Northmen had strange ways. Their behavior bordered on disrespectful—as if they served by choice and not decree. The lower soldiers and guards seemed to respond properly to their leader, but those of higher rank were given much more leeway. It would never be so with the Dor. She couldn't imagine a warrior speaking to her father as this Gunnar had just done Jarl. Not even her elder brother, Lothor, would be permitted such transgression.

The next rattle of the thin boards requesting permission to enter was one of his guards bringing food. Nena's mouth watered as the smell of roasted pheasant filled the tent. Though her throat was raw and parched from the smoke and the battle, for a moment her hunger overpowered her thirst. After

Jarl's maps were removed from the table and the large tray of food placed there, the guard exited.

Jarl came to stand in front of her. "I know you're hungry and probably more than a little thirsty, so can you behave long enough to eat if I release you?" he asked.

Nena only stared at him. Though she longed for nothing more than to say yes, a warrior did not beg their captors.

Jarl contemplated her a moment longer, cocked his head then grunted, "I didn't think so. I'll eat first, then deal with you." He returned to the table and took a seat facing her.

Nena watched him pull tender strips of meat from a drumstick with his teeth, then suck the ends of the greasy bone before laying it on the side of his plate. Her stomach growled painfully. He washed each bite down with a large swallow of wine, clearly savoring every mouthful. His eyes met hers as he reached for another piece. "You could be eating now, too," he said. "If I could trust you."

Nena did not respond. The savory smells swirling around inside the tent had fanned her hunger to a raging flame, and she was sure he was intentionally eating as slowly as possible to torture her. It seemed an eternity before he had eaten his fill. After multiple portions of meat, he ate several small fried cakes, chewing each one slowly and deliberately. The cakes were foreign to her but appeared to be made from some type of ground grain. Finally, he pushed his plate aside.

She watched with great interest as he cut off both sides of the pheasant breast and laid the chunks on a second plate. She doubted it was by accident that he gave her no piece with a bone she might use as a weapon. Just as Altene had refused to give her a clasp with the new dress and made her tie it in a knot behind her neck instead. After adding two of the fried cakes to the plate, Jarl picked it up, grabbed a nearby waterskin, and came to stand before her again.

"It's been a long day, and I'm not up for another fight right now. You can eat here tonight. We'll try out your table manners tomorrow."

He set the plate and water bag on the floor, just within her reach, then stepped back as if she were some wild animal that needed coaxing. It wasn't necessary. With her hands still bound together, she grabbed the waterskin and gulped down long deep swallows of the lukewarm fluid until it was almost empty. Then without acknowledging him, she picked up a whole breast and tore off half of it with her teeth. She chewed it quickly, swallowed, then stuffed the other half into her mouth and did the same. It was followed immediately by the first grain cake, then the second, and finally the last piece of meat. She picked up the plate and tipped it to her lips before swallowing the remaining traces of juice.

"Do you want more?" Jarl waved toward the platter on the table, but she shook her head. "Then give me the plate," he said.

She hesitated.

"Not that I think you can make a fair weapon from a plate, but I'm not taking any chances. Hand it to me," he insisted.

Nena set the plate on the floor and pushed it with her foot to the edge of her circle of restraint.

"Now the waterskin."

Nena lifted the bag to her lips and drained the last of the water before tossing it at him.

"Very good," Jarl said, then carried the plate and bag back to the table. He returned to the bed and his sleeping furs with his back to her. He pulled his tunic over his head and dropped it to the floor, then bent his head while he unlaced the front of his trousers. When his trousers joined the tunic, Nena eyed his muscular buttocks and back warily, watching his every move lest he come in her direction. But Jarl never looked at her again. After briefly rearranging his furs, he crawled beneath them. Within minutes he was asleep, snoring softly.

As soon as she was sure it was not a trick and that he was actually asleep, Nena began to gnaw at the hardened leather bindings on her wrists. The new braided leather was thick and strong, and tied so tightly to her skin, it was difficult to get a good angle to bite. Forcing herself to be patient, she chose one small section at a time, wet it with her tongue and lips to soften it, then worked at it with her front teeth. For the longest time she seemed to make no progress. Eventually though, the leather would give and she would remove a tiny piece, then start the process over.

Nena lamented the first rays of gray light that filtered through a thin crack in the tent wall. She was out of time, exhausted, and only halfway through one binding. She knew she would not get another chance. If he awoke and called for Altene, the other woman would see the chew marks immediately—of that Nena had no doubt. That was, if he himself did not notice it first; he did not seem to miss much. She needed to make an attempt now. She stood up silently and carefully placed one foot on the end of the chain to keep it from rattling. Using her second hand to support the wrist with the chewed binding, she pulled upward against the weakened leather with all of her might. She thought she felt the leather give slightly, but couldn't be sure. She renewed her grip, took a deep breath, and pulled again.

Nothing.

Her wrist on fire, Nena frantically calculated her next move. The quiet sounds of his breathing changed behind her. She turned. He was staring at her, his expression intense and lustful. It was too late.

Nena had more than once overheard the women of her village laughing about a man's desire when he first awoke, but couldn't recall their words exactly. Was it stronger than a man's night desire? She wished now she had paid more attention to the gossip, but had always assumed she would find out for herself one day. She did not want that day to be now.

Jarl threw back the furs and swung his legs out sideways to the short drop to the floor. His erection was clear for her to see, but he seemed not to care. He stood and walked naked to the tent flap. Holding it open just a few inches, he spoke to one of the guards stationed outside. "Send for Altene."

As much as Nena did not wish to see the other woman, or be forced to witness what she was sure they were about to do again, she was relieved for his having an outlet other than her. Though it made no sense for him to have brought her here if not to force himself upon her. He hadn't known her identity then, so it had not been for the ransom, and he made no attempt to hide the fact that he found her desirable.

Jarl returned to the edge of the furs and picked up his trousers. Nena looked away as he pulled them up over his erection, more concerned by her own body's issues at that moment, than his. The water she had consumed the night before was threatening to burst within her, and she wondered where they relieved themselves. She had seen nothing in the tent.

Altene arrived in a flash, immaculate and scantily dressed, as if she'd been waiting for his summons. Nena realized she probably had. The other Dor woman did not appear to have slept any more than she had—probably fretted all night about her chastising and what Nena and the Northman were doing in her absence. Altene carried a leather warrior dress, though not the same soft doeskin Nena had been wearing when she was captured. This one was made from a poorly-tanned, thick, coarse hide. Altene draped the dress over a chair, then smiled at Jarl. "Shall I pleasure you this morning, my lord?" she asked, her voice low and sultry.

"Not today. Get your women and take her to the latrine," he commanded, but his voice was softer and carried none of the bite from the previous evening.

"Yes, my lord," Altene said. Her half smile and deep exhale as she turned away revealed her relief that his anger had abated. She exited and returned again quickly with four women. Two Nena recognized from the night before, but the other two were new.

"My lord, she has chewed her bonds," Altene reported as the other women secured Nena with the rope harness. Her eyes were wide, pretending to be shocked, but Nena could see the hard glint within them.

Klarta bitch.

"Yes, but only halfway," Jarl responded without looking at her wrists. "They will hold. I will fix it when you return."

So he had noticed.

Once he was satisfied that Nena was suitably harnessed again, Jarl left the tent for the latrine, leaving the women alone.

As the previous evening, the women did not address her as they walked through the camp, and Nena used the silence to focus on holding her bladder and taking in every detail of this new route. The direction was opposite of the way they had taken her to the baths the night before, but this side of the camp appeared to be laid out almost identically. Rows of small tents, a fraction of the size of Jarl's, were pitched side by side, with shared campfires centrally located in the middle of every eight or ten. Men lounged about outside. Jarl's message of a week of rest had clearly been well received.

Nena studied them. Some sharpened weapons, some cooked, some shaved. Some were already drunk, though it was early morning. Many were shirtless in the heat, and the hair on their exposed chests ranged from thickly matted to sparse, but all of them had it to some extent. Some even had thick hair on their backs, she noted with disgust. The amount of hair on their heads also varied. Some were shaved bald, but many were shaved only on the sides, with the long hair on the tops of their heads held in a ponytail or braid high on the back. Most were tattooed to some degree, but unlike the Dor, the Northmen's green and black symbols appeared to be random pictures and designs that were spread all over their bodies, even extending to the faces and heads of some.

Altene led the group of women among the men with no apparent concern, and not one of the men made any attempt to address them. Nena tried to look past how repulsive they were and estimate their numbers, but without knowing how many rows of tents were present, it was impossible to tell. One thing she did know. There was no short or easy path back out to the open plains. From what she could see today, what she had seen the night before when they took her to the baths, and the little she'd been able to see when she arrived thrown over the front of his horse, Jarl's tent seemed to be located dead-center in the camp.

Nena could smell the latrines long before they reached them, but her need overran her disgust. At least they were private—single canvas stalls with a circular hole cut in wood over a shallow dug pit. Or they would have been private had Altene not insisted on two of the other women escorting her inside the small cramped foul space.

When they returned outside, Altene led off, with Nena and the women holding her ropes following behind. Nena hurried her step to catch up but felt the ropes tighten around her neck before she could reach Altene. "Release me," she called to her.

Altene slowed and turned to face her, but continued walking. "For what? You will not escape here. Unlike the foolish plains tribe you were visiting, this camp is heavily guarded at all times. Rings of their soldiers extend far out into the plains. There has never been a successful escape, and some far more capable than you have tried."

"You have no idea what I'm capable of, and what do you care? If I'm recaptured maybe he'll be angry and do as you suggest and keep me with the other prisoners. Or maybe I would be killed in the attempt. In any case you would have your Northman back all to yourself."

"You will not escape on my watch. I will not risk having Jarl angry with me." Altene paused. "And I'm not worried; his preoccupation with you will not last. Even though it is acceptable among his people, he will not force you to his furs, and I will not offer again to make you willing for him—that was a mistake on my part," she admitted with a frown. "And since I do not foresee you going to him willingly, soon enough he will tire of the inconvenience of having you in his tent and probably give you to one of his men. For your sake, after your little escapade with his blade, you'd better hope it's not Tryggr, though he's the most logical choice as Jarl's second."

"But he said he intends to ransom me to my family."

Altene smiled. "And I'm sure he will. Though it won't be right away. Jarl's no fool. He won't alert the Teclan to your presence here until he is safely away from your lands and your warriors. And there's no reason his men cannot have their fill of you until then. Your family will pay without ever knowing of your well-used condition. Or maybe he'll ask for extra to cover the red-haired giant's seed sure to be in your belly." She gave Nena a long sideways glance, satisfied with the horrified expression she saw there. "And if they won't pay, then you'll be sold with the other prisoners as slaves once we reach port."

"What about you? Are you also not a prisoner? Will you not be sold as well?"

"Jarl has other plans for me."

Nena shook her head. "Why do you do it? Why do you stand for his animal rutting? You may be Klarta but you are still Dor. Where is your pride? Is it because he is a leader? Is it status you seek?"

"Animal rutting? Jarl?" Altene seemed truly confused and her eyes searched Nena's face for her meaning. "Ah." She nodded as she understood. "I suppose you would think that after last night, but that was not typical. Well, it was typical for after a battle." She shrugged. "But only when the battle fever grips him, is Jarl ever hurried in the furs. Any other time he's the most meticulous man I've ever lain with." She lowered her voice confidentially before adding, "and you were correct last night in referring to how large my circle would be. There have been many to compare him to." She smiled and seemed almost proud of the admission.

"I won't say I don't care about status," she continued. "Being Jarl's only chosen elevates me far above the other prisoners. It even earns me a certain level of respect among his men. But I would lay with Jarl any time he asked, even if he were a lowly camp cook; he is that skilled." Her voice faded off temporarily as she reminisced, then her lips widened in a malicious grin. "Though I don't need to explain it to you. You'll soon get an eyeful of anything

I could possibly describe if he keeps you chained to the pole for very long. Prepare to see unimaginable pleasures and to see them often, Princess; Jarl has a healthy appetite." Altene laughed out loud at the shocked expression on Nena's face as her words sank in.

"You are disgusting," Nena spat.

"And you are a fool," Altene answered. "Teclan—so fierce in battle, yet so naive as to the true ways of the world."

Their arrival back at Jarl's tent ended their discussion. The guards nodded them past, and Altene pressed on a well worn spot on the side of the tent near the door. Nena heard the thin boards rattle within, and Jarl's voice bid them enter. He was seated at the table with maps in front of him. He looked up, saw it was them, and went back to studying.

"Change her dress," he said to Altene, without looking up again.

"As you wish, my lord." Altene retrieved the stiff leather dress from the chair where she had laid it earlier and returned to stand just out of Nena's reach. "Remove your dress," she ordered.

Nena did not move.

"Are you deaf? Or would you like some assistance?" Altene taunted, then leaned in close to Nena's ear and lowered her voice to a whisper. "Perhaps from my lord, Jarl?"

Nena's fierce gaze met the other woman's triumphant, laughing eyes and held them. She would kill this woman one day, she vowed. She would see the smirk fade from her face as she choked the life from her. She prayed for the gods to give her that pleasure before she escaped. Keeping her mind filled with image of Altene's' bloodshot eyes bugging from her head, Nena reached up over one shoulder with both bound hands in a slow resolute move, and untied the knot of the dress behind her neck. The thin gauzy material floated down her body like a cloud, pooling on the floor around her feet. She stood with her chin raised, her jaw set, her eyes fixed on Altene, waiting for her to hand her the new dress, but Altene delayed, leaving her to stand naked in front of him.

Jarl hadn't given it any thought when he gave the order. He had assumed Altene would change the dress once she had resecured Nena to the pole. When it became clear Altene intended to do it there in front of him and use the opportunity to humiliate her, he almost intervened. Almost. The challenge had been issued, and he, like Altene, watched and waited to see what Nena would do.

Jarl sucked in his breath as the soft material slid down her body, caressing every inch of her golden skin on its journey to the floor. For a brief moment he had an unadulterated view of what he had only imagined before. Her perfect firm breasts. Her trim waist flaring to the curve of her hips. The dark patch of her womanhood. Altene handed her the baggy leather replacement and Nena donned it in a flash. The sight was lost, but the image still burned clearly in his mind. Jarl took a deep breath and reached for the jug of wine even though it was early.

"Shall I also replace her chewed binding for you now, my lord?" Altene asked.

"No. I've made other arrangements for her. That one will hold until then."

Nena's mind raced at Jarl's words and their implication. Had Altene been right? Had he already grown tired of her presence and given her away? Would it be Tryggr? She'd bested him before, but she'd had her hands free to fight. Or would it be the fair-colored one, Gunnar? By his own words, he had no reservations about lying with an unwilling woman. And he shared Jarl's physique; he would be a difficult fight in the best of circumstances.

She could tell Altene was barely able to contain her excitement, and knew she was thinking the same. Nena prayed she would ask what his 'other arrangements' for her were, but Altene had learned her lesson from the night before and did not question him. After she verified Nena was firmly reattached to the chain on the pole, Altene instructed the other women to leave and turned to Jarl.

"I've asked among the new prisoners and have information about the tribe you attacked," she said.

"Give voice to it," Jarl said, looking up.

"They are the Eastern Plains tribe, and the celebration your scouts described was a tournament of warriors. The Teclan chief, Meln, and his daughter, her," she thumbed in Nena's direction, "were attending as guests of honor. The Plains tribe had hopes that she would choose one of their warriors, and an alliance with the Teclans could be secured. It's highly unusual for a Teclan woman to be present at a lesser tribe's tournament, but she had grown so old without choosing, her father must have been desperate and feared the gods had forsaken her."

The recent image of the dress sliding down Nena's firm young body flashed to the forefront of Jarl's mind. There was nothing about it he would describe as old. He fought it aside and asked, "So there were other Teclan there? How many?"

"I do not know, my lord," Altene said.

"But you are certain Meln, himself, was there?"

"Yes."

"Are there any other Teclan among the captives?"

"That I also do not know. None that I have seen so far, but there are many new prisoners in this latest batch."

"Gratitude, Altene. Your information is most valuable. Go now and ask among the prisoners if any know the fate of the other Teclan." He paused. "And Altene, if your methods do not prove adequate to obtain the information I seek, use the prisoner guards. Tell them you are working on my behalf, and they are to assist you in whatever ways you deem necessary. This information is very important to me."

"Yes, my lord," Altene murmured, unable to hold back the smile at his compliment and trust in her as she turned to leave.

Jarl waited a few moments then followed Altene outside the tent. Nena heard him speaking to one of his guards, his voice low. She strained her ears, trying to focus on his words. "Yes, a star and a lightning bolt, on the upper left arm," he said.

The guard's response was too muted for Nena to make out.

"Report exact numbers back to me once you are finished. And you are to search every single one. Am I clear?"

Did he not trust Altene? Was he sending a guard to double check the prisoners? More importantly, if Altene's words were true, then her father and brother must still be free! Surely had the chief of the Teclan and his son been captured, Altene would have heard of it right away.

Chapter 3

The remainder of the day was a steady procession of men to see Jarl. Nena soon realized that what she had assumed was a grossly oversized tent to fit his ego, was, in fact, at times far too small. Some men had disputes. Some requested new orders or clarification of old. Some offered suggestions or requested permission to take on a new project. Others presented Jarl with problems for him to solve: problems with supplies, problems with weapons, problems with other men. Jarl addressed each issue calmly, though sometimes she could tell he was irritated or disinterested. He was easy to read.

Unlike the Teclan who were trained from an early age to reveal nothing— to keep their faces and bodies inexpressive, the Northmen were the opposite. Jarl was no exception. His face, body and even his energy aura clearly transmitted what he was feeling, though the other Northmen seemed not to be able to see it. The way the muscle in his cheek tensed when he was angry. The way his left shoulder dropped a fraction when he was bored. The way the small lines in his forehead became deeper when he was interested and giving careful consideration. Nena could read it all. Foolish, untrained, undisciplined Northman, she thought with disdain.

Every detail of every encounter, she filed away to potentially use in her escape. An escape, since being bloodsworn to the girl, had become a hundredfold more difficult, but still possible. She just had to be ready to seize the opportunity when it arose. To do that, she needed to learn everything she could about them.

When the next man entered, Nena was struck by how filthy he was, but the way Jarl reacted to him, sitting up and giving him his full attention, told her this was a man of importance. She took closer note of him. His thick dark beard and clothes were covered in a fine black soot. She smelled an acrid burnt smell even across the tent where she was secured. He was a large man—not near so tall as Jarl, but his body was much thicker, like the trunk of a tree.

"Is this what you had in mind, Jarl?" The dirty man asked as he held out something for Jarl to examine. Nena could not see what it was. Jarl took the item, and Nena heard the clink of metal. So this man was a forger—able to create and repair their weapons. No wonder he was so important to Jarl. For that same reason, he could be important to Nena. When she escaped, she would need a weapon. If she could locate the forger's tent, there should be many there to choose from.

"Yes. These are perfect. Gratitude, Eigil," Jarl said. "I shall see you properly rewarded."

"No reward required. It was a pleasure to create something other than dagger and sword." The man dismissed Jarl's offer and smiled, his teeth appearing very white beneath the soot in his mustache.

Nena could tell Jarl was, in fact, very pleased by whatever it was this man had made for him. Her curiosity grew. Was it some unique weapon? If so, it had to be very small—and small appealed to her.

After the man left, Jarl stood and walked toward her, the item hidden inside his bulging fist. Her eyes darted from his hand to his face to his body, trying to identify not only the metal object, but also his intentions toward her in time to react, if necessary.

"I have a gift for you," Jarl said. "Something to keep you safe." He opened his hand and there in his palm was the forger's masterpiece. Two small metal wrist shackles connected by four short links of chain. They were unlike any she had ever seen. Each one opened in the normal fashion with a hinge on one side and a lock clasp on the other, but they were delicate—more like bracelets, and each was lined with a soft rabbit fur cuff.

Jarl's eyes searched her face to see if she recognized the significance of what he held, but her face remained a smooth mask. How could she show nothing? She was such an enigma to him. Did she not understand his intent or know what they were? With these, there would be no gnawing herself free. He reached for one of her wrists, but she jerked it away and stepped back, her eyes locked on his in clear defiance. Jarl nodded and smiled, satisfied. She knew.

"I'm going to replace the rawhide on your wrists with these. I had them designed for your comfort and to not mar your skin, as I fear you may be wearing them for awhile. At least until the day I can trust you, as I trust Altene."

"That day will never come," she seethed.

"Perhaps." Jarl acknowledged with a smile and shrug. "In the meantime, I cannot be forever worried that you have chewed yourself free when I am busy or preoccupied. Believe it or not, I do have other things to worry about besides you." He took another small step toward her. "This is going to happen now, but I'm giving you a choice. You can accept them willingly, or I will put them on you like I did the first ones, rolling in the furs—which I quite enjoyed," he added. "You decide."

Nena rapidly evaluated her limited options. The shackles, though delicate in appearance, would be extremely effective. If she allowed him to place them on her, she would not be able to get free of them without a key. If she tried to fight, already bound as she was, she would be no match for him, and any injury she would be able to inflict would be minimal. The end result would be the same, but she would have endured being manhandled and groped by him again.

Her heart raced as she fought back the panic that threatened to overwhelm her. She had to remain calm. Panic served no purpose. She had no choice. She would not be able to chew free, but she would find another way. Later. Secure the key. Something. Like being bloodsworn to the child, this was another setback, but it would be overcome. They said the camp would move in a week. In that certain chaos could be opportunity. Making no attempt to hide her hatred of him, Nena offered up her wrists.

The guard bringing dinner, entered with another heaping tray of food. After he set the tray on the table and left, Jarl picked up his set of utensils and a second set, Nena assumed were for her, and placed them on a smaller table behind his chair, near the chest where Altene had chosen her ruby. He poured himself an oxhorn cup of wine and took a long swallow, wiping the excess from his lips with the back of his hand while he studied her.

Seeming to come to some decision, he leaned the horn against its short wooden stand, walked across the tent and stood in front of her, his body tense. "It's time to eat, Princess. Let's try to play nice, alright?" he asked, though Nena could tell he was not really expecting a response. He started to unhook the long chain from her cuffs, then paused and looked her straight in the eye. "Know this. If you make a move on me, you'd better be certain you can finish it, and kill me. Am I clear?"

She stared back at him in silence.

"Here goes nothing," he murmured, as he unhooked the chain. Leaving her hands bound together with the cuffs, he led her to a chair across from his, and sat her at an empty plate. She eyed the utensils behind him. The Northmen utensils, other than the knife, were strange to her, so she did not need them to eat, but had hoped to have access to the pronged one. Perhaps he would give her an oxhorn cup like his. The intricate silver decoration around the top rim would not make it heavy enough to kill him with a blow to the head, but the sharp silver-tipped curved point on the bottom could surely be driven into his eye—maybe even his ear.

Tonight's feast was a roasted shoulder of wild pig. Jarl cut off two large slabs of the steaming meat, placing one on his plate and one on the plate in front of her. He returned his knife to its sheath when he noticed her eyes on it, then added a large scoop of tender grains boiled with small wild onions to each plate. He poured wine into a shallow silver cup, slid it in front of her, and nodded for her to drink.

Nena frowned, disappointed that he'd had the foresight to not provide her with one of the oxhorn cups. She took a small sip. She was thirsty, but did not want to dim her wits around him. She picked up the piece of hot meat and bit off an edge. When she finished that piece, he cut her another. She had to scoop the onions and grains up to her mouth with her hands, but she didn't mind. They were delicious—heavily salted and seasoned with some other spice that was unknown to her.

Jarl sat watching her, his full plate of food untouched, though he did continue to drink his wine and soon had refilled his oxhorn several times.

"What were the Teclan doing out on the plains?" he asked. "Altene said earlier, in hopes you would choose. What did she mean by that?"

"Ask your whore," Nena responded between mouthfuls.

Jarl sat back and smiled, seeming to be relaxed, but Nena could feel the tense awareness emanating from him. She could tell that even with the wine he had consumed, he was poised to react within a split second to any move on her part.

"How many of you were there? Who is left guarding the Teclan mountain stronghold?"

"Ask your whore that, too."

"Perhaps I will, but that will have to wait until later. I do not wish for Altene to disturb us now."

What did he mean by that? What was he planning to do now? Altene had said he would not force her—had that been a lie? Deceitful Klarta bitch couldn't be trusted. Nena delayed eating her last few bites to postpone as long as possible what was to come after the meal.

As he led her away from the table, Nena planned her defense strategy. If he ventured past the pole toward his furs, her best bet with her hands cuffed was to go for his eyes.

Jarl stopped at the pole and reattached her chain. He stood back and admired her. "You are exquisite." He reached out to stroke her hair, but she shook her head and stepped back, glaring at him. "Hnf," he grunted with a nod and a hint of a smile, then turned and went to the door. "Send for Altene," he said to a guard outside.

He met Altene at the door and the two made their way to his furs, shedding clothes along the way. Nena watched only long enough to be sure they were not coming in her direction, then picked a spot on the floor midway between the pole and the furs and stared at it. She dared not close her eyes and be completely without warning sight in this place, but she would not endure Altene's promise of witnessing their intimacies. She stared blindly at the spot, clearing her mind, blocking out as much as she could.

Nena employed a warrior's tactic, learned, so that if ever captured, she might endure torture. She took her mind far away to a place that was soothing to her—the green banks of the cool stream where she used to play as a child. She was there again, smelling the tangy spring grass, feeling the warm earth between her bare toes, seeing the small silver fish darting beneath the clear surface of the water. She was only dimly aware of their whispers, their groans, their sighs, the increased tempo of their bodies coming together, their mingled cries of pleasure, then their panting breaths. When it was silent, Nena brought back her focus, but still did not look at them.

"Are you hungry?" she heard him ask Altene.

"Why yes, my lord," Altene murmured surprised.

"Come. I have not yet had time to eat. You can tell me what you've discovered over food and drink."

"Gratitude, my lord."

Nena looked up as Jarl pulled on his trousers and Altene her dress, again to verify they were not coming for her. She was numb, her mind clear and calm. As her eyes followed them to the table, her contempt of Altene returned. The woman seemed not to mind that he served her food on a dirty plate or poured her wine into a used cup, as he might have given table scraps to a dog. Could she not see it? Did she truly not care? He did give her clean utensils, though— the ones Nena had not been permitted to use. And more important than that, he gave her a knife; Altene's sickening behavior had earned his trust. As much as Nena would have liked to have had the weapons, it made his suggestion that she would one day be trusted the same as that groveling little snitch, even more insulting.

"They said there were nine: her, Chief Meln, her younger brother, and a small escort contingent of six Teclan warriors," Altene began.

"Who is in charge in their absence?" Jarl asked.

"Her eldest brother, Lothor, remained behind. He has a formidable reputation. I would not anticipate any lessening of their defenses. Rumor has it he is as strong a warrior as Meln."

"Strong warriors do not necessarily make strong leaders," Jarl responded. "Are there any other Teclan among the captives?"

"No, my lord."

"Does anyone bear witness to what happened to them in the battle?"

The battle? Did they call massacring unarmed opponents—women and children—a battle?

"None that I have spoken with thus far, but I have yet to question them all. By end of day tomorrow, I will know all that they know," Altene promised.

"Very good." Jarl cut another bite of the now cold pork. "You said earlier the tournament was in hopes that she would choose. What did you mean by that?" Jarl asked.

"Tournaments are a way for Dor men to safely demonstrate their fighting skills and gain status. It's also a time for them to impress the gods and offer themselves up to be chosen. All tribes have them. We....," she began, then corrected herself. "They...believe the gods choose a woman's first union and reveal their choice through the woman, when they are ready."

"When you say choose first union, what is that? Sex? Marriage?"

"Usually it is both. After the first union is complete..."

"By complete, you mean they have sex," Jarl interrupted to clarify.

"Yes. After that the woman will make a statement in front of the village, that she accepts the union and then it is final. Then it is a marriage."

"Does that always happen?"

"Almost always. There would have to be severe extenuating circumstances for a woman to go against the gods and not agree with their choice."

"Like rape?" he suggested.

"Yes, that would be one reason." Altene lowered her voice. "But that is very, very rare. Men will rape married women of a tribe they have conquered as an additional way to show their dominance, but it is never acceptable to rape an unchosen woman. They are considered sacred by the gods."

"Are all Dor men so fearful of the gods that you've never heard of it happening?" he asked in disbelief.

"It is not only the gods they fear. It is the punishment. One of the few punishments that is universal among all the Dor tribes, at least all those I've ever heard of." Her voice was barely above a whisper now. "The punishment for such a man is castration and to live out his remaining days as a slave of the lowest order in the tribe."

"And the woman? What happens to her?"

"Nothing." Altene looked bewildered by the question. "She would not make the statement of union, of course, but the gods still chose for her. The Dor believe the gods recognized a poison within the man, and in order to cull him from the tribe, picked the one woman he could not resist to bring it to light. Such a woman would be revered to have been so chosen by the gods, and would be rewarded in her next choosing being far above her station."

Jarl nodded as he digested the information.

"If the women choose the men, are they in charge? I've seen women in battle but never heard of a female Dor chief."

Altene laughed as if the idea were ridiculous. "No, my lord. A Dor woman could never lead. That is only for men. Yes, all young women are trained to fight. It comes to serve later when they are mothers and left behind in the villages while the men go to raid. If they were ever attacked, they would not be defenseless."

"So the men are in charge, make all the decisions, but not who they marry? They must wait for a woman to pick them?" Jarl asked.

"Yes." Altene nodded.

Jarl frowned and shook his head. "Can the woman choose anyone? What if the man doesn't wish to be chosen?"

Altene laughed. "Of course the man must also be willing. He would indicate his willingness in advance to the woman, as would others. Higher ranking men usually will only do that with women of equal or higher status." She paused. "But it is a great honor for a man to be chosen, and the younger he is chosen, the greater that honor. Because of this, many men have an open willingness to being chosen by any woman. Though they will go to great lengths to impress a woman they prefer. They bring gifts to show they can support her. They compete in tournaments like this one to demonstrate their superior battle skills over other men. To vanquish a rival in front of a woman is powerful medicine in the eyes of the gods."

Altene's words transported Nena back to her trip to the tournament only three short days before. She was astride Nightwing again, still a day's ride out from their destination, when her brother had dropped back to ride beside her. Her younger brother, Ruga, so brave, so sure of himself. "I shall fight hard, Sister. If there is a man in this village who can defeat me, then the gods will know he is worthy of your immediate choice. Unfortunately, that means you will yet have to remain a warrior, because none will best me." It was his first tournament outside of their own tribe. His excitement at being chosen to attend as his father's second, an honor normally reserved for their older brother, Lothor, could not be contained.

"Eventually the gods will have to choose one for you, of course—but a second place champion to be sure." Though said in jest, Ruga's words were true. Her brothers were both great warriors; Lothor undefeated. And even though Lothor was not present, any man who could defeat Ruga would have to earn the gods' strong consideration. "And when I win the tournament, I shall find the most beautiful woman there and offer her alone my willingness, so that I am not chosen by the wrong one. Not like Belka."

Nena knew the story, but listened as he told it again, as if she did not. "Belka entered a tournament with his eyes on the chief's beautiful daughter, but left himself open to the choosing. When he won, a big fat maid claimed him before any other could, and he had to marry her." Her younger brother rolled with laughter. Nena had no idea of the truth of the tale. Belka was, in fact, married to a large woman, but she had given him many strong sons, and he seemed happy. Besides, it was the gods who chose, and in Belka's case, she felt it was a good match.

Nena could still see the sunlight shining on his dark hair as he teased her. Ruga, so sensitive and carefree underneath the well-trained surface—so different from the stern Lothor. Was he dead? Was her father dead? If she trusted Altene's words, she knew now they were not enduring the shame of being taken. They could still be alive. As much as she wanted to hold onto that hope, Nena knew in her heart the men of her family would never run from a fight, much as she had intended to fight until her last breath—until Jarl had intervened. Nena felt her throat constricting. Tears threatened her eyes. She grit her teeth. She would not cry, not in front of this Northern dog and his Klarta whore.

"Do men ever take more than one wife?" Jarl's next question interrupted Nena's thoughts. "I mean, can a man be chosen by two women?" he clarified.

Altene shook her head adamantly at first, then paused. "When I was in the pleasure house in Anbai, I heard of such things in far off tribes, many moons ride from here, but only there. A Dor man may have more than one woman under his roof, his mother or sisters, but only one wife."

"So women usually choose from within their own village?"

"The gods can choose anyone, but usually it is from within their tribe, yes. There are also great tournaments once every few years where friendly tribes meet and compete. Blood is mixed that way," Altene added.

"And that is what was happening here?"

"Not exactly. No other tribes were invited to this tournament, only the chief of the Teclan and his family. The Eastern Plains chief would not have wanted to risk her choosing a warrior from another tribe; an alliance with the Teclan would have meant a very prosperous change in their fortunes. The men would have been competing for their own women also, but the top contenders would have all put forward their willingness to be chosen by her. And I am sure the local women would have been under strict instruction to delay their choosing until after she had done so."

Nena listened deep into the night as Jarl continued to ask specifics on their customs, their beliefs, their lives. Anything and everything Dor. She could tell by Altene's elated expression and almost giddy responses, it had never happened before. She was eager to tell him anything he wanted to know, thrilled by his attention, however motivated.

When Nena thought she could not possibly keep her eyes open another moment, Jarl sent Altene away and retired to his furs.

Chapter 4

The next morning Nena was awakened by the clatter of the entry boards. Upon Jarl's bidding, a guard entered, his clothing and boots covered in dust and blood. Nena was instantly alert. Were the Northmen under attack? She strained her ears but heard nothing out of the ordinary outside the tent. She looked back to the man. He did not appear to be overly excited. Nor did he have any injuries or damage to his clothing from fighting that she could see.

"I have the report you requested," he said to Jarl.

Jarl rose and hastened to meet him at the doorway. "Outside," he directed.

The two men moved far from the tent, and though she could hear their voices, no matter how hard she tried, Nena could not make out their words. When Jarl returned, his mood seemed pensive. He looked at her as if he were about to say something, but was interrupted by a second excited rattle of the boards.

"Come in," he called out. It was Altene.

"My lord, I have news," she said in a rush.

Jarl held up his hand. "First. What is the significance of placing a body off the ground on a raised platform made out of sticks?" Jarl heard Nena's chain rattle behind him, a sound he only heard when she changed positions abruptly, which was rare. It was actually uncanny how she was able to move most of the time without the slightest clink. For him to hear it so loudly now, he knew it had to be in response to his question.

"I do not know, my lord," Altene answered quickly, clearly more eager to give him her own news than give much consideration to his question.

"What do you mean, you don't know?" he demanded.

"It's not a Dor custom I know of," she offered, sensing her mistake. "but I was taken from my tribe when I was young."

"Do the Dor burn their dead on a pyre?" he asked.

"Not that I've ever heard. We always buried them."

"Wait outside. I will call for your news in a moment."

He moved to stand in front of Nena. She remained kneeling, balanced on the balls of her feet, a position he had seen her hold for hours at a time. She seemed composed, but her face was drawn.

"You know what it means," Jarl stated without asking.

"Why did you ask her that?" Nena responded without looking up from the floor.

Jarl hesitated. "There is no trace of your father, but your brother and six other Teclan were killed in the battle."

She looked at him then, her eyes searching his face. "You lie."

He shook his head. "Why would I? If I wanted you to feel alone and vulnerable, I would have told you all were dead. If I wanted you to be happy and have hope of rescue, I would have said all lived. I will not lie to you. I sent men back to the village to examine every body. Six men bearing the Teclan star on their arms were discovered among the dead. The seventh's body was found on the platform I described. His arm bore the star and also bore the lightning bolt, as does yours." He paused. "He was young."

Nena fought back the wave of pain that threatened to choke her. It was her brother, Ruga. What the Northmen had mistaken for a funeral pyre, was in fact a sky grave, the final resting place for a warrior killed far from home. Only the Teclan believed this, and for her brother to have been so placed meant another Teclan yet lived. If she believed him about the identity of the six dead, then it would have to have been her father. But why would he not have taken care of the others?

Her face was so pale, Jarl felt compelled to say something. "It did not appear anyone had attempted to set it on fire, or by my men's accounts, that it was even complete enough to hold a flame. Perhaps they ran out of time. I can have my men return to finish building it, and light it, if you wish."

Her head snapped up. "No. They must not touch him."

"Explain to me why and I will make sure it is so," he reassured her.

Nena did not want to talk to him of this, of all things, but her brother's body could not be disturbed. She began to speak, her thick accent blurred with obvious pain, making some of her words difficult to understand. "When a Teclan warrior dies, our spirit makes the great journey to the sky to join our ancestors in the afterlife. From our mountain home the journey is short and the path easy to find. But if a warrior falls on the plains, too far from the mountain for their body to be returned there, then sometimes the spirit can be lost making the great journey. The sky grave separates the body and spirit from the ground, allowing the wind to pass beneath it and show it the way to the afterlife."

Jarl nodded. "I understand. We will leave him."

He turned to the door. "Come in, Altene. What is your news?"

"I have found a man who saw the Teclan fall to your soldiers. All are dead. Meln from a battle-axe to the head, and Ruga, his son, to a sword," Altene said with great relish.

Jarl looked to Nena, trying to gauge the impact of Altene's words, but the Teclan woman remained unmoving, as if she had not heard or understood. He turned back to Altene. "Is that all?" he asked curtly.

"Yes, my lord," she said, confused by his unexpected response. "But do not pity her. She does not mourn them, I assure you. The Teclan believe it is a great honor to die in battle. Though that is probably easier for them to believe when their own losses are usually few and their victims' are many," she spat, unable to hide her true feelings.

"Then they are much like us, the Norse, in both of those regards," Jarl said. "We also know our kinsmen live on fighting and feasting in Valhalla in the afterlife, but it does not always soften our grief at their passing."

Altene clamped her mouth closed, upset that she had inadvertently drawn a connection between the two of them.

"You may go, Altene." Jarl dismissed her.

Later that afternoon, Altene returned with the four women to take Nena to be bathed. Nena stood quietly while the women fitted the rope harness to her body. She did not fight them. There was no point. She was very familiar with the hobble harness; the Teclan were quite fond of it. Loose and flowing, it allowed a prisoner free movement to walk, sit, even labor, but the loops, knots and twists provided incredible leverage. With even the smallest amount of pressure on either of the two longer lines, the prisoner could be choked and immobilized on the ground in a matter of seconds—a fact she had been emphatically reminded of on her first trip to the baths.

Even as she'd lain gasping on the floor, she'd felt it had been worth it at the time—to have been able to reach Altene and slam her cheek into the side of a post. Now she could see it had probably been a mistake. Altene had been furious. The two women who had held her ropes too slack that day had been replaced with new ones, and Nena could only assume by the way the women now fearfully regarded Altene, the first two had been punished severely. Nena didn't particularly care about the other women's poor circumstances, but her actions unwittingly had serious consequences for herself. All the women's eyes now followed Nena's every move with grim determination.

As they made their way to the baths, Nena scrutinized them—which women watched her the closest, who were friendly with one another, who might be distracted. Most importantly, she looked for any sign of sympathy—whose trust she might be able to win—who could perhaps be turned to ally. Altene she had already dismissed, though it didn't stop her from pressing Altene to release her whenever they were away from Jarl.

Each time Altene refused with disdain. "Things have never been better for me. Why would I risk that?" Altene scoffed. "For whatever reason, your presence has sparked his interest in our culture. It is an interest I'm happy to fulfill. He asks my opinion now, listens to me when I speak, even invites me to share some of his meals."

"So is it *our* culture again, then? Before you seemed eager to distance yourself from your people," Nena pointed out.

"Yes, and it will remain *our* culture until it no longer suits me," Altene said.

Once in the bath tent, Nena's dress was removed by one of the women while two others stripped naked and stepped into the knee deep water ahead of her. The two women holding the long lines remained outside the water on opposite sides so that Nena could never have access to them both at once.

None of the women addressed her, only pointed to indicate when they wanted her to do something. They actually spoke very little even amongst themselves. Nena wondered if it was because she was Teclan and they were intimidated, or if Altene had given orders forbidding it. But they did not need to speak for Nena to know quite a bit about them. By the marks on their arms, she could see they were all from the smaller, weaker tribes of the plains—all tribes that would have been victims of the Teclan in the past, and all tribes easier for a Klarta to dominate.

They bore no bruises or scars that Nena could see, yet appeared almost tranquil—accepting of their fate. Nena could not comprehend it. How could they so easily embrace servitude and not be plotting to escape? How could they be surrounded by so many potential weapons and not arm themselves? Nena made no attempt to ask them; she knew they would not answer. Again she told herself she must be patient. As with everything else in her life now, she had to watch, learn, and wait.

Though the water was warm and their touch was gentle, Nena was uncomfortable being the recipient of the slaves' attentions. She sat stiffly on the edge of the low bench under the water while the two women lathered and scrubbed every inch of her. No place was missed. As one slave lathered her hair and massaged her scalp, the second used a dull quill to clean underneath her fingernails. Her arms were then lifted to wash her armpits and the sides of her breasts. Her feet were each held out of the water and care was taken to scrub between each toe. Nena grit her teeth as the soapy rag was run between her buttocks, and again when her legs were spread to better accommodate the probing rag in her private places. It was all done quickly and efficiently, but Nena found it degrading just the same.

All the while, Altene sat lounging on the side, well out of her reach, making sure the task was done to her satisfaction, but never getting involved in the work. "If I were rich, I would have slaves bathe me every day. I wouldn't lift a finger to tend to anything myself," Altene imagined out loud.

Nena didn't respond but couldn't help but be struck by how different they were. The Teclan felt it showed weakness to have others perform labors for them. Because of this, they were the only tribe she knew of that did not keep slaves. Young children, the elderly, and the sick or wounded needed to be attended to, but for any who were physically able, to accept such care was disgraceful.

One of the women held her fingers over Nena's eyelids to keep them closed, while the second used a bucket to rinse the lather from her hair. After twisting her hair into a large tight knot and squeezing the excess water from it, a vial of scented oil was pulled through her long strands, and any tangles were removed with their fingers. She was then allowed to step from the pool and stand while they dried her entire body with soft hides. The final step was to rub her skin with more scented oil until it glowed. Altene snapped her fingers, and Nena was provided a fresh baggy leather dress. She hadn't seen her original soft doeskin since the first night, though she was sure, by now, it had to have been cleaned. After the two slaves who had bathed her donned their own dresses, Nena was returned to Jarl's tent and secured to the pole.

Nena counted off the days until the camp would move—each one seeming to drag on forever. Every day she listened in silence as Jarl and Altene pieced together her life and the life of all Dor. Every day she continued to do the same about the Northmen, watching, listening and learning. Every seemingly insignificant detail, she committed to memory for her escape.

As the guard entered with their evening meal, it was an escape she hoped would come on the morrow. One more sleep and the day the camp was to move would finally have arrived. Everything would be disorganized. She would be free of the pole. Jarl would be preoccupied. She would have to slip among the prisoners and find the girl, but with the plain dresses Altene kept her clothed in, she would not stand out.

Jarl unhooked the chain from her cuffs and led her to a chair at the table. There were only two places set, which meant Altene would not be joining them. Nena breathed a thankful sigh of relief; she would be able to eat her meal in peace tonight. After she was seated, Jarl took his place opposite her, facing the door, as he always did. Nena knew it was so that he could see anyone who entered and keep her in his line of sight at the same time. During meals, though, intrusions were rare and usually brief. Once he ascertained it wasn't an emergency, Jarl would send the person away with instructions to return later.

When the entry boards rattled, Nena turned to look, ever hopeful. Who knew when and in what form opportunity to escape would avail itself. Nothing she had seen so far prepared her for the woman who entered.

Jarl was, in fact, just about to send her away, but Nena's response made him hesitate. For all her practiced mask, Nena was clearly shocked. She stared openly at the woman. Puzzled by her reaction, Jarl beckoned the blond Northwoman closer.

"Yes, Osa?" he asked.

"Apologies to bother you, my lord, but there is a question on the guard rotation when we break camp tomorrow."

Nena was only barely aware of their words, so focused was she on this woman. Her blond hair, the same shade as Gunnar's, was fastened with intricate braids coiled on top of her head. She wore light armor stained with blood from previous battles. Tall and strong, she carried sword and dagger and talked to Jarl as a man would. When their conversation was over, Nena's eyes followed her to the doorway until the last trace of her disappeared beyond the flap.

She turned back to her plate of food, trying to process what she had just seen. Her curiosity was intense, but she dreaded the thought of having to ask Altene about it. She could clearly imagine Altene's smug, superior look as she relayed the information as if she were speaking to a child. Or worse, if she thought Nena wanted to know badly enough, she would refuse to answer at all.

Jarl watched Nena pick at her food. Had he not just witnessed her strange reaction to Osa, that in itself would have told him something was amiss. Normally she wolfed down every bite to be away from him as quickly as possible. He wondered what had affected her so, but did not ask. There was no point. Her response to every single question, other than on the subject of moving her brother's body, was always the same. *"Ask your whore."* So he was shocked when she spoke.

"That woman," she began, "she is a warrior?"

Jarl hid his amazement and took another bite, as if nothing were out of the ordinary, before answering. "Osa? Yes. She's a warrior and a good one. We call them shield-maiden."

Nena considered that information for a long moment. "So, she is unmarried?" she asked.

"No, Osa is married to Hansted. He is another warrior here," he elaborated.

"Are they recently married?"

He thought about it briefly, then shook his head. "No, not recently. I don't know for sure, but I think they've been married quite awhile—ten years, perhaps."

Nena nodded as if it all suddenly made sense to her. "Then she is barren."

"Osa? No, she has two children. They remain with her sister in the north while she and Hansted are on this expedition."

Nena's face was so shocked by his latest admission that Jarl felt obligated to defend them. "Between the two of them they will earn as much on this one journey as they would in three lifetimes of successful farming. Their children are with family and well cared for, and would continue to be so, should they fall and not return."

"Are there others here—female warriors?"

Jarl loved the strange way she pronounced his words, each rolling of her tongue with guttural undertones. He wanted nothing more than to keep her talking.

"Yes. A few. Why does that surprise you? Are not all of your women raised to be warriors?"

"Yes."

"Then what?"

"Our women fight only until they choose," she said. "Or rarely until they are with their first child, if the number of men in the village is very low, and they are needed to fight," she added.

That explained the barren question. "What if a woman does not wish to give up being a warrior? Can't she continue to raid?" Jarl asked.

"No. And no woman would want that. Once a woman chooses, she no longer wishes for such things. She wants only to be a mother and to remain in the village to tend to things there," she finished, trying to seem matter-of-fact, but coming off more as well-rehearsed.

"With most of our women it is also so," Jarl said. "But not all. They are trained to fight as young girls, and as they grow older, many do not care for the danger and prefer to remain at home." He paused, then added. "But with our people, it's the woman's choice...well, hers and her husband's. Do none of your women ever want the same?"

Nena shook her head.

Jarl could tell the conversation was winding down. He didn't want it to end. "That seems a great waste. Some of our women are even leaders."

His last statement did not have the desired response of initiating further discussion. After her initial shock and search of his face to see if he was lying, Nena became silent, contemplating the new information.

Chapter 5

The next morning Jarl was up and gone before first light. Nena could hear activity going on outside the tent in all directions. She could barely contain herself. When the tent flap next opened, it was not Jarl who returned, but two men she had never seen before. They propped open the tent flap, revealing an empty wagon parked outside. Without even seeming to notice her, they efficiently began to pack Jarl's belongings. No move was wasted. No time was spent pondering the best way to fold something or what to pack together. Everything was tied in bundles or neatly fit into crates as if it had a predetermined place.

She evaluated each man closely as they moved about the tent. Her hopes rose even higher. The older one was stronger and more aware, but he moved stiff in his right shoulder. The younger one had no injury that she could determine, but glanced at her nervously whenever he had to walk near her, and averted his eyes quickly when she looked back at him. Neither would be a match for her. She waited, tense with anticipation. Soon, she would be the only thing remaining in the tent for them to move.

When the last bundle was stowed on the wagon, the two men remained outside talking under their breaths. The younger one cast an unsure glance at her, and they conferred again. Perhaps they were trying to decide which one was going to unchain her. Perhaps it would only be one of them. How fortunate for her that would be. She waited to see what they would decide. But instead of coming back inside, they gave her one final look, then moved from her view. She heard them untying some of the smaller support ropes on the outside of the tent. The canvas wall to her left sagged slightly. Nena wanted to scream with frustration. Were they not going to release her? Surely they weren't going to just drop the tent around her ears.

She heard a horse's hoof beats approaching and stretched to the end of her chain to gain a better view out of the tent opening. There were the reddish-brown and black legs of Jarl's stallion, then Jarl's boots as he dismounted. He said something to the two men, tied the horse's reins to the wagon, and entered. He surveyed the empty tent with satisfaction before walking toward her.

"Don't look so disappointed," he said in response to her expression. "You didn't really think I'd trust one of them to release you, did you?" Nena scowled at him, and he paused, reading her face. He chuckled. "Ah, you did." He shook his head. "I know better. And I like them both far too much to subject them to that."

Jarl unhooked the chain from the pole and started to lead her toward the door. "Remember to behave yourself, Princess," he warned. "The furs may have already been packed, but I'm not above rolling around on the ground with you if you try anything."

He untied the horse's reins and led both the stallion and Nena half a dozen paces away from the tent. He pulled her closer to the horse and tied her hands off to the front of the saddle so he could watch the final step uninterrupted. The two men disappeared inside with long poles. The top of the tent jiggled and changed shape, then the men reappeared dragging the heavy center pole between them. They loaded it, splitting the wagon lengthwise down the middle, and while the older one lashed it down to keep it from rolling side to side, the younger man returned inside alone. Nena heard two quick tapping sounds, then he reappeared, racing back through the doorway. Within seconds, the tent collapsed to the ground with a whoosh of air from the opening, and the men began to roll it up.

Without waiting for them to finish, Jarl led Nena to the wagon and climbed into the back, tugging on her cuffs for her to follow him. He pointed for her to sit on one side of the pole, then produced a shorter length of chain from his pocket.

"You'll be sitting, so you won't need the extra length," he explained as he replaced the longer chain on her shackles. "Besides, it would likely only get you into trouble." After securing the new chain to the pole, he climbed down from wagon and smiled at her. "Comfortable?" he asked.

She glared at him and looked away.

He laughed.

Nena heard the squeak of leather as he remounted, then the sounds of the stallion's hooves moving away. She jerked the cuffs in frustration. She had hoped to be free of the pole for the move, yet here she sat, as secure as ever. And this shorter piece of chain didn't even allow her enough length to wrap around someone's neck.

One such someone appeared at that very moment. Altene watched as her own belongings were stowed, then took her place in a pile of Jarl's furs on the opposite side of the wagon. Nena grimaced, then looked away, refusing to acknowledge her. The day could not get any worse. Jarl's security measures would deny her the escape she had desperately hoped for all week. And not only was she utterly humiliated at being loaded like some common piece of Jarl's chattel, now she would also have to endure Altene.

The two men who had packed the tent climbed up onto the driver's bench, and the wagon lurched forward. Creaking and bouncing, they fell into line with others from the camp, continuing their journey north. The pace was slow to accommodate the walking prisoners, among whom Nena was still sorely disappointed to not find herself. After hours of bumpy, silent travel through the unchanging plains, Nena stole a glance at Altene.

The Klarta woman stared out of the opposite side of the wagon, clearly no more happy with her traveling companion than Nena was. That Altene found her presence irritating made Nena feel somewhat better. A plan began to form in her mind. Perhaps Altene's unwelcome company could be turned to opportunity. If Jarl could gain information from her about the Dor, why couldn't she do the same about the Northmen?

"Where are we going?" Nena asked.

Altene looked at her without replying, then looked away again.

Perhaps she didn't know. Nena tried something else. "I thought that the word Jarl was a title, like King or Chieftain, not a name. Did I learn this incorrectly?"

Altene gave her a long measuring look, then surprised Nena by answering. "No. You are correct. Normally it is a noble's title, but for him, it is his given name."

"How did you know Jarl would not force me to his furs?"

"Because everyone knows it."

"But why?"

"Why should I tell you?"

"Because we are stuck on this wagon together." Nena rattled the chain on the pole for emphasis. "Because we have nothing else to do, and perhaps it might speed the journey."

Altene heaved a great sigh. "I suppose." She thought for a moment. "Truly, I do not know why. Rumor has it his mother was raped in front of him when he was but a boy, too young to defend her—that she made him swear to be a better man than that." She paused, then shrugged. "But you know how rumors are. The truth could be far removed."

"Was it also the same with you then? Did he keep you a prisoner at first? And what changed to make you now serve him so willingly?" Nena asked.

Altene smiled and shook her head. "Jarl had only to ask to lie with me. No man before him ever did. I was a true prisoner for many years before that."

"Why do you hate me?" Nena asked. "Do you think it's somehow my fault, or the fault of the Teclan, that you spent your life a prisoner? The Teclan don't take slaves. We're not responsible for you being here."

"And that probably lets you rest easy at night, doesn't it?" Altene asked, her voice hard. "The Teclan don't take slaves, so they are not responsible for what happens to a village after they attack. Did you know there are other tribes and bands of slavers who follow Teclan warriors like the great buzzard follows the lion? When the men are killed and a village is left decimated and defenseless by the Teclan, these others appear within days, stalking their wounded prey.

"You wouldn't know anything about a village's desperate attempts to flee— to find some place to hide or defend. But these men who follow the Teclan are skilled, and they hunt with no more mercy than if they were hunting a rabbit. Every man, woman, and child, regardless of age, is captured. For all those who survive, a buyer will be found, the price dependent on the individual's abilities. Even the weakest and the youngest are capable of performing some menial task.

"Do I hate you?" Altene considered the question out loud, then nodded. "Yes, I do. Though I suppose it is a hatred born much of envy. I envy to be you—to have lived your whole life in privilege and without fear. Even now, if you were any other woman, you'd have been taken by half the Northmen camp, yet because you're Teclan, you've been spared again."

"Then release me. You want me gone—to have Jarl back to yourself. Now, during the move, in the chaos, I could find the child and escape with her."

"You are a fool," Altene said and looked away.

Nena waited for many minutes, then started a new line of questioning, sure that Altene would spite her with silence. "Where do they come from? How far north are their homelands?"

"I do not know exactly." Altene surprised her by responding. "I believe the journey takes them months. To get here, they follow a maze of rivers from the far north and west through a wild land they call Rusland, far beyond where any Dor has ever ventured. In places they must carry their ships across land to the next river until they reach the last river they call the Volga. That river brings them here, to the Great Sea, though they call it the Caspian. I have heard them say it's small compared to the seas of their homeland. Each time they come ashore in a different place and make a sweeping arch through these lands, acquiring treasure and slaves on the way. Their ships await them on the coast."

The Great Sea. Nena had only beheld it one time. It was the year she had first become a warrior. The journey north to the sea was one her father insisted all Teclan warriors make at least once—to see the great body of water that held power to rival their mountain. Her father had accompanied the novice warriors that year to refresh ties with the Sea Tribe's chief, whom his sister had married years before.

The Great Sea was beautiful, Nena recalled, but terrifying at the same time. She remembered wading out into the clear turquoise waters while children from the sea tribe paddled around her in tiny boats, laughing and playing. Though she knew how to swim, she'd kept her feet planted firmly in the soft sand, feeling the power in the small waves that pushed and pulled at her like a living thing—a living thing so vast, one's eyes could not take it all in with a single look. That power had frightened her, as she was sure it also had the other young Teclan warriors who waded with her, though none admitted it.

Her father had explained to them that the Great Sea protected those of the sea tribes as the Great Mountain protected the Teclan. He cautioned all the warriors that any attempt to ever pursue a sea tribe out onto the water would be fatal, even though they made navigating it appear easy. The Great Sea, when angered, could raise walls of water taller than three men, destroying anything in its path.

So how had the Northmen been able to cross it? And Altene said they came from a land that had seas larger than the Great Sea? Impossible. She returned her focus to Altene. "So there are more of them on the ships? How many?"

"I don't know, however many it takes to sail them. At the port they will sell everything they do not wish to take back with them, including most of the prisoners for slaves."

"They don't sell all the prisoners? They take some with them?" Nena asked.

"Yes, for labor when they must move the ships over the land." Altene smiled. "And for other things they may be good at."

"Have any who have been taken ever returned?" Nena asked.

Altene paused. "Not that I know of."

"What do you think becomes of them?"

"How should I know?" Altene snapped. "I'm sure many die on the journey. The labor of moving the ships is supposed to be nigh impossible."

"And yet you wish to go?" Nena asked.

"My labor will be of a far more delicate nature."

"Hmm," Nena murmured. "Has he shared with you then, his plans to take you with him?"

"Not in so many words, but his intentions have been plain."

Nena looked out over the endless grasslands and reflected on Altene's words as the wagon continued its agonizingly slow pace. "Before I was here, did you ride in the wagon or walk with the others?" she asked.

"I always rode. Jarl prefers me well-rested at the end of the day. As you will soon discover."

Nena scowled and Altene laughed.

For Nena, the long days in the wagon seemed never to pass. The landscape afforded little relief with only occasional trees when they were close to a river. On days when the air was still, the clouds of dust raised by the caravan threatened to choke her. Some days Altene was talkative. Others she sat in surly silence, refusing to answer a single question. Jarl had refuted her earlier claim of wanting her well-rested. She had yet to share his furs even once, and Nena could see that disturbed her greatly.

Every night, Jarl's tent was set up, though most of his belongings remained packed on the wagon, and many of his men slept under the stars. Nena soon realized the tent was not for his comfort. It was a battle planning station and scouts reported in at all hours of the night. Maps were perused, routes were adjusted.

Even had she not been privy to every conversation and every plan, Nena would still have known when the next target village was close. The men were tense and excited, eager to fight. It came as no surprise to her when Jarl ordered the halt of the procession and a full camp to be set up. The same two men unpacked the wagon, placing every item exactly where it had been before, and Jarl returned her to the pole.

The routine in his tent picked up much where it had left off, with Jarl settling grievances and dealing with camp business. The most significant difference were the many reports from the reconnaissance teams. Every activity of the next village was documented and relayed to him. Nena couldn't help but wonder what the scouts had reported when her small party had arrived at the Eastern Plains tribe the day before the tournament. Seeing the minute details his men provided him with now, she was sure it would have been noted. What had they said to him? *"Nine other natives arrived today. Armed, but no threat."* It was difficult for her to accept that was all it would have appeared to be to an outsider—that such a major event in her life could be reduced to nothing more than those nine words.

While the last minute plans were made, Nena again could only watch and file away the details of how things changed when they attacked—how many men went to fight, how many men stayed behind to guard things. She waited and prayed for an opportunity to escape.

The next village fell quickly. From all reports, the Northmen suffered few casualties and Jarl ordered only two days of rest—time enough to take a full accounting of their most recent acquisitions. Then they were packed and traveling again.

The next time the full camp was set up, it was expected to be for a longer stay than any of the previous ones. Scouts had reported several potential targets in the vicinity. Jarl chose a campsite near a wooded area and a fork in the river. It was a good location, centrally located from which to attack, and able to sustain the camp for an extended period of time. As the days dragged by, Nena continued to learn about the Northmen, about Jarl, about other Dor, even about herself. Many of the things uncomfortably contradicted what she'd been taught and had known her entire life to be true, and much of what she learned she would have preferred not to know.

After being so long in his nearly constant presence, it was impossible not to have learned the most about Jarl. It was easier in the beginning when she thought of him as an ignorant cruel barbarian, with no code, no honor. A savage grunting man-beast, as all Northmen were known to be. But now she knew none of those things were accurate in describing him. From all accounts he was fearless in battle. And while she had witnessed him to be strict with discipline, he was fair in his dealings with the men. Those were traits to be respected, not despised or feared. Those were Teclan values. That he shared those characteristics with the Teclan surprised and disturbed her.

In other ways he was as opposite of a Teclan as he possibly could be. Nena had never seen anyone even remotely like him. Every emotion manifested itself clearly on his face and body. When he was amused, the fine lines in the corners of his eyes crinkled, and unusual sharp depressions formed in his cheeks a short distance on either side of his mouth, even before he smiled. And his eyes. They were a unique blend of colors—shades of browns and greens with flecks of yellows and even dark blues, like the gods could not decide which color to make them, so had given him all instead. Even stranger still was that they changed color with his mood. Nena had no idea eyes could portray so much depth, so much feeling. Though he usually held his actions in check, Jarl's feelings were never secret. It was something Teclan were schooled against from the time they could walk—to show your feelings was weak. But Jarl could never be called that. Somehow, it just made him more alive.

Something else Nena soon came to easily recognize was his arousal. It wasn't so much a single defined thing that she could see. It was more the way he carried himself as he moved around the tent, the air around him charged with a tense masculine energy. Some nights he consumed large quantities of wine and sat staring at her, brooding. These nights he would go to his furs alone. Other nights he would look at her longingly, then call for Altene. But these nights were becoming less and less frequent.

That fact pleased her, and not because it had anything to do with them. On the nights Altene shared Jarl's furs, what Nena learned about herself was even more difficult to accept. She had never thought of her body as being anything other than an obedient tool to her mind. It wielded her knife to skin a kill, or her spear to kill an enemy. It vaulted effortlessly onto Nightwing's back. It did anything she required. Sometimes it might fail her by being too slow or too weak, but it was never independent. Other than thirst and hunger, it had no demands or desires that her mind did not give it, and with training even those could be ignored.

But thirst and hunger were the closest things Nena could come up with to describe how her body responded to him. While her mind still formulated ways to kill him, her body reacted to him of its own accord. It tingled when his eyes caressed it from a distance. And when Jarl called Altene to his furs, it was filled with a deep aching hunger she had never experienced before. Her body disgraced her.

Nena had known before what happened between men and women in the furs. Teclan women were not shy about their intimacies, especially the older ones. It was something they did not discuss in mixed company, but many an experience had been shared in private. Even with all their talk, Nena was not expecting this. She knew, in general, how the act was performed and that it would be pleasurable—how pleasurable seemed to depend on the individual man. But no one had ever described anything close to what she saw Altene and Jarl experiencing. For all of Altene's falseness, she'd apparently been honest in this. Her ecstasy was unmistakable, as was his.

Nena still used her warrior tactic to take her consciousness away, but when the increased tempo and intensity of their sounds intruded on her peaceful scene—their soft gasps, the moist sounds of their lips and then intimate places meeting, her stomach clenched involuntarily. Though her eyes remained averted, Nena could clearly see the taut muscles of his straining back, his muscular buttocks thrusting and thrusting, from other times when she had stolen a look.

She had looked more than once, truth be told. At first she told herself it was to identify any weakness in him, an old injury perhaps that she could later use to her advantage. And maybe it had been initially—though he was not shy around her; she could have seen everything she needed to see in that regard, one of the many times he moved around the tent naked—and she had. Now, after all this time, she knew every detail of his lean body. Every detail down to how the hair on his chest and abdomen swept in from both sides, meeting in the middle of his rippled stomach before angling downwards. How each individual muscle in his upper arms bulged, smooth and well-defined. How his battle scars were fewer than she expected from his reputation, and none seemed to hinder him. She knew all of those things, so there was certainly no reason to look now, yet she still did. Her lack of discipline in this regard disgraced her even more than her body's responses.

The time Nena spent away from Jarl when the women took her to the baths was no less disconcerting. Increasingly confident around her that she was not going to escape and get them punished or killed, the women's tongues were loosened. They were from many different villages, but their stories were shockingly the same.

Nena knew them to be true, but had never once considered life from the perspective of the vanquished. The Teclan were never raided; their families were never torn asunder by outsiders. No outside force had ever made it past the Bloodcliff Gates of their mountain stronghold, much less to their village high above. The Teclan had losses but they came as a result of their own initiated actions. Loss was a way of life for these women, and had been for as long as they could remember.

It was their belief and acceptance of melding with their captor's tribe that was most shocking to Nena. They expected that after their initial grief, if they could be taken as a wife, it was for the best. Not only had the gods chosen it, but the new tribe was obviously stronger than their previous one, so they should be better off. Some viewed it as an almost accepted way of mixing blood. Coming from a strong tribe, Nena found their attitudes baffling. The idea of living in a weak, fearful tribe to start with, and then submitting to being a captive were difficult enough, but to embrace the enemy as your own was inconceivable to her.

Yet the more she listened to them, the more she began to understand, and even agree, that for them, perhaps joining a new tribe was better. What was their alternative? With limited fighting skills, vengeance was not an option. And if they could escape, where would they go? Back to the remnants of an already weak tribe and wait for the next attack? If they could find peace and happiness in a stronger tribe, was that wrong? Nena could have accepted it easier had they not applied the same logic to the Northmen. To them, the Northmen were only a tribe of a different skin color. That, Nena could not accept.

Two of the women who regularly bathed her, shared tents full time with Northmen, and Nena had to admit, they appeared happier than those who did not, often chatting away at how well they were treated and their hopes for a future with these men.

Some days it was too much for Nena to take in. Her mind was stretched with so many facts, so many details, so many new ideas. Northwomen warriors—

even leaders, if she believed Jarl's words. Jarl not being the beast-man she had assumed all Northmen to be. Her body's traitorous response to him. The way these women accepted their lot and their bizarre ideas on assimilating with their captors. Had this always been the way of the world? Had being a Teclan so shielded her? Was she truly as naive as Altene said? Sometimes her mind hurt when it was time to sleep at the end of the day.

"What do you think of that, Princess?" Altene's voice interrupted her thoughts. She always used Jarl's pet name for her, but when Altene said it, it was more as an epithet. "Have you ever feared for your life when you went to get water? Or wondered where your next meal would come from because your village was gone? I think not. You Teclan have no idea of what others endure in their everyday lives."

"I know I will never accept being a captive, and I will never forget who I am. No matter how long it takes—weeks or years, one day I will escape and return to my people."

"And that may be fine for you; you have some place to go back to. We must find a new home, a new tribe."

"The Northmen are not a tribe," Nena maintained.

"Aren't they?" Altene countered. "I would say, not only are they a tribe, they are the strongest tribe."

Several of the other women nodded in agreement.

Nena didn't argue. She wasn't up to it. It took too much effort and her own thoughts were too conflicted to mount a proper argument. Every new thing she learned challenged the black and white world she knew, each new concept adding another shade of gray.

Chapter 6

Jarl reached for the tent flap to call for Altene, then changed his mind and stepped out into the warm night air. He needed a release, but Altene was not who he wanted. The prospect of spending an uninterrupted evening alone in the tent with Nena was a physically uncomfortable one, and tonight, it would most likely be uninterrupted. The first village from this latest grouping of targets had fallen with little resistance to their swords that morning. His men would all be celebrating.

After the ease of today's victory, he knew the men were already eager to move on the next settlement. He would finalize the plans tomorrow and they would attack it soon, maybe even the following day. Jarl nodded to his guards and made his way toward the loudest sounds of revelry. He found Tryggr there.

"Ah, Jarl. Come to join us for a drink. It's been too long. Come, come." Tryggr waved him to a chair.

"Is there any left?" Jarl asked dubiously, noting the flushed color of Tryggr's face nearly matched his hair.

"Plenty," Tryggr answered and handed Jarl a half full bottle.

Jarl took a swig without waiting for a mug. His face twisted and he coughed at the stoutness of the brew. "What the hell?"

Tryggr laughed. "Horace just finished this fine concoction. Only the gods know what's in it. I, myself, am too afraid to ask. Probably not quite the quality fare you're used to?"

"It'll do." Jarl said and took another swallow. "Where's Gunnar?" he asked after he caught his breath from the second dose of the burning liquid.

"He was here briefly, but you know Gunnar—unable to resist a beautiful woman. Some new one caught his eye today, and he couldn't wait long enough to even share a proper drink with friends."

Jarl nodded. Gunnar's appreciation of women was well known. "How fare you after today's battle?"

"Not a scratch today. I am fully returned to form. And you? How fare you with your wild Teclan woman? Still have her chained to the tent pole? Or have you finally been able to secure her to your man pole yet?"

"I'm getting there," Jarl replied.

"That's a no, then."

"You do not understand the principles of taming, Tryggr. It's the same as breaking a fine horse. Choose a strong-willed one and take your time, and the results will far surpass your expectations. Rush the process, and you will be left with little of worth." Jarl took another long pull from the bottle and exhaled sharply through his clenched teeth. "Though that is probably why you still ride an oversized plow horse. My stallion fights beneath me like an additional weapon, often taking down more foe with his hooves and teeth than my sword. He does this now, but trust me, when I first captured him, he was as eager to kill me as the woman is."

"I ride an oversized plow horse because that's the only thing big enough to carry me," Tryggr objected. "And no matter what the method, Jarl, everyone gets around to riding them sooner or later. Maybe it's time you just threw your saddle on her and see what happens." Tryggr laughed and slapped his leg, then reached for the bottle and took another swig.

Jarl shook his head. Tryggr would never understand. He was a good and trusted friend, but they were very different men. Tryggr lived and fought by brute strength alone, and it had served him well. His only battle loss had come at Jarl's hand, and from that Tryggr had sworn his undying loyalty, but it had not changed him.

"No, but seriously," Tryggr continued when his laughter had abated. "I'm telling you, you're not thinking clearly. She's not like your horse that will fight by your side for years to come. What difference does it make what she thinks of you, or if she's a bit battered by the experience? She'll recover; they all do." He shrugged and took another drink. "And soon we'll be returning home." When Jarl did not respond, Tryggr paused and regarded him closely. "You can't possibly think to have a future with her? As what? As bed slave? As wife? Do you think to marry her and take her home to the North? She's never even seen snow, Jarl. She knows nothing of surviving in the cold, and nothing of our ways. Will she gather wood and keep a fire in your hearth? Tend to your cottage and rear your brats? Is that what you see?" He didn't wait for Jarl to answer. "No, it's not, because you haven't thought any farther ahead than fucking her. So do it. It's consuming your thoughts. For the sake of the gods, man, go do it now. Throw her to the furs and get this madness out of your system."

Nena was kneeling, balanced on the balls of her feet, when he entered. She looked up at him. It was early for him to be retiring to his furs. But Jarl wasn't looking at the furs. He was looking at her. Her pulse quickened. Something was off. Something had changed. She stood in one fluid movement to face him.

Every fiber in her body sensed him. Her eyes. Her ears. Even her skin felt for tiny wind currents. It was her warrior training. The Teclan were thought by their enemies to have reflexes of lightning, but in truth they were no quicker than any other Dor. They were just taught from a young age to be aware—to sense their opponent with all their senses, not just their eyes. And even with their eyes, they learned to see differently. Not to see the sword blade as it was pulled from the scabbard, but to see the fingers as they twitched or trembled before they gripped the hilt. To see the slight flaring of their enemy's nostrils as they inhaled before lunging. Through those small silent almost invisible signals, the opponent telegraphed what their next move would be long before they made it. The Teclan saw and felt it all.

Without a word, Jarl came closer, not stopping until he stood only inches from her. Her senses screamed at his nearness. She could not turn them off, and they continued to bombard her with signals of imminent danger. His eyes were the deep green of when he was aroused. She smelled the smoke on his clothes from the cook fires outside, the harsh scent of lye soap on his skin, and the alcohol on his breath. His masculine energy ran unchecked between them, filling the small space like a living thing. Nena did not step back or shrink away. There was nowhere for her to go—a few feet in either direction to the end of her chain, and the result would be the same. She would not show fear. She dare not excite the predator response in him. Every warrior knew that if attacked by the lion, never to run, but to remain as still as possible and hope the beast would lose interest. Nena called upon that training now.

Jarl reached up and touched her face, stroking from her temple down over her cheek to the line of her jaw. She remained perfectly still, but the track of his fingertips left a stinging burn as if he had slapped her. His touch was gentle, but Nena could see his entire body was as taut as hers. She held his gaze, unmoving, grasping at every shred of her discipline to do so.

With Tryggr's words fresh in his ears, Jarl stood before her, taking in every detail. Her eyes, dark unreadable pools, held his. The curve of her lips, her exotic scent and her warmth beckoned him. Her proud strength combined with her almost innocent sensuality filled his senses, and it was far more intoxicating than the liquor he had just consumed. He could only imagine how having her would feel.

"Do I frighten you?" he asked, his voice husky.

"Free my hands and give me a weapon, and I will show you," she murmured.

Nena's senses first reported the unusual indents in his cheeks beginning to form, then the softening at the corners of his eyes, before his lips twitched and he smiled a rueful smile. He grunted and nodded, appreciating her response. Her words had broken the spell.

"Yes, I imagine you would. But know that I will tame you. There has never been anything in my life that I wanted that I could not win." He paused and exhaled slowly as his eyes gave her one final admiring exploration. "Though I must admit, you are turning out to be a far greater challenge than I had anticipated."

The next morning a messenger arrived from the healer, bringing word of a sickness spreading among the prisoners. The cases were few, he reported, so Nena was surprised at the level of Jarl's concern—even more surprised when he postponed the attack on the second target within their range. As the number of cases grew, the senior healer became a frequent visitor to Jarl's tent. Each of his reports were more grim than the last.

"It's the Curse, my lord, worse than I've ever seen in years past, but it is definitely the Northman's Curse," he announced one evening.

"How many have we lost so far?" Jarl asked.

"Twenty, with more every day."

"And still none of our men sick?"

The healer nodded.

Jarl stretched and rubbed the back of his neck. "We've had this every trip; why is it so much worse this time? And so close to port? I thought we had avoided it."

"I don't know, my lord. In many ways it is the same as before, but in others it's different. Instead of infecting blocks of prisoners, it will affect only one out of a small group that share a tent, then skip the rest and affect another somewhere else. Quarantine has been ineffective, as unfortunately has treatment. Unlike before, when many would be sickened but few would die, this time fewer contract the disease, but death is certain. I've tried leeches, sandalwood, ratfish oil, arsenic, burning wormwood, even trepanned a few, to no avail. I also attempted some native remedies received from a captured medicine man, but nothing has worked."

"Keep trying," Jarl said.

"Of course."

"And none of our men are affected, you're sure?"

"Not a one, sir. Just as before."

Jarl nodded. "If there is anything you need—anything special, send word to me and you shall have it. Whatever you require."

"Yes, my lord." The healer excused himself and left the tent.

As the news from the prisoner compound continued to grow worse, men worked around the clock, digging pits for the bodies. Under normal circumstances, they would have constructed great pyres to burn the dead, but Jarl feared the smoke from such large fires would alert the next villages to their presence.

Each day Jarl's face grew more drawn. His men were also disturbed, but Nena knew from listening to their conversations, that their concern centered only on the amount of wealth they were losing per day. They even raised the suggestion of making one extra sweep to the east instead of going straight to port, to replenish the slave population before they made sail. Jarl agreed to consider the proposal and make a decision—once these quit dying.

After the last of his higher ranking men had left for the evening, Jarl drained his cup and pushed his chair back from the table. Altene remained. She moved to stand behind him and began massaging his broad shoulders. He closed his eyes as her nimble fingers unknotted the tension from deep within his muscles. "Shall I pleasure you tonight, my lord?" Altene whispered in his ear and pressed her breasts against his back.

Nena grimaced. It had been quite a while since Jarl had taken Altene to his furs, a fact that clearly disturbed Altene. Jarl did not respond. Altene traced her fingers along Jarl's neck just inside his collar, then unlaced the front of his tunic and moved her caresses to his chest. Still he made no move to stop her or take her to the furs. Becoming more bold, she reached down and unlaced the front of his trousers, then extended her hand inside, stroking and pulling.

It was what she did next that shocked Nena, who thought she could no longer be shocked by anything Altene and Jarl did. Keeping one hand engaged inside his trousers, she unclasped her dress with the other. After it fell to the floor, she moved around in front of him, then knelt before him naked. Slipping her upper body between his legs, she spread them slightly, then lowered her head and took him into her mouth. Jarl's face tightened in immediate response. He groaned.

Nena closed her eyes and tried to go far away, but the image remained vivid in her mind's eye, kept there by the sounds of his pleasure. She had never heard of such a thing, even from the boldest of the older Teclan women. She took a deep breath and tried once again to go to her warrior's tranquil place, but was overcome by a sudden wave of dizziness and nausea. She thrust out her hands and grabbed the pole to steady herself.

The sudden jangling of Nena's chain set off Jarl's alarms. He shoved Altene aside and stood to gain clear view of the center of the tent. His first thoughts were split evenly on responding to Nena's escape and her attack. But Nena remained standing like a statue—her shackled hands gripping the pole—her eyes staring at him, unfocussed.

Nena didn't know what was the matter with her. Three blurry Jarls edged toward her with three Altenes close behind him. All six wore horrified expressions on their faces. She shook her head, trying to clear her vision. The motion caused her to lose her balance. She clawed at the pole for support, but her fingernails were unable to find purchase on the smooth wood. As her hands fell away, the last thing she was aware of was Altene's terrified whisper.

"It's the Northman's Curse."

Chapter 7

"Nena," Jarl shouted as he jumped forward to keep her suddenly limp body from crashing to the floor. He gently laid her down on her sleeping furs, and pushed a few strands of hair from her face. "Nena, can you hear me?" He lifted one eyelid with his fingers, but her glazed eye was unresponsive.

"Get the healer," he called over his shoulder to Altene, then bent to check her breathing. Her chest rose and fell as normal. When he did not hear the tent flap move, he turned to find Altene still standing where he'd left her a few paces back—still staring horrified at Nena. "Altene!" he shouted.

Her eyes flickered to his face.

"Move! Go get the healer, now!"

Altene gave a quick nod and fled the tent.

Jarl unclasped both shackles from Nena's wrists and carried her to his own furs. He could feel her body burning even through both layers of their clothing. He found a small rag near the table, soaked it from the waterskin, and returned to her side, wiping her forehead and neck. He felt helpless. He had attended many an injury on the battlefield, but with no wound to address, he was at a loss for what to do. *What was taking the damn healer so long? Had Altene even found him?* A rattle of the boards at the entrance answered his question. "Enter," he called out, irritated that they had bothered with the formality when the situation was so urgent.

"Jarl?" the healer asked as he entered with Altene close behind him.

"Here," Jarl directed him to the furs. Altene waited at the doorway.

"What happened to her?" the healer asked as he set down his bag and rolled up his sleeves.

"I don't know. She was just standing there." Jarl pointed to the pole. "Then with no warning, she started to sway and collapsed."

The healer nodded and felt her forehead. When he lifted her eyelids, Jarl noticed both of her eyes were now bloodshot. The healer parted her lips and checked her gums. He listened to her breathing, first with his ear close to her nostrils, then with it flat against her chest. He checked her skin all over, focusing on the palms of her hands, then her fingernails. Other than her eyes, he found nothing out of the ordinary that Jarl could see. But when he finished, he looked up at him, his expression grave.

"Is it the Curse?" Jarl asked softly, not wanting to know the answer.

The healer only nodded.

"What can you do?"

"I don't know. First we can bring down the fever. I've had luck with ground willow bark for that." He dug in his bag for a small vial, pulled the cork and stuck his finger inside, rolling it around until was coated in the fine grayish brown powder. Pulling open Nena's lower lip with his other hand, he rubbed the coated finger along her gums.

"Then what?" Jarl asked.

"Then, when it returns—and it will, we will do it again. And when the chills take her, we will keep her warm." His shoulders sagged. "Eventually, though, nothing will work. The pain will come next. Thyme will hold it at bay for awhile, but after that only juice of the poppy will make her comfortable."

"That's it?" Jarl asked.

The healer looked at Jarl, exhausted and a little exasperated. "Jarl, we have discussed nothing but this for almost a fortnight. You know I do not have a cure."

"What else have you tried?"

He shook his head. "Everything. You know that, too."

"What has worked?"

"Jarl...."

"What has worked the best then, dammit? Surely you have learned something with all the hours you've wasted. Have you not saved even one?"

"Apologies, Jarl, but you know that I have not."

"Get out. Leave the vial and get out."

The man stood as if he were going to say something more, then headed for the door.

"Altene," Jarl called.

"Yes, my lord," she whispered.

"Go to the prisoner compound and find any among them with healing knowledge. I know the healer has already questioned a medicine man there, but there may be others, midwives, someone with a special tribal remedy. Find them for me and take them to the healer. This time, let them know the reward for their success will be their freedom. And yours," he added.

"Yes, my lord," she said, her deflated tone reflecting her feelings on the dismal project.

Altene and the healer returned together in the gray light of predawn. Jarl had given Nena several more doses of the willow bark during the night, and though she remained unconscious, for the moment her fever was stable. Jarl met them at the table and poured each a cup of wine.

"Has Altene brought you any treatment of merit?" he asked the healer.

"Nothing new. All remedies she has discovered I have already tried, whether I thought they had merit or not. Contrary to what you might believe, Jarl, I have not ignored any treatment, no matter how strange, out of some egotistical need to prove my own expertise."

"Apologies, my friend, for my earlier words," Jarl said sincerely. "I know you are doing your best. Keep looking."

The following days for Nena were a blackened blur of fleeting images, half awake dreams and fragments of awareness. Once she awoke to find her skin on fire and Jarl carrying her through the camp.

"Is she dead?" she heard a voice ask.

"Get out of my way," Jarl snarled in reply.

The next thing she knew, he held her body submerged in the cool waters of the river, her head resting in the crook of his arm above the surface while her body dangled beneath.

Then darkness.

She lay covered with some bristly fur, near a fire she could not seem to get close enough to. Her body shivered and her teeth chattered uncontrollably. She burrowed deeper, pressing closer to the heat, unsure of why she could not reach it. As she became more aware, she realized it was not a flame, but Jarl's body that provided the heat. The bristles were not those of fur, but the hair on his chest and legs. She pushed against him, trying to push him away, but he only murmured something soothing in her hair and tightened his arms around her, pulling her back to the warmth she so desperately needed.

Darkness.

A hollow reed was between her lips, with Jarl dribbling tiny amounts of water into her parched mouth. His face was gaunt with worry.

Darkness.

The senior healer's face suspended over her, his expression bleak, before he turned to Jarl and shook his head. Dimly she heard Jarl shout something unintelligible, his voice twisted with fury. The healer's face was yanked from her sight.

Darkness.

Jarl's voice raised in anger. "We will attack when I say. When—I—say!" Jarl shouted, emphasizing each syllable. "Do not ask me again. Get out! Get out now, Tryggr. And know this—any man who thinks of trying to move her, I will kill him. Any man. Are we clear?"

Darkness.

Jarl cooling her forehead with a damp rag.

Darkness.

Unendurable pain coursing through ever fiber of her body. Nena couldn't take it—could not stand to be touched. Even the feel of the softest fur against her skin was agony. She longed for the darkness. She longed to die.

Darkness.

The suffering was unbearable; the afterlife beckoned her with sweet relief. The pain would be gone, and she would see her brother, Ruga, and the mother she had barely known. She would ride Nightwing again. They were all near. She could feel them reaching for her—welcoming her. She was ready. She let go.

Something held her fast and pulled her back. Back to the fire. Back to the ice. Back to the pain. Back to Jarl's haggard face and, one night his voice.

"I will not let you go. You are mine, and no one—not even the gods are going to take you from me," he whispered, his voice feverish, not from sickness, but from desperation as he held her head and dribbled cool water laced with something bitter into her mouth.

He was mad. Why did he care? Why did he not let her die? No one fought the gods. No one could. And no one dared try.

Then everything went completely black.

Nena awoke to light that did not burn her eyes and a body that did not ache. She took a moment to focus on her surroundings. She was in Jarl's furs. He sat on a stool at the side of the bed watching her closely. But it was not the same Jarl. This Jarl was bleary-eyed, and his gaunt face was covered with an unkempt ragged short beard. Nena tried to sit up but could not.

"I'll help you. You're too weak," Jarl said, his voice hoarse. He stood and rearranged the furs behind her, then lifted her effortlessly so she could sit upright. "Are you thirsty?" he asked.

She was and she nodded, still confused and disoriented. He brought a small cup and held it to her lips. She tried to gulp the refreshing cool liquid, but after several sips, he pulled it away.

"That's enough for now. Let's see how you do with that first," he said as he sat back down on the stool. "How do you feel? Are you hot? Or cold? In any pain?"

Nena shook her head to each of his questions.

"Good. That's good." He ran one hand through his hair, then leaned back and watched her. "How is your stomach with that water?"

"Fine." She tried to say, but the word came out as a barely audible whisper.

"I have some broth here if you think you can keep it down. Do you want to try?" he asked.

She nodded.

Jarl stood again and went to the table behind him, returning with a small bowl of tepid broth. He knelt down and lifted the spoon to her lips, but she shook her head and tried to reach for the bowl herself.

"Just eat," he scolded, and pushed her hands away. "You're too weak to feed yourself, and you'll never get any stronger if you don't eat." He offered her the spoonful again. She took it.

He was right. Her arms felt weak as a baby's. The tiny effort of lifting them had exhausted her. She finished the bowl, then slid back down in the furs, instantly asleep.

When she next awoke, Jarl was still sitting slouched on the stool, but now Altene stood behind him.

"I will tend to her, my lord. You need to sleep," Altene said.

Jarl started to protest.

"If anything changes at all, I will awaken you immediately," Altene reassured him.

Jarl nodded and stretched out across the furs at the foot of the bed. Within seconds he was snoring softly.

"You have survived the Northman's Curse," Altene murmured. Her voice was both awed and disappointed. "No others did, though they did not have Jarl attending to their every need." The resentment in her last words was unmistakable. "There is much talk among the men that you have put some Dor spell on him. He would not eat, not sleep, not speak or listen to reason while you were ill. He even threatened to kill any who tried to remove you."

"There is no such spell," Nena croaked.

"You and I know that. I have no idea where they would get such a notion." Altene smiled, and it was clear to Nena exactly where the *notion* had come from. "But Jarl's men are very concerned by it. If he cannot be rid of you on his own, maybe they will be able to convince him—or take matters into their own hands."

"That would be my wish, too."

"Perhaps," Altene said, measuring her.

"Let me go and you shall see."

"You are too weak to even stand; helping you now would serve no purpose. Besides, Jarl would kill me. Of that, I now have no doubt."

Over the next few days, Nena's strength slowly returned. When she could walk without assistance, she was returned to her place at the pole, though her relationship with Jarl was now one of an uneasy truce. He still chained her at night or when he left the tent, but the rest of the time she was free to move about inside. When they ate their meals together, he still allowed her no utensil other than a spoon, but they were speaking...somewhat.

"Surely there is some Dor law that binds you to a man when he saves your life?" Jarl teased as he attached her cuffs for the first time.

Nena had denied it, but knew her answer was not entirely truthful. There was more to it than that. While there might be no such binding law, the Dor valued honor, and the Teclan valued it more than most. To kill someone who had saved your life would be beyond dishonorable, and for that she would spare him. She had no doubt he had saved her. He had pulled her back from the afterlife more than once, though she still had no idea how that was possible. He had challenged the gods themselves. Who dared do such a thing? Who could do such a thing and have the gods listen? That question was very disturbing and she tried not to think about it. Instead she focused her thoughts once again on escape—though now her plans would require leaving Jarl alive.

Chapter 8

That afternoon the tent was filled with his officers. Though Nena remained secured to the pole as they pored over the maps and finalized their battle plans, she listened to every detail.

"Does she have to be here?" Tryggr complained. "I don't like discussing our plans in front of a Dor—any Dor."

Nena thought it strange. They had discussed their plans in front of her many times before, and while Tryggr had often looked at her suspiciously, never had he voiced his disapproval. Nena knew it had to be in response to Altene's rumor. Before she could look to Jarl and gauge his reaction, Gunnar spoke.

"You worry too much, Tryggr. Who's she going to tell?" Gunnar laughed. "It's not as if our fearless leader is going to let her out of his sight. If the past weeks have shown us nothing else, they have shown us that."

"Put your mind back to the business at hand and have the men ready to move on the next village tomorrow," Jarl said. His voice had a hard edge to it that Nena had not heard him use with them before.

"Tomorrow?" Tryggr asked.

"Is that a problem?" Jarl challenged. "You've done nothing but press me to attack for more than a week. Surely you would not have done so if the men were not ready." Jarl's eyes dared Tryggr to deny it.

"Of course they are. It's just..."

"Good," Jarl cut him off. "We'll move at first light."

After the last man had filed out for the night, Jarl released her, then moved to the table to clear it for their evening meal. Nena glanced at the last map as he rolled it up.

"Are those the last villages you will attack?" she asked, pointing to the circled marks.

"Yes," he said.

"Will you capture another chief's daughter and chain her to the pole next to me?"

Jarl shook his head and grunted. "No. I've quite learned my lesson there. One chief's daughter is plenty for a lifetime."

Nena had said the words in jest, hoping to cover her reaction to the last mark on the map. Though the scale of Jarl's map was different than her father's, the two long crooked fingers of land that jutted out into the Great Sea were unmistakable. She knew what the X marked where they joined the mainland represented. Her aunt's tribe would be the last to fall to the Northmen's swords. She changed the subject.

"Your man has often regarded me strange, but tonight he seemed quite vexed. Why?" She had not mentioned Tryggr by name, but Jarl knew who she was referring to.

"Perhaps he is entranced by your beauty and wished he had fought harder to keep you." Jarl judged her response carefully. Many native women found the red-haired giant's coloring irresistible; they had no such coloring here in the south, though Tryggr swore it was the legend of the size of his cock that kept them flocking to him.

Nena sniffed with mild distaste. One edge of Jarl's mouth twitched in a small smile, appreciating her response, before he continued.

"More likely he is curious as to why I keep you here. I have never kept a woman in my tent."

"You keep Altene."

"Not here."

"Why do you keep me chained? You know that so long as I am bound to the girl, I will not escape. Why don't you release me?"

"I do release you."

"To eat. To use the latrine. To be bathed by your whore. That is not release."

"I release you whenever I am present...and awake. Even with the girl, I don't trust you not to be able to find some way out—and to be quite honest, I still don't fully trust you not to try to kill me. And I told you before, when I first put them on, you would wear the cuffs until I could trust you as I trust Altene."

"I've had multiple opportunities now to kill you and have not. Does that not show I am trustworthy?" Nena asked. "What more would it take to convince you? What if I gave you my word?"

"I think not." He smiled a wry smile. "I've learned much about the Dor, far more than I ever planned to. A Dor's word to their enemy means nothing. And I am still your enemy. Your eyes are not as fierce, but I still see it there within them plain enough." He paused. "You asked me what it would take to convince me? There is one way." He grinned at her devilishly. "Share my furs willingly and you will have run of the camp any time you wish."

Nena scowled at him.

"So I must assume by your refusal that you do not find your bondage so undesirable after all," Jarl teased.

"The only thing you can assume is that I find you even more undesirable than being a captive," Nena retorted.

Jarl laughed out loud. "When you change your mind, you know how to make your chains disappear.

The second village also fell with few casualties to the Northmen. This one was larger than the last and many new prisoners were taken. It was a good start in replacing the numbers that had been lost to the Curse, Jarl thought, as he finished putting his stallion away. Perhaps they would not need to lengthen their trip after all. He was walking past Gunnar's tent on his way to his own when Gunnar and Tryggr hailed him. "Come, Jarl, have a drink."

Jarl hadn't noticed them. Though he was in a hurry to get back to his own tent and Nena, he stopped and took a seat. Tryggr handed him a cup filled with wine while Gunnar stood to retrieve something from inside his tent. He came back out carrying a sword and offered it up for both men to see. "Have you ever seen its like?" he asked.

Jarl looked at the golden hilt encrusted with fine jewels that sparkled and winked in the sunlight. The scabbard itself even appeared to be woven from gold metal thread. He shook his head. "I have not," he admitted.

"And wait," Gunnar said. He pulled the blade from its sheath.

The light bounced and danced on the silver as Gunnar rolled it with his wrist. Jarl had never seen such a blade either. Sharpened to a razor's edge, the steel was perfectly smooth, free of any flaw.

"I've never seen such fine workmanship, not in adornment or blade," Jarl confessed.

"You must have a feel." Gunnar turned the sword, holding the blade in his hands as he offered Jarl the hilt. "You would expect it to be heavy with the extra gold, but feel how light and well balanced it is."

Jarl took it and made several practice slashes through the air. "It is remarkable," he concurred and handed it back to Gunnar.

"Tryggr, would you like to have a feel?" Gunnar offered.

"No, it's a bit too fancy for my tastes," Tryggr declined. "Looks like something a woman would carry."

"And you got this from the last village?" Jarl asked.

"Yes, and I would keep it as part of my share. That is, of course, if you do not wish it for yourself." Gunnar said, offering the sword back to Jarl but clearly hoping he would refuse it.

"The sword is yours," Jarl declined. "That was not the point of my question. I saw nothing else there today to indicate they were capable of this level of craftsmanship. I cannot imagine that they forged it, so where do you think it came from? I truly have never seen its like. If we could find its creator, a man such as that making weapons for us would be of great value."

"I don't know, but I don't think it's anywhere near here. See this stone?" Gunnar pointed to a small olive green stone in the hilt that Jarl hadn't noticed. This stone is from the far, far East. I have only seen it come from traders who ventured there. They call it jade. It is possible the stone was brought west and used by the maker, but more likely since we have never seen anything similar, the whole thing was made there."

"I thought you reserved such close inspections for women, my friend. And yet even after this battle, I see none here. Are you so enamored with this beauty that you will go to cold furs tonight?" Jarl asked with a smile.

Gunnar flushed and nodded at the truth in Jarl's words. "Aye, I must admit, I've had a hard time taking my eyes from her," he agreed.

"And does *she* have a name?" Jarl asked.

"Not yet."

"Call it Maid's Plaything," Tryggr suggested, then laughed out loud. "That's what it looks like to me."

"I would, but that name's already taken," Gunnar replied without a moment's hesitation. "That's what the men call you now, behind your back, after Jarl's woman cut off your ear."

Jarl snorted into his cup, shocked at Gunnar's boldness. He struggled to keep from laughing so as not to fan Tryggr's fury any further, but it didn't help. Tryggr's face lost all trace of amusement and turned beet red.

"Why you little fuck," Tryggr roared. "I'll show you a maid's plaything." He stood to his full towering height and glared at Gunnar. Gunnar held his ground and stood with an easy smile, his hand casually resting on the golden hilt. He was no small man himself, and he still held the sword.

"That's enough, you two. Save your hostility for the enemy. We've had great success today, and I'll not have it spoiled with blood spilled now." Jarl intervened without taking sides.

Both men took their seats with Trygrr still grumbling under his breath.

"In line with Tryggr's suggestion, I could call it Maid's Dream, although I'd probably forever be getting it confused with my other blade that should naturally go by that name." Gunnar grinned and took a swallow of wine.

"No fear of that," Tryggr disagreed. "There's nothing so special about your tiny cock that maids would ever dream about it, unless it was the nightmare of being unsatisfied."

"Maid's Dream, it is then," Gunnar said, as he lifted the sword and scabbard once more to admire them.

"Do you have the final tally, Tryggr?" Jarl shook his head with a smile and changed the subject.

"Close enough." Tryggr relayed the number of horses and prisoners they had acquired that day. It was higher than Jarl had expected. The talk of their increasing wealth improved Tryggr's mood. "The men were getting a little worried about you, but I have to say, this success will put their minds at ease," Tryggr confessed.

"Worried about what?" Jarl asked.

"Worried that woman had put some kind of a spell on you. You've been acting like a man possessed."

"And they were worried about what exactly?" Jarl repeated. "My leadership?"

"Your sanity," Tryggr responded.

"Were any worried enough to pick up a sword and confront me with their fears?" Jarl's smile had faded.

Tryggr shook his head. "No, none were quite that worried. And when you put it that way, I guess you'd call it more of an unease. I won't deny it though, Jarl. I felt it, too. That woman has done something to you, and I don't understand it—from all accounts you haven't even fucked her yet."

Jarl's jaw tensed. Tryggr didn't see it but Gunnar did.

"Pay him no mind, Jarl. Tryggr knows naught of what he speaks. He and most of the other men here only know women with their cocks, but I, too, have had a woman in my blood before, and there is no experience to match it. No victory, no treasure, nothing else compares."

"I didn't know that of you, Gunnar," Jarl said.

"Obviously it wasn't the same," Tryggr interrupted. "Because Gunnar can survive without his woman; his presence here alone is a testament to that. So where is this fine woman, Gunnar?" he asked.

"She's dead, Tryggr, or I assure you, I would, in fact, not be here. She was killed by the Germanian chieftain, Ulther von Glossen, when I was away raiding to the west. They attacked our village, killed many, and captured others. My wife was among the dead when I returned." Gunnar's eyes were far away.

"Apologies. We have fought many battles together, but I never knew," Jarl said.

"Did you kill the bastard?" Tryggr asked.

"I killed all who called him family or friend, but sadly, no—Ulther escaped my sword. By the time I found him, he was already dead. They said he died slowly from an infected wound he received attacking our village. I like to think it was my Brigitta who wielded his deathblow, but I could never know. She was willful and strong. Much like your woman, I suppose." He nodded at Jarl.

"How did you meet her?" Jarl asked.

"I captured her on a raid in the Baltic." Gunnar's eyes were soft with remembrance. "I had never seen anything like her—red hair, similar to Tryggr's, but much darker, like the color of a spring sable."

"And did you take her home and baby-coddle her for months, like Jarl here, or did you get the job done in the heat of her burning village?" Tryggr asked.

"Neither. We'd taken her village by surprise and had grabbed great spoils, but they were regrouping. I was not about to risk losing her back to them, so we retreated to the boats and returned home as quickly as we could."

"And then?" Tryggr prodded.

"Yes, Tryggr. I was young and did not wait. I was like you then, and only knew women for the physical pleasure they could provide me. Though I had to do much to make up for that later."

"In the end, she forgave you?" Jarl asked.

"Yes. We were married. I can only pray that one day the gods will so bless me again. To feel a woman in my blood, in my heart, as if we are one. Perhaps that's why I'm always so active in sampling. Leave no stone unturned." Gunnar grinned at that and raised his mug, his brief moment of melancholy passed and the roguish lieutenant returned. "I used to be sure it was not possible, but now?" He turned to Jarl. "After seeing you, of all men, so smitten with your she-wolf. Now I am hopeful again."

"Is that why you joined us years ago? Is that when she was killed?" Jarl often wondered what motivated men to risk their lives. For some, it was the obvious wealth, others the glory, but for still others, like Gunnar, there was more to it—a yearning for the battle itself. This explained a lot.

"The first trip, yes." Gunnar answered. "No one expected you to return—assumed you would die at the hands of savages. In those days, I sought to die a good warrior's death, to be reunited with Brigitta in Valhalla as quickly as possible. The agony I endured every day after learning of her death was like a living thing, eating me from the inside. Finding Ulther dead and killing his brethren did nothing to slake its appetite. So when the opportunity arose, I joined your crew—to quiet the thing inside once and for all." He paused. "But somehow we survived. The second trip was for more gold, and this third…I have come to know nothing else," he admitted.

"And the thing within? Does it finally sleep?" Jarl asked.

"It's quiet most days. When it does awaken, it is more of a gnawing now. But I do have to agree with Tryggr and the others on one thing. A battle camp is no place for a woman. It is dangerous for her, and for you, and any men who follow you, if you allow yourself to be distracted."

Jarl thought about how he had chafed to stop here tonight and share a drink with his men, an act that would have been commonplace before. *Had Nena changed him? Was he distracted?*

"On the other hand," Gunnar continued. "With my own experience, I cannot, in good conscience, tell you to leave her somewhere safe. There is nowhere safer than by your side, so I have no answer for you."

"Perhaps you think I should retire? Maybe you could be the next leader?" Jarl asked.

"Me?" Gunnar laughed. "No, thank you. I'm very happy with the way things are right now. I have plenty of authority and very little of the responsibility. Never have my coffers been so swelled or my fighting so successful. The gods favor you, and thus they are favoring me. Gratitude for the consideration, but I like things just the way they are.

"Speaking of retiring though, there are more than a few men who will not be returning with us to the North. They have taken women and plan to settle here on the northeast coast of the Caspian. Their thoughts are toward building a trading community. A link between the far far East and Constantinople—and also a place for future Norse voyagers to rest, resupply, and trade for goods at a fair price. I think it an ambitious undertaking for a few, but I cannot fault them. If they succeed, it will be a good life. If I could better tolerate the heat, I might have even considered it for myself." Gunnar paused and studied Jarl. "I am curious, though, as to your plan with this woman?" Gunnar unknowingly echoed Tryggr's earlier question. "Do you truly think she will become affectionate toward you, simply after time remaining chained? Brigitta was my captive, but she had run of my village, and after the first, I worked very hard to win her."

"Nena is too resourceful to turn loose, and we are still within her lands. I do not have the luxury of having sailed her many miles away to mine. And I'm making progress," Jarl added.

"How long do you think that will take?"

"I don't know, Gunnar. Believe it or not, I've had a few other things on my mind. I'm still responsible for an entire raiding expedition," Jarl responded gruffly to the perceived criticism.

"Unbelievable." Tryggr, who had remained silent during the interchange, could no longer hold back. "Now Gunnar thinks you should woo her. What the hell is happening here? This is a woman we're talking about, and a slave to boot. The fact that we've spent any time even discussing it at all is ridiculous. Who cares what she thinks, or likes? What's happened to you, Jarl? Just have her and be done with it. Even Gunnar said you could satisfy yourself now and make it up to her later, if you are still so inclined. Though my coin says, once you have her, you will cease this nonsense and forget all about her."

"I did not say that, and I did not say woo," Gunnar corrected. "I merely asked what Jarl thought was going to change her mind."

"I treat her well," Jarl offered.

"Do you still bring Altene to your furs?" Gunnar asked.

Jarl nodded.

"Thank the gods for that, at least, or I would be worried," Tryggr muttered.

"Though not as often as before," Jarl admitted. "Since capturing Nena, I find the encounters with Altene less…satisfying." He shook his head ruefully at the admission, seeming surprised by the realization itself and to be sharing the fact, even with his closest.

"And say the situation was reversed," Gunnar asked. "Say she was trying to entice you to her bed. Would you find her more or less appealing if she were fucking another man in front of you every night—say Tryggr here." He nodded toward the burly second with a grin.

Jarl's eyes flashed with anger at the thought of Nena with anyone else.

Tryggr bristled. "Don't be mixing me up in this bullshit. I have no interest whatsoever in that woman, and Jarl knows it."

Gunnar laughed out loud at Jarl's expression and obvious response. "It was only conjecture, Jarl, not a question meant to be answered, though I think you already have." Gunnar shook his head and drained his mug.

Chapter 9

"**C**ome." Jarl removed her cuffs and made his way to the tent opening.

"Where are you taking me?" Nena asked, remaining by the pole.

He stopped and turned back to face her. "Would it matter? I would think any place would be an improvement from here." He waved his hand around the tent. "But you can stay if you want." He left the question hanging in the air.

She nodded and followed him. Outside, two horses stood saddled and ready. One she recognized immediately as his magnificent bay and the other was a shorter stockier sorrel. "That one is for you." He indicated the sorrel.

Nena hesitated again. Was this a trick? Would he laugh at her at any moment and return her to the pole? She found it hard to believe he would go to this trouble to torment her—for whatever he was, Jarl was not cruel. He nodded toward the horse again and raised an eyebrow. Nena approached the animal slowly, allowing it to sniff her hand before she stroked its face, then its neck and shoulder. She climbed aboard the unfamiliar leather saddle without further delay. Jarl mounted his stallion and took the reins to her horse, leading it behind him.

So—she was to have no control over where she went. But Nena couldn't complain. Even with the hard uncomfortable Northman saddle, she could feel the power of the animal beneath her. That power made her feel more alive than she had since her capture. Free of her bonds, free of the tent, her spirits soared. She chafed at the slow pace as they made their way through the camp, drawing more than a few curious stares. When they passed the last sentry on the hill overlooking the camp, Jarl stopped and handed her the reins, his expression a mixture of speculation and uncertainty.

"Lead off. I'll follow. Wherever you want to go, whatever speed you choose, just keep heading in this general direction," he instructed and pointed to the southwest.

Was it true? Was he really trusting her to go wherever she wanted? Before he could change his mind, Nena kicked her horse up into a gallop, the animal's short legs churning beneath her. She drank deep of the wind in her face, losing herself in the sound of pounding hooves in the soft grassy soil. The horse was working very hard, but Nena was surprised to note they were not covering much ground. She glanced back at Jarl. The tight rein on his stallion confirmed her suspicion. She leaned low on the sorrel's neck and urged him faster.

The fat little horse responded gamely, spurting forward, his short legs now a blur. But the burst of speed was brief, and Nena soon felt him flagging beneath her. When his breathing began to labor, she sat up and drew in rein. As he slowed to a walk, she patted his neck, rewarding him for his effort. He had tried for her, but was physically not capable. Nena thought of Nightwing and how she would have tossed her head with impatience at having been slowed so soon. But this little horse plodded along dutifully, more than happy with their new pace.

Nena turned to Jarl who had ridden up beside her. "This horse is fat...and slow," she accused.

Jarl laughed openly at her expression. "Yes, he is. I picked him out myself."

Nena pursed her lips, fighting a smile of her own. He hadn't really trusted her. He suspected her first thoughts would be to escape, even with the child in the camp. Only Nena knew that concern was unfounded. Escape beckoned her, but she would remain bound by her word. Though from what she now knew of Jarl, she doubted he would actually kill the girl. If Nena had already escaped, the child's death would serve no purpose other than spite. And spite was not Jarl—Altene perhaps, but not Jarl. Even believing that, Nena would never leave the girl behind. She could never be sure, and she couldn't live with the shame of knowing that she'd been able to escape by counting on a Northman's honor to be greater than her own.

Nena squirmed in the uncomfortable saddle, hating the bind and pinch of it, but refusing to complain; she never wanted the ride to end.

"Are you alright? Would you like to go back?" Jarl asked, noticing her discomfort.

"No," she answered quickly. "It's just…your saddles…your saddles are very uncomfortable." Jarl watched as she again tried to reposition herself.

"Then take it off, if you want."

Nena looked at him sharply. "May I? Really? But how will we carry it?"

"Just lay it in the grass. We'll get it on the way back." The hope in her face was so sincere, Jarl would have been willing to throw the saddle and ten more just like it off a cliff. The idea of removing it had not only made her extremely happy—she seemed happy with him.

Nena was off in a flash, pulling at the unfamiliar straps but making little progress.

"Here, let me help you." Jarl dismounted and moved to her side to demonstrate how the saddle rigging was secured. For a moment they were close, with Nena's horse broadside in front of them and Jarl's stallion standing right behind. The earthy smells of leather and horse mingled around them in the small area. His arm brushed hers. Even though the straps were disconnected,

Jarl delayed removing the saddle. Nena felt the now familiar response of her body to his nearness.

"Gratitude," she murmured as she moved a half a step away.

"Will you need help getting back on?" Jarl asked, hoping to have feel of her calf as he helped her to mount, but instead she frowned, indignant at the idea.

"I would not be much of a warrior if I required assistance to mount a horse, would I?" With that, Nena grabbed a handful of mane and swung aboard the sorrel's bare back in a single fluid move. She took a deep breath and sighed as she settled into the living softness of the animal beneath her.

"Better?" Jarl asked, though the answer was obvious.

"Much better," she replied.

They rode for hours, meandering through the plains. When they came to a stream, they stopped and dismounted to allow the horses to drink and graze. Jarl watched her pull her horse's head up out of the deep grass. Long stems hung from both sides of the animal's mouth as it chewed. Nena stroked the sorrel's nose and adjusted his forelock. "You do not have to eat every blade of grass in sight," she admonished the little horse gently. "That is why you cannot run with the wind, my friend. You could be a great warrior's horse if you ate a little less." The placid little horse looked at her affectionately, appreciating her soft touch, then pulled his head down to take another mouthful. Nena laughed and allowed him to pull away, though he soon returned his head to her hands for more stroking as he chewed.

Jarl couldn't help but think of her fingers so gentle, so tender, on him. He felt his gut tighten. This was the side of her he had seen reassuring the child who was bloodsworn to her. This was the side he could only imagine being the recipient of.

"This horse is a lost cause," Nena laughed, totally at ease. "He has no shame and doesn't care to ever be a warrior's horse." She shook her head, unaware of how much the shared relaxed moment was affecting him. When she did finally look over at him, the intensity in his eyes startled her, but he recovered quickly and smiled.

"We need to get back," he announced unwillingly.

Nena nodded and swung aboard her horse. Though there was no tension between them, they did not speak on the return ride, not even when they reached the saddle and he reattached it for her. When they arrived back at his tent and dismounted, Jarl sent one of his guards for Altene. He saw Nena frown. Would that Gunnar was right. Would that she disapproved because she was jealous, though he knew that was not the case.

"You are dirty from the ride. Altene will take you to the baths," he explained and saw comprehension smooth her brow.

Altene arrived and took in the scene with barely concealed anger. Word had spread through the entire camp like wildfire; Jarl had taken his Dor captive for a ride, and they had been gone for hours. Altene had scarcely believed it, but here was the evidence right before her. With great effort she smiled a tight smile at Jarl and asked, "My lord?"

"Please take Nena to the baths," he instructed.

"Yes, my lord." She nodded, then hesitated. "Um, shall I still use the other women and the rope harness?" she asked, referring to her rival's new freedoms, not sure how far they were to be extended.

"Yes. I'll have her shackles replaced before you return." He turned to Nena. "Come."

Nena followed him inside the tent to the center pole and waited while he bent over to retrieve the cuffs from the floor and remove them from the chain. He turned back to her, and she held up her hands in silence. As he closed the second cuff around her wrist, Nena studied him while his attention was on the clasp. His wavy brown hair, the color of dark clay, fell forward as he bent his head down. There was already a dark shadow of beard on his well-defined jaw, though she had watched him shave that morning.

"Jarl," she said.

He looked up and met her gaze, his eyes the mixed colors of contentment.

"Gratitude," she murmured.

She seemed almost disturbed to say the word, but clearly meant it. For Jarl it was immeasurable progress. She had never thanked him before, not even for saving her life. Though he was careful not to show it, he was elated.

"You're welcome. Perhaps we'll do it again if you would like," he offered.

"Yes, I would like that very much."

Altene entered at her last words. Nena wondered how much she had overheard. The way Altene seethed in silence the entire way to the baths, she guessed quite a bit, but couldn't be sure; she'd already been angry after their return. Once Nena was safely in the water, Altene left. It was something she had never done before.

"Where has Altene gone?" Nena finally asked one of the other women.

The woman looked around nervously, then answered in a whisper in case Altene was still within earshot.

"I do not know. She was very upset that you and Lord Jarl went riding."

"Upset angry or upset sad?"

"Again I don't know. I would imagine both."

Altene returned as they were finishing and stood silently surveying them from the doorway. When they were ready, she turned on her heel and strode off without waiting to see that they followed.

"Where did you go?" Nena called to her.

"None of your concern; I was busy," Altene snapped haughtily without slowing.

"Were you busy out riding horses with Jarl?" Nena heard several of the women behind her gasp.

Altene stiffened and stopped, then turned back the few paces to confront Nena, face to face. "Be careful, Princess," she warned.

Nena ignored the threat and referred to her own question. "You know you were not," she whispered so the other women could not hear. "He is losing interest in you. Help me to get free. Now, before it's too late for you. You know where the child is kept. You have run of everything. You could arrange it. Bring her to me. We will slip away, and you can have your Northman back."

Altene glared at her, then turned on her heel and continued toward Jarl's tent without looking back.

The evening meal had already been delivered by the time the women returned from the baths. Jarl was in a good mood and offered for Altene to stay and eat, oblivious to the tension between the two women. Altene's mood improved at the invitation and even more as the meal went on. Soon she was chatting with Jarl about Dor customs again. Nena remained silent.

They were almost finished when Jarl asked Altene, "How is it that you have never had a child? Are you barren?"

"No, my lord. I take an herb that keeps the seed from taking hold in me. Once I stop, I can become pregnant. Perhaps, I could quit taking it now and give you a strong son."

Jarl almost choked. Nena watched as he struggled for words. "A crying babe is the last thing I need right now," he finally managed to say.

"What he really means is that he wants no son from a whore. No man would want that," Nena scoffed.

For the first time Nena's barb hit a nerve, and the normally thick-skinned Altene winced, her eyes welling briefly before she regained her composure.

Jarl swore under his breath and slammed his fork to the table. His eyes flashed with anger at Nena, but she returned his stare coolly.

"Give her back to Tryggr, my lord." Altene pleaded in a rush. "He is healed now, and she vexes you constantly. And she was his by first claim."

"Enough! The two of you," he shouted. He turned to Altene and lowered his voice. "She is mine now. Do not speak of it again."

Sleep would not come to Nena that night. The contradicting events of the day had left her feelings jumbled in confusion. Her captor had released her from all restraints. She'd been free, though not free. Had felt a horse beneath her, though not much of a horse. And Jarl—away from camp he had been so different, so relaxed. He'd seemed much younger and more...handsome. There was nothing wrong with admitting it. It was a simple fact, no more significant than his hair was brown or that he was tall. Jarl was handsome. It didn't change anything. And neither did his incredibly thoughtful act. Or did it? Even now the sense of pure enjoyment she had felt on the ride still filled her, and her thoughts toward him were softened.

You must not dwell on that. You must escape. You are running out of time.

She thought back to his maps. Only two villages remained after they were finished here. Not only did her aunt's life hang in the balance, but if she were unable to escape by the time they met the ships at port, her own prospects were frightful. Jarl had given no recent indication that he intended to ransom her, and she doubted she would be sold as a slave. That only left being loaded onto a ship bound for the North, a place by all accounts, that even the gods forsake in winter.

That could not happen. Altene was the key. Nena's previous appeals to Altene's sympathy had fallen on deaf ears, but today she had changed tactics and had seen the first favorable results. She had pushed Altene and would keep pushing her. A desperate Altene might be willing to take a risk the complacent Altene would not. Though Nena had said the words of Jarl losing interest in her as a jab, there was much truth in them, and Altene had to know it. If she had not resumed her place with Jarl by time they reached the port, her future was also in serious jeopardy.

Chapter 10

Nena and Jarl rode almost every day, usually in the afternoon after he had dealt with camp business, but occasionally in the morning. Nena lived for those hours. She tried to remain focused on the experience itself and not who provided it, but every day the strain between them became a little less. The time they spent together a little more comfortable, a little easier.

Between the discussions of the men in his tent and the talk of the women in the baths, Nena stayed apprised of everything that went on in the camp. Much of the talk of the men was on future attacks or meeting up with their ships and returning home, while the women's conversations centered around their personal lives—their hopes and fears for the future. Seldom did the content of the two overlap. That was until the day the upcoming arrival of the slaver was announced. From that moment forward, he was the only subject on anyone's lips. The men excitedly made preparations and estimated their wealth to be received. The women whose fate hung in the balance repeated every rumor ever told of the merciless trader.

The man dealt not only in slaves; he would convert all assets the Northmen didn't want or didn't have room for on their ships into gold and jewels. Slaves were his specialty but he traded for anything. He was expected any day now to get a preliminary assessment of their inventory so he could gather proper payment. Later he would meet them where their ships were anchored for the final exchange. Nena wondered if she would be included in the tally.

Jarl was the only one who seemed ambivalent about the slaver's arrival. Nena did not understand his attitude until she overheard Jarl and Tryggr discussing their last encounter with the man. Apparently Jarl had insulted him on the previous trip, and Tryggr'd had to work hard to get him to come back. He was the largest slaver in the area—the only one who could afford to acquire the number of slaves they would have to offer at one time.

Tryggr was desperate to make this transaction go smoothly and counseled Jarl repeatedly on the importance of remaining civil. The incongruity of Tyrggr being the more rational one was not lost on Nena. She had never seen Jarl so disagreeable. She wondered what the slaver could have possibly done to so anger him that he would have lost control and insulted the man in the middle of bartering. Jarl was not one to be easily rattled.

With the slaver's arrival imminent, Tryggr returned to Jarl's tent to present the final preparations for Jarl's approval. Nena listened as Tryggr outlined his plans to provide the man with some of their finest wine and food. Jarl agreed to all of Tryggr's suggestions without much thought—until Tryggr suggested they send Altene for his pleasure for the few days he would be there. Jarl balked.

"Oh, for the sake of the gods, Jarl, what is your problem now? Altene is a whore and a good one. You've said yourself, the best, so why on earth not send her to help smooth things over? It's not like I'm suggesting we send him her," he thumbed his hand at Nena. "Has she made you soft to all women now?"

"I'll think about it," was the only response Jarl would give.

"What do the Teclan do with the slaves they capture?" Jarl asked Nena once Tryggr had left and they sat down to their meal. "Surely you don't keep them all."

"We do not take slaves. When we raid we take only things we want, or can use: horses, furs, jewels, weapons. Occasionally we will take a particularly good supply of food if it is something we cannot grow on the mountain."

Jarl stopped chewing and looked at her to see if she was serious. "But all Dor keep slaves," he said when he saw that she was.

"Not the Teclan."

"Why not?"

"Having others do labors for you makes one soft. We feel that softness has been the downfall of many."

"That may be true, but even if you didn't keep them, surely you must recognize their value. You could trade them for something you did want."

"We do not trade either. We will sometimes take a prisoner to ransom if they are from a particularly wealthy or powerful family, and occasionally we'll take one if they carry some valuable knowledge we seek. But we don't take them to trade."

"What information would you consider valuable enough to keep someone?"

"Their language and customs, if they are strange to us."

"So you had a Northman prisoner?"

"Three of them—at different times."

"What happened to them? Do they live?"

"No."

"How did you convince them to teach you? By torture?"

"The first one, yes, but once we were able to learn more of your culture, we offered them what they all wanted most. A good death."

Jarl leaned back and rubbed his chin. "What do you know of that?"

"I know that your gods reward you for dying with sword in hand by sending you to a better place in your afterlife, Valhalla."

"So these men, your prisoners, were given a chance to fight?"

She nodded. "Trial by combat."

"And none won?"

She shook her head.

"Were they fair fights?"

She frowned at him, insulted. "Of course."

She seemed sincere. He changed the subject. "Surely there is something that you need or want that you cannot always acquire in raids. Is trading forbidden?" Jarl asked.

"Forbidden? No." She shook her head and thought for a moment. "My father does not trust other tribes to meet with them to barter. Such meetings, wherever they took place, would ultimately make us vulnerable to betrayal. Either out in the open, in their lands, or if we allowed them through our defenses onto the mountain." She paused. "But it is more than that. My father would be insulted to sit with a lesser man and have him dictate or negotiate terms as an equal. Teclan do not negotiate. We take. Even friendly tribes who we have marriage alliances with, we do not trust. We do not raid them, but they are not our equals."

"I've never known a people who did not always want more—more jewels, more horses, more something."

"A man can only ride so many horses, Jarl, but he must feed them all. And you can only wear so many jewels. Gold and gems never spoil or die. Every jewel that has ever been taken by a Teclan warrior, since the beginning of time, remains with the Teclan. Most are passed down from mothers to their daughters."

"So do you have your own stockpile of jewels?" he asked with a smile, still not fully believing her.

"Of course. My mother was the daughter of a chief and then wife to a chief, so mine may be even larger than most," she said matter-of-factly.

"And do you have so many that you keep them in a chest like that?" He nodded to the chest on the table behind him where he kept the jewels from their raids.

Nena looked at it, gauging its size, then shrugged. "Something similar, but much larger."

Jarl set down his fork and leaned back in his chair, sure now that she was having sport with him. "And all Teclan women have such a collection," he reaffirmed.

She nodded.

"So all a man would have to do is take the Teclan stronghold, and he would be wealthy beyond his wildest imagination."

Now it was Nena's turn to smile. "Yes, that is all a man would have to do." Her smile grew larger at the thought.

"I've heard that it's well fortified, but for that kind of wealth, surely it is possible," Jarl said.

"Surely it is not," Nena disagreed. "Since the Teclan have been on the mountain, as far back as even the oldest stories can recall, never has a foreign force been successful in taking the mountain. Never. And many have tried."

"Hnf," Jarl grunted.

"My family could afford a great ransom for my return," she said, suddenly serious. He had not mentioned it again since she had first been captured.

He looked deep into her eyes while he considered her offer.

"I think I now understand your people's position on trade, and in this I must agree with you. When you already have what you want, there is no reason to barter for even a large quantity of something else—even something of great value. Especially if what you have is irreplaceable. I already have what I want. And it is not a ransom."

Chapter 11

The slaver's caravan set up camp on the northern edge of the Northmen's tents, and from what Nena heard, it was quite a spectacle. Her rides had been curtailed until the business with him was over, so she had yet to lay eyes on it, but the other women said the slaver's tent was as red as the reddest sun before it sank in the west. And they said he dressed himself in silks and jewels finer than any woman. The women who bathed her were all more talkative than usual—with the sudden unexpected absence of Altene.

She'd been sent to please the slaver.

Nena shivered in the warm water. What was Altene experiencing in that very moment? What was she having to do? How could she do it? Where did her spirit go when it was happening? Did she have a warrior's soothing place? And while she did it, did she smile and moan and pretend to want him as she did Jarl? For all of Altene's bravado, Nena knew she cared deeply for Jarl. A feeling that, while he was affectionate toward her, Jarl did not return. And to be given by the man she cared for to service another? And not just another—a slaver?

For the first time, Nena truly felt sorry for Altene. She was nothing more than an animal to these Northmen, and while Jarl may have been kind to her, he was no different. Nena knew she had to remember that. In the face of his kind words and acts, she had to keep her feelings hardened toward him. If she did not escape, that could very well be her one day. Jarl pretended to care about her now, and maybe he even did, but had he felt the same once for Altene?

Nena had thought her only two possible futures were to escape or to be loaded onto a ship and taken to the frigid North. Now she realized there might very well be a third option. This slave trader dealt in all goods, and, if he was smart, he would surely recognize her value to her family. Perhaps he would help her to escape—for his own substantial reward, of course. Nena couldn't wait to see him. Couldn't wait to see if he was from a tribe who was friendly, or would want to be friendly with the Teclan. To slip him a message to negotiate ransom with her father or brother. But wait she did. It was two days before he was presented at Jarl's tent. Two days while he took preliminary inventory of the other items. Two days that Altene remained absent.

When the guards outside the tent announced his presence, Nena saw Jarl scowl. Tryggr looked up from filling two polished silver chalices with some of their finest wine and saw it, too. "For the gods' sakes, Jarl," he whispered, "if you can't be nice to him, at least try not to look like he is some animal scat you just scraped off your boot. You may be the greatest at acquiring treasure, but you're the worst at bartering it."

"But he does remind me of something I stepped in," Jarl replied.

"I know. He's disgusting," Tryggr agreed. "There's no doubt about that, but he'll be bringing us chests of gold in a few weeks. I choose to focus on that, and you should, too. Everything is set here; there's food and wine, and I've already shown him everything outside: the slaves, the extra horses, the weapons. All you have to do is work out the price."

The guard shifted his weight at the entrance at the delay.

"Do you want me to stay?" Tryggr asked hopefully.

"No. I'll be fine," Jarl said.

"Just try not to insult him like you did last time," were Tryggr's parting words under his breath.

Nena's eyes were riveted on the tent opening. In a cloud of red swirling silks and cloying fragrance, the slaver made his entrance. Her hopes were dashed as soon as she saw his face. He was a Worick.

"Liars, murderers, thieves and poisoners." Her father had described them. *"They are cunning and cruel, but cowards to a one. Never trust a Worick."* He had counseled her and her brothers repeatedly. *"They will not fight like men, but are equally as dangerous as the most skilled Teclan warrior. Never forget it."* Nena never had.

Woricks' skin color was only a few shades darker than the Dor, yet they were easily distinguished from any other people of the region. Their custom of binding the sides of the heads of their children produced a characteristic oblong skull, further accentuated by their naturally long narrow faces. If the bulging back of their heads were not enough, the Woricks' fascination with body piercing truly set them apart. They did not wear their jewelry as others did around their necks or on their fingers and arms. They attached it to themselves permanently, and they believed more was better. Though only his face and hands were exposed, it was enough to see this Worick was no exception.

On his face were three nearly solid lines of penetrating gold rings. Some were so thick and heavy they left sagging dark holes in his skin. The first line began at the top of both of his ears, ran across his temples and along the full length of both of his eyebrows. The gold arches met in the middle between his eyes, joined there by a single gold-rimmed ruby. The second line started mid-ear and coursed across his cheekbones, meeting on the bridge of his nose, then running in a single line down to the tip. The final lines started at the base of both ears and traveled along his lower jaw, stopping just shy of his chin. From there, his thin black beard was greased stiff and pulled to a long point. Even it was adorned at the bottom with a large gold nugget woven into the tip.

The Worick hadn't seen her. His eyes were on Jarl. A false smile covered his thin elongated face as if he were greeting a long lost friend. With Tryggr's words fresh in his ears, Jarl attempted to smile back, but managed only a grimace. His lips parted in the normal fashion, but no depressions formed in his cheeks, and there was no crinkling around his eyes. His eyes were hard. Nena had never seen him this way. Not even when he was freshly returned from battle. She could feel the open hostility simmering just beneath his surface.

"Greetings, Piltor," Jarl acknowledged the stranger and waved him toward the table.

"Greetings, Jarl," the Worick replied. "I must thank you for your most appreciated and generous gift of Altene. I understand she is your most often chosen, and I can see why. As a man in my position, I did not think I could be surprised by a woman's talents, but she is a gem, and a varied one at that. My appetites tend to be…shall we say…unique, and I found her to be most accommodating."

Jarl scowled and Nena cringed.

After the initial pleasantries, for what they were, were exchanged, the Worick continued, "I hear you have a tiger skin. Is it here? May I see it?"

A tiger skin? Her tournament gift from Dorac? It seemed a lifetime ago and she had not seen it since, but of course the Northmen would have recognized its value and taken it.

Piltor glanced around the tent, his eyes seeking the hide, but finding Nena. "And what have we here?" he murmured in appreciation and moved toward her before Jarl could respond. His eyes were like clammy hands touching her everywhere, leaving cold slimy trails on her skin. Nena shuddered. The Worick was close now, circling her, taking in every inch of her. His eyes discovered the Teclan star, the lightning bolt, and the open circle on her arm. He sucked in his breath.

"Unbelievable," he whispered. "I see you have saved the most valuable for last, Jarl. She is splendorous," he said, drawing out the final "s" to a soft hiss.

Nena stared at his thin wet lips, fully expecting to see a forked tongue slither from between them. He turned to look toward Jarl, giving her a full close up view of his profile and the freakish egg-shaped bulging back of his head. He was the most revolting human being she had ever seen.

"She is not for sale," Jarl said.

Piltor laughed. "You're negotiating has improved, my friend. That is one of my favorite and most successful tactics when I see a customer openly covets one of my treasures. First, frighten him with it being unavailable, then the price will not matter. But everything is for sale." His voice trailed off. "I must admit, she so took me by surprise that I have shown you my desire, and know I will now have to pay dearly for it. What is the price?"

"I said she's not for sale," Jarl repeated, his voice tight.

Piltor laughed again. "That is not how this works, Jarl. Now you are to pretend to consider to sell her, as if it had only just crossed your mind. Then make up some lie about how maybe you could do it, but only for a good friend, such as I. I'm sure you must think you know what she's worth, but I doubt you truly do. The pleasure houses in Anbai will pay more for her than everything else you have here combined. And not because she's beautiful—though she is that. You have many beautiful captives. She is Teclan. And not only a Teclan, but the virgin daughter of Meln." He whistled between his teeth and shook his head as if he still could not believe it. "I don't think you can imagine what they would pay.

"The Teclan may be respected, Jarl, but they are not loved. Many men have lost things at the ends of their spears and swords. Many who would relish the opportunity to get back at them." He nodded at Nena. "She would provide a most enjoyable way to do so."

Piltor mistook Jarl's silence for consideration. "She will be as well-cared for as any slave ever was—to ensure her longevity, of course. And she will be trained," he murmured, lost briefly in his own imaginings. "Perhaps as good as Altene. If you would like, I could include in our negotiations a free night with her, or two, on your next visit to our lands. I can guarantee I will include at least one for myself. Though not her first night," he sighed wistfully. "I could not come close to being able to afford that."

Piltor reached out toward her breast as if to sample the quality of the wares.

Nena shrank away, sure now that a passage north and a lifetime in a frozen hell were much preferable to spending any time with this vile man. She twisted her body out of his reach to the full extent of her bindings, unable to heed her earlier council to stay still for the lion and not excite the predator's urges. The slaver only smiled and stepped closer.

Nena stared down horrified as his hand closed the distance between them. His energy, she sensed, was dark and twisted—as alive as Jarl's had been when he was close. But unlike Jarl's that was warm and vibrant, the Worick's energy was cold and wriggling. Any second his hand would touch her, and she would feel the cool slime she had only imagined before. So focused was she on his fingertips, she did not see Jarl moving across the tent toward them. Out of nowhere, his hand slapped down on Piltor's wrist, seizing it and jerking it away.

The Worick grunted in pain. Jarl's eyes were the color of dark slate, and his face bore an expression Nena had never seen before—a cold hard fury she had not known him capable of. She could see the muscles of his forearm bulging as he applied more pressure to the man's wrist. She wondered if at any moment she would hear bones breaking. She hoped so.

But then Jarl released him, a smaller version of the false tense smile back on his lips. "As I said before, she is not for sale." His eyes glittered dangerously, challenging the man to ask again. But Jarl had made his point. The Worick only nodded as he rubbed his wrist.

"I stand corrected, Jarl. Perhaps everything does not have a price."

The negotiations after that were brief. The price the Worick offered for the remaining items seemed low to Nena, but she had no way of knowing. As he moved toward the tent opening to leave, he paused and took one last lingering, appreciative look at her before he exited. Nena again felt the slimy tracks of his eyes where they touched her. Jarl bristled. Then, in a flash of red silk, the Worick was gone.

Tryggr entered soon after, an expectant smile on his face. "Well? How did it go? Will we soon be rich men? Piltor seemed to leave in a twist; did you drive a hard bargain?"

Jarl relayed the offered price.

"What?" Tryggr said incredulous. "That's impossible." He shook his head while the number slowly sank in, then exploded. "What the fuck happened in here? It should have been twice that, at minimum, and you know it."

"It doesn't matter," Jarl said.

"Doesn't matter? Yes, Jarl, it does matter. Acquiring wealth is the whole purpose of our little expedition. We don't come all this way to enjoy the weather. What happened? Did you insult him?"

"Not exactly."

"Not exactly? Not exactly?" Tryggr blustered. "What does that mean? You only insulted him a little?"

"I may have almost broken his wrist," Jarl admitted.

"Broken his wrist? For what?"

"He was sticking it where it did not belong."

Tryggr glanced at the chest full of gems, then followed Jarl's eyes to Nena.

"Her?" he asked, his voice very low. "Do not tell me it is because of her that he offers half. Do not tell me that my labors for the past months are now worth half because of some Dor bi...."

"Tryggr!" Jarl cut him off. "Mind your next words."

The two men stared at each other in hard silence.

"So that is the way of it then?" Tryggr asked, his jaw clenched.

"It is," Jarl said with finality.

Tryggr turned without another word and left the tent.

Jarl paced the tent like a caged animal, then slammed his fist down on the table so hard the plates and untouched cups of wine jumped and rattled. He ran his fingers through his hair and gave her a long look. Then he, too, left the tent, leaving Nena alone with her racing thoughts.

Her heart pounded in her chest. She could not stay here a moment longer. She struggled against the overwhelming urge to scream and jerk wildly against the cuffs until her wrists were bloody. She had to escape. The slaver was no hope. Jarl had made it clear he was not going to ransom her. The port loomed ever closer. She was out of options.

Chapter 12

The next morning, Jarl called his higher ranking men to the tent to discuss the slaver's offer and make plans. Tryggr was present, and though he pointedly ignored her, he and Jarl seemed to have come to some understanding.

"I'm sure you've heard that the Worick's offer was half of what we expected," Jarl said to the assembled men. "Even with the Curse, we've made very good time on this trip and are well ahead of schedule. There is plenty of time to make an additional short sweep to the east, here." He pointed to one of the maps. "Or I would hear other thoughts." He looked to the men.

"Can't we deal with someone else?" one of them asked.

"No one but the Worick can handle the volume we offer," Tryggr rejected the option.

"Then why not split it up and deal with several? It would be more time-consuming, but we have the time; Jarl said we are ahead of schedule. Even if we made deals at three-quarters of expected value, it would be half again more than what we will get from the Worick. Surely, at that price we could find someone who would take them. I request permission to take several men and proceed to port to try to secure other buyers."

"I feel no obligation to stick to the deal offered by the Worick," Jarl considered out loud. "What say the rest of you?"

The tent was filled with murmurs of agreement from the other men.

"And you, Tryggr?" Jarl asked him specifically. "You have the most effort into this last deal."

"I think it's a good idea, but I don't think we should count on it. The Worick wields a lot of power in this area, which is another reason we've been forced to deal with him in the past. If he gets wind of what we are up to, I think considerable pressure will be brought to bear on any who would barter with us—and we might not find them nearly so accommodating."

"That's a good point." Jarl turned back to the man who had made the request. "Permission granted to take some men ahead to port and seek replacements for the Worick's purse, but do it under the guise of checking on the ships. Keep your true purpose concealed. The Worick thinks we have a deal, so he should not be looking to intercept our negotiating with others. Let's keep it that way.

"In the meantime, the rest of us will take the last villages as planned. Depending on what the men are able to come up with at the port, and our final tally, we will make a decision then on whether or not to make additional raids."

***

That afternoon, Nena sat in the baths while the two women lathered her hair and scrubbed her skin. She tried to relax, but the excitement and drama of the past few days had left her knotted with tension. She longed for a horseback ride, but Jarl had been too busy to take her. One of the women who was in the water with her, chatted away while the other said not a word. It would not have been unusual except their roles were reversed. The normally talkative one was silent.

"Sven has told me I will not be sold," Gineesh reported excitedly. "He will use part of his share of the bounty to buy me, and we shall settle on the northeast coast of the Great Sea together. There are quite a few Northmen who are taking wives and will remain behind there."

Nena understood her excitement. Gineesh had long feared and expected her Northman to dispose of her with the other slaves in the end. He had never treated her badly, but was not prone to any displays of affection, and had never made any suggestion toward keeping her. Unlike the other woman, Lenta, who was always sharing glowing reports of her Northman's generosity and kindness. Today she remained quiet. Nena turned to her, but her downcast eyes remained fixed on her duty.

"And what of you, Lenta?" Nena asked. "Do you have news from your Northman?"

The woman looked up and nodded. "Yes. Though I have shared the furs with Ralgon for months now, he has made no such offer toward my purchase." She tried to hide it, but Nena could see the fear and disappointment in her eyes.

Realizing the talk of her own good news had caused the other woman sorrow, Gineesh tried to comfort her friend. "Perhaps he has just not yet done so. Perhaps he waits to tell you until after the deal is secure. Ralgon has always been so good to you."

"Gratitude for your kind words, Gineesh, but it is not so. Ralgon already has a wife in the North. I will be traded with the others to the slaver and then sold."

Nena seared Lenta's expression to memory. She had fallen for a Northman, had shared his furs and expected an impossible future. Nena thought back over Lenta's previous conversations in the baths. How happy she was with Ralgon. How well he treated her. All had assumed she would definitely be one who was taken as a wife, if any were. Yet here she was, to be cast aside with no more consideration than a trinket.

The Northmen could not be trusted. Even if they had not planned it all along, as Ralgon clearly had with a wife at home, Jarl, with Altene was no better. His affections had simply faded and moved to another. The end result for Altene was the same. Nena had to keep the plights of these two women fresh in her mind. When Jarl plied her with kind gestures and things she enjoyed—like riding, she had to remember it would only last until another woman caught his eye.

Nena had just stepped from the water when Altene arrived, returning to her duties as if nothing had happened. Nena's acutely trained eyes searched the other woman's body for marks of what she had endured, but found none, only a subtle stiffness in her movements that Altene tried to hide. Nena had assumed by the slaver's comments that he had been cruel and Altene would be covered with the evidence. But only in Altene's eyes did she occasionally see a fleeting pain—though whether it was physical or emotional, Nena could not be sure.

Do not pity her. Altene is as heartless as these men, and would have been ecstatic to hear you'd been sent to the slaver to satisfy his…unusual appetites. Do not become soft. You must push her again. Now while she is vulnerable.

Nena considered what she would say. She assumed she would have to wait until they were on their way back to Jarl's tent to be able to speak to Altene without the others overhearing, but after the women had finished rubbing Nena's skin with the scented oil and dressed her, Altene dismissed them. "Leave us and wait outside," she said. "I would have words with Nena alone."

The women holding the two long ropes hesitated.

"Go." Altene waved them off. When they were safely out of earshot, she turned to Nena. "I have a plan for you to escape," she whispered.

"You will bring the girl and let me go?" Nena was incredulous.

Altene frowned and shook her head. "Don't be an idiot. I'll not risk my neck for you."

"Then what is your plan?" Nena asked, exasperated. "Shall I turn into some great bird and take the whole tent with me? If another way to escape with the girl was available, I would have taken it by now. But your loose tongue with Jarl has thwarted any opportunity I would have otherwise had."

Altene nodded in agreement. "I regret many of my words now. Would that I could take them back. But that is in the past. Do you want to hear my plan or not?"

"Yes." Nena nodded.

"You must lay with him. You must choose Jarl for your first union. It is the only way he will trust you to let you go. Once you have run of the camp, you'll be able to find a way to escape and take the girl with you. You'll need to leave the mother; you're not bloodsworn to her and Jarl will not punish her. The child will be enough of a dead weight slowing you anyway. And I'm sure the woman will happily give up her daughter if it means saving her life." Altene eyed her speculatively. "Then you will be rid of him, and I will be rid of you."

"I can't," Nena whispered, and shook her head, imagining for one brief moment what Altene proposed—her beneath Jarl, instead of Altene.

"Then stay here forever," Altene hissed. "You said you wanted to escape and I gave you a way to do it. I knew it was a lie."

Altene's words burned in Nena's mind. "*Choose him for your first union or stay here forever.*" It seemed like forever already. Could she do it? How could she not, if it meant being free? She had no doubt of her ability to escape if she could move about the camp as freely as Altene did. And Jarl had told her he would free her. So what was stopping her? If Altene had offered for her to be branded or whipped or some other normal form of torture in exchange for freedom, she wouldn't have hesitated before accepting. So why was this even a choice—much less a difficult one?

The vision of his lovemaking to Altene crept unbidden to her mind. One of the times she had sworn not to look but had stolen glances anyway. She knew the answer. Because it might not be torture. Nena, who was afraid of almost nothing, was afraid of this—afraid of her body's independent response to him—afraid of losing control and being humiliated—afraid of it not being painful at all, but enjoyable. Nena knew she could withstand torture—maybe even in silence for awhile, though to scream in pain would not dishonor her. To whimper and roll beneath him as Altene did, would do nothing less.

Yet she was a warrior! How could she stay here now when an escape had offered itself so plainly? She had waited months for Jarl to be negligent to no avail. She did not have more months to wait. She must not be weak.

"He will never trust me to do it. He'll know I'm plotting something." Nena shook her head as she expressed her doubt with the plan.

"Perhaps. But he has a fire for you—a heat deep within that he fights. He will take you if you offer. I have no doubt." Altene seemed both sad and bitter at the admission. "I will even make sure your dress is more suitable for the task." She reached out and fingered the baggy hide Nena now wore. "Though nothing too nice, so as not to arouse his suspicion—your original doeskin should do nicely."

"What if I can't escape and I take your place in his furs?" Nena voiced one of her many concerns.

Altene laughed. "I have considered that, too. Briefly. But I'm not worried. Once he has you and realizes you are no different than any other Dor woman with a wet spot between her thighs, you will be no competition for me. Even with my skills, I cannot compete with you now—not with the virgin pedestal he has placed you on. But once the playing field is equal...Jarl will soon tire of you. And if you do not escape quickly enough, he may yet give you to Tryggr or one of the other men."

"What if I got with child?" Nena whispered forlorn.

"We can't have that, now can we? Not some other reason for him to keep you. I will give you the herb. It will keep his seed from growing."

"This plan will never work. He does not ask me."

"His eyes still ask you all the time. And if you're worried about being refused, wait until the next battle. It will come soon, and his lust will be strong. He will not refuse you then. Though he will not be as gentle as he would on another night."

"I don't care about that. Even better," Nena said vehemently, then was silent for a moment. "But that is only two days away."

"Yes, it is." Altene nodded. "You know, under different circumstances you and I could have been friends," Altene said, her voice softer, reassured by Nena's clear lack of interest in Jarl, and her near acceptance of the plan. "If it makes you feel any better, you'll be well-served to have Jarl be your first. He's the best lover I have ever known, and I've known many. I was not so fortunate in my first union." Her voice trailed off, her mind momentarily far away, but then she recovered and smiled. "Then when you escape and marry some Dor brute with hands like clubs, you will always have your first to go back to in your mind."

"But what of the gods? Won't this anger them? I would be taking their choice from them," Nena whispered. Even as she said the words, she wondered if it were possible.

"Do not speak to me of the gods. Where were the gods when my first union was sold to a fat old man in Anbai? Or do you think he was the gods' choice for me? The gods are nothing more than a bitter joke," Altene spat.

"Do not say such things. The gods had a purpose—even with you."

"Then your decision should be easy. When you choose Jarl, it will have been the gods' choice all along. You can even tell yourself that is why the gods' saved your choosing for so long—knowing this was coming and you would need it to free yourself." She could see Nena struggling with that. "You can't have it both ways, Princess." With that she turned and called for the other women to return.

Jarl watched Nena pick at her food. She had eaten this way and had few words for him since the incident with the slaver. She'd seemed truly terrified of the man, but he wasn't sure that was what was upsetting her now. The more he thought about it, her demeanor had truly changed when she returned from the baths with Altene. He swore under his breath. The deal with Altene had been a mistake. He should have never listened to Tryggr. And for what? They had certainly seen no gain from the sacrifice.

He had offered Altene another choice of jewels, which she'd accepted, but with none of the enthusiasm of when she had chosen the ruby for her bruised cheek. That time, Altene had seemed as if the reward had far exceeded her efforts. This time, though she bore no visible injury that he could see, she acted as though the gem was nowhere near worth the price.

What had the women discussed in the baths? Had Altene horrified Nena with tales of the slaver's twisted appetites? He wished he could have taken Nena for a horseback ride. That always seemed to make things better between them, but there had been no time for it. They were to attack the last target within reach of their current camp in the morning and the planning had taken up every minute of the day.

"You don't like the food?" he asked her.

"Hmm?" she responded, so lost in thought she had not heard the question.

"The food," he repeated. "Don't you like it?"

"Oh, no. It's fine."

"Are you ill?"

"No, I am well." She took another bite to show him but did not meet his eyes.

When they were finished eating, she stood and returned to the pole, waiting there for him to come and reattach her cuffs and chain. Jarl shook his head. She never fought having them put on anymore, but she was never in a hurry. He tried to catch her gaze while he clipped the cuffs around her wrists, but she did not look up.

When it was done, she sat cross-legged, absently running a loop of chain between her fingers. Jarl felt bad as he watched her, but had no time to root out the true source of her reticence. He would only get a few hours of sleep now, as it was, before he needed to be up coordinating the pre-dawn attack. Nena would have to wait until he got back.

Chapter 13

It was late when Nena heard Jarl's stallion approaching. That meant the latest village had put up a fight. His battle fever would be strong.

Her mouth went dry.

Jarl entered the tent and shed his bloody battle armor in a heap in the corner. She had tried to prepare for this moment since Altene had first suggested it—what she would say, what she would do. And today, since the moment he'd left for battle this morning, she had thought of nothing else. He seemed poised to return to the tent flap, but then turned and looked at her, his eyes filled with longing.

Do it now. Say the words.

She faltered.

He had not been with Altene in many weeks. He would not be gentle, Altene had warned. Perfect. She did not want him to be gentle. It was now or never. If he called for Altene, she would miss her chance. He reached for the flap.

Do it now! Say something!

"Wait," she called out to him, her voice shaky.

"What is it?" He dropped his hand and turned back to face her.

"Don't call for Altene." It was only part of what she needed to say, but the next words stuck on her lips, refusing to pass. She forced them out. "I will pleasure you tonight. I will take the battle fever from your blood."

Jarl raised his eyebrows in disbelief and suspicion, but Nena also saw the hope flash in his eyes and knew Altene was right.

"And why would you do that?" he asked.

Nena chose her words carefully. "The truth?" she asked.

"Yes, the truth."

"Finally captivity has become even less desirable than you." It was partially the truth and she hoped enough of it would carry in her voice to be convincing.

Jarl moved closer to her, so close that they were almost touching. Nena could feel the heat emanating from his body. She could smell the salt of his sweat and the coppery tang of blood from the battle. He reached a hand up and traced his thumb across her breast through the soft leather material of her warrior dress. She gasped involuntarily, but did not pull away.

"And you will be willing?" he asked, his now green eyes so intense they were almost frightening—almost.

"Yes," she whispered.

"Is this some trick?" he asked, still suspicious, but wavering.

"It is no trick. I choose you."

Jarl reached for her wrists and removed her cuffs. Nena wasn't sure what to do next. She knew, of course, what was about to happen. If she hadn't before, his nights with Altene would have filled in any blanks. But what did she need to do? Altene was right to not feel threatened by her.

Jarl led her toward the furs, then turned and pulled her to him. Drawing her head back by her thick braid, his lips descended onto hers, his kiss hard and aggressive. It was exactly what she had hoped for. It should be over quickly; she would only need to endure for a little while. She had mentally prepared herself for this all day. She could do it. She forced her thoughts to the cool grass banks and the stream with the small silver fish.

Jarl broke off the kiss and took a half a step back away from her. He was breathing hard. Nena could tell he was gritting his teeth. Why? She knew from other battles, he was quick and rough on these nights. That was what she was counting on—had been why she had chosen tonight. She did not want to enjoy it, or to go back to it in her mind when she was married, as Altene had suggested. She wanted to get it over with and put this all behind her. So why was he waiting? He would have had Altene down, thrusting deep inside her by now.

"Remove your dress," he said.

That made sense; Altene would have undressed immediately. Nena untied the dress behind her neck and let it fall to the floor.

Jarl sucked in his breath as his eyes took in every inch of her. He reached for her braid and untied it, separating each section, one by one, until her hair fell loose and wavy around her shoulders and down her back. He ran his hand up her back and tangled his fingers in the thick tresses behind her head, then pulled her head back, baring her throat and immobilizing her. He kissed her again, gentler this time, but she could feel his barely restrained tension. As her body leaned into him of its own accord, she once again squeezed her eyes tight and forced her thoughts far away.

The tip of his tongue probed between her lips. Her lips parted, accepting him. Though she tried to focus on her safe haven, details of the moment— details of him, began to intrude. His masculine scent mingled with, then supplanted the sweet tangy smell of the spring grass. The feel of the soft earth between her toes was driven out and replaced by the full length of his rock hard body pressed against her. The walls of her mental refuge began to fracture. She fought to hold onto it, but bit by bit, piece by piece, her sanctuary began to crumble. The strength of his need, of his desire, were impossible to block out.

Keeping his one hand entwined in her hair, he held her still while his lips continued their exploration of hers. His other hand found one of her breasts. He cupped it, then stroked and pinched her nipple gently, rolling it into a firm point between his fingertips. The exquisite sensation that rocketed from her breast was so intense, it was almost painful—almost. She moaned.

The sound affected him profoundly, and his grip tightened in her hair. "Nena," he murmured through clenched teeth as he moved his lips to the base of her ear. The feel of his breath alone on the tiny hairs of her skin sent quivers throughout her body. He suckled her earlobe. The quivers intensified and her legs threatened to fold. The last shred of her refuge fell away, leaving her defenseless against his assault.

She felt the pulse in her neck bounding against his lips as he moved his kisses down to the hollow at the base of her throat. She was shocked at the sensitivity of the areas he lingered over. Normal places that had never been especially sensitive before—her ears, her neck, now responded so strongly to his touch that she felt it difficult to draw in a full breath.

Jarl pressed her down onto the furs, then stood and stripped out of his remaining clothes. Nena tried to recover her bearings, but the reprieve was too brief. He slid next to her and his hands continued their onslaught—touching, stroking, caressing, pinching. His lips and tongue followed where his fingers had been only seconds before, nuzzling her neck, teasing her tight nipples. He sought out areas she had no idea would respond as they did—the insides of her wrists, the soft skin on the inside of her elbows. Nena felt herself spiraling out of control, wanting him to continue, needing him to continue, begging him to continue.

She didn't think she could take another moment of the intense pleasure. Her body writhed beneath him and the sounds it made were not her own. The places he discovered—that he seemed to already know. How much more would he make her endure? Was there no end to this yearning? It was even worse than she had feared, but nothing about it was shameful—and no part of her wanted him to stop. Yet surely it had to be over soon. How much more could she bear?

But Jarl wasn't even close to being finished with her. His lips moved down over her flat stomach to her belly button, then lower. He found the pulsing moistness between her thighs and tasted her. Softly at first, with the just the tip of his tongue, he explored every fold and crease until he came across her swollen node. As his tongue flicked over its surface, her back arched. A guttural moan escaped her lips. His own manhood throbbed in response, straining for release, but he held back, teasing her, licking her, then sucking gently. When she could take no more, when her body began to convulse and shudder and she made a sound like none other, only then did he leave her. Parting her legs wider with his knees, he guided his shaft between her soft folds. He intended to be gentle, but seeing and hearing her intense pleasure, hurled him beyond the limits of his restraint. Unable to hold back any longer, Jarl drove deep within her in one powerful stroke.

Nena's cries of pleasure changed pitch briefly to a cry of pain, but still she clung to him, pulling him closer, holding him to her as he drove inside over and over. His release came quickly, carrying him on a raging tide of pure blind deaf sensation. It was many seconds before his senses returned and he was aware of her beneath him. Her breath still came in gasps, but was slowing. Their sweat mingled between their chests. "Did I hurt you?" he whispered.

Hurt? Had he really asked that? He had just taken her to a place that she had no idea existed, and the first union was always painful for the woman. She'd been expecting that. Though now she could remember nothing of pain, only of…. Her pulse, even now, still pounded in her ears. She looked at his worried face and reached up to touch his cheek, having no words, but wanting to comfort him. He smiled at her.

Jarl pulled out slowly and rolled over on his side to lie next to her. He reached out with one hand to stroke her hair. "Nena, my princess," he murmured.

Nena turned to look at him. His eyes were slowly returning to the mixed shades of all colors of when he was content. She had made the right choice. This had to have been the gods' choice. They wanted this union even if only to allow her escape. Why else would it have been so magical?

A trickle of blood running down his neck caught her attention. She followed the blood trail and noted a shallow wound on one of his shoulders. He seemed unaware of it.

"You are wounded. Let me see it," she said.

"It can wait. It is small—but a scratch."

"Even small things have a way of becoming troublesome. Come, I will tend to it for you."

Jarl groaned and sat up on the edge of the bed. He knew she was right but would have given anything not to move at that moment. He watched as she slipped naked from the furs and went to retrieve a water bag and rag. She moved about the tent totally at ease, showing no sign of modesty in her nakedness or what had just transpired. His eyes followed her every graceful move, admiring her long lean legs and the way her thick dark hair cascaded down her back.

He prayed the entry boards would not rattle and send her scurrying for cover. In his mind he threatened death to anyone who interrupted them now—anyone who caused them to lose this moment. Although as much as he enjoyed watching her, he also couldn't wait for her to return to him. He wanted her near him, touching him. Even the short distance that separated them now seemed too much.

He could not believe what an affect she had on him. He could not believe she was finally truly his. She was such an amazing woman—a beautiful blend of contradictions. As tough as any man he'd ever known, but at the same time gentle and tender. Innocent, yet her passion had matched his own. Intelligent and learned in so many things—tending his wound being just a small example, yet naive in so many others.

Nena's lips curved into a smile as she returned with the water bag and a cloth, reading the general path of his thoughts by the intentness of his expression. She crawled onto the furs behind him and knelt to better reach the wound on the back of his shoulder.

"It was close to your neck," she commented with disapproval. "You left your back unprotected."

He knew she was right; the careless mistake had almost cost him dearly. "He paid for it," was his only response. Jarl ignored the sting as she wiped away the dried blood and dirt. "Will I live?" he asked, teasing.

"Yes, I'm afraid so," she replied with a smile and continued to clean. When she was finished, she looked at the wound, unsatisfied. "That's better, but I would prefer to have willow bark to pack in it, to be safe."

"There is some in that vial." He pointed across the tent to a spot near the jewel chest. "I got it from the healer for your fever when you were sick."

When she was sick. When he had saved her. Nena's stomach constricted at her planned betrayal.

She retrieved the powder and poured a thin line into the length of the wound, tamped it with her finger, then blew the excess away. Her soft breath tickled the back of his neck, and Jarl felt his groin twitch in response. He fought it. He had to control himself now. She would be sore. They had forever to work up to all-night lovemaking. He smiled at the thought.

He made love to her again in the morning. This time slower and with less intensity, but with the same leg-tangled results. When she was finally steady enough to rise, Nena checked her new boundaries. "I would go to the latrine and to bathe," she announced tentatively, more than half expecting him to refuse or call for Altene. He did neither.

"Fine." He rolled onto his back and smiled at her with the most contented smile she'd ever seen on his handsome face. "I should, too, but I think I'm just going to lie here instead and die a sweet death."

Nena still couldn't believe it as she tied her dress behind her neck and exited the tent unescorted, but he made no move to stop her.

She groaned as she slipped into the hot water of the bath. Every muscle ached and complained, and the water stung her tender womanhood, but the pain was brief, and soon she felt it melting away. She was free. Perhaps not all the way free, but well on her way—the hardest hurdle overcome. And the price had been—she smiled and flushed at the memory—had been more than easy to pay.

As much as she would have liked to stay and enjoy the water, Nena finished quickly. She did not wish him to worry about the length of her absence and have second thoughts about her new freedoms. Everything she did from now on needed to be toward building and maintaining his trust.

"I will need ink," she said when she returned to the tent.

"I will have Altene find some and bring it to you." Jarl moved behind her and nuzzled her neck. "You know Altene wished to share you with me, and while I must admit at first the idea intrigued me, I know now, I could never share you with another. Not even a woman could I tolerate seeing bring you to the long moan."

"You are jealous," she said and smiled.

"Beyond jealous. You are mine and only mine."

Until I am gone.

The difference in Jarl was astonishing. He was tender and affectionate, bordering on playful. Throughout the day, his eyes followed her everywhere, as if he feared the previous night had been a dream, and he had to keep verifying it was real. It revealed an almost vulnerable side to him that she had never seen before. Gone was any trace of tension in his face or body. Even when they were interrupted by camp business, his mood remained exceptionally high and his dealings very lenient.

Nena responded in kind. She told herself, as she allowed him to pull her onto his lap and shared wine from his oxhorn cup, that it was to lull him into a false sense of security, and to not arouse his suspicions. But being this close to him was easy. Far too easy.

She expected the camp would pull out after a few days of rest, but when the first scout reported that a potential fourth target had been discovered—one that might be reached from their present location, Jarl was quick to delay their departure. He sent full reconnaissance teams to bring him reports before he made a decision as to the next move.

Altene brought the ink and graciously offered to fill in the circle for her. Nena accepted and bit her lip at the repeated penetration of the inked needle.

At first Jarl hovered nearby, watching the process closely. "Make sure you fill it in plenty dark," he instructed Altene. "I don't want there to be any doubt when other men see it. And where will you record my name? Above or below?" he teased. He was full of himself.

Altene laughed at the ridiculousness of the idea before she replied, "Nowhere."

Undaunted, he persisted, "Perhaps just my initials then. There's plenty of room for that."

Altene only shook her head.

"But I thought you said all of a woman's important life events were recorded," Jarl persevered.

"And they are; her circle is being filled in," Altene agreed.

"But no credit given to who was responsible for the feat?" Jarl asked.

"Only when a woman makes the statement of union in front of the village and becomes married is the man's family line listed there. No one asks a woman who her first union was with. If a circle is filled in and not followed by a husband's lineage, then it is known that it is something not to be talked about."

Jarl frowned as he considered her words. There was clearly no way such a statement of union would ever be made. Even if he could convince Nena to say the words, which he realized was a stretch—and at best, a very long way off, she would never stand in front of her village again. Did that mean every Dor who saw her from now on, with the dark circle and no husband marked upon her arm, would assume her first union had been something unpleasant? The thought disturbed him. Even knowing that soon he would take her far away and there would be no other Dor to see it—or that his people would never recognize the significance of a circle with no marks below it, did little to ease his troubled mind.

Nena watched the frown crease his forehead. She knew it meant he was contemplating something very deeply and wondered what he was thinking about. Before he could offer any clues, he left, saying evasively he had business to take care of. Nena wouldn't have thought twice about it, had his behavior before he left not been so peculiar. She wondered what business he could not attend to in his tent, or what was so important that it needed to be handled now.

Altene shook her head and smiled as he left. Nena was surprised she was not more upset. She wondered briefly if it was Jarl's unusual boyish behavior affecting her, too, but then quickly discounted it. Altene was happy because her plan was in motion. She was probably already counting down the days before she would return to Jarl's furs.

"He seems very proud of himself," Altene commented once he was gone.

"Yes." Nena nodded.

"And he already allows you to move about unescorted? As we had hoped?"

"Yes."

"Good. Don't push it by asking for too much too soon."

"I know. I won't." Nena sat in silence while Altene continued to work on her arm. "Perhaps you could escape with us. I could find a way," Nena offered.

"Escape?" Altene laughed derisively. "And go where? Back with you to the Teclan? And have them look down on me as you do? My village is long gone. I have nowhere to go."

"There are other tribes of Klarta."

Altene shook her head, neither option seeming to please her. "I think not. Do not pity me. Many moons from now when you are gone and lying beneath your grunting Dor husband with his club hands, I will be enjoying Jarl's touch in his new lands of the North."

And any other man he chooses to give you to. "But how do you know he will take you with him to the North? How do you know you will not be sold with the others to Piltor?"

Altene frowned at the mention of the Worick's name. "Jarl will take me with him. He has more than once said he has never met my equal in the furs. Once you are gone, I will remind him of that regularly. And if for some reason he does not, I have enough jewels now to buy my own freedom."

Nena changed the subject. "I need the herb."

"Be patient. I have it here."

"How much do I take?"

"Pick one leaf from the stem and hold it under your tongue every day for an hour. Then spit it out. Do not swallow it." Altene held out a small branch with stiff tiny olive green leaves protruding from either side. Nena glanced at it only briefly before plucking a leaf and placing it under her tongue. The plant was unfamiliar to her and the leaf had a bitter flavor.

"Do you have more?" Nena asked.

Altene looked at her suspiciously. "You will not need more. You are escaping, remember?"

"Yes. I only wondered if it took longer than expected..."

"See that it doesn't," Altene threatened as she stabbed the needle again into Nena's upper arm. "So was it as good as I said?" she asked.

Nena flushed again at the memory, though she knew better than to admit the experience to Altene. "It doesn't matter. The sooner I can forget it and leave this place, the better."

Altene took her redness and response for denial. "I warned you. I was worried he would be rough from the battle."

Nena could tell she had not been worried at all, but had hoped—and was pleased.

"That is all the help you will get from me, so do not think to ask for ways to please him. I worked hard for those secrets and will not share them."

"I would never..." Nena began, then stopped. "Gratitude," she said, instead.

"For what? For not sharing?"

"For everything. For pushing me to see the means to escape. For the herb. Perhaps you were right that under different circumstances we could have been friends. How is it you came to be here? How are you not married to a Dor with club hands raising his children?" Nena flinched as Altene again drove the inked needle beneath the surface of her skin.

"After the Teclan raided our village, slavers caught up with the survivors a few days later. I was very young, only eight summers. I was sold to a pleasure house in Anbai, where, until I was old enough to work in the house, I was taught other things—foreign languages and customs, so as to better understand the demands and wishes of my future customers. And I was also taught the many ways to pleasure women and men—ways that do not require penetration.

"When I was old enough, my first union was sold to the highest bidder. He was no Jarl. He was a panting, slobbering old man, and I took no pleasure from it. I worked in the house for several more years until I was purchased by a regular customer. He was taking me to his home when we were attacked by these Northmen, and I was taken prisoner again. Jarl has an eye for Dor women, and I was soon to catch it—much as you were. Which is why you must go."

Chapter 14

"**I** have a present for you," Jarl announced.

Nena smiled at his excitement. "I do not need a present. And besides, your last gift to me were the cuffs."

"I know, but I want to give you one. I want to see you as happy as I am. And the cuffs were a gift of necessity, for your safety—and mine," he added. "This is a gift purely for your enjoyment."

Nena hesitated. Would he give her a giant ruby as he had given Altene when she pleased him? The thought hardened her heart.

You are nothing more than a favored slave to him. Do not forget it. He even thinks to appease you with trinkets, now—as he did Altene.

"Come." He motioned for her to follow. "It's this way." He held open the tent flap.

Nena followed him out into the bright sunlight and had to shield her eyes with her hand for a moment. There was Jarl's stallion, saddled and ready, and beyond was the shadow of another horse. She assumed it would be the fat little gelding she had grown fond of, and moved around Jarl's horse to mount. Her present must be out on the plains, or for some reason he chose not to give it to her here.

As she stepped around Jarl's stallion, Nena saw a creature more beautiful than she had ever imagined. The mare standing saddled was the color of polished steel, with lighter dapples distributed evenly throughout her glossy coat. Where Jarl's horse was tall and muscular, this one was sleek and refined. Nena's eyes scanned the entire animal, finding no flaw. The mare's legs seemed almost delicate compared to the thick bones of Jarl's warhorse, but they were straight and perfect. Her hooves were flinty and tough, able to withstand the roughest terrain. But it was her face that drew Nena's longest regard. The mare's head could not have been finer had it been chiseled by the most skilled sculptor. Huge intelligent eyes were set wide on a broad forehead that tapered to a tiny muzzle with large nostrils.

Nena had never seen anything like her. She had to be one of the legendary Bedouin horses from the lands far to the south. She had heard of them but had never seen one in the flesh. The horses that could carry a man for days without rest. Horses that could survive in the harsh desert with little food or water. They were the toughest, and some argued the fastest, horses the gods had ever created. So prized by the Bedouin who bred them, they even slept in their tents with them as family. Nena had heard all the stories, but never that they were so beautiful.

The mare wore a Dor sheepskin saddle. It was plain, with no adornments of ivory or zebra hide as her tournament gift had been, but the thought behind the additional gift moved her even more. She approached the mare and took her bridle. The mare lifted her tiny muzzle and sniffed Nena's face. The two stood bonding, exchanging breaths for a long moment.

Nena turned to Jarl, unable to hide the emotion his gift had elicited. "She is for me?" she asked in disbelief.

"Yes."

She held his gaze, looking deep into his eyes. "But she can outrun your stallion." She said the words quietly, her eyes searching his face the entire time. It was a simple observation to an outsider, but both of them understood the significance.

"Perhaps not on a short stretch, but yes," he nodded. "She could outrun him—if she wanted to. Would you like to ride now?"

Nena nodded and smiled a small smile, still deeply affected by his gift and trying to overcome it. "Yes," she said.

Compared to the other thick tribe horses, Nightwing had been sensitive and willing, but this mare was even more so. Jarl had no way of knowing that her beloved mare had been killed in the raid. And yet he had chosen the one gift that would move her more than any other. How had he done it? How did he know her so well in so little time?"

After miles of riding, when even Jarl's stallion had a sweat, the mare seemed as fresh as if she had just been saddled. What the Teclan warriors could do with horses like these. She was a weapon beyond value. What Nena herself could do with a horse like this to escape.

They rode for many hours, stopping at a turn in the river where trees grew tall and the water pooled in a lazy slow moving current. There, they unsaddled the horses and turned them loose to graze on the lush river bottom grass. They did not fear them running away. Jarl's stallion was trained to many commands, and coming to Jarl's whistle was one of his lesser ones—the same trick that Nena had thought unique to her previous mare, Nightwing.

They watched the bay stallion circling the gray mare, bowing his neck and striking high with his foreleg in the air, trying to get her attention—trying to impress her. The mare regarded him coolly while she nibbled the tender blades of grass, but was quick with a reprimanding sharp nip or kick when he pushed too close. Finally, the stallion, too, began to graze, though he remained ever hopeful. Taking short anxious bites, he kept his eyes fixed on the mare and nickered softly at her whenever he raised his head.

Jarl laughed at his antics. "It seems my great warhorse has also found a southern beauty who rejects him. He's almost embarrassing to watch." He turned and smiled at Nena. "Though I'm sure I never acted quite so foolish."

Jarl pulled off his tunic, revealing his well-contoured chest and arms. He turned and stepped to the water's edge, then bent to remove his boots. The sun danced on the rippling muscles of his back and shoulders, and Nena felt an overwhelming urge to run her hands over his skin—to feel the firm ridges of muscle beneath her fingers.

"Do you swim?" His voice interrupted her reverie, and she flushed guiltily. Jarl grinned at her obvious thoughts and her embarrassment at having been caught in them. He stood with one hand carelessly resting on the front of his half undone trousers, his eyes laughing at her.

"I…uh…yes, though not since I was a child," she answered. "The water in the mountains is cold."

"It'll be much warmer here. And if you get a chill, I'm here to warm you. Though you look quite warm, now," he teased, referring to her flushed face. With that he shed his trousers and turned to wade out into the water. He stopped when it was just above his knees.

While his attention was focused on his next step on the river bottom, Nena resumed her admiration of his naked body, safe for the moment from being discovered again. Her eyes started at his broad shoulders and worked their way down to his muscular buttocks and lean, haired thighs.

Suddenly he leaped into the air. His body curved into a perfect arch as he dove, his hands and arms slicing through the surface of the water. With barely a splash, he was gone. There was no sign of him for many seconds. Nena looked with consternation at the water that had swallowed him without a trace. Still no Jarl. She ran to the water's edge. There was no sign of a struggle, no thrashing that she could see. She didn't know what to do. If something were to happen to him now….

Then, as suddenly as he had disappeared, he resurfaced on the far side, spitting out a mouthful of water and shaking his soaked locks like a great bear would shake his mane. "You're still dressed," he observed. "Hurry. Come join me. The temperature is perfect." He called out encouragement to her and began to lazily make his way back toward her with slow sure strokes.

Nena tentatively undid her dress, not at all looking forward to the frigid water. But Jarl was not gasping or shrieking from the shock of the cold that she still remembered vividly from her swims as a child. She had told him she could swim, and it was true, but her rapid frantic dashes and splashes in the water did not resemble what he was doing.

Nena tested the water with her toe. Jarl was right; it was quite warm in the shallows, almost the temperature of the baths. Slowly, she waded out further, feeling the temperature drop with every step, though it still remained comfortable. Jarl waited for her in the deeper water beyond. When the water was waist deep, she hesitated and looked to him, unsure.

Jarl was mesmerized by the sight of the water slowly creeping up her naked body. It concealed a tiny bit more of her with every tentative step she took. When it passed above her thighs and the dark triangle of her womanhood, he let out his breath. Standing there now, the water lapping against her trim waist, with only her upper torso still exposed above the surface, she seemed a vision of some golden water goddess. He could see she was waiting for further encouragement from him, but his mouth could not form the words that would end the alluring display.

"How deep is it where you are?" she asked.

"I can touch the bottom," he lied.

"Can I?" she asked. Jarl was a full head taller than she was.

"I think so, but if not, you can hold onto me." This was the first time he had seen her afraid of anything other than the slaver, and he enjoyed her vulnerability—enjoyed being in the position of her needing him to protect her.

Nena took a deep breath and lunged forward, her arms and legs moving in an odd combination of flailing and dog paddling. When she reached him, she turned her body vertical and reached with her toes for the bottom that wasn't there. She shrieked with terror. Just before her head went under, Jarl grabbed her firmly by the arms, keeping her face safely above the surface. He shook the water from his hair again, thoroughly soaked from her erratic thrashing. "Easy. I've got you," he reassured. "It's alright. Hold on to me." He pulled her toward him and felt her arms wrap around his neck. Her breasts and body pressed tightly against him. Keeping one arm around her waist, he tread water with the other. "I thought you said you could swim," he chuckled.

"I can, but what you are doing is…" she marveled, at a loss for words at how he was keeping them afloat while barely seeming to move his legs and one arm.

"No," he corrected her. "What you did was not swimming."

"I did not say I was a fish," she retorted, more comfortable now that it was becoming clear he truly could support them both and she wasn't about to drown.

He reached for the end of her braid and pulled loose the tie, allowing the water's gentle current to undo the sections.

"Can you teach me to swim like this?" she asked.

"Yes, I could. But then you wouldn't need to cling to me so tightly, so I don't think I will," he teased. His eyes were the multicolored mixture of grays and blues of when he was amused, but she could see the flecks of green becoming more predominant the longer he held her. She felt his hardness growing between them.

Wrapping her legs around his waist, she kept his goal suspended just beyond his reach. He kissed her deeply, water droplets mingling with their kiss, then began to paddle them closer to shore. He could easily keep them both suspended in the water, but to do anything more required some traction. Her dark hair fanned out around them now like a veil in the water. Jarl could feel its thousands of tiny fingers caressing his skin, tickling, teasing, tingling everywhere it touched him.

"Nena," he groaned under his breath.

Her entire body, to her core, reacted to his tone, his need, and she felt it become her own in an instant. In that moment, there was no Teclan, no Northmen, no camp waiting for them, no slaver, only the two of them as one. She felt a fluttering weakness within her that she knew now could only be quelled when his strength was inside her. Slowly she loosened her grip with her legs around his waist and allowed him to push her lower until his shaft was buried deep within her. Their bodies firmly connected, he paused and kissed her again, his eyes now the color of emeralds. With his hands tight on her hips and buttocks, he began to move with firm upward strokes, slowly at first, then increasing in intensity.

Nena twisted her fingers into Jarl's thick dark chestnut hair, feeling the explosion building with each sure thrust. She clung to him, her parted lips pressed against his cheek, lost in the ecstasy of her senses. When her body began to shudder, she felt him join her with his climactic release.

Neither moved or spoke for many moments. Jarl remained locked inside her. Even when his manhood fell away, they remained embraced, motionless in the cool water.

"I think I will definitely not be teaching you to swim," he said with a smile, his eyes once again a playful swirl of blues and grays.

Nena smiled back and gently bit his lower lip. She pulled it back toward her slightly before releasing it. "I have changed my mind," she whispered. "I no longer wish to learn."

Jarl nodded, appreciating her response. "Lie back," he said, "until you are flat on top of the water." He felt her tense. "Don't worry, I've got you and I won't let you go. I promise." He kept one hand under her neck and the other under the small of her back. "It's alright, just enjoy the water. Feel how it lifts you." He moved behind her holding her only by her head now. "If you feel like you are sinking, just take in a deep breath and hold it; you will float without even trying." As her body began to sink, she did as he suggested and soon felt her chest breaking the surface. It was amazing. "The salty waters of the sea are even easier to float in," he said. "They lift you without your hardly having to draw in a breath at all."

Nena couldn't imagine doing something like this in the unpredictable shifting sea. Even wading with her feet firmly on the bottom had disturbed her, but she did not doubt that he was telling her the truth, or that the sea was different with him. She had thought before that their mastery of the sea was due to the strength of their ships, but seeing him here, so at home in the river and hearing him describe the sea as being the same, Nena knew it was more than that. These Northmen had a powerful connection—almost a kinship to water.

She felt him crouch down behind her, and then his strong arm was around her ribs. Gently he pushed off the bottom, pulling her with him, until he floated next to her on the surface with her head on his shoulder. Nena fought the urge to thrash, every instinct telling her that one of them needed to have their feet on something solid. His arm tightened around her.

Then they were both floating together. When she was finally able to relax, the experience was like nothing she'd ever felt before. The sensation of pure weightlessness. The quiet. The strange feeling of buoyancy while remaining perfectly still. Jarl occasionally paddled with his other arm and moved them lazily around the pool. Nena didn't want it to end. She'd never been able to enjoy water like this before and was disappointed to find he had maneuvered them back to the shore.

"Come," he said as he dropped his feet to the bottom and helped her to stand. "Too much time in the water and your skin will wrinkle." He began to wade to the bank.

Nena didn't care if her entire body looked like a piece of dried fruit, and followed him only reluctantly. She watched as Jarl gathered their clothes and then spread them out side by side on the grass in the sun. They lay together on their backs, looking up at the cloudless blue sky, while the sun dried and warmed them. He rolled up and gently kissed the dark circle on her arm. It was still raised and tender.

"Why do you not have tattoos?" she asked.

"I have a few," he responded.

"But not like your men."

"No. Not so many as most of them do."

"Why not?"

He shrugged. "I don't know. I'm not opposed to them, and I understand why other men get so many; I just never cared to."

"Gunnar has a great many, and I've often wondered why you did not decorate yourself in a similar manner."

"Why? Do you like them?" Jarl asked, disturbed that she had taken such close notice of his second.

Nena thought for a moment. "The black ones I do not mind, but the green ones I do not care for. From a distance they look like bruises to me. Though perhaps it is because my people do not use any color other than black, and I'm just not used to seeing them." She paused. "But it is strange to me that they have no meaning."

"They do have meaning," he disagreed.

"I misspoke. I understand they have meaning, but only to the bearer. And if they have no meaning to those who look upon them, then why have them at all? A man does not need them to remember things—his memories are forever within him. With the Dor each one tells something specific to all who look upon them. They are not for decoration."

"Our men get them for many reasons. Some are to remember something important and, even though you're correct and they do have their memories, by looking at the symbol, it keeps the memories fresh in their minds. Others bear marks that show unity or brotherhood. But some are for nothing more than decoration or to frighten the enemy."

Nena thought of the Northman she had seen in the camp who had filed his teeth into sharp points and tattooed his entire face with scales like a serpent. It was repulsive to her, but not frightening. "Teclan do not need such marks, we believe in frightening the enemy with our weapons."

Jarl chuckled. "As do I."

They lay in silence a while longer.

"We need to get back," he said, but made no move to rise.

"Yes," she agreed, but also did not move.

He smiled at her and shook his head. "You're a terrible influence on me. I could stay here forever."

Tryggr was waiting for them on the outskirts of the camp, pacing back and forth, clearly agitated. He glanced at Nena, then at both of them, taking in their recently wet appearances. He scowled. "Nice ride in the country?" he asked sarcastically.

"What is it, Tryggr?" Jarl asked, not taking the bait and not amused.

Tryggr looked at Nena pointedly and remained mute.

Jarl turned to Nena, "Return to the tent. I'll see you there. Have the guard take care of the mare. I'll show you where she is kept tomorrow so you can do it yourself the next time."

Nena nodded, nudging the mare forward with her heel.

When she was safely out of earshot, Jarl raised his eyebrows, not about to repeat his question. Had his afternoon not been so perfect, he would have given Tryggr a strong reprimand. Friend or no friend, Tryggr was pushing his boundaries and was going to have to be dealt with. Jarl took a deep breath. Some other time.

"You're not going to believe who our men have found skulking ahead in a canyon." Tryggr waited a few seconds to build the suspense. "Piltor."

"What's he doing there?" Jarl asked.

"I don't know, but they said he's not traveling with his whole caravan, just a small well-armed force."

Jarl stroked his chin. "That's very unlike our friend to travel without his comforts, more like how a raiding party might travel."

"Exactly. What do you think he's up to?" Tryggr asked.

"I don't know," Jarl lied. "But I plan to ask him. Bring him to me and increase the security around the camp."

Chapter 15

Piltor entered the tent in such a rush, Nena knew he must have been shoved. He paused and readjusted his disheveled robes in a huff. She had wanted to go to the baths to avoid his unpleasant presence altogether, but Jarl had refused, not wanting her out of his sight until he knew what was going on. She sat cross-legged on Jarl's furs, on the opposite side of the tent from the table where Jarl conducted his business, to be as far away from them as possible.

Without even acknowledging Jarl, Piltor's gaze flew to the center pole. Confused to find it empty, the Worick brazenly continued his search of the tent, his eyes darting to every corner until he found her. He focused on the dark circle on her arm. His face fell.

"Have you seen enough?" Jarl interrupted his examination.

"What?" the slaver mumbled, his thoughts still in disorder after his recent discovery.

"Why are you here?" Jarl demanded without repeating his first question.

"I, uh, I came to make sure partial payment in rubies would be an acceptable substitution for the gold we agreed upon," Piltor stammered.

Both men knew rubies were more valuable and lighter to carry; they would be an acceptable substitution for gold in any situation. It was clearly an excuse and not a very good one.

"Rubies will be fine. Though I am surprised you would make such an arduous journey simply to ask that. Was there something else you wanted?" Jarl asked.

"Uh, no. You are such a good customer, I only wanted to ensure that the transfer at the port went smoothly," the Worick proceeded, relieved that Jarl seemed to have accepted his explanation. An uncomfortable pause followed. "I see you have sampled your greatest treasure." Piltor changed the subject, then shrugged. "Though I can hardly blame you. Even with the prospect of a mountain of gold, that temptation would be too much for any man to resist for long." He brightened visibly as a new thought came to him. "But perhaps she will be for sale now? The price will not be what it once was, of course, but it will still be substantial. Her first union would have brought nearly a king's ransom, but only that once. She will still have great value every night for as long as she lives. As I told you before, the Teclan have made many enemies over the years—in fact, their actions continuously beget more. Their raiding will ensure her a never-ending supply of customers." His eyes moved back to her and Nena felt them crawling over her skin, leaving the same slimy tracks as before.

Jarl was managing to hold his temper better this time, though Piltor did not press it by trying to get close to her. "She's still not for sale," he answered the original question.

"Pity." The Worick paused. Then his eyes gleamed again. "But perhaps we could work out something else? In the past, you so kindly shared your previous favorite, Altene, with me." Piltor licked his lips in anticipation as his eyes undressed her. "Perhaps…" Piltor struggled to find the best way to word his request. "I will not be leaving until the morrow, and would pay handsomely for time with her. Very handsomely indeed," he added.

Nena saw the cords of Jarl's neck become taut. One of his fists clenched and unclenched under the table. Using the utmost restraint, he smiled at Piltor—a dangerous smile, then spoke through gritted teeth that left no doubt of his position. "Our business is done here." He stood and moved toward Piltor as if to toss him from the tent. The slaver recognized it and scurried for the door. "And Piltor," Jarl added.

"Yes?"

"You are mistaken. You will be leaving tonight, and I don't expect to see you again until we meet at the port."

"Yes, of course," the Worick said as he bobbed his head and backed out the doorway.

That night Nena could not sleep, and though she tried to think of anything else, her thoughts continued to be drawn back to the slaver. He was a harsh reminder of the reality of her situation in the face of her recent idyllic days. She had to escape. Now. While she could still find her way home. Before she was too far away in the cold strange lands of the North. It was only a matter of time before Jarl tired of her—before a new woman caught his eye and she was given away as Altene was.

You are not Altene. He is different with you. He keeps you with him all the time. He is careful to do things you like—to give you things you like; he gave you the mare.

And he gave Altene jewels, which was what she liked...and then he gave her to the slaver. What has happened to you? You are a Teclan warrior and the daughter of Meln. Yet you have gone from seeking any way to kill him to sharing his furs willingly every night. To taking rides, and waiting in his tent for him to return, like some woman waiting for her husband. You are his slave. And like the other women here who you used to ridicule, you have become complacent with your bondage. Remember what happened to Lenta.

All men are not like Lenta's. Gineesh's Northman is taking her as wife. Jarl will not hurt you. He fought the gods to save your life.

And he doesn't think he is hurting Altene any more than he is hurting the chair when he sits upon it. That is its function in life and he is merely using it. When his infatuation with you fades, he will use you in the same manner.

Jarl is different.

Even if he is; what happens to you if he is killed? Even the greatest warriors fall in battle when the gods choose for it to be their time. What happens to you then? Do you think Tryggr will hesitate to claim the handsome price the slaver offers?

No.

No. Her stronger inner voice repeated for emphasis.

The internal debate only reinforced what Nena already knew. She had to escape, and she had to do it soon. Any longer and she might lose her resolve. She realized she was dangerously close to it now. She looked over at Jarl sleeping next to her. His face so relaxed, his hair tousled like a boy's. She resisted the urge to touch it.

She needed a foolproof plan. She would get only one chance, and if she failed....

She could not fail.

The gift of the mare gave her the excuse she needed to fully exercise her free run of the camp without raising any suspicion. Though she was not allowed to ride without Jarl, at least twice daily she visited the mare to groom her or bring her a treat. The mare's coat responded to the attention and glistened in the sunlight like a polished silver coin. Soon the horse guards were barely acknowledging her, and Nena knew her presence among the horses would not raise concern when it was time.

Caring for the mare brought another unexpected bonus. The horse enclosures were beyond the prisoner compound on the back side of the camp to reduce the number of flies in the main camp itself. In order to reach them, Nena had to pass directly through the prisoners. Each time, she varied her course slightly, hoping to see where the girl and her mother were kept without having to ask. She trusted no one with her secret—not even her own people. She could not risk being betrayed.

On the third day, she saw the mother and girl from a distance. She did not approach them. Instead, without slowing her stride, she scrutinized them and the area around them closely. There was no sign of a guard on the girl, as she had feared. Perhaps Jarl had rescinded the order when she chose him. Why or how didn't matter; one by one her obstacles were crumbling in front of her.

Her only problem left to solve was the location of the camp sentries, and after the unexpected return of the slaver, the increased number of them. She knew from the maps and hearing the men talk in Jarl's tent, the camp was set up within four circles of guards. The men were stationed closer together along the innermost circle nearest the camp, then fanned out in ever-widening circles until the outermost ring of sentries on the plains. While the distance of each circle from the camp remained relatively fixed, the location of each individual sentry within that circle was fluid. They constantly moved along the perimeter of their ring, never staying in one spot.

Not being able to predict their exact location was bad enough, but it was their warning system of whistles and horns that was Nena's biggest concern. It was designed to alert them to any attack, and allow men to converge on a particular area to repel intruders. The furthermost sentries' signals were rapidly transmitted to all the circles, and men from other areas would move swiftly to bolster the area under siege. But the same alarms could also be used in reverse, in the case of an escape attempt.

Nena was standing in the mare's pen when a horn sounded, quite close, from somewhere inside the prisoner compound. The mare spooked and raised her head, her tiny ears pricked toward the sound. Her nostrils flared. Initially, Nena could neither see, nor hear what caused the alarm, but the quick succession of whistles and horns, and the mare's ever-moving attention, told her which direction to look. At last, she saw a young dark-skinned man break free from the tents and sprint through the grass. Even though he was fleet of foot and had managed to evade the first row of guards, from where she stood, Nena could see he never had a chance. Sentries from the outer rings, alerted by the alarms, closed in on his location. He was quickly surrounded and recaptured.

She had to somehow account for that in her plan. If the sentries were alerted before she was clear, her plan was doomed. To outmaneuver so many in close quarters would be impossible. Her mare's strength was in the open and going a distance—the longer the better. Once she was free; not even Jarl with his great stallion would be able to catch her. But how to get there?

Then even that problem solved itself. That evening in Jarl's tent, she sat listening to the scout reports that were just beginning to come in from the next village. The potential fourth target from this grouping had not been worth their while, and the first scouts had returned from the next target on Jarl's map. The last one before her aunt's tribe. These early reports described the next village as much larger than any of the previous ones and its defense fortifications more significant. All agreed it was still well within their capabilities, but would require more men. Nena listened carefully as Jarl and his officers discussed just how many men would be needed. The number was substantial.

She could not believe her ears. When the men left for this battle, the camp would be poorly guarded, the sentries spread very thin. Jarl would be gone. She could make her escape with the girl and have at least half a day's head start before he knew she was missing.

Jarl gave orders for the camp to break at dawn. They would move to within easy striking distance of the next target, make the final adjustments to their plan, then attack.

That night as they lay languorously entwined in the furs, with Jarl's finger absently tracing an imaginary pattern on her stomach, Nena brought up what had been on her mind.

"Tomorrow, will I be riding the mare when the camp moves?" She knew it was a big test of her new freedom. She was not allowed to ride without him, and though he would also be riding that day, he would never permit her to ride with him. Having his slave woman riding along beside him—and that's what she was—while he dealt with the men, was not an option. Still she had to ask. The thought of riding in the cramped wagon with Altene was unbearable.

She held her breath.

Jarl could tell she was waiting with considerable anticipation for his answer. He hadn't given it any thought and had assumed she would ride on the wagon, but he could see why she would not want to. On the other hand, he didn't want to have to worry about her. With the camp on the move, the sentry system dismantled, and her with the mare, there would be a lot of variables to worry about.

Jarl wondered briefly if she had intentionally waited until this moment when he was sexually sated to ask him, to manipulate him, then dismissed the thought. She did not seem to possess that particular feminine guile; her straightforwardness was another thing about her he found irresistible. He looked at her now, her thick lashes hiding her dark eyes while she waited for his verdict. Things had been so perfect between them. She did not push or ask for anything. He knew he could not deny her.

"Yes, you may ride the mare," he acquiesced.

Her eyes flew open and she snuggled closer to him. "Gratitude, Jarl."

"You're welcome," he said, and kissed the top of her head. *Don't make me regret it.*

Nena had the mare saddled and ready before dawn. She led her back to the tent and waited, staying out of the way while the two men dismantled it. She watched as the younger man went in and dropped the two temporary poles, then raced out as it collapsed. She had seen it many times now, but their precision still amazed her. She soothed the mare when the horse snorted and spooked at the great gust of air that blew from the tent opening.

Jarl arrived just as the tent flattened to the ground. He spoke with the two men, verified all was proceeding according to schedule, then approached Nena.

He glanced at the mare, only briefly, but his eyes took in every detail. There was only a smaller waterskin tied to the front of the saddle. No provisions, no large waterskin, no extra clothing for inclement weather that one might take if they were expecting to travel far. He turned to Nena. She wore her usual simple warrior dress. Everything seemed in order. Still he cursed himself for his weakness the night before. What had he been thinking? Why risk it?

This was one thing he did not have to be worrying about right now. One thing he had control over—unlike every other thing that had gone wrong that morning. Since he had left the tent, he'd been confronted with one disaster after another. As he looked at Nena now, he certainly hoped that streak did not bode poorly for the rest of his day.

"Jarl. There you are." One of his men jogged up to him out of breath. "Tryggr needs you at the front. He said it's urgent."

"I'll be right there." He dismissed the messenger and turned back to Nena. He had planned to accompany her initially, when the wagon train first got moving, but knew it wasn't really necessary. It had been more for his own peace of mind. Perhaps it was a sign. Perhaps he should put her on the wagon after all. He knew she would be disappointed, but he could make it up to her later.

He looked at her standing expectantly next to the mare and couldn't do it. "Just stay close to the wagon," he muttered.

"I will," she agreed, sensing his indecision and praying he would not change his mind. "Gratitude, Jarl," she added to further reassure him.

He shook his head, then kissed her before turning to mount his horse. "I will come and visit you during the day, as I am able."

Nena knew it was his way of letting her know he'd be checking on her. She nodded.

Altene arrived as he was leaving. She looked with raised eyebrows at Nena's traveling arrangements, then smiled a huge smile as she followed her bundles onto the wagon. Nena wished she could speak to her, to tell her that today would not be the day, but could not see how to do so without having the two men overhear. Nena knew her plan to escape during the next battle was so much better—so much more likely to succeed. It wasn't like she would get a second chance if she tried today and failed. Jarl would never trust her again. At least not while they were still within her lands and escape would do her any good.

She could understand Altene's excitement, though. She felt it, too. For the first time since her capture, escape was easily possible—if it weren't for the girl, Exanthia. All she would have to do was peel the mare off and run. No one could catch her. Nena wondered briefly if she could find the child now in the commotion. But even if she could, it wasn't as if she could just ride in and pick her up. She dare not be impatient. She had waited this long and had to stick to her plan. Now was not the time.

As the wagon pulled out and Nena fell in beside it, she soon realized Jarl wasn't as trusting of her in his absence as he had seemed to be. One of the men driving the wagon turned to look at her frequently, and there were two extra foot soldiers following a few paces behind who had never traveled with them before. Each carried a curved warning horn on a tether around his neck.

Nena pretended not to notice them. This could work out for the best. If she pretended to be dutiful and content, it would further reassure Jarl that he had no cause to doubt her. After days of such trust being rewarded, when it came time for him to leave for battle, he shouldn't give it a second thought. Nena relaxed and enjoyed the comfortable stride of the horse beneath her, each step taking her closer to her escape.

True to his word, Jarl rode back to check on her multiple times during the day. Each time, she saw his stern expression soften with relief when his eyes found her riding where she was supposed to be. Each time she was careful to reinforce his faith in her, by smiling and showing she was happy to see him. That was not difficult; she was happy to see him. The slow pace and lack of conversation were boring, but even she had to admit there was more to it than that; she enjoyed being with him. After riding with her and making small talk for a short way, he would leave again to check on the rest of the caravan.

Later in the day, when he approached and his eyes rested on her, they were decidedly warmer. As he rode the stallion up next to her this time, she could see the unmistakable flecks of green within them.

"If I had my way, we would stop and camp now. I was actually ready to stop at the last watering hole, when there was still probably six hours of daylight left," he admitted. "The journey would take ten times as long and I wouldn't care. All I could think about was taking you to the furs." He looked at her and shook his head. "You have bewitched me."

"I, too, look forward to the end of the day—and to the night," she murmured, her eyes meeting his and holding them. She saw him shift uncomfortably in his saddle.

"Your words are not helpful, woman," he growled.

Nena laughed. "They were not meant to be," she teased, enjoying having such an affect on him.

"You think it's funny, do you? Tonight, I will remove that smile from your face," he warned. "You'll pay for your shameless teasing." His eyes were a deep green now as he brought his stallion closer and their knees bumped, momentarily pinned together between the two horses. She thought he was going to kiss her, but he smiled and shook his head, then kicked his stallion up to a canter to check on the rest of the procession.

Nena was still smiling at the encounter when she turned and found Altene's eyes boring holes in her. Her smile faded. She didn't think Altene had been able to overhear them, but their body language had probably been clear enough. She knew Altene was upset there had been no escape attempt today. But she also knew Altene was even more upset by the fact that, since Nena had chosen him, Jarl had not once accepted any of Altene's repeated offers to pleasure him. Her prediction that Jarl's lust for Nena would fade had not proven true. Jarl and Nena had spent every night together, and the passion they continued to share was evident.

That night in the makeshift trail camp was no different. When Nena was with him and they were alone, his sensitive, intimate side that no one else saw, made it easy to forget her circumstances and lose all sense of urgency to escape. But every morning when she stepped outside the tent, the reality was a slap in the face. She was a slave. Whether Jarl treated her like one or not, the fact remained.

She longed to reach the next full campsite—longed for the day of the battle to be here so she could escape. To finally put an end to the push and pull of her contradicting feelings. Before something happened and the opportunity was lost. Before Jarl's tender acts chipped away further at what remained of her slowly eroding resolve.

It was the middle of the fifth day of travel when Jarl rode up beside her and announced, "We will be stopping up ahead in about an hour."

"For the night?" Nena asked.

"No, to set up the next full camp. We're close enough now."

Nena nodded as she digested the information. The next full camp—for her, the last full camp.

Like Jarl's tent, the camp was set up almost identically every time, varying only slightly with the differences in the terrain. Over the next few days, Nena verified that was the case this time as well. The horse enclosures were in the same place in the rear of the camp. The prisoner compound was laid out in the same rows of temporary shelters. It made it easy for Nena to locate the mother and Exanthia. She confirmed with relief there was still no guard on the child. With so many men needed for the upcoming attack, Nena did not anticipate that changing before the raid.

Jarl made time to ride with her every day. Most days they stayed close to camp, as his time was limited, but a few times they rode further—always to the south, away from the next target so as not to accidentally alert them. Daily she sucked the bitter leaf. The second branch she had received from Altene was almost bare. With her escape near, it appeared she would have just enough, depending on when Jarl gave the order to attack. Nena knew it would be soon.

She listened as each of the last detailed scouting reports came in. The men were excited at the prospect of a larger score and a tougher opponent. Jarl gave the order. They would attack the following day. When the men left and Nena was alone, she pulled out the branch. There was one leaf left. It would cover her for today, but she would need one more for tomorrow. She set out to find Altene.

"I need more herb," Nena said when she finally discovered Altene leaving the baths.

"I don't have any more," Altene said, her voice cold.

"But I need it," Nena said, shocked at the other woman's obvious lie.

"And I need you to be gone, yet here you remain. You swore to escape, but you do not—do not even make attempt. Days with the camp on the move and you with a horse. No Jarl. No guard. Yet you rode so close to the wagon you might as well have been chained to it. I should have known. You'll never leave him. You plan to take my place at his side in the North."

"He was having me watched when we moved, and besides I could not have found the girl."

"Then you should have left without her. Watched or not, you could have made it easily. I don't care a piss pot about some stupid little girl's fate; certainly not more than I care about my own!" Altene hissed.

"I only need one more leaf. I'm going to escape during tomorrow's battle. Everything is set." Nena confessed the plan she had shared with no one, fearful even now, that Altene would betray her.

"Good, then I hope for your sake his last night of seed within you does not take."

"Why are you doing this?" Nena asked.

"You've given me no choice. I risked everything for this plan, but once you felt his touch, you changed your mind."

"That's not true."

"Isn't it?" Altene was openly hostile now. "I have waited and waited for you to either fulfill our deal, or for him to tire of you, but neither has happened. You say you will escape, but you spend your days on joy rides and your nights in his arms. Meanwhile, I am running out of time. We shall make the port soon. Not having the herb will give you a little more incentive to follow through with your word. And if you fail—or change your mind and stay, we'll see how he likes your bloated stretched body after you are with child. Even married men stray when their wives are pregnant. And you are nowhere close to being his wife. You are still just his slave. Either way, he will soon call me back to his bed."

———◆———

That night as they ate their last meal, Nena forced herself to engage in conversation with him and to eat normally, though every bite sat in her stomach like a stone. Every minute seemed an eternity. When he took her to the furs, it was easier. Easy to get lost in his embrace and forget what the dawn meant for her. She was sure as he held her in the crook of his arm, still warm from the afterglow of their lovemaking, that she would not sleep that night. But the next thing she was aware of was being awakened by his kiss.

It was dark, but she could hear the activity outside the tent as the other men prepared for battle. She knew he would rise right away and get dressed; he was always the first to be ready. She reached for him, returning his kiss, then lifted her leg over his, holding him down and pressing her body against him. She felt his hardness.

He groaned under his breath at her unexpected initiation. "You will make me late," he murmured.

She did not answer, but moved her pelvis tighter against his. He pulled her hips to him and entered her as he rolled onto his back with her on top of him. Nena sat up astride him, his hands tight on her buttocks, holding her to him as he moved inside her. She leaned forward and kissed him, pressing her breasts against the hard muscles of his chest. She shifted her body sideways, indicating she wanted back on the bottom. Jarl obliged. Nena enjoyed being on top, but this last time she did not want any space between them. She wanted to feel the full weight of his body pressing down on her—to have full contact with the entire length of him—to better commit the feel of every inch of him to her memory.

As they lay side by side catching their breath, Nena couldn't help but wonder. With no more herb, would she get with child from this last joining? Why did the thought of it not distress her? Why was she only concerned with the fact that this was the last time she would caress his sculptured shoulders or look into his multicolored eyes. The last time she would feel his touch. The last time she would feel the strength of their connection.

You must not waver now. Everything has come together. You will not get another chance. Escape this place. Do not allow Jarl's affections to make you weak.

The pang of sadness felt like a large hole in her stomach.

Jarl mistook her melancholic distraction for concern for his safety in the upcoming battle. "Do not worry, my princess." He kissed her forehead and tenderly stroked a long section of her hair away from the side of her face. "I will return safe. And knowing you are here waiting, I will make this the quickest victory of the raids."

Nena did not want him to leave. Did not want this to be the last time she saw him. She kissed him softly on the lips. "Keep your guard up today. Do not let haste leave you open to needless danger," she murmured.

Jarl kissed her back, the effect of her unusual gesture evident on his face. His voice was husky with emotion. "When I am with you, I feel...you make me feel as if nothing else matters. Things that were so important to me before, now mean little, and I could forsake them easily. It is in many ways disturbing to me."

The boards rattled, breaking the mood.

"Jarl? Are you ready?" It was Tryggr.

"I'll be out in a moment," Jarl answered. He grinned at her. "See what you have done. Now I am very late." He stepped from the bed and dressed quickly. Nena watched as he strapped on his hardened leather armor plate.

"Jarl? Will you be joining us today?" Tryggr called out again.

"Be right there." Jarl returned to the furs and bent over to kiss her one last time. "The men are waiting. I must go."

"As must I," she whispered as the tent flap fell closed behind him.

Chapter 16

After the last of the men had filed from camp, Nena gathered her things for the bath, then waited. She could not afford to arouse suspicion now by acting hastily. She must go about her normal daily activities as if nothing were amiss. The single guard outside the tent acknowledged her as she exited, noted the bath supplies, and nodded. Nena breathed a sigh of relief. Normally the guards paid her little heed, though she was sure they took notice of her comings and goings, but she'd been worried that Jarl might have given some special instruction to watch her more closely in his absence today.

She returned from the bath and stalled again. Though she was anxious to get as big a lead as possible, she had to make sure that Jarl and the men were far enough away not to hear or respond to the sentry call—if there was one, when she escaped. She went over every step of her plan one last time in her mind. Her biggest unknown, and therefore her biggest concern was, of all things, the reaction of the mother and child to her sudden arrival and ultimatum. What if the girl refused to leave? Or the mother refused to let her go?

Nena knew it was going to be a shock for them. She prayed the woman would do what was best for the child. She was sure she would, if she had time to think it through, but Nena hadn't dared forewarn them. She had even tried to think of a way to include the mother in the escape, but had come to the same conclusion as Altene; the mother would be too much. Taking her would require a second horse and that would not only slow her down, it would also double the chances of them being seen. The girl she could take behind her on the mare.

Finally it was time. Tucking a small waterskin, a pouch of dried meat and a coil of thin rope under her dress, she exited the tent with the normal bread treat she would take to the mare. She didn't look to the guard for permission, but made sure the treat was clearly visible in her grasp. Nena held her breath, and counted off each step in her mind. *One, two, three, four...*

She feared any second to hear the guard's voice hailing her to return or be accompanied. There was nothing.

Fourteen, fifteen, sixteen...

She was almost to the closest row of tents that would block his sight of her. *Nineteen, twenty...*

With the tents between them, Nena's stride lengthened with determination. She was committed now. There would be no going back.

Nena went straight to the prisoner compound. She was relieved to see very few guards here also, and no one questioned her as she made her way among the captives. The mother and Exanthia were squatted near the remains of a tiny fire in front of a small tent when Nena approached. The mother looked up, shocked and then hopeful as she read the resoluteness on Nena's face.

"Apologies," Nena answered her unspoken question. "I cannot take you both. I only have one horse."

Fear, denial, then resignation flitted across the mother's face as she quickly processed Nena's words and what they meant for her.

"I will see that she is well cared for and raised a Teclan. You have my word," Nena promised. It was an elevation in status far beyond anything the girl could have ever hoped for. Not only would her future be secure, but it would also be far above her humble beginnings. Nena hoped that knowledge would provide some comfort to this mother's wound.

The mother nodded and turned to the girl, taking her by the shoulders. "You must not cry, and you must be strong. You will be Teclan now. You must do as Nena tells you, as if she were I. The gods have chosen to spare you."

Exanthia's lower lip began to tremble. Nena looked around nervously to see if their meeting was drawing any attention. No one seemed to be paying them any mind. She was sure that wouldn't last if the girl began to cry. "We must go," she urged.

"My spirit will always be with you, here." The mother touched Exanthia's chest with the flat palm of her hand. "That is what you must remember. Not this." She waved her hand at the camp around them. "You must be brave, as I know you are. And you must live." The mother reached for Nena's hand and placed the girl's hand within it, clasping them together. "Go now," she said, then turned and disappeared inside their small tent.

Nena felt the girl stiffen to rebel and gave her hand a gentle but firm reassuring squeeze. She was careful to not squeeze so hard as to feel constricting. Everything hinged on the child's actions in those next seconds. Both of their lives and futures hung in the balance. Nena took a step and pulled, praying the girl would follow.

Exanthia choked back a sob, but did not move. Nena waited and held her breath. If the girl refused now or sounded an alarm, her escape would be over before it started. Then, without making another sound, the girl turned and obediently followed her as if in a trance.

One more hurdle overcome.

Nena led the way to the horse enclosures. As they approached the pen where her mare was kept, Nena was shocked to find a guard. His back was to them and he was walking away, down the row of mostly empty pens. Her warrior senses evaluated him quickly. Stiff movements indicated an unseen injury, which probably explained his being left behind. His sword was sheathed sloppily at his side, and a dagger was slung haphazardly from his belt. He was clearly not expecting to have need of them this day. Nena hoped he was right.

He turned around and stopped when he saw them. His hand moved to the hilt of his sword. He made no move in their direction, but eyed her suspiciously, then glanced at the girl. Nena realized his initial reaction had been one of instinct and defense; they had taken him by surprise. Now he seemed more irritated than anything. Nena breathed a small sigh of relief. He was not guarding the mare. Tucked away here, out of sight from the other guards, Nena guessed he'd been looking for a place to take a nap when they had startled him. She acted totally unconcerned with his presence and turned to the mare who had come to greet them.

"Here she is—the mare Jarl gave to me. Isn't she as beautiful as I said?" Nena spoke loudly to Exanthia in the Northmen's tongue, though she doubted the child understood a word. She didn't need to. The words were not for her. "And here are her brushes. You can help me groom her today," Nena continued, as she bent over to pick up the two brushes that were on the ground outside the pen.

Though she pretended to pay him no mind, Nena carefully gauged the guard's response to her words from the corner of her eye. Every fiber in her body tingled. She did not want to kill him, but if he moved against them now, she would have no choice—and it would have to be quick. He must not be allowed to cry out. Her fingers and palm already itched for the hilt of his dagger. Her shoulder already imagined making the upward sweeping arch to draw the blade across his throat.

Nena untied the gate to the mare's pen and pulled it open, but remained in the entryway, balanced lightly on the balls of her feet. The guard muttered something unintelligible under his breath and limped away. Soon he was around the corner and out of sight.

Nena closed her eyes and exhaled. Thank the gods. That could have been disastrous. She continued to make small talk with the girl under the subterfuge of a grooming demonstration, in case the guard was still close enough to hear, but Nena was moving quickly now. She removed the small coil of rope from under her dress and rigged a slip knot loop on the mare's lower jaw. Then she ran the long end of the rope over the horse's head behind her ears and back down through the jaw loop on the other side, forming a makeshift rope bridle. It only gave her one rein, but Nena could not risk trying to retrieve the mare's real bridle and saddle. And one rein would be enough; the mare was so sensitive to Nena's commands, she probably could have been guided with no bridle at all.

Taking one last glance in the direction the guard had disappeared, Nena grabbed a handful of mane and swung onto the mare's bare back. She reached down and quickly pulled the girl up behind her. "Lean down against me and hang on tight," she whispered as she leaned forward and pressed her own face into the horse's mane. "And no matter what happens, do not make a sound."

Lying flat against the mare's neck with the young girl plastered to her back, Nena wrapped one hand tightly in a section of the horse's thick dark gray mane. Using her legs, she guided the mare out of the pen and into the herd of spare horses that had not been taken to battle. A few of the animals raised their heads and eyed the newcomers with mild interest before returning to grazing.

Nena felt as if she would explode. Every nerve in her body was taut as a bowstring. She wanted desperately to gallop, but kept the mare to a slow walk as they quietly moved among the other horses. Any second she expected to hear a warning horn followed by multiple coordinating whistles. She lay poised to dig her heels into the mare's flanks and ask her for top speed when the alarms came, but the only sound continued to be their muffled hoof-beats in the soft soil.

Nena pointed the mare south for two reasons. The battle was going on somewhere to the north, so the remaining sentries should naturally have more of their attention focused in that direction. She also knew from her rides with Jarl that the river to the south cut a notch in the hillside. Once she made it past that ridge, she would be out of sight of even the most outlying sentries.

Nena held her breath, knowing each step was critical progress toward their success. The slow moving horse in the group of horses had yet to attract any attention, even with the slouched riders on its back. Soon they were approaching the southernmost edge of the picket line fence that kept the spare horses corralled—the single last obstacle to their freedom.

"Hang on," Nena whispered to the girl as she sat up and threw one leg forward over the mare's neck and slid to the ground. She reached for the nearest post, pulled it swiftly, and laid it down on top of the rope line. Leading the mare behind her, she hastily pulled four more posts and did the same, leaving a large section of the rope fence flat on the ground. Shimmying back up in front of the girl, Nena carefully guided the mare over the rope and resumed their southward travel. When the other horses found this hole and escaped, as she was sure they would, it should cover their tracks and create an extra diversion for the remaining guards.

She would not be missed until Jarl returned.

Jarl. His tender smile as he'd left that morning came unbidden to her mind. Nena felt the sharp pang again in her stomach, but quelled it. There was no going back now. She was doing the right thing. She must put this behind her. Raising her chin, Nena pointed the mare toward the distant ridge.

Jarl entered and felt the emptiness of the tent before his eyes verified it. Nena's presence was a warmth that spread to everything around her, and he did not feel it now. The tent was cold. He was beyond disappointed. Her unexpected tenderness that morning had dangerously filled his thoughts all day with distraction, and he needed her now. She must be bathing. He unbuckled his armor, shrugged it off, and piled it in the corner. He paced the tent for a few moments, waiting for her to return, then went to find her in the baths.

Women shrieked and hurried to cover themselves as he barged in. Nena was not among them. Jarl felt the first fingers of unease begin to tighten around his gut. He returned quickly to his tent and sent for Altene. She arrived in a flash, wearing a low cut pale green dress of soft swirling silk.

"Where is Nena?" he asked.

"I have not seen her, my lord. Would you like me to pleasure you?" Altene offered with a sensual smile, her lips remaining parted.

"No. I want to find Nena. What do you mean you haven't seen her? Where is she?"

"I truly do not know, my lord." Altene bowed her head and waited while Jarl threw open the tent flap and stepped outside to question the guard. She couldn't make out the words, but heard the fear in the guard's voice as he relayed something to Jarl.

"And how long ago was that?" Jarl asked, his words very clear and very loud.

The guard mumbled something in reply, and Altene heard Jarl swear. She waited for him to reenter but after a few minutes realized he was gone. She settled down to wait for him with a smile on her lips, her fingers caressing the soft furs. He'd be back soon enough.

Jarl strode through the camp toward the prisoner compound. He fought the urge to run. The first of the new prisoners were just arriving and being processed. No one noticed Jarl in the midst of the hubbub. He made his way directly to the child's tent. The child who he had ordered guarded for so long—until Nena had chosen him and there no longer appeared to be a need.

The mother sat staring at the remains of a dead fire. She did not look up, even as he approached. Jarl swept open the tent flap and searched inside for the girl, but there was no sign of her, as deep down he had feared and known there wouldn't be. "Where is she?" he demanded. Only then did the broken woman raise her eyes to meet his. The grief he saw there was all the answer he needed.

Jarl did run now. An injured guard sauntering along the row of empty pens, snapped to attention on his arrival. "Sir," he said.

Jarl's eyes scanned the mare's empty pen. "Where is the gray mare?" he asked.

"The mare?" The guard looked at the empty pen. "Well…uh…I don't know. She was just there. I mean, before the other horses got out, and I had to go help round them up, she was there."

"Was Nena," Jarl began, then stopped. "Was a Dor woman here?"

"Yes," the guard stuttered. "She came with a girl to brush the horse earlier today." Seeing the rage on Jarl's face he added, "but they left well before the other horses got loose. The mare was still there then; I'm sure of it."

Jarl's quick perusal of the guard led him to the same conclusion Nena had reached earlier; the man would have been no match for her. If she could take Tryggr's knife from him and cut off part of his ear, this man would have offered her little challenge. But none of that mattered to him. Better that he had found him dead and known that he had at least made an attempt to stop her, than to find him here now. He grabbed the man by his throat, furious with him for lying, and for letting her escape—wanting nothing more than to kill him himself. The man gurgled and thrashed in his grip. After a moment Jarl released him and shoved him away. The guard cowered on the ground, holding his throat and gasping for air.

Jarl reined in his fury. "Find both Tryggr and Gunnar and send them to my tent. Make that the fastest thing you have ever done," he commanded. The guard sprang to his feet and ran, showing no evidence of the injury that had kept him from being able to fight earlier that day.

"You knew this was going to happen," Jarl accused Altene as he reentered the tent.

"What has happened, my lord?" she asked, her eyes wide.

"Don't play stupid with me." Jarl grabbed her by both arms and shook her. "Nena is gone and you knew this would happen."

"No, my lord," she denied. "I thought being bloodsworn to the child would keep her here, and it did."

"The child is gone, too, but I'm sure you already knew that as well. Now, tell me what you know," he threatened, his voice low and his grip still painfully tight on her arm.

"You're hurting me," Altene whined.

"It is nothing compared to what I will do to you if I'm unsatisfied with your answers. Do you understand me? Where is she?"

"I know nothing," Altene repeated. "She begged me many times to release her—from the first day you brought her, but I would never cross you. Then when she filled in her circle, she quit asking and I did not worry."

Jarl continued to stare at her unsatisfied. "You know something. I can see it in your eyes."

Altene was desperate. She had expected him to be upset about Nena's absence, but had never expected his reaction to be this violent, or to have his temper directed at her. She had planned all day on how best to console him. Perhaps it was the battle fever. Whatever it was, it had Altene scrambling for something to tell him that would diffuse his rage. She latched onto the first idea that came to her frantic mind.

"She came to me yesterday and mentioned her moon blood was late. She was worried she was pregnant." It wasn't a complete lie. They had at least discussed Nena becoming pregnant.

Jarl's expression was one of such shock, Altene proceeded in a rush, eager and sure that she was on the right path. He had been clear about how he felt about children. How had he worded it when she herself had suggested giving him a son—a crying babe was the last thing he wanted?

"She asked me if there was an herb to shed the baby," Altene lied. "There is, but I did not give it to her."

"Why did you not tell me this yesterday?"

"You were going to battle. I did not wish for you to be upset or distracted. I could not bear for an enemy's sword to find you because of my careless words.

And I assumed she would tell you. If she did not, I would have, of course, told you once it was safe. As I am, now."

Thoughts exploded inside Jarl's skull, each so huge it barely left room for the next. *Was she truly pregnant? Carrying his son? With her strong blood it would have to be a son. Their son. But why had she run? She seemed happy.*

His thoughts were interrupted by the arrival of Gunnar and Tryggr. Both men still wore their bloody armor.

"Nena is gone." Jarl explained their sudden summons. "Tryggr, find our best tracker and have him locate her trail. Have him begin his search to the south, where apparently the spare horses got out earlier today. Then ready a small contingent of men. We're going after her. Gunnar, you are in charge until we return."

"How long will we be gone, so I know what supplies to take?" Tryggr asked, surprisingly without any argument.

"As long as it takes. But we travel light," Jarl said, then turned to Altene. "Change into whatever garb you can ride in. You're coming with us and it will not be an easy pace." He turned on his heel and went to re-saddle his stallion.

Jarl stood next to his horse, on the south side of the rope picket fence, with a small group of men and Altene, waiting for the tracker's results. He boiled with impatience and had to school himself repeatedly to remain still. He watched his stallion tearing off large mouthfuls of grass with his teeth, barely seeming to chew, before he took another bite. He knew the horse was hungry after the long day, and normally would have removed the stallion's bridle so the bit would not interfere with his eating, but he wanted no delay when the tracker finally gave the signal—not even the few seconds it would take to put the horse's bridle back on.

Even now he wanted to mount up and ride—to be making some progress toward finding her, rather than sitting still. He knew Nena would ride south. That was home to her, and that was where his men had reported the horses had escaped. He was sure it was not a coincidence. Still he waited for the tracker's confirmation. He could ill afford a mistake now. She already had a significant head start, and if he charged off in the wrong direction on a hunch, he might never find her.

He glanced around with approval at the men Tryggr had assembled. They were his best fighters, though many were already clearly exhausted from the day's battle. It could not be helped. The tracker whistled and motioned for them to follow. He had picked up Nena's trail heading south.

"Finally." Jarl released an agitated breath. He remounted and rode after the tracker, holding his stallion to half a dozen lengths behind the other man's horse so as not to interfere with his scrutiny. The tracker maintained the lead at a long trot, his eyes remaining fixed on the ground.

They followed Nena's trail southward for an hour at the same pace when suddenly the tracker slowed and held up his hand for them to stop. Jarl watched as the man followed tracks in a new direction for several hundred yards, then rode in large circles, before returning to give his report.

"She's turned due west," the tracker said. "I don't know why. There's no change in the terrain ahead that she would have to go around, but she's definitely heading west now, and her tracks don't double back."

"That can't be right. She'll go south, like she has been," Jarl disagreed.

"I'm not mistaken, Jarl. The mare has a unique hoof print and an odd stride. Her back hooves are longer and narrower than a normal horse. And where most horses' back feet step into the same tracks made by their front, her back feet fully overstep her front tracks by several inches. These are her tracks heading west," the tracker reaffirmed. "And there are no human tracks splitting off, like they let the horse go to throw us off the trail."

Jarl did not doubt the last part. He knew Nena would never give up the mare.

"Maybe she's lost," Tryggr suggested. "Got turned around. She is a woman after all."

Jarl shook his head. "She's Teclan. She won't be lost." *But where was she going?*

Chapter 17

The escape had been easier than Nena imagined possible. Other than the brief scare with the guard at the mare's pen, everything had gone according to plan. The men left behind to guard the camp had been so preoccupied with the battle they were missing, and spread so thin, no one had noticed them. She and the girl had ridden south for an hour when Nena drew in rein. She could safely change directions here. Feeling the strong pull of her home to the south, she hesitated a long moment before turning the mare west. She knew what she had to do.

She had known it from the moment she had seen the last X on Jarl's map.

For three days they had followed her rambling trail. First south, then west, then north. It made no sense to him, and that worried Jarl as much as anything. Where was she going? Was she lost as Tryggr had suggested? He couldn't believe that, but her erratic direction changes were clear. Was she injured? None of his men, other than the pathetic excuse for a guard had reported even seeing her, and Jarl doubted that man could have injured her if he'd wanted to. And there had been no blood trail. But what else could explain it? Was she sick? Delirious? That would make him feel better about the why, but he knew it wasn't true. She'd been perfectly lucid that morning, and there was no way she could have pulled off such an escape without her full faculties and planning. After riding hard all morning, the tracker stopped to deliver his latest report.

"Jarl, we'll soon be approaching the village on the Great Sea. It's the last village we were to attack before port. If we proceed any further, we are likely to warn them of our presence before we move on them later with our full force."

"If she's gone there, I think it's too late for that already," Jarl conceded.

Tryggr drew in a deep exaggerated breath and stroked his red beard. "Hmm. What was it Gunnar said when we were making plans in front of her? Who can she tell?"

"You were right, my friend. It appears this village is lost." But Jarl was elated. He cared not a whit for the bounty Nena's warning to this village would cost them. There were plenty of other villages. Now he knew where she was going and why. Now her path made sense. Most importantly, he also knew that once her mission there was complete, she would resume going south, back to her home in the Teclan stronghold.

Jarl knew from the tracker, that even though he was pushing them hard, Nena was making better time and had increased her initial lead. But now that he could predict her next move, that changed everything. He thought back over his maps of the area. The village should be another half day's ride to the northwest. If he headed straight west now, he would save that time, plus whatever time it took her to deliver her message and ride south. And from the village she would ride straight south, of that he was certain. Even with her head start, he had a chance now to cut her lead significantly—maybe even cut her off.

Jarl ordered the two men with the slowest horses to continue following her trail to the northwest, so as not to lose her in case he was mistaken. Keeping the rest of the men, the tracker, Tryggr and Altene, Jarl spurred his stallion due west.

It was late when he finally ordered them to stop. In his excitement and anticipation he would have ridden all night, but he knew the tracker could not perform in the dark. Starting with first light, Jarl would relinquish the lead back to the man. Following her trail was one thing—even a less experienced tracker could do that in most circumstances. If a few tracks were missed here or there, the trail was still easy to find. But to pick up a trail they were crossing over was a different story. If a few tracks were missed then, the entire trail could very well be passed over and lost. Jarl did not trust his own eyes with that responsibility.

He shook out his furs under the stars, as all the men had done since they left the main camp. The weather was fair so tents were unnecessary, and the time it took to set them up and tear them down was precious time to sleep. Jarl heard light footsteps approaching from behind him and turned to find Altene. She smiled at him, though he could see she was weary.

"Good evening, my lord." She stepped closer to him, stopping just shy of touching him. The light pleasant scent of her floral fragrance filled the small space between them. The breeze lifted the soft material of her dress and Jarl felt it brush against his hand at his side. She tipped her face up to look at him and whispered. "Shall I pleasure you tonight?"

Jarl looked at her thick braided hair and dark almond-shaped eyes in the moonlight and pictured Nena. How could he have ever thought they looked alike? Other than basic coloring, he could see virtually no similarities in them now at all. Jarl reached up and gripped both of Altene's arms firmly above her elbows. Gently he pushed her back half a step and held her there.

"Do not offer yourself to me again. You will not be returning to my furs. Whether I find Nena or not. There will be nothing more between us. You need to look to your future and it is not with me."

Altene just stared at him.

"Do you understand?" Jarl asked.

She nodded.

"Very well. Go get some rest. Tomorrow will be another long day."

Nena halted the mare in the middle of a clearing. Someone had been pacing them in the bushes for the past half mile, but had yet to reveal themselves. She knew by the lush vegetation that they were close to the Great Sea. She hoped it was someone from her aunt's tribe, but in case it was not, she wanted to meet them in the open, where she had room to maneuver. She sat and waited.

Within minutes a short heavyset warrior with a spear stepped from the bushes in front of her. He was too far away for her to see if he bore the wave tattoo of the Sea Tribe on his arm.

"What is your business, woman?" he demanded.

"Are you of the Sea Tribe?" she asked.

"I am."

"I need to speak with your chief."

"Give me your message; I will relay it to him."

Nena was already irritable from lack of sleep, and she chafed at the delay. She didn't have time for this. She pushed the mare forward. Using the height of being mounted to her advantage, she spoke in her most imperious tone. "Tell him the daughter of Meln has an important message for him. Yet you felt he did not need to hear it, so she is being detained outside the village and he will have to wait."

Another warrior with a horizontal scar across his forehead appeared from the bushes on her left in time to hear her last words. He glanced uneasily at the shorter man, and Nena knew she would not be kept waiting after all.

"Come closer," the short stocky one instructed.

Nena stopped the mare within feet of him. She felt the eyes of both men on the star and lightning bolt on her arm as they verified her identity.

"Follow me," the short one grumbled, and turned back into the underbrush.

After almost an hour of following him through the dense green foliage, they broke out of the bushes on the crest of a hill. Though the warrior in front of her did not pause before dropping over the edge and continuing on the winding trail below, Nena pulled the mare to a stop. The Great Sea spread out before them, even more vast than she remembered. It filled her view and extended all the way to the distant horizon. The breathtakingly beautiful water sparkled like a blue jewel. Nena felt Exanthia stiffen behind her and heard her gasp.

"It is wonderful, is it not?" she asked the girl.

"Yes," Exanthia replied, her voice filled with awe.

"That is the Great Sea," Nena explained.

From their vantage point on the hillside, Nena could make out the two long spits of land she had recognized on the map, though she could not see all the way to their tips. There, nestled between their bases on the shores of the protected bay, was her aunt's village. Nena would have liked to linger, to further admire every aspect of the panoramic view, but she tore her eyes away and pushed the mare down the hill toward the village below.

As she followed the warrior between the tents, villagers stepped out of their way and watched as they passed, more curious than alarmed by the arrival of a single strange Dor woman and child. Nena wanted to shout out her warning so they could begin packing or preparing their defenses, but she continued to follow her escort in silence. It was not her place as an outsider, and certainly not as a woman, to address these people. She knew her news would alarm them soon enough.

It had been many years since her previous and only visit, and Nena was unfamiliar with the layout of the village. Still, she recognized the tent with the gold banner and blue wave on top as the one she sought. Only a chief's tent would be so adorned. The short warrior indicated for them to wait and disappeared inside.

A barrel shaped man with graying hair and shrewd eyes exited the tent shortly thereafter. He looked vaguely familiar to her, but she had only met her aunt's husband once before. She glanced quickly at the extensive tattoos that identified him as the chief, then slid from the horse and knelt with her head bowed. Nena felt his eyes on her arm verifying the stocky warrior's report of her own identity.

"Rise, daughter of Meln. To what do I owe the honor of a visit from the daughter of my most powerful ally?" the chief asked.

Though she was sure the warrior had already told him she had an urgent message, a fact further supported by her soiled appearance from hurried travel, the chief kept up the pretense of formality, giving no indication he was anxious for her news.

"I bring you warning of great danger," Nena began.

"Has your father sent you?" the chief asked.

"No. I have come on my own. I, and this child," she nodded at Exanthia, "have been held captive by powerful Northmen for months now, and only days ago made our escape. In that time, I learned of their plans to attack your village within the fortnight. With you being a friend to the Teclan, I could not in good conscious return home with this knowledge."

"I see. And you are certain they are coming here?" he asked.

Nena wanted to scream at him to dispense with propriety and sound the alarms, to begin moving his people to safer ground this very second, if they even had such a place. Neither of them could afford to delay right now. But this was the stoic way of the Dor and she knew it well. Her father would have probably reacted much the same.

"Yes, I am certain," she said. "I have overheard their leader making plans and seen their maps. The two spits of land extending out into the Great Sea were unmistakable," she added for emphasis.

The burly chief took stock of her for one long moment, then spoke to the short warrior who had escorted her. "Summon the council immediately."

"Yes, my chief." The stocky warrior ran to do as he was bade, leaving the one with the thin blade scar across his forehead.

The chief turned back to Nena. "You must be tired and hungry. I will have Heldor show you to a tent, and he will have someone bring you food and water. It will take some time for everyone to pack, so you should have the remainder of the day to rest. Under the circumstances our hospitality will not be as gracious as we would normally extend to the daughter of Meln, but once we are safely settled, and I can spare the warriors, I will have you escorted home to your father."

Nena chose her next words carefully, having no intention of remaining in this village for a single second longer than necessary. She hoped he had too much else on his mind now, dealing with her news, to be insulted or to disagree.

"This woman greatly appreciates the chief's kind and generous offer, but must refuse. If I could ask for any hospitality, it would be only for travel food, a sword and spear, and an extra horse for the girl."

The chief eyed the mare with the child still aboard. Nena saw his eyes widen slightly as he evaluated the animal. "Of course," he said. "And I shall do better. I shall give you two horses. One for the girl and one to replace the tired animal you are riding."

Nena fought back another wave of irritation. Even after she had risked her life to save his, he would still try to take advantage of her, hoping she did not recognize the value of the mare. She focused on the good news—that he was letting them go.

"Again, I appreciate the chief's most generous offer, but this mare is a gift for my father, when I return." She hoped the mention of her father would stem his greed, and that he would not risk angering Meln. It worked.

"Of course." He looked at the mare with resignation. "Give my best to your father. And thank him for your warning. I am in his debt."

Nena nodded.

After the chief relayed his new instructions to the other warrior and both had left, Nena's aunt, Darna, arrived in a rush. "Nena. It is true." The two women embraced, then Darna held her out at arm's length. "I have not seen you since you were but a girl. It was your first summer as a warrior, as I recall."

"Yes," Nena agreed. She looked at her aunt who so resembled her father, not necessarily a good thing for a woman. Her face was round and flat and her nose a little too large, but her eyes were honest and warm.

"And here you have grown into such a beautiful woman, so much like your mother," Darna said, then glanced at Nena's arm, "and chosen." She nodded in approval before she looked closer and realized there was no lineage of a husband in the marks below it. She tipped her head and shrugged to cover her mistake. "There will be many fine warriors awaiting your second choosing."

"Gratitude for the kind words, Darna, but you must not delay. You must pack and leave this place at once. It is not safe."

"My husband has heeded your warning and is summoning the council as we speak. Are you sure you will not stay with us until the threat is past? You will be safe here among our warriors. We could become reacquainted and then send a proper escort with you back to your father."

"Gratitude for the offer, but I cannot stay. I must resume travel immediately. And you must press your people to make haste. Do you have a safe place to go?" Nena asked.

"I'm not sure what they will decide. Either the winter grounds in the hills, or an island that is not far out in the Great Sea. We have avoided danger there before, but it is only suitable for short stays. We cannot take many of the animals in the boats."

"Anything you leave behind will be lost. And I fear from this particular threat, the island might not be the safest place for you either. These men are very powerful."

"I know you do not trust the Great Sea, Nena, but it protects these people—now my people."

"It's not that. The sea also protects these Northmen. They navigate its depths even farther and easier than you."

Darna shook her head, disturbed. "We've never faced an enemy also favored by the sea. Perhaps the winter lands would be better. I will speak to my husband. Is there anything else you need?"

"I would have a travel hide, if you can spare one—just large enough for the two of us." Nena motioned toward Exanthia. "Your husband has already made arrangements to provide an extra horse and provisions, but the weather has been so favorable, I forgot to ask for a hide."

"Of course. I will have one sent to you immediately. Anything else?"

Nena hesitated. "I would also have root of the Taymen."

Darna stiffened and examined her closely.

"I am not a habituate." Nena reassured her. "You may check my eyes." Nena stepped closer and lifted one of her upper eyelids with her finger, then looked down to expose the surface of the white of her eyeball. She wanted her aunt to know her eye did not show the characteristic purple streaks that came with prolonged use of the addictive root.

All Dor knew of the Taymen root. Every Teclan warrior carried a small piece in their war packs, but only to be used in extreme situations where prolonged awareness was needed. Other tribes used it for rituals and even for festivals. Unfortunately, the stimulus of the root was too much for some to resist. Habituates, they were called, partook of the root regularly, and soon became unrecognizable to all those who knew them. No shame, no honor, no care for anything in life other then obtaining more root. Worse, there was no saving them once they reached that point. No bringing them back, even with extreme measures. Because of this, the Teclan banned all non-emergency use of the Taymen root. Any who were caught breaking that law were punished severely. Though her aunt was no longer Teclan, and the Sea Tribe's laws were known to be more lax, her disapproving frown clearly expressed how she still felt about it.

Darna nodded after examining Nena's eye. "Why do you want it then?" she asked.

"I believe we are being pursued. I need it to stay awake until we reach the safety of the Teclan mountain."

"You cannot stay awake that far," her aunt disagreed. "To use the root for that long could kill you. Your body will need to sleep."

"I know. I would not use it every day—only in an emergency."

Her aunt looked unconvinced. "They are but men who pursue you, Nena. They will also have to sleep. The root is too dangerous."

"I cannot be recaptured," Nena whispered.

Her aunt wavered.

"I will be careful and only use it sparingly, if I use it at all," Nena added to further persuade her.

"Very well," her aunt conceded begrudgingly. "I will find some and have it delivered with the hide."

"Sincerest gratitude," Nena said.

"Travel safe, Nena." The two women embraced again.

"And you, Aunt."

True to her word, Darna sent a young slave woman to deliver the hide and a small leather pouch. After the woman left, Nena untied the thong on the pouch and peered inside. There was a short chunk of the gnarled pale gray Taymen root. Nena tugged the string, resealing the pouch, then tied it to the sash of her dress at her waist.

When there was still no sign of the scar-faced warrior with their provisions, Nena led the mare into the shade between tents. The grass grew taller there, and she allowed the mare to graze while they waited. What was taking him so long? Had he gotten sidetracked? Or been given some other order?

Nena tried to remain calm and not fidget, but it was almost as if she could feel Jarl's army bearing down on them—the great warhorses pounding across the plains, drawing closer with every second she tarried.

Stop it. Even if they are coming, you had at least a half day's head start and you were rested. They would have started tired, their horses tired. With the speed of the mare, you should have at least a day's lead on them by now. And you are assuming Jarl will even waste the time to chase you. You may be already dimming in his memories as Altene replaces you in his furs.

Before she could proceed any further down that line of thought, the scar-faced warrior appeared leading a horse with two travel packs of food, extra skins of water, and a sword and spear. Thankful for the interruption of her thoughts, Nena took the second horse's reins from him. He did not address her, but nodded and turned away.

Without wasting another second, Nena took a quick inventory of the food in the packs. If rationed properly, there would be plenty for her and Exanthia to make it back to the Teclan mountain without having to hunt. Nena then turned her attention to the weapons. They were not the highest quality, but both were smaller and well-balanced. They would suit her purpose if she had need of them. Her last inspection was of the horse. Compared to her mare, it was a disappointing creature, but its legs were clean, its wind sound, and its temperament appeared to be suitable for a child. After she made sure Exanthia was safely mounted, Nena swung aboard the mare and led them out of the village, heading due south.

Jarl's stare burned holes in the back of the tracker's neck as he bent over the deep tracks that crossed their path in the soft soil. The man stood up and reluctantly turned to meet Jarl's eyes. "The tracks are hers, approximately half a day old, and she has a second horse now."

"Half a day?" Jarl exclaimed. "How can it still be half a day? She started with little over a half a day's lead. Though we lost ground initially, we should have shaved off all the time it took her to ride the additional distance to the village, and whatever time it took her to convey her warning."

The tracker only looked down, waiting for Jarl to finish his tirade.

A sense of helpless rage filled Jarl so completely, it threatened to consume him. He had fully expected to cut her off here, or at least be close. His stallion reared beneath him. Even though Jarl knew the horse was only reacting to his own chaotic charged feelings, he had to fight to keep from disciplining the animal harshly. Something had to pay. He needed an outlet. He dismounted and dropped the great horse's reins before stalking out into the sand away from the group. His hands itched to throw something, to beat something, to kill something. Barring some miracle, they would never catch her now. He had to pull himself together. He had to think. Jarl ran his hand across his forehead. Unless…

He returned to the group and remounted before making his announcement. "We ride south. The mare has already carried two riders with little rest." Before Tryggr could point out the condition of their own animals, Jarl continued. "Even more importantly, the second horse will be a common tribe horse. From now on, she can travel only as fast and as far as that second horse can keep up." It could be just the anchor he needed.

Nena glanced at the sun and the shadows on the grass to gauge her direction. Since they had left the lush vegetation of the coast, the terrain had been much of the same; dry grasslands merged occasionally with the sand and stone of the edge of the desert. She knew it would remain that way for the next few days. Then she would see the first of the low mountains in the distance. As she continued south, those mountains would become taller and closer together. Navigating would be easy from that point, but for now, she had to double check her bearings frequently.

After finding her tracks and realizing they had lost more ground to her, Jarl became even more merciless with the pace. Horses and men started to show the effects; horses were gaunt, men silent. As he saddled the stallion in the first light of dawn, Tryggr approached him. He pointed to Altene, struggling to lift her saddle.

"This pace is too hard for a woman, Jarl," Tryggr said.

"And yet it is a woman we are unable to catch," Jarl responded as he tightened his cinch.

"A normal woman." Tryggr glowered.

"With a child," Jarl countered abruptly and turned to face him. "Can our men not even outride a child now?"

Tryggr did not respond. Jarl looked to Altene and shook his head. "I will not slow the pace. She's tougher than she looks."

Tryggr scoffed and stomped away toward Altene. Jarl watched him lift the saddle and secure it to the horse for her. They exchanged a few words that Jarl could not hear, then Tryggr walked to his own horse and packs, before returning to her with a small vial.

"Here, rub this ointment on the raw spots. It will help with the healing and the pain," Tryggr said as he handed her the vial.

"Gratitude, Tryggr," Altene murmured, clearly surprised by his offering.

"None required. It's just a simple cream and some I had left over," Tryggr said gruffly as he turned away.

"Gratitude all the same," Altene said to his retreating back.

Since leaving the village, Nena had increased their brutal pace. Her energy was boosted by the relief that no obstacles that hinged on anyone else's actions remained in her path. Her anxious worries over whether Jarl's guards would be sufficiently negligent for her to escape, or if the Sea Tribe chief would insist she delay, were all behind her. Her destiny was finally in her own hands and all she had to do was ride—something she was born to do. Nothing could stop them now.

Her thoughts moved ahead to what things would be like at home. For most of the tribe, life on the mountain would be relatively unchanged. Even though it seemed like a lifetime had passed since she had left for the tournament on the plains that spring, it was still within the same summer. The tribe would be preparing for winter—drying meat, tanning hides. Life would be going on as it always had. But what would that mean for her? She was a far different woman now than the warrior who had left only months before. And what remained of her family there?

Ruga would be gone and that thought pained her deeply. She knew she should not mourn him—that he was riding among their ancestors in the afterlife, but she couldn't help it. She would miss him, miss his fun-loving carefree attitude, his antics, his teasing. It had been easier before when she was in Jarl's camp, to imagine that he was home and alive, but when she returned home, she would have to face the truth. Life without him on the mountain would never be the same.

And her father—had he returned home? His fate had never been determined. Jarl swore he was not among the bodies, but Altene had sworn he was dead. Who was right? Someone had built the skygrave for Ruga. It had to be her father. If it was not, then her older brother, Lothor, might be chief. He would do well in that role, but between his responsibilities there and his new family, he would have little time for her. She would need to start thinking of starting her own family.

Her own family. A husband. Children. With the gods' choice behind her, she would be expected to choose again; she knew that. And while the gods' choice was never questioned as far as timing or suitability were concerned, second choosings were given no such leeway. It was not acceptable or practical for a chosen, but unmarried woman, to remain alone. She would be expected to choose from among whoever were the most qualified available men in the tribe at the time, and she would probably be expected to do it fairly soon. Her imagination moved on to sharing a tent and furs with a nameless Teclan warrior. She felt ill.

You must push that from your mind and focus only on your journey. Your thoughts are all twisted and backwards. Jarl has done this to you. Lack of sleep has only made it worse. Once you are home and rested, there will be no more doubts. You will be back among your people where you belong and everything will be clear again. One day you may even look back on this confusion with a smile. Look back to the time when some mysterious magic had ahold of your senses, but you were able to fight through it.

Nena prayed it would be true. It had to be. The gods had shown her the path to escape and then ensured she was successful. Surely, had she not been meant to do this, her plan would have failed. Comforted by that, she refocused her thoughts on the long journey ahead. She was doing the right thing. She just had to make it home.

When the scout reported they were still not gaining on her, Jarl slammed his fist into the map in frustration. He was running out of time. Her hard ridden trail was clear to follow and he knew where she was going. Like the flight of an arrow, she was headed straight for the Teclan mountain stronghold. If she made the Bloodcliff Gates, she would be lost to him.

"She's moving too fast, Jarl." Tryggr pointed out the obvious. "Even with the child. They are lighter than armored men, and our horses started out tired."

"I don't want excuses," Jarl snapped.

"They're not excuses, Jarl; they're facts," Tryggr exclaimed. "You used to be able to tell the difference when you weren't thinking with your cock."

Jarl's eyes flashed with fury, but Tryggr wasn't backing down this time.

"Go ahead. Glare at me. You haven't kept me around this long because I blow smoke up your ass, and I'm not about to start now. If you wanted someone to fan your soft woman follies, you'd have brought Gunnar instead. You knew I'd tell you the truth. That's why I'm here and he's not. So when are you going to start listening to me?"

"Not today." Jarl rolled up the maps and strode to his waiting horse. "Mount up," he called over his shoulder to the other men and put the stallion back on Nena's trail.

<hr />

The report from the tracker the next day was worse. Though he had pushed them even harder, they had lost more ground. Jarl did not understand how it was possible.

"What do you want to do?" Tryggr asked after the tracker had left.

"Keep going."

"For what? We'll never catch her now before she makes the Teclan stronghold."

"We keep going."

"What are you hoping for, Jarl? That after how many miles she suddenly changes her mind and comes back to you? Or that her horse breaks a leg, and she's waiting for us to pick her up by the carcass? Who gave her that fucking horse anyway? Besides, she's got a second horse now. She could just ride it."

Jarl remained silent.

"And when we get to the Bloodcliff Gates, what then? Will we keep going then, too?"

"I don't know."

"Jarl, these men have shown many times they are willing to follow you to their deaths, but never before was it a suicide."

"Send a messenger back to Gunnar. Tell him of our plan, and that he is to proceed to the port and make the exchange with Piltor—or with the other traders, if any have been found. If we do not meet him there after four weeks, he is to divide the treasure, and send all but three of the ships and The Treasure Huntress home, before it is too late for them to make it. He can decide which other three stay."

"You said to tell him our plan. What exactly is *our* plan that you would like me to tell him?" Tryggr asked.

"Just send the fucking messenger," Jarl snarled, his patience at an end.

Jarl didn't have a plan. Didn't have a clue of a plan. He knew Tryggr was right. He knew they would never catch her. She was so far ahead now, even if both of her horses broke legs and she and the girl had to walk, they would probably still make it through the gates before he could get to her. So why did he keep going? Why didn't he turn around?

Because he couldn't.

Because he could not imagine his life without her now.

Because he could not just give up and let it end this way.

Because since becoming a man, he'd never wanted for anything he could not have. Many believed it was because the gods favored him. Jarl thought that reason was as likely as any other, and he could not imagine the gods would deliver him such a treasure only to yank it from his grasp.

His thoughts were interrupted by an odd heavy sensation in his lungs and chest that signaled an impending change in the weather. He glanced up at the clear sky. There were no dark clouds on the horizon and no wind—no physical signs of a storm, but Jarl knew one was coming. Years at sea had taught him how to feel them.

Nena stood in the calf-deep water, holding both horses as they grazed on the tender water grass. The horses would have preferred to remain on dry ground but the dark green stems were a Teclan secret, packed with concentrated nutrition that enabled a horse to perform better with less feed. The second horse was already considerably tucked in the flank, but the mare seemed no worse for wear.

Nena looked at the girl, curled up on the bank, sound asleep. She rubbed her own swollen tired eyes. They had ridden hard for many days now, yet the girl had never once complained. Nena thought back to the day before, when she had glanced back just as Exanthia was about to fall from her horse. She had stopped and pulled the exhausted girl up behind her on the mare, and led the second horse for the remainder of the day. Exanthia had slept soundly against her back, her arms wrapped around Nena's waist, her hands clasped in front, held securely there in Nena's grip.

Nena looked at her now with fondness and respect. She was strong. She would make a good Teclan. Her life had been ripped asunder, but she had never once complained. Nena felt bad she'd been unable to provide her with more support. It had not been intentional. Initially she'd been too driven and focused on their escape to offer the girl much comfort. Now she was too exhausted. When they made it home, Nena vowed to make it up to her, to lavish her with the attention she was unable to give her now.

Nena felt her eyelids closing. She fought to keep them open, but they seemed to have weights attached to them. She felt for the chunk of root in the pouch tied around her waist, but did not pull it out. Not yet. She was afraid of how it would make her feel. She knew the root would keep her awake, but also knew there would be a significant price. She had only tried it once before as a young warrior in training. She and the other trainees had been kept up for three days straight, then given the root and pushed for another two. Even now she remembered vividly how it had made her heart race uncomfortably in her chest. How it had drained every bit of strength from her body and took her days to recover. She did not want to experience that again—not if she could help it. The short catnaps she'd been able to take had been sufficient so far.

In the mountains, the cold water would have helped to shock her awake, but this water was a soothing tepid temperature. Her earlier determination to focus only on the journey faded, and Nena's exhausted mind drifted to another time in the warm water with Jarl. His offer to teach her to swim and then his retraction. She smiled at the circumstances preceding that retraction. What was he doing now? Life in the camp after a battle was always relaxed and easy for several days. Or would they be moving again? Toward her aunt's village that hopefully was no longer there?

He's probably sharing his furs with Altene at this very moment.

Nena tormented herself with the vision of Jarl and Altene together. Of Altene nestled in the crook of his arm, her head on his shoulder. Of Jarl's fingers absently caressing her skin.

If you truly believed that, you wouldn't be running. Wouldn't be pushing yourself, the child and the horses, to the brink of collapse. You know in your heart—Jarl is coming for you.

The thought pained her almost as much as the vision of him and Altene together.

Even if that were true, he'd only be coming to recover a prized possession— just as he would if someone had stolen his stallion or the tiger hide. If he does, in fact, follow you, it is only because you are a valuable slave.

Her inner voices had waged this war for control of her heart many times, but no matter which one was victorious, she always ended up in the same place—as Jarl's slave.

Chapter 18

Thunder cracked above them, so close and so loud, it seemed as if the clouds were being ripped apart over their heads. Nena felt Exanthia flinch behind her and wondered if she had done the same. The storm had threatened them for hours, blasting them with wind and shocking them with lightning, but so far the rain had held off. It wouldn't be long now, though. Nena could smell it.

When the first scattered drops hit them, Nena looked ahead and saw the main body of the storm for the first time—a black wall of water bearing down on them from the south. They were headed straight into it and had maybe a few minutes before the deluge reached them. She glanced around one last time for any cover in the near vicinity, but none was to be had—as she had known there wouldn't be. She regretted her earlier decision to not detour and seek shelter in the forest to the west. At the time, without knowing if Jarl pursued them or not, she'd felt she could not afford to take the risk and add the extra miles to their trip. But she'd had no idea then of the size of the approaching storm.

Nothing could be done about it now, other than to keep pushing forward toward the Bloodcliffs of the mountain. It would be miserable travel, but there would be plenty of time later for rest and comfort. Nena halted the mare and pulled Exanthia's horse up alongside. Without dismounting, she untied the travel hide from the girl's saddle and shook it open.

"It's about to get very wet," she said over her shoulder to Exanthia, her voice raised to be heard above the wind, even though the girl sat right behind her. "There is nowhere to stop here that will provide any protection for the horses, so we'll keep going. This should keep us dry for the most part." She pulled the hide over the two of them. Meant to be used as a tent, the hide was soft and pliable. It draped down over the legs of both riders on the sides, and half of the mare's hindquarters in the back. Nena tucked the front lower edges, where they split at the mare's withers, under each of her thighs, pinning them against the horse with her legs.

She gave the hide a gentle test tug. It held. It should work as long as the wind continued to blow from the front. If it changed direction and came from the rear, they would have to roll the back under Exanthia for her to sit on. Satisfied, Nena gathered the two sides of the hide together under her chin with one hand, leaving only a small hole for her face. She held the horse's rein and the edges of hide together with her other hand, midway down her stomach. She was ready.

The first soaking blast of water temporarily blinded her. She blinked hard and tightened her grip on the hide. The mare balked and tried to turn around, not wanting to face the onslaught. Nena pushed her forward. Water squeezed between the hide and her face, running down her neck and arms. Soon her entire front was soaked. She could still feel Exanthia's warmth pressed up against her back.

"Are you dry?" Nena twisted her head inside the hide and yelled.

"Yes, I am fine," came the girl's muffled reply.

As the wind and rain whipped around them, the few scattered landmarks quickly became invisible. Nena lost her bearings and stopped, unsure of what to do. She could continue to head into the wind and hope it remained coming out of the south, but if it shifted in the darkness, she could end up going the wrong way. She had to think. The river! The shallow river flowed almost all the way to the Bloodcliff Gates and, though she could no longer see it, she knew it was still somewhere to her left. If she rode along the water's edge, it would keep her heading in the right direction.

She turned the mare and strained her eyes to see ahead, but saw nothing of the river until the mare's hooves splashed into deeper water. She steered the horse back to the soggy bank and continued south. Battered by the storm and using only the river to guide them, they rode for hours. Even with the wet and cold, Nena felt her eyes closing. She had pushed her body to the point where it would no longer obey. The short catnaps she had managed to take along the way were no longer enough to keep it going. Her body demanded sleep—real sleep, but she could not stop now. Nena reached for the pouch at her waist and pulled out the root.

She hesitated.

Her head nodded forward. She jerked it back upright and lifted the root to her lips. She bit off a small piece and felt her lips and tongue go instantly numb.

"It's about to rain like a cow pissin' on a flat rock." Tryggr shouted his warning to be heard above the wind. "We should set up the tents now and let this storm pass before it's too late."

Jarl stretched his neck from side to side and glared at the dark clouds bearing down on them.

Tryggr rode up next to him, but still had to yell. "Come on, Jarl. You know it has to be done. We can't track her once this hits. We won't be able to see a damn thing."

"Tryggr is right, Jarl." The tracker joined them. "It will be dark soon anyway; with the rain and no light, her tracks will be impossible to find."

"And tomorrow? Once this storm passes, will there be any tracks left?" Jarl shouted.

"Probably—yes. She's riding hard and has made no attempt to hide her tracks so far. They will be washed out but there should be enough remaining to follow," the tracker affirmed.

"Even if there's not, it's not like we don't know exactly where she's headed," Tryggr added. "Since she left that village, she hasn't deviated an inch from a straight line to the Teclan mountain."

Jarl didn't respond though he knew they were waiting for his decision. He hated to stop for multiple reasons. He hated the feeling that he was standing still while she was drawing further away. He hated the coldness of his furs without her. He hated the emptiness of being alone—something he had never experienced before. Nights were always the worst, and it kept him in the saddle every day for as long as possible.

"She won't be able to ride through this either, Jarl. She's heading straight into it. She'll have to stop, the same as we do," Tryggr nudged.

Jarl nodded, though he wasn't happy about it. "Pitch the tents. And make sure the horses' picket lines are extra secure. We're in for a rough night, I'm afraid."

"You heard him, boys. Make camp and make it quick. Thor's about to pay us a visit."

Jarl rolled out his own small travel tent while the others rushed to do the same. This was the first time they had needed them since leaving the main camp. Jarl was pounding his last tent stake into the ground when Tryggr returned.

"Um...what do you want to do about her?" he asked, nodding toward Altene.

"Set up a tent for her," Jarl said.

"I didn't bring a tent for her. I assumed she'd be sleeping with you."

Jarl looked up at him annoyed.

"Well, why else does a man bring a woman along with him on a trip like this, if not for his comfort at night?" Tryggr defended his decision.

"I brought her to translate if we needed it, or to explain any strange Dor customs or items we might come across."

"How was I supposed to know that?" Tryggr complained. "You said travel light, so I did." He glanced back at her. "She can't stay out in this."

"It's your mistake, so you fix it," Jarl responded.

"Fix it how?"

"However you want, Tryggr." Jarl went back to pounding the stake. He was still convinced Altene had played a part in Nena's escape. The thought of having her in close proximity to him all night was not the least bit appealing.

Tryggr grumbled something under his breath and moved toward Altene.

"Um, I made a mistake in the tent count," Tryggr shouted to her as another harder gust of wind hit them.

Altene only nodded and pulled at her pack.

"The weather is about to be unfit for man or beast out here. I...um...have my tent and it's large enough for two. You can put your sleeping furs there tonight—next to mine—not mixed up with mine. Just to be clear."

"That would be much appreciated, Tryggr," Altene yelled back at him. "Gratitude, yet again."

"It's nothing," he said. "It was my mistake, after all, and I had to set a tent up for myself anyway, so it was no extra trouble. And I'm probably the only one who has a tent big enough for two...because I'm big, you know."

"Yes, I know," she agreed.

"I think I just felt the first raindrop. Here, let me have your pack. I'll get soaked if I have to wait for you to carry it." Without waiting for her to accept, Tryggr hoisted her pack and her saddle onto his shoulders and strode off toward his tent.

Altene followed him, but paused at the tent flap to cast one last glance at Jarl. He was standing outside his own tent taking stock of the makeshift camp. She smiled and waited for his eyes to find her, but when they did, they were cold and his gaze didn't linger. Her smile fading, Altene turned and ducked inside Tryggr's tent.

"You can sit there," Tryggr said and pointed to a narrow spot between their packs. Once she was seated, he brushed past her and began to tie the flap closed. He had just finished and was surveying his handiwork when the first wave of rain hit. He waited for a moment, watching for leaks, then satisfied that it would hold, he stumbled back to his bundle of furs. Crammed inside with two sets of gear and tack, there was little room for either of them to move. They sat in awkward silence in the dim light as the rain pounded against the outside of the tent.

"Is that blood?" Tryggr asked, when she shifted her position and her dress fell away from her leg.

"It is nothing," Altene said and pulled the material back to cover it.

"People don't bleed for nothing," he disagreed.

"The saddle has rubbed me raw on the insides of my knees. Your cream has been most helpful with the pain," she elaborated.

"Let me see," he said gruffly.

"It's nothing," she repeated.

"I'll decide that, now let me see," Tryggr demanded. Altene pulled up her dress and revealed the ugly purplish wound on the inside of one of her legs. Tryggr exhaled sharply. "I've never seen it so bad before. Your skin must be very soft." He turned and rummaged through one of his packs. He pulled out a shirt and began ripping it into strips.

"Tryggr, really you don't need to..."

"Hush up, woman, and present your leg."

Altene did as he commanded.

Using a small strip of shirt and water, he first wiped the wound carefully, then smeared a thin layer of salve over the top. He wrapped a clean strip around her leg and tied the knot on the outside of her knee to secure the bandage. "Now the other leg," he directed.

He frowned when he saw that it was worse, then cleaned and bandaged it, too.

"Gratitude, Tryggr," Altene said when he was finished.

"Don't go getting all soft on me. I would have done the same for one of the horses. You couldn't ride for much longer like that, and when you started to slow us down, it might have been just enough to push Jarl over the edge. He's halfway there already," he muttered and shook his head. "I only tended to you to spare myself from having to listen to his ranting later, so don't thank me. Get some sleep."

"She did not stop," the tracker reported to Jarl and Tryggr. "You see, these tracks here were made while the rain still fell. You can see the way the water poured into the print when the animal lifted its foot."

Tryggr raised his eyebrows and shook his head, amazed. "I don't see how that's possible. You couldn't see a damn thing in that rain."

"She couldn't either," the tracker disclosed. "She was riding almost blind."

"Almost?" Jarl asked.

"She used the river to guide her. I've found several places where she accidentally rode into the water. She couldn't see a thing."

"But she didn't stop," Jarl said, resigned to the fact that any news from the tracker these days was going to be bad.

"No," the tracker confirmed.

"How far back are we now?" Jarl asked.

"It's too hard to tell with the tracks being so wet. Once things dry out a bit and we get to tracks that were made on drier soil, I can tell you for sure, but she was not making good time."

Jarl twisted his head and rubbed the back of his neck with one hand while he did the calculations in his head. The storm had kept them pinned down the first afternoon and night, and all the next day and night. Even if her pace was only at half speed, that put them at least another day and a half behind her. An additional day and a half on top of the lead she already had. How could she not have stopped?

"I know what you're thinking, Jarl, but it's not as bad as it sounds," the tracker continued. "She'll have to stop and rest some time. No one can go on forever without sleep. The time she made in the storm was very slow at best. We are all fairly rested now, and if we ride at normal speed today, we'll have gained on her by nightfall—maybe quite a bit, depending on how long she stops for," the tracker added.

Chapter 19

Nena stopped the horses at the base of the tall red cliffs. The Bloodcliff Gates. How many times had she returned from raids and felt their welcoming security? Why did she not feel it now? Where was the relief that her exhausting journey was at an end? Where was the elation that her escape was successful and she was free? Why did she not feel anything but numb? It had to be the Taymen.

"We are here," she said to Exanthia who was back on her own horse, trailing at the moment. "We've made it. These are the Bloodcliffs that keep us safe on the mountain. No enemy has ever passed through them and lived. You see on the top." Nena pointed up to the rim. "Warriors man these cliffs day and night. When you are older, and a warrior, you will do the same."

Exanthia said nothing, only stared at the imposing red monoliths.

"Come," Nena said, as she led the way into the narrow canyon between the sheer rock walls. They had made it only a short distance inside when the trail turned and wove through a patch of large boulders. "These are here to slow an enemy. They prevent wagons or large groups of men from being able to pass in a rush," Nena explained. Before she could continue, she was interrupted by the sound of pounding hooves. She looked further up the canyon, beyond the boulder field. Hard riding Teclan warriors bore down on them. In that moment Nena could see how terrifying they must be to an outsider. In her current state, still jittery and numb from the Taymen root, they were almost intimidating to her. She turned back to Exanthia and reassured her. "Have no fear. You are safe with me, and these are your people now."

Teclan warriors surrounded them, their faces stony masks, though Nena could tell they were excited to see her. She recognized them all. There was Gentok, who, though only a few years older, had been one of her weapons trainers. Nena regarded him with fondness and respect. Then there was Baldor, a larger heavily-muscled warrior, whose sister had chosen her older brother Lothor. He was a fierce warrior, and though he was brother's closest friend and her own brother-in law, Nena had never particularly cared for him.

"You have returned, Nena. Your father will be very pleased," Gentok welcomed her.

"My father? He lives?" She tried, but could not keep the emotion from her voice.

"Yes," Gentok replied. "Your father is a strong man, and though his injuries were grave, the gods have mended him."

"And my brother? Ruga?" The words were out before she could stop them.

Gentok shook his head. "Your brother rides in the afterlife."

Nena nodded.

Baldor rode beside her, interrupting them. He made no attempt to hide his examination of the circle on her arm, before taking an exaggerated look around, pretending to look for a husband who was clearly not there. "It is just the two of you then?" he asked.

"Yes," Nena replied, and fought back a wave of annoyance.

That brought a hint of a smile to Baldor's lips. He looked her over again with more familiarity than she cared for. Men from her village had looked at her before, but when it was the gods' choice, it had been more with a wistful longing—never this kind of boldness. It would be an adjustment for her, but she had to accept the fact that men would be this way now—and Baldor was one of the more qualified candidates. Her stomach twisted.

"And what have we here? A prisoner?" Baldor turned his attention to the girl and bumped his horse into hers. He raised his hand as if to strike her. Exanthia's eyes were wide with fright, but she kept her chin up and did not flinch away.

"Leave her!" Nena's command rang out in the narrow canyon. Baldor hesitated, his earlier familiarity with her gone. Nena drove her mare between Baldor and Exanthia's horses, forcing his mount to back away to make room for her. Her hand rested ready on the hilt of her sword while her eyes remained fixed on Baldor's face, daring him to defy her. Nena did not fear him, and not because she was the daughter of Meln. Though he was nearly twice her size, she knew Baldor relied too much on his size and strength and less on skill. She was fully confident in her ability to back up her command. "She is no captive. She is my ward and under my protection. Any who take issue with her, take issue with me."

The other warriors looked to Baldor with interest, awaiting his response to her clear challenge. Nena's reputation as a skilled fighter was well known—not to mention how it would look to the tribe if Baldor were to exchange blows with her on her long awaited return home. Baldor nodded curtly and turned his horse away. Without another word, he moved to the front of the group and waited for the others to fall in behind him.

Though she outranked him, Nena did not challenge him again or assert her claim to lead the small band. Nor would she have done so had any of the others taken that position. She was too physically exhausted and mentally drained. She did not wish to be responsible for any more decisions, even simple ones. For now, she was content to follow. With Exanthia riding close behind her, and Gentok and the other warriors bringing up the rear, they began to make their way up the mountain.

As the horses climbed the rugged, but well-worn trail into the trees, Nena waited to feel at home. Everything was so familiar. There was the large boulder that had rolled across the trail last year after heavy spring rains. And the great pine whose trunk took three men to encircle with their arms. It had been struck by lightning four summers ago and survived, but since then, stood only half of its previous height. There was even the same small patch of purple wildflowers that grew in the boggy spot on the edge of the trail. Nena could have been blindfolded and dropped at any point along the way and known exactly where she was within seconds of opening her eyes. So how, though she recognized it all, did it somehow still feel foreign to her?

Her father was waiting for them outside of his tent with her brother, Lothor, standing slightly behind him. As her father stepped forward to greet her, Nena slid from her horse, struggling to hide her emotions and to not react to the hideous scars that covered what had been his right eye and the upper right half of his face. Even the bones of his skull beneath them were sunken and misshapen. How had he survived such an injury? Perhaps Altene had not been lying after all when she reported a man saw Meln fall to a battle-axe. That would explain so much—why the other six fallen Teclan warriors had not been placed in sky graves. How had he possibly managed even one for her brother, Ruga?

Nena knelt before him, and Meln placed his hand on the back of her head in an uncharacteristic emotional gesture.

"Nena, my child. It is good to see you well."

"And you, Father," she acknowledged. She stood then, but they did not embrace.

"And who is this child?" Meln nodded to the girl who had also dismounted and stood behind her.

"This is Exanthia." Nena reached back and pulled her forward, then stood with her hand protectively on the girl's shoulder. Her father had been fearsome to strangers before, but Nena was sure his mangled, scarred countenance had to be truly terrifying now. "She is brave and strong, and I bring her as my ward to join the Teclan."

Meln's brow furrowed. It was an extremely unusual request. Very few outsiders were ever accepted into the tribe, and usually only then as the result of marriage.

Sensing his indecision, Nena continued. "I was bloodsworn to her by another Dor when I was held prisoner. I could not escape and leave her to suffer the penalty for my actions. But she is more than that. She is strong deep within. Teclan strong, and I make this a formal request."

Her father paused for a moment, then nodded his acceptance. Nena breathed a sigh of relief. The chief's blessing was required for any outsider to join the tribe.

"The gods have chosen for you?" her father asked.

Nena was caught off guard by the sudden shift in conversation. "Yes, Father," she answered.

Lothor scowled.

Her father nodded, seeming disappointed but not surprised. He knew the circumstances under which he had last seen his daughter. He knew only capture by the Northmen, or an injury such as his, would have kept her away from home for so long. She was clearly not so injured.

"With the gods' choice behind you, there is no reason for you to delay choosing a warrior from among the tribe."

"Yes, Father," Nena replied, biting back all the things she wanted to say. *After thinking she was dead, that was his first concern?*

"And you have used the Taymen?" he asked, shifting the conversation again suddenly, as direct as ever.

Her brother looked away, his scowl deepening. Lothor had yet to say a word, which was not unusual, but something about his demeanor was off—something more than his normal stern manner. Nena sensed disapproval when he looked at her. She tried to read his face to pinpoint the source, but he would not meet her eyes. Was it the girl? Or that she had used the Taymen? She couldn't be sure. In her current wrung out state, she couldn't even be sure that what she was feeling was real.

"Yes, Father. It was a long journey home, and I feared pursuit. To avoid recapture, I used the Taymen to stay awake. We have just come all the way from the Great Sea. While we were there, Darna provided me with a small piece," Nena explained. She hoped the mention of her strict aunt would alleviate any concerns he had about her being a habituate.

Her father nodded. "Then you will need rest. We will talk more later."

Her aunt, Jalla, rushed forward and hugged her, then held her at arm's length to take in her whole appearance. "Nena. It is true. You live, and you are well. Come. Both of you. You must eat and rest. You will both share my tent from now on. It will be so nice to have female company and the fresh energy of youth," her aunt babbled without waiting for a single response. "What a beautiful girl," Jalla said as she turned to Exanthia and stroked her hair. "And if Nena says you are brave, then you must be nigh as brave as Meln himself. Nena does not speak such words readily."

Exanthia seemed to melt before Nena's eyes, responding to Jalla's soft comforting words. She looked to Nena, awaiting her approval before she followed this new woman. Nena had given no thought to where they would live when they arrived. Her focus had been only on reaching their destination. Though her father's youngest sister, Jalla, had always been her favorite, and had practically raised her and her brothers after their mother died, Nena balked at the idea of living with her. Her father had asked no questions about her time as a prisoner, but she knew her aunt would have no such reservations. She would expect to hear details of the last few months.

Nena had shared her father's tent with Ruga before the tournament, but how could she ask that now of Exanthia? Or her father? She glanced back at the young girl who was awaiting her decision, her eyes filled with hope. After everything Exanthia had endured—losing her mother, their hell-bent travel pace, Baldor's terrifying welcome and then seeing her frightful new chief, Nena knew she could not deny her this. She nodded and they followed Jalla back to her tent.

Jalla dished them each a bowl of rabbit stew. Nena could feel her aunt's eyes on the circle on her arm as she fluttered around them, but she made no mention of it. Nena knew that would not last. "And did I hear you say you saw Darna?" Jalla asked. "How is she? Is she well?"

"She was when we left. The Sea Tribe was preparing for an impending attack."

"An attack? From who?" Jalla asked.

"The Northmen," Exanthia volunteered. "The same ones who held us as prisoners. We delivered a warning to the Sea Tribe to save them."

Jalla looked to Nena to elaborate, but she was eating mechanically, staring unfocussed into her bowl. "It is early. Would you like to go to the baths when you have finished eating?" Jalla asked.

"I need to sleep," Nena declined, her response clipped. Even though she knew she would sleep better without the layers of travel grime on her skin, she could not face other women right now. Could not answer their questions or feel their probing eyes on her. Could not see their pity as they imagined her treatment at the hands of the Northmen. Could not hear their suggestions about who she should choose. "I used the root of the Taymen," she said to excuse her behavior and her absence.

Her aunt nodded. "Of course. And how about you?" Jalla turned to Exanthia. "Are you also too tired? Or would you like to have a nice relaxing bath with me and see some of the village?"

"I am not too tired. I was able to sleep while we rode. Nena let me ride behind her on her horse and held my hands so I would not fall while I slept." It was clear Exanthia had no intentions of letting Jalla escape from her sight.

"Very good then. You and I will go, and we will let Nena rest," Jalla said. "And on the way back, we'll gather more sleeping furs so there are enough for the three of us."

After the two had left and Nena heard their voices becoming fainter as they moved away, she looked around the tent. It was filled with things she had known since she was a child. Colorful carpets, hand woven in intricate patterns, covered the walls and floor. Large clay pots, filled with grains and herbs, lined the walls along the floor. A tall rack for drying meat stood folded and empty in the corner next to the shelves that held Jalla's many assorted jars and vials of medicinal ointments and powders. Her survey faltered as it passed over the tent flap. There were the three small red hand prints she and her two brothers had made with war paint on the inside of the flap when they were young.

Her eyes welled with tears. She dashed them away with the back of her hand and shook her head, but they continued to flow. What was wrong with her? She had not cried since she was a child. And she would not cry now. She was home. It had to be the Taymen root that was making her irritable and emotional. She just needed to sleep. Without undressing, Nena curled up on top of her aunt's furs and closed her eyes.

Exhausted as she was, her thoughts continued to race on. Her father's words echoed in her mind, over and over again. *"There is no reason for you to delay choosing a warrior from among the tribe."*

With those few words, he had made his expectations clear. He hadn't said choose one this very moment, but Nena understood he might as well have. Having voiced it was basically a decree. And he was right; there was no reason—at least no logical one. It was their way and she'd been expecting it, so why was she surprised? Had she really thought to be like Jalla? Her aunt had lost her husband soon after Nena's mother had died, but had never been required to choose another. Instead she had taken over much of the rearing of Meln's children—a duty that should have gone to his next wife, but her father had never offered his willingness to be chosen by another.

But Nena knew her situation was different. She hadn't lost a mate. She'd been a female prisoner of the loathsome Northmen. Her father would have no way of knowing what her captivity had actually been like, and naturally, would assume the worst—that she'd been raped and tortured for months. He probably even thought she would want a husband quickly to put that behind her.

Nena's thoughts took a darker path and, for a brief moment, she wondered bitterly if his haste had anything to do with her at all. Seeing her circle filled in with no husband's symbol below would be a constant daily reminder of his own horrific defeat. He, and everyone else, would think of it every time they saw her. Once she chose and had a warrior husband's lineage on her arm, things would, at least on the surface, appear to be normal. They could all go on with their lives as if nothing had ever happened.

Nena shook the angry thoughts from her head, realizing they were irrational. Again, it had to be the lack of sleep and the Taymen affecting her judgment. Her father had nothing to gain by covering the miniscule evidence of his defeat from her arm. Not when his own skull was a shocking daily reminder to all.

Nena's bladder awoke her in the darkness. She sat up disoriented and looked around the tent to get her bearings. Embers from a small cookfire illuminated the small space with soft orange light. She still slept on top of Jalla's furs, though someone had covered her with a thick soft wolf pelt. Jalla and Exanthia slept together in a separate pile of furs on the opposite side of the small firepit. A new flat pan and two freshly washed plates sat tipped on their sides against a stone of the fire ring, and Nena smelled traces of wild onion and antelope. She had heard nothing of their return or the meal they had obviously prepared and eaten.

She stood and moved quietly toward the flap without waking them. As she exited the tent and walked toward the trees, she glanced up at the moon to gauge the time. It would soon be first light, though she couldn't be sure of which day. At minimum, she had slept the entire day of their arrival and almost an entire night. She did feel more rested, and though she knew she could sleep more, she decided against returning to her furs. Instead she went to the baths, making the most of her early rising to avoid the other women there a bit longer.

When she returned to the tent, Jalla was just leaving with a fired-clay pot of tea. She glanced at Nena's clean appearance with approval.

"Nena. I wondered where you'd gone so early. Perhaps you would take this tea to your father for me. It helps with his headaches."

"Of course." Nena took the tray from her.

"You will usually find him by the bend in the stream in the Meadow of the Idols," Jalla suggested. "And I was going to take Exanthia to the training grounds this morning, if that is alright with you? She is eager to start her warrior training, and I see no reason for her to delay."

Exanthia appeared from the tent at that moment, her hair freshly braided and wearing a new young warrior dress. Her face was filled with excitement and anticipation. Both seemed to be waiting for her permission.

Nena nodded and smiled.

Nena inhaled the sweet smell of ripe and rotting fruit as she passed between the twin obelisks that marked the west boundary of the Meadow of the Idols. The fruit trees planted within the sacred space to ensure the gods had sufficient nourishment, were laden with fruit this year and much had already fallen to the ground. The gods would be pleased. Carefully balancing the tray on her hip,

Nena reached up between the branches for a dark purple plum and plucked it from its hidden place nestled between the glossy green leaves.

She rubbed it briefly against her dress, then raised it to her lips. The tart skin burst as soon as her teeth touched it, spraying the sweet juice into her mouth. She closed her eyes and savored it. They were better than she remembered. Though the trees were maintained for the gods, the people of the tribe were allowed to share in the bounty, but only by taking the fruit from the west half of each tree. The sweetest fruit that was first touched by the sun every morning was always left for the gods.

Still sucking the last shreds of sweetness from the pit, Nena made her way through the tall carved stone idols. She found her father exactly where Jalla had described, sitting where the creek made a sharp turn, with his back leaned against the gnarled trunk of an old pear tree. He looked up at her approach.

"Ah, Nena—and you have brought my tea. Very good. Sit and join me." He patted the grass next to him. "When Jalla first made this for me, I did not care for its flavor, but now I have acquired a taste for it. Would you like some?" he offered.

"No, thank you," Nena declined as she sat cross-legged next to him. "Jalla said it helps with your headaches. Are they severe?"

"Not so bad anymore. The tea helps to keep them at bay. Initially she put other stronger things in it—juice of the poppy I am sure was one, though she knows how I feel about it, and still will not admit it. Now I believe it is down to just a few ingredients."

"As injured as you were, how did you ever make it back here?" Nena asked the question that had been on her mind since first seeing his scars.

"Survivors of the Eastern Plains tribe discovered me among the bodies. I regained awareness only long enough to explain to them how to build the sky graves, and to request that they return me here, if I still lived, when they had completed them. I fully expected not to even begin the journey home, much less to survive it. They told me later they had found your brother, Ruga, but not you. All this time I feared they had not looked hard enough, and that your spirit might still be lost trying to make the great journey. They were so terrified the Northmen would return. They wanted nothing more than to flee the place. Only later did they admit they had not prepared sky graves for our escort warriors. Every day I worry for them, and part of me worries even for Ruga, if they truly did as they claimed."

"Ruga is safe with our ancestors, Father. There was a point when I was a captive that I approached the afterlife. I felt Ruga there. And Mother." She shook her head and frowned at the recollection. "Which was strange because I barely knew her. Yet I recognized her spirit as if we had been close."

"So you were badly wounded, too," he said, nodding as if he had expected no less. "Your body has healed well; you show no signs of mortal injury."

"I was not wounded, Father. I became very ill with a deadly sickness they called the Northman's Curse. Many among the prisoners contracted it. I was the only one to survive."

Her father cocked his head and looked at her curiously. "Never before did I believe people could return from being so close to the afterlife. But I, too, felt your mother when I was injured. Ruga was not there, so your words bring me great comfort. It was strange, though. Your mother did not welcome me. It was as if she was trying to tell me it was not my time. Was it the same for you?" he asked.

"No," Nena said. Her father's words disturbed her; they confirmed her earlier suspicion that Jarl was the only reason she yet lived. For her, the afterlife had been very welcoming, but Jarl's hold on her had been too strong—stronger even than the gods. He had pulled her back.

"Ah, probably just the delusions of a wounded old man," her father said as he took another sip of tea. "You know, with only one eye, I will never raid again, and worse, something is wrong inside my head. I can no longer ride a horse. The world spins uncontrollably if my feet are not firmly on the ground." He paused and looked at her. "No one else knows that."

Nena opened her mouth to argue with him. He was not old. He was Meln. He was strong and powerful. But as she looked at him now with the shock of white hair growing from the injured area of his scalp, quietly sipping his tea, she realized that even though he was also home and still chief, much had changed for him as well. Most telling was the fact that he was having such a heartfelt discussion with her at all. Her father was a different man.

"Are the survivors of the Eastern Plains tribe who brought you home, still here?" she asked.

"No. Once their wounded were healed, they were sent on their way. They were well-rewarded for their efforts and well-supplied with provisions for their journey. I will always be grateful to them, but they are not Teclan."

Nena nodded and was thankful again for Exanthia's easy and unobstructed acceptance.

"Have you given thought to your decision?" he asked.

She knew he referred to her next choosing. "Yes, but no decision has been made."

"I know you think my words about choosing another so soon to be callous, but know that I am not unsympathetic to what you have endured, or your feelings on this matter. You must trust me that my decision is for your own good."

"Yes, Father." Nena nodded, but her mind raced. He would never have spoken so to her before—never felt the need to justify his decisions. That he did so now was staggering to her.

"When one is left alone with certain memories, those memories can become like the iron vine growing inside," he explained. "If left unchallenged and not replaced, their vines grow very quickly, and eventually they will strangle your spirit. Even the greatest warrior cannot fight them. You must make new memories, now, before their grip on you is too strong to break. Only when new experiences fill the places within you, will the others wither and fade. Only then can you have your life back as it was before. Only then can your spirit have peace. Do you understand?"

"Yes," she murmured. *Her life back as it was before. Was such a thing possible? But it had to be; that was why she'd escaped and returned here. How did her father know these things?*

"And the warriors here are not unfamiliar to you," he continued. "You know them all—have known them your entire life as warriors and as men, so you will not be making a hasty decision from strangers. I expect you to choose one soon. It is the best thing for you, Nena. If too much time is allowed to pass, it could be too late."

She nodded. "I understand, Father."

"Good. Now you should go and reacquaint yourself with your friends, and not waste any more of your first day home sitting here with me. There will be many who are pleased to see you."

Nena nodded and stood. As she left the Meadow of the Idols, she saw Lothor approaching and paused to wait for him. He looked up, then turned suddenly and walked in a different direction. That was odd. She was sure he'd seen her. She followed him, adjusting her own course to head him off in the trees. Maybe he had just recalled something else he had to do, and she was being overly sensitive, but even upon her return, she had felt his attitude toward her had been strange. She quickened her step. She would know the truth soon enough.

"Lothor, may we speak?" she asked when she caught up to him.

He stiffened but nodded.

"I fear you are angry with me. Have I done something to offend you?" she asked.

"No," he replied.

"Then what is it?" she asked.

"There is nothing, Nena." He shook his head and turned to leave.

"I have never known my brother to be a coward," she said to his back.

He stopped and turned back to face her, his eyes blazing, but his mouth set in a firm tight line.

"Yet that is the only explanation I can find for why he is afraid to confront his sister."

"You wish to know why I am angry?" he seethed. "There are too many reasons to count. I am angry that the gods did not choose for you here—that the trip to the Eastern Plains tribe was ever made. I am angry that I was stuck here and could do nothing. I am angry that Ruga is dead. I am angry that our father, a great warrior, is now a shadow of his former self. I am angry that the Northmen responsible will sail away and possibly never return for me to have my revenge.

"I am angry that these things happened and you did not stop them. Instead you allowed yourself to be taken prisoner. At first, I was also angry for you, fearing your unimaginable torture at their hands. Yet here you return, months later, your circle filled in, your body unscathed. No scars from even so much as a scratch that I can see. Did you fight at all? Did you fight when our brother was being killed or our father's head bashed in? Or could you not wait to offer up your first union to save yourself?"

"How dare you!" Nena hissed. She had been so taken aback by his initial attack, it was the first she could gather her thoughts and retaliate. "How dare you question the gods without fear of their reprisal. And how dare you question me! I am the daughter of Meln! The fighting blood that flows through your veins, flows equally through mine! I had eight kills that day. Eight!" she repeated, her voice nearing a shout. "How many battles can you ever claim the same?"

Lothor only stared at her.

"Answer me!" she demanded.

"In no battle have I had eight kills," he admitted, his voice still choked with rage.

"Had the other warriors present averaged but a single kill each, the Northmen would have walked this earth no more. And no, I did not look for Ruga or Father in the fighting. Had I done so, maybe I would have killed only seven, and the last one would not have bashed in Father's head, but cut it off instead. To suggest you would have done differently is a lie. You know that, and yet you shame yourself with this outburst and these accusations. Luckily for Father, he could not hear you, or it would have wounded him deeper than the enemy's battle-axe ever did."

Lothor took a deep breath and closed his eyes for a brief moment. "Eight kills is an impressive feat. But then what? How many did you kill after you were captured?"

Nena didn't answer.

"Any?" he prodded. He could tell by her expression and silence the answer was no. "How is that possible? How is it possible that you killed eight within hours, but then managed not to kill even a single one in months? Were you chained the whole time? Your arms do not show evidence of shackles. And when you escaped—could you not even kill one then?"

At his reference to being chained, Nena's mind skimmed back to the special fur-lined cuffs Jarl had the forger craft to not mar her skin. She could not tell Lothor of those. Her mind moved to her escape and Jarl's guard outside the tent or the wounded guard by the horses. She could have easily killed either one of them.

Lothor stared at her, his face twisted with pain and disbelief at her silent pondering. "How could you become soft to them, Nena? They killed Ruga! They almost killed Father! I, unlike you, Sister, have a hatred for the Northmen that burns so hot in my chest, I fear it can never be quenched. I pray to the gods every day for the opportunity to kill them—to avenge Ruga's death, my father's injuries, and my sister's dishonor."

"Do not speak to me of dishonor! Or criticize how I fought, when you've been sitting here safe on the mountain, doing nothing," she spat. Lothor winced. Nena knew her brother—knew pointing out his inaction would wound him deeper than anything else she could say. She didn't care. His words had cut her deeply and, in her own pain, she lashed back. "The day I escaped, I could have easily killed several of their warriors, but to do so would not only have jeopardized my escape, the discovery of their bodies could have led to my absence being noted too early. I could not afford that—could not afford to lose even a single moment. Because when I escaped, Lothor, I was thinking beyond selfish revenge and my own desire to return home. I was thinking of saving a fellow tribe—our blood. Had I killed a few Northmen for retribution that may have never happened. Though I suppose you would consider that an acceptable loss? Our aunt's entire tribe for a few Northmen?"

They glared at each other for a long moment, both breathing hard.

Lothor proceeded, his words quieter, but no less angry. "Ever since the plains tribe returned with Father and word of the attack, I have wanted nothing more than to take our warriors and fly from this mountain in a wave of death never seen before. But since Father clung to life, and I was not yet chief, the council would not allow it. So you are correct, Sister, I sat here *safe* and helpless, unable to do anything until Father awoke. When he opened his eyes, I was overjoyed—not only that he still lived, but that my time had finally come. Then he, too, forbade me to pursue them, as he has continued to do every day when I petition him. It is almost as if he is afraid," he said, his voice filled with bitterness.

"But know this. When I am chief, it will be my mission in life to rid the world of Northmen. I pray the ones responsible will return so they, too, can fall to my blade. But even if they do not, I will bring my wrath down upon every single one of them who ever dares to come here again. Spilling their blood is all I think about from the time my eyes open in the morning until they close at night." He paused and stared at her. "These are the words I should be hearing from you, and Father, and it sickens me that I do not." He turned on his heel and strode away.

Chapter 20

Nena returned to Jalla's tent, still shaken by the confrontation with Lothor. She found Exanthia sitting alone outside.

"Why are you not practicing with the other girls?" Nena asked

Exanthia chewed an edge of one of her fingernails. "They are in-between lessons," she mumbled.

"But surely the next will start soon." Nena remembered her own classes as a youth.

"I do not wish to return," Exanthia murmured with her head down.

"Why not?" Nena could not believe it. Exanthia had been so excited to begin her warrior training.

"The trainer said I will not make a warrior because I have weak blood. He said it is a waste of his time to try to train me."

Nena smoldered with barely controllable fury. After they had endured so much to return here, she and Exanthia had both been met with disparagement and doubt. She fought to not let it show. She did not want Exanthia to see how serious she felt the words were, or to give them any credence.

"That's nonsense. And who would you believe—me or someone who just met you? Your trainer does not yet know you, like I do. I have known many great warriors, and you possess the inner strength and bravery that set them apart from others. You lack only the skills that anyone can learn. Strength and bravery, on the other hand, cannot be taught. You must be patient."

Exanthia nodded.

"And I will help you, so you can catch up to the other girls your age more quickly. Perhaps I will even go to watch your next lesson so I can gauge where you need the most work," Nena lied. She knew Exanthia needed work in every aspect of combat. She wanted only to see this instructor. "Then tonight, you and I will start working on those areas together. How does that sound?"

Exanthia smiled and nodded, her spirit bolstered.

"Now run along, so you are not late. I'll be there shortly."

Exanthia rose and trotted back toward the practice area. After a few minutes Nena followed. She had not accompanied Exanthia intentionally. She wanted to observe the practice unnoticed, to witness the cause of Exanthia's sudden change in attitude. Nena knew if they arrived together it would cause a stir, and the true actions of the culprit might not be revealed.

As she stood watching the young man, it was all she could do to keep her anger in check. He was demonstrating the use of poles—Nena's favorite and one she excelled in. He was young, perhaps sixteen or seventeen summers, but it was customary for young warriors to be trainers. It allowed them to continue to work on their own skills while they educated others. But this young warrior was not educating at all. He was humiliating them and reveling in his own expertise. She watched as the second young girl was tripped and thrown to the ground. No explanation was given as to what she had done wrong or how she could improve.

Still rankling from her brother's words, Nena made her way to the young man at the front of the group. "It appears you have no equal with which to give proper demonstration," she said as she approached. She recognized him as being from a lower ranking family, but could not recall his name.

He smiled and nodded, thinking she was complimenting him.

"Perhaps you will allow me to join you as your aide, to better show these girls proper form and technique?" Nena knew she could not join the class without his invitation. It would cause him insult, and she did not have the right. She also knew with the way she had worded it, he would not refuse.

"Yes, that would be most welcome," he said. "These girls are poor students." Nena could not believe how cocky he was and again had to bite her tongue. She thought back on how her own instructors had always said the students were a reflection of the teacher—how they needed every student to do their best, to do them proud.

Nena picked up the sticks he had allowed the girls to use against him. They were knobby and poorly balanced. She noted his were smooth and perfect.

"The first thing I will add to this lesson, is to know your weapon," she said to the girls. "Your instructor has given you inferior weapons to use. They are poorly balanced and far more difficult to wield."

She saw him scowl from the corner of her eye.

"But I am sure he has done this on purpose to simulate battle, where often you must use whatever is available, and you may face an opponent with far superior weapons than yours." She turned back to him. "I am ready."

"Would you like a different set?" he offered.

"No, these will be fine and will better make your point." *And mine.*

He tapped at her with the sticks, tentatively at first. Nena blocked each blow but did not counter. He grew more bold and pressed her, his blows coming faster and harder. He twirled one pole in an unsuccessful attempt to distract her while he struck with the other. Nena continued only to block. With no warning, Nena went on the attack, in three strikes, the instructor was on his back on the ground. Nena turned to the group.

"Always aid your sparring partner to rise when they have fallen. It shows you have no hard feelings and are only training." She reached for his hand, but he rolled away and bounced to his feet. Nena smiled to herself.

Gone was all trace of the cocky smile now. He came at her hard this time. Their sticks clacked and clashed, the sounds resounding in the small meadow. Nena made him pay with multiple hits to his body this time before she humiliated him again and threw him on his back. She reached out her hand. Again he refused it.

The third time, she beat him severely, raining blows against all parts of his body. She wanted to make sure that his aches reminded him of this lesson for days after it was over. She spun to one side and put her whole body into a blow across his back. He stumbled forward in pain, but did not cry out. When he faced her again, she saw the fear and defeat in his eyes. He clearly no longer wanted to continue, but didn't dare say so. He had yet to reach her with a single blow. When he was on his back for the third time, Nena pounced and straddled him, using a pole against his neck to cut off his wind. He held up the first two fingers of his left hand to signal his submission.

Nena leaned down and whispered in his ear. "This is how you teach them. Do you think this is a good way? Did you learn much today? I suppose you did, but what I meant was, did anything I taught you today improve your skills with the sticks? No," she answered for him. "You are these girls' instructor. It is your job and should be your pride to see them excel. Any failings they show are a direct reflection on you. This is not a game. One day your life and mine may depend on the level of skill they achieve. Do you understand me? From now on, I expect to see you take care in teaching them properly. Their weaknesses are not to be exploited for your amusement; they are to be corrected."

He nodded, his eyes bulging. Nena released him and stood, extending her hand. He took it this time, and she pulled him to his feet. She heard single slow hand-clapping behind her and turned to find Gentok approaching. "That was quite a display," he said.

Still angry from the session, and caught off guard at being witnessed, Nena tipped her head to acknowledge him.

"You are done for the day," Gentok said to the instructor. "And I will have words with you tomorrow before you return." The youth nodded, his hand still on his throat, then limped away. Gentok turned to the wide-eyed girls. "Take a short break, but do not leave. It will only be for a few minutes and then your training will resume." The girls all split up and moved to the shade, whispering excitedly. He turned back to Nena. "What was the subject of today's demonstration, might I ask—how to thrash someone?"

"I merely continued the lesson he was already teaching, exactly as he was teaching it. The only change I made was to make him the recipient." She defended herself. "He is not a suitable trainer. The girls will learn nothing from him."

"I'm not judging you. I've heard other complaints, and I will speak to him tomorrow. If he does not change his ways, he will be replaced. And I will make sure he knows it will bring great shame on him if that happens. Though I think you made the point well enough today; my words may not be necessary." He paused and looked at her. "Now for the matter at hand. Would you like for me to aid you in giving them a proper demonstration? Was that truly your intent? Or would you rather try to give me a thrashing, too? If it's just a good fight you need, I'm willing to oblige that as well, though we should probably conduct that somewhere else, so as not to intimidate them."

Gentok spoke in a teasing tone, but Nena could see he was serious. He knew her well. He could see the tension bottled beneath her controlled surface. She considered his offer. She would appreciate a good fight, and might, in fact, take him up on that later, but at the moment teaching the girls was more important to her.

"Your offer to assist in their instruction today is most appreciated," she said.

"Very well then. And my other offer still stands for another time."

Nena nodded and called the girls back. "As a female warrior, you will often be called upon to fight a male opponent who is bigger and stronger. To do so you must be faster. But you cannot rely only on quick reflexes. You need to read ahead, to anticipate the opponent's moves by their subtle signals. Gentok and I will now demonstrate. Every time we identify a tell sign of the other, we will stop the fight and point it out. You should all come closer and try to see what we are talking about."

Nena and Gentok each picked out a set of poles and twirled them to check for weight and balance. Then each dipped the ends into colored chalk to better show when a blow was landed. Nena chose red, Gentok blue.

"When you are ready," he said and tipped his head, deferring to her.

Nena scrutinized him. He appeared relaxed, but she was not fooled. It had been many years since she had sparred with Gentok, but she remembered her lessons well. He was as fast as lightning. But she had learned more than a few things since she was that young warrior in training. She called upon all of her senses to read his moves, then struck.

Gentok deflected the blow and countered with a strike of his own.

Nena ducked and felt the swoosh of air as the pole passed over her head.

"Stop," she called out. "Did anyone see what I saw before Gentok swung the pole and I ducked?" she asked their audience. "His little fingers tighten on the pole." She smiled at him. "Again," she said.

They circled each other, each making and deflecting multiple strikes.

"Stop." It was Gentok this time. "Did anyone see how Nena plants the heel of her left foot before she strikes with her right hand?" He smiled back. "She was once my student and has done that since she was a girl your age. Improving your fighting is not only seeing the opponent, it is disguising your own moves. When you know you make a particular sign, you must try to hide it."

Nena flushed and in that moment felt like the young girl he had schooled long ago.

For the next twenty minutes they sparred, each occasionally landing a blow on the other. Every time they stopped and explained what had transpired, what signals their opponent had telegraphed prior to making a move that allowed them to avoid it or land it.

"Now I am going to put you all in pairs and you are to practice what we just showed you," Nena said. "The goal is not only to win, but to improve your partner as well. So, whenever you are able to land a blow, I wish to hear you explain to them what you saw or what they did not do, that enabled you to do so. Is that clear? Gentok and I will move among you to observe and give tips. You must all strive to excel individually, but success in battle depends on the entire group. Every member must be strong. Do you understand?"

The girls all nodded.

"Very well." Nena walked among them. "You and you." She pointed to two taller girls who both had similar serious competitive expressions on their faces. "And you and you." She paired two other girls of similar age and build. "And you and you." She pointed to Exanthia and a girl about the same age. She could have paired her with one of the younger girls who would be less skilled, but Nena did not want to embarrass Exanthia by pairing her with a child.

The girl Nena chose to pair her with, though athletic, had an expression Nena remembered well from her days at this age. This girl had no fire, no desire to be a great warrior. She would be one of the girls for whom the gods chose very early, probably as soon as she became a woman, and probably before she ever made a single raid. She would hopefully be a good partner for Exanthia. She could share her knowledge, but would have no competitive desire to best her.

For the next hour Nena and Gentok coached the girls. They moved among them observing and occasionally stepping in to show a particular hold or technique. When the girls were all perspiring from the exertion, Gentok called an end to the lesson. After the last girl had put away her practice sticks in the wooden storage crate on the side of the field and left, he turned to Nena and smiled. "Their parents will thank us. They will all sleep well tonight," he said.

"Yes," Nena agreed as they began the walk back to the village together. "Gratitude, for your help today," she added.

"None required. I enjoyed it."

"As did I," Nena admitted. For the first time since her return she did not feel on edge. She knew it was because, like the girls, she, too, was physically spent, but still it felt good. For the moment she was free of all worries and doubts. She thought of how happy Exanthia had been when she'd left with her new friend, Shia, after the lesson was over. "Exanthia lacks skill, but even more lacks confidence. Once she has that, she will catch up quickly," she said.

"Yes," Gentok agreed. "She is fortunate you take such an interest in her training. To be trained by Nena, one of the greatest Teclan female warriors ever," he embellished with a grin.

"You tease me after pointing out my many mistakes today. I have grown sluggish," Nena said ruefully as she rubbed the multiple blue marks on her arms and dress.

"You were not without success today." He pointed to the red evidence. "You have improved much since your lessons as a girl. In many ways." Nena turned and found Gentok's dark brown eyes on her. They were warm with appreciation, like Jarl's eyes used to be. She recognized the significance of the look and waited for her body to respond. Gentok was handsome and very expressive by Teclan male standards. She felt nothing. Gentok covered the awkward pause with a smile, and they continued to walk for a short distance in silence. "I understand you will be inducting Exanthia into the tribe tomorrow," he said.

"Yes. There is no reason to delay, and it will bring her great peace of mind." Nena was grateful for the change in subject. "Will you be there?"

"Give her my apologies, but I will not. I must take my turn at the cliff gates. Tell her I will be sure to bring her my welcome gift."

They came to a fork in the path and paused.

"Nena," he said.

"Yes?" She turned to look at him.

"I professed my willingness to be chosen by you before, when it was the gods' choice. I want you to know for your next choosing, that willingness still stands."

Nena remembered his earlier declaration well. The entire tribe had whispered about it for a long time—not because Gentok had professed his willingness to her; he was a very qualified and suitable candidate. Everyone had whispered, because he had professed his willingness only to her and no other. Many feared that his attempt to force the gods into only one choice would anger them. She wondered if he had professed to any others in her absence. "Gratitude, Gentok. But I am not yet ready to choose."

"I understand. I just wanted you to know, when you are ready, I will be waiting."

Chapter 21

"I, Nena, hereby declare you, Exanthia, as my ward. From this day forward you shall be known as Exanthia of the Teclan, Ward of Nena, Daughter of Meln, Chief of the Teclan tribe. Your previous life is forgotten. Your blood is now as true Teclan as any born to the mountain. You are one of the Teclan people, deserving and entitled to all rights, equal in every way.

"To welcome you, I give you this set of combat poles carved from the black oak of the Teclan mountain. They were my training sticks, and I hope they teach you as much skill as they taught me."

Nena stepped back and watched as her father approached next. "I, Chief Meln, welcome Exanthia of the Teclan with this gift." He held up a leather cord necklace with a single long lion's fang dangling from the center. "This is a tooth from the Great Lion. It is mate to the one I also wear." He lifted his own up from his neck, and held them close together for a moment, before placing hers over her head . Murmurs rippled through the crowd. Even Nena was impressed by the thoughtfulness and symbolism of his gift. He had worn the two large teeth around his neck since he had killed the lion as a youth, long before she was born.

Lothor and his very pregnant wife were next. Nena held her breath, praying that her brother's bile would not ruin this moment. "I, Lothor, welcome Exanthia of the Teclan with this dagger. The blade is knapped from the black stone that is found only on the Teclan mountain. May it keep you safe and service you well." Lothor handed her the dagger and stepped to the side. "And I, Belda, wife of Lothor, welcome you with this cape made from the pelt of the high goat, also found only on the Teclan mountain. May it keep you warm and bring you comfort wherever you find yourself." Baldor's sister handed Exanthia the fur.

One by one, people from the tribe stepped forward to present Exanthia with a gift and to welcome her.

"There is so much," Exanthia murmured, when it was over, overwhelmed by the generosity and thoughtfulness of the gifts. "This is more than my whole family ever had."

"There will be more," Jalla said. "Those who could not attend the ceremony today will come later with their gifts."

"They accept you, Exanthia. You are one of the people now. Never doubt that and never doubt yourself. You have much to learn, but plenty of time to learn it, and plenty who will help to teach you. I could not be more proud of you if you were my own daughter." Nena hugged her. "Though where we're going to put all your things, I'm not sure. There will be no room left for Jalla and I."

Jalla called them to eat as Nena picked up an armful of gifts and followed Exanthia inside the tent.

"If you choose Gentok, will we all live together in the same tent?" Exanthia asked as she took another bite of smoked fish. She had changed into a new beaded dress and had the mountain goat cape draped around her shoulders, even though it was quite warm. She had barely stopped chattering during the whole meal.

"When Nena chooses—whoever she chooses—you will remain here with me," Jalla said quickly, saving Nena from having to answer. "A man and woman in a new union will not want the company of a child. There is a reason it takes nine moons for a baby to be born, so the new couple can have privacy—to get to know one another."

A baby? And time to get to know one another. Nena lost her appetite. *As she had gotten to know Jarl?* The thought was like a knife twisting in her heart. What was wrong with her? She was free. So why did she not feel free? Why did she feel more trapped than ever? More trapped than when she'd first been chained in Jarl's tent. Was her father right? Were the vines of her memories with Jarl already strangling her spirit? Was the answer really to choose? If so— why did it feel so horribly wrong?

"Well, I would choose Gentok," Exanthia continued. "He is strong and brave and very handsome."

"What do you know about handsome?" Jalla chided her. "You are still a girl."

"I'm not a blind girl," she quipped, full of sass. "So, will I join them after nine months, then?" Exanthia asked, cheerfully oblivious to Nena's distress.

"Perhaps," Jalla agreed, though her concerned eyes remained on Nena.

"You have changed," Jalla said when the meal was over and Exanthia had been sent to wash their plates in the stream.

Could everyone see it then? Could everyone see her inner turmoil?

"It is for the better," Jalla continued. "You are more sensitive and compassionate. Exanthia has softened you. You will make a great mother one day. I was worried about you before—just a bit. You were always so tough, so hard. It made you a great warrior, but it concerned me to never see your softer side. You were always so much like your father and brothers, and nothing like your mother. Your mother was strong, too, but she was also gentle and kind. I feared for you growing up without her influence. Feared that with only your father and brothers as examples, it had shaped you too much in their like. I tried to provide as much feminine influence on you as I could, but you were always so headstrong and stubborn. It has taken a great affection to crack through your shell and release the gentleness within. I'm glad to see it. Exanthia is a treasure in many ways."

Great affection? Yes, she had felt great affection, but not in the way her aunt assumed. Exanthia was the beneficiary of the change within her, not the cause. Nena remained silent. Better Jalla thought that, than for her to know the truth.

And Nena did not agree this softer side was an improvement at all. The old her had been so sure of everything. Had been prepared to choose an unknown warrior from the plains tribe and leave her mountain home altogether. That version of her had not felt physically ill at the prospect. She may have had her doubts, but she never would have considered shirking her responsibility, or pining for a different future. The old her would have scoffed at how she felt now. The old her was strong—one to be admired. This new her was pathetic.

"Baldor brought a haunch of venison for you earlier," Jalla interrupted her thoughts.

Nena glanced at the empty meat drying rack, then at the small simmering pot of leftover rabbit stew.

"Oh, he didn't leave it. When you weren't here, he said he'd bring it back later, so he could give it to you personally. What did he think—that I would take credit for his kill? Or give it to someone else?" her aunt fumed.

"Nena." Baldor's voice hailed her from outside.

"I hope he heard me," Jalla muttered under her breath as Nena stood and made her way to the tent flap.

Baldor stood with legs spread and arms crossed over his muscled chest, the leg of venison lying on the ground beside him. The hindquarter lying in the dirt was not the most impressive presentation, but Nena knew it didn't really hurt the meat. The hide protected most of it, and the dried outer edges on the exposed cut end would be trimmed away anyway. Far more dangerous and likely to lead to spoilage was that fact that it had sat out in the heat while he waited for her to return.

"I brought this for you," he said without moving. His body language and what it implied was clear. He would not hand it to her. He expected her to bend over next to him to retrieve it.

Nena thought of telling him she knew he'd been there earlier—maybe even put him on the spot and ask him why he hadn't left it then, so she could have been enjoying venison stew for dinner instead of leftover rabbit. She said nothing. She didn't want to argue with him, and she didn't care to try to make him a better man. She knew she would never be his wife, and there was no sense antagonizing him. He would already take it as a personal insult when she chose another.

"Gratitude," she said as she knelt and hoisted the leg over her shoulder.

Baldor seemed to be waiting. It was not an awkward wait, like he was embarrassed or trying to say something—more like he was expecting her to say something. Did he really think he would bring her a chunk of meat and she would choose him on the spot? Nena realized he probably did. He had heard her father's directive to her upon her return, and his ego knew no bounds. He was physically one of the strongest warriors, and the gods had chosen her brother, Lothor, for his sister. In his mind, Nena had probably chosen him already and was only waiting for the opportunity to voice it.

"This is an impressive kill," was all she could muster.

Baldor frowned, then nodded, pleased with her compliment but unhappy with the lack of results.

Jalla was waiting for her just inside the tent and reached for the meat to begin cleaning it. Nena pulled out her own knife to help, but her aunt waved her off. "Exanthia will be back soon; she can help me. She needs the practice."

The costliness of Baldor's mistake of not leaving the meat with her aunt soon became abundantly clear. Long after the last shred of flesh was removed from the bone, her aunt pointed out every flaw in the meat, real or imagined. It was too stringy, too tough, too lean, had a foul taste. He should have killed one from the sweet grass meadows instead of the dry rocky cliffs. He should have killed a young one instead of an old toothless one, but this old one was probably the only one slow enough he could club to kill instead of using his bow. Nena knew she referred to Baldor's reputation of enjoying violence. Though she could taste nothing of what her aunt was referring to, she did not disagree. Truthfully, most of the food she ate was tasteless to her.

Gentok was smarter and brought a trio of cleaned quail—Jalla's favorite. He had no problem leaving them for Nena when she wasn't around. The quail were followed by fresh fat speckled trout and a small practice bow he had carved for Exanthia. Nena heard nothing but good things about Gentok.

Nena sighed after the latest round of Gentok's accolades. She knew Jalla was right. Gentok was a good warrior and a natural, gifted hunter. His acts with the meat and the bow were thoughtful and kind, if not calculating. And, unlike Baldor, he was at least smart enough to be calculating. With the field seeming to be narrowed down to these two suitors, Nena knew she should just choose Gentok and get it over with. Putting off the inevitable was foolish—and it was inevitable.

Her thoughts skipped ahead to moving into Gentok's tent—to sharing his furs. Her stomach clenched and she felt a small wave of nausea. But even that was a vast improvement over the gut-wrenching torment of her dreams.

Chapter 22

Nena's dreams always started the same. She felt the luxurious softness of Jarl's furs against her naked back. Sweat mingled between their bare torsos as the roar of her pulse in her ears slowly subsided. Jarl was still locked inside her, but had propped himself up on his elbows to better look into her eyes. His eyes were emerald green as he leaned down and tenderly kissed her lips. Nena was overwhelmed by the intensity of the bond she felt between them.

The intimate moment was shattered by the rattle of the entry boards. The guard outside announced the arrival of the slaver, Piltor. Jarl rolled off to the side, but seemed only mildly frustrated by the interruption. That was strange. Normally, Jarl bristled with animosity at the mere mention of Piltor's name. Nena stood and stepped from the furs to retrieve her dress from where it had been discarded earlier in their haste, halfway across the tent. She had just reached it when Jarl beckoned for Piltor to enter. She scrambled to pull the dress up and cover herself, though not before she felt Piltor's cold slimy eyes on her bare skin. She spun around to face Jarl, shocked at his oversight, but he had stood and was pulling on his trousers, utterly unconcerned with Piltor's roving gaze. She would have to take it up with him later.

"Jarl, my friend," the slaver said with a smile.

"Piltor," Jarl responded. The two men clasped hands in a hearty handshake, the red silk of Piltor's gown swirling against the bare skin of Jarl's arm. Gone was any evidence of the thick tension that normally choked the air between them.

Nena's earlier anxiety at what she had perceived to be Jarl's simple oversight grew into a distinct deep unease. This wasn't right. Nothing was right. She retreated back to the furs as the two men moved to conduct their business at Jarl's table. When they had finished, Jarl produced a bottle of wine and poured them each a cup while they continued to visit.

"You know, I must ask again, Jarl. It has been a long time, and I've made you a rich man many times over. Surely I am due for an extra reward. Will I be allowed to share furs with her this time?"

Nena waited for Jarl to explode, to reach across the table and grab Piltor by the throat before dragging him to the door. But Jarl only took another swallow and stroked his chin as he considered Piltor's request.

"The words you speak are true, my friend. You've been very patient and I've been greedy. Apologies." Jarl was smiling. He was not angry. Not upset. Not anything.

"No apologies necessary, my dear Jarl. I can only imagine the pleasure of the experience—and I have done so many times, I must admit," he chuckled. "Especially when I saw how much she had affected a great man such as yourself."

Jarl shook his head. "I don't know what came over me. It is true, I could not get enough of her for the longest time. When I first captured her, it was almost as if I were under some spell. But now...well, now time has passed and you know..." He shrugged. " I will have her sent to the baths and then to your tent."

The slaver looked back at her, his eyes filled with sadistic longing and triumph.

No! The voice inside Nena's head screamed. *No! No! This couldn't be happening!*

"And," Jarl added. "I will send Altene as well, to make her willing. Nena was a handful when I first captured her, and I would hate for her to harm you. Altene assures me that with initial restraint, she can make any woman willing."

The slaver's eyes gleamed with sick excitement. "Jarl, my friend, you honor me too greatly."

"Nonsense. This has been a long time coming. You deserve it." Jarl stood and moved to the tent flap. He summoned the guards. "Take Nena to the baths and then to Piltor's tent. Make sure she is well secured there before you leave."

"Yes sir." The first guard entered and moved toward her.

Nena frantically searched the area around her for a weapon, but nothing was close. She looked back at the guard. She did not need a weapon. She was Teclan! Her own body was weapon enough—her teeth, her thumbs. The guard grabbed her hand. She twisted her body and brought her other elbow down hard on his wrist, sure that the blow would break his hold. She waited to hear his grunt of pain, but he never even flinched. Instead he laughed, and his grip remained on her like iron. Nena swung her fist at his chin, but before it could reach its mark, he grabbed it, too. She kicked at his shins, but felt the feeble blows doing no damage. Though Nena fought with all her might to free herself, in her dream she had no more strength than a small child.

"I won't need any help, sir," the guard said to Jarl as he began to drag her effortlessly toward the door.

"Jarl!" She screamed his name. "Jarl, please! Please don't do this!"

Jarl had been watching the scene with mild interest, but turned his handsome face away to better hear something the slaver was saying, utterly unmoved by her pleas. The guard dragged her out into the blazing sunlight.

Nena awoke in a pool of sweat. Her breath came in short ragged gasps. She was in her aunt's tent. She was home. She was safe. She lay for many minutes in the darkness while her pulse slowed. Her hair was damp and tangled from thrashing. Her chest hurt from the thumping of her heart, but that pain was minimal compared to the sorrowful ache of her spirit. Jarl had been so cold. He had looked at her as if she were nothing to him. How could he feel that way when her feelings for him were so strong?

It doesn't matter. You are home. None of that matters anymore.

Nena doubted sleep would come to her again and was more than a little afraid if it did. She sat up in her disheveled furs. Slipping silently into her sandals, she moved toward the door. She felt her aunt's eyes upon her before she could see them in the dim light of the last fire embers. Their worry for her was a clear question, though Jalla said nothing.

"I'm alright," Nena whispered to her as she stepped out into the darkness, wondering even as she said the words if the assurance was for her aunt or herself.

She moved swiftly through the silent village to the horses. There she found the mare in the middle of the herd, dozing with one hind leg cocked. Nena straightened her forelock and rubbed her forehead absently, needing only to feel the mare's nearness to draw from her strength. The horse turned and nuzzled her face, her delicate whiskers and warm damp breath caressing Nena's skin. She held the side of the mare's soft muzzle to her cheek. "It was only a dream. A bad dream," she murmured.

Or perhaps it was the gods' way of showing you your future had you not escaped. It would have been nothing but pain. You were his slave and he would have tired of you. The idyllic time you shared with him was not to last, either way. You did the right thing.

And now you must do the right thing again. You must put these thoughts behind you. You must not be weak. You were not raised to be weak. Look at Exanthia. She has lost everything, and yet she does not mope around and pity herself. You are Teclan. It is time to start acting like one.

Her father's words about her memories strangling her spirit came once again to mind. She did not doubt his wisdom, but he assumed she was recovering from abuse. Was the path to recovery from abuse the same as to recover from... what? What was she recovering from? What left this pain in her chest? Jarl had never abused her—the opposite, in fact. So was the solution the same? Her memories with Jarl were still so fresh and vivid. Was it because they were they growing like the iron vine inside her? Was being alone nurturing them and condemning her to a lifetime of this pain and doubt? It was the only thing that made sense. Her dreams were a warning. She knew what she had to do.

She would choose Gentok tomorrow. She would let him know her choice in the morning. She would put this behind her. She would be strong.

Chapter 23

As Jarl examined the looming red sandstone cliffs, it was easy for him to see how they had come by their name. The Bloodcliffs. Stained from centuries of the blood of those who tried to pass, Altene had explained. Even from where he stood, he could see the guards along the top rim. There was no sense attempting to go any further. Nena's trail clearly disappeared within the protected narrow canyon between the walls.

"We'll make camp here, rest the horses, and weigh our options." Jarl announced the welcome news to his weary group. Their campsite was within sight of the opening, but safely outside of the Teclan bow range. While the others set up camp, Jarl pulled out his scope and walked toward the cliffs to take a closer look. After several minutes, Tryggr joined him.

"Found a way in yet?" Tryggr asked.

"Not yet, but I'm working on it," Jarl replied.

"I take it there's more than a few of them up there?" Tryggr asked as he looked up at the top of the cliffs.

"You could say that, yes."

"You already know I didn't bring a tent for her, so what do you want to do with her this time?" Tryggr nodded at Altene.

Jarl lowered the scope from his eye and frowned, irritated at having to interrupt his inspection for this. "We've been through this before, Tryggr. I don't care. She can share your tent again, or one of the other men's. The weather is mild; she can sleep outside—like we've all done for most of the trip. I don't care. Just take care of it."

Tryggr stood with one eyebrow raised. "You're sure you'll be fine with her pleasuring another man while you sleep alone in cold furs? And more importantly, you'll stay fine with it?" Tryggr asked, not wanting to make any assumption where a woman was concerned.

"I'm sure," Jarl said and resumed scanning the cliffs.

"Very well then." Tryggr shrugged in disbelief and turned away.

"And Tryggr. As soon as the camp, for what it is, is set up, send out two hunting parties to gather food. We might as well be eating better if we're not moving."

Nena glanced at the woman's weaving loom next to her. Though they had started at the same time, the woman had made ten times her progress with a far more intricate pattern than the simple rug Jalla had assigned to her. She watched the woman's shuttle fly between the upright warp strings, watched her efficiently batten down the newly delivered thread with the wooden comb-like reed, then shoot the shuttle back in the opposite direction after shifting the loom frames. She made it seem effortless.

Nena looked back at her own loose sloppy work. She couldn't understand it. This should be easy for her. Her mother had been renowned for the quality of her weaving, and Nena herself was dexterous with all forms of weapons. She and Jalla had both assumed she would be a natural at it, and Jalla had been ecstatic when she had voiced her interest to try that morning. An interest that had quickly waned. It was unbelievably boring. Nena had yet to put in a half a day and could barely stand to look at the tall frame. She had no aptitude for the unbroken focus required for the monotonous job. No matter how hard she tried, soon after starting, she found her thoughts drifting, while her body continued to awkwardly go through the motions.

She envied the young girls who had the job of beating the fleece with long forked paddles to separate the fibers for spinning. Even though it was a lower status job, at least they were moving and doing something. Standing still for hours was torture in itself, but worse was that she could not control her wandering thoughts.

How could her life that had seemed so full, so complete and on track before, feel so hollow? Her warrior days were over, or practically over, and the prospect of life as a tribal woman extended out before her now as interminable monotony. She would be expected to bear children, and many of them, and while the idea of remaining in the village rearing children had never sounded exciting to her before, now, after this time with Jarl, it seemed absolutely dismal. She found herself wondering if she could find the herb. She would recognize it now if she saw it growing. Altene always had a ready supply, so it had to grow freely.

Do not dare to think such things! The gods will be furious. You should want to have children with a Teclan warrior. It is natural.

Natural or not, Nena did not feel it. Altene's words echoed in her mind. "*While you are lying with your Dor husband with club hands, I'll be enjoying his touch.*" When Altene had first said it, Nena had thought the idea ridiculous. Now when she thought of Jarl's tenderness, of their passionate connection, then imagined herself with a stone-faced Teclan man, her stomach convulsed.

You could have such a relationship with Gentok. You do not know how he is in the privacy of his tent. Maybe he is sensitive and playful, too, after sharing furs. None of the other Northmen would have believed how Jarl was with you in private—that their strict warrior leader could have a side like that. You don't know—Gentok could be the same.

But Nena did know. Before her capture, she had listened to the women of her village talk in the baths about their private time with their men. Not one had ever described a man like Jarl. Nena closed her eyes and tried to will herself to clear her mind of the troubling thoughts and focus back on her task.

Fast approaching pounding hooves interrupted her deliberation. An outrider slid his lathered horse to a stop in front of her father's tent, its hooves leaving deep furrows in the soft ground. She watched the man leap from his horse, shout something through the tent opening, then hurry inside. His urgency was strange. Her father and the outrider exited together shortly thereafter and made their way to the council tent where another messenger was dispatched. Soon warriors from all over the village were joining them inside.

Nena knew she could still enter the council tent as a warrior, and though she was beyond curious, she didn't join the others she saw on their way. She would not hold that position for long; there was no sense becoming involved in that capacity now. She would choose Gentok today—would have chosen him already if he had not been on guard duty at the gates. She reminded herself this was the natural order of things, and that she needed to concern herself with more feminine pursuits from now on. She tried to ignore the excited activity, but the mysterious events unfolding inside the council tent beckoned her with far more appeal than the tedious task in front of her.

"There are Northmen at the cliff gates." A young man made the breathless announcement to the women in the weaving area.

"How many?" Jalla asked.

"Only a small scouting party," he replied.

"What are they doing? Are they trying to enter?" A woman holding a newborn baby asked nervously, her face tense with worry.

"No one knows why they are there. They have not yet tried to pass. They seem to be setting up camp there, just outside."

Nena's heart lurched. *Jarl.* She felt a sudden crazy urge to find a horse and race to join the cliff guards so that maybe she could catch a glimpse of him—to know for sure if it was he who was there. But what would be the point? Nothing had changed. Even if he had tracked her here, so what? He wouldn't be able to pursue her any further, and he would not be able to stay. Once he saw she was inside the gates, surely he would go.

Only dimly aware of the questions flying around her, Nena hung the thread shuttle on its hook on the side of the loom frame and walked toward the council tent. Feminine pursuits would have to wait. Lifting the flap to the council tent, she stepped inside. She heard her brother talking before she could see him. The excitement in his voice was unmistakable.

"What are we waiting for?" Lothor demanded. "We can easily wipe them out. I'll gather a group of warriors and we'll ride out right now and finish them."

"You will do no such thing," her father said.

"Why not? They are but few."

"You will send out scouting parties in all directions to confirm the Northmen's numbers, and to verify there are not more waiting somewhere else. This is not like them—more like one would expect from a trap."

"Yes, Father," Lothor deferred, but Nena could tell it took great effort for him to do so.

"Once we have that information, I'll make a decision." Her father paused, having seen her enter. "Good, your sister is present," he said. "Perhaps she can explain their actions."

"If it is a small group. I would assume it to be a scouting party sent to track me. I told you I feared pursuit when we escaped."

"But you said they were near the Great Sea. Why would they travel so far to retrieve two escaped prisoners?" Lothor asked.

"They knew I held a great ransom value. They were probably hoping to recapture us before we made it here."

Everyone nodded in agreement. It made sense.

"Once they see I have returned safely home, they should not stay."

"Then why are they setting up camp?"

"Our pace was very hurried. They will need to rest and gather supplies. After that is done, I would expect them to leave and return to the others. I often heard them discussing their trip back to their home in the north. They travel by rivers and must make it back through all of them before they freeze. Otherwise they will be trapped somewhere along the way. They were still ahead of schedule when I escaped, but every day that passes now, is precious time lost. They will have to leave soon or risk not making it home at all."

The first foraging parties brought back good news to the small Northman camp. The lands surrounding them were rich with game and wild vegetables. The river that trickled out of the canyon created lush meadows and thick stands of trees for miles until it reached the great plains. Such land could sustain even their full force for months, and with just the few of them, indefinitely.

Jarl concentrated on his primary order of business—to find a way in. He sent scouting parties to examine the Teclan defenses in both directions, then rode out himself to make his own observations and try to come up with a strategy. He knew they were too small a force to fight their way in through the cliff gates. Besides, if the legends were correct, that tactic hadn't proven successful for anyone with larger forces in the past. He needed a plan—an alternate route, a diversion, or some way to sneak past the guards. None was forthcoming. Every day the scouts returned with reports that mirrored the information he noted on his own forays. The jagged cliffs extended for miles in both directions. The mountain was an impenetrable fortress.

"How long are we going to stay here?" Tryggr asked one night after they had finished their meal of roasted grouse, steamed grains, and tender cattail shoots dug from the nearby muddy marsh. "Not that I'm in any hurry to leave," he added. "I must admit, since we stopped that insane pace, this has become an extremely pleasant respite for me. The food is plentiful. The work is easy and the nights are...relaxing." Tryggr leaned back and stretched. "If only we had some ale," he sighed. "Or some mead."

"You were the one in charge of packing," Jarl reminded him as Altene removed their empty plates.

"Your orders were to travel light. That usually doesn't mean ale."

"A lot of good that did," Jarl grumbled. "What did she beat us here by? A week?"

Tryggr didn't respond to Jarl's exaggeration. "Back to my original question. How long are we going to stay?"

"Until I get her back."

Tryggr nodded and pulled at his beard as he digested that information. "Well, we'll have to move camp or start sending scouts on longer trips to probe their defenses further away. They're dug in pretty tight here, and we've found no weak spot for miles in either direction. Maybe further around to the southwest," he suggested. "Or northwest, who knows." He shrugged. "It's just not going to be here." When there was no acknowledgment from Jarl verifying the wisdom of such a move, he continued. "Or do you have another plan? Perhaps you are hoping that by some miracle, out of that whole mountain she knows you are here and will take pity on you? Or is so in love with you that she will suddenly change her mind and come back?"

"She knows I am here," Jarl said.

"If you are certain of that, then...um...not to point out the obvious, but she isn't coming out, Jarl. That, when combined with how she ran here without pause to escape you in the first place—to me, might indicate she doesn't wish to see you. But perhaps you see it as a sign of something else?" Tryggr asked.

Jarl did not respond.

Tryggr scratched his head. "Do you intend to camp here and hope until you are gray? What has happened to you?" he asked his voice softer. "Look at yourself, man. You're acting completely irrational. This is not you. I've been your friend for a long time, and I'm speaking to you now in that capacity. I cannot say I understand what you are feeling, because honestly I don't have an inkling, but one thing is clear to me—she's not coming back to you. You must see that. Whatever you think you had with her, it was false.

"Look at the facts. At the first opportunity she left you. Then she rode so fast, even the gods themselves would have had a hard time keeping up with her. Those are not the actions of a woman who is unsure of purpose. She is lost to you, my friend. And all the hoping and waiting in the world isn't going to change that, nor is it going to reduce the number of warriors lining that ridge."

"Gratitude, Tryggr, for your counsel and for your loyalty. Know that I do hear you, but you are wrong about one important thing. She is not lost to me until she is dead—or I am—and maybe not even then."

Tryggr shook his head.

Nena stared up at the loom. Every morning she approached it with the same dread as one would approach a torture rack. She was sure the mental torture she endured throughout the day was no less than any physical torture she could imagine from its war counterpart. Nena glanced enviously again at the young women thrashing the fleece. They were sweating and exerting—and getting to pound something. She longed for a physical release. Every day the Northman camp remained outside the gates, the tension only built inside her. Every day she remained bound to this hated loom allowed no escape from her painful reveries. It had been hard enough to keep Jarl from her mind before, but now with Northmen being the only thing anyone talked about, it was impossible. It may have been easier, had she been able to choose Gentok as she had planned, but with the arrival of the Northmen outside the gates, he had yet to return.

Perhaps tonight she would take the mare for a long ride. She imagined herself galloping down a moonlit trail, far from the cliff gates where she might catch a glimpse of him—because she was sure now, it was Jarl who was there. Had it only been trackers who needed to rest, they would have left already.

So why didn't he go? Why did he linger? What did he hope to gain? He had to know by now he could not make it through their defenses—and that he was in danger. The Northmen force was small and in an indefensible position. Even a poor strategist could see that, and Jarl was a master. The longer he remained camped there, the greater the chance Lothor would win over her father—or worse, disobey him.

But Nena knew her desire for Jarl to leave was not based solely on fear for his safety. She needed him to leave and take her doubts with him. Doubts about her decision. Doubts about her future. Once she had returned home, all was to have been clear and right—as it was before, but that hadn't happened. Jarl needed to go to put an end to the inner turmoil and constant seesaw of her thoughts and emotions. So why did he not?

Her thoughts wandered down a new path. Did the memories of their time together choke Jarl's spirit as they threatened to choke hers? In many ways the idea appealed to her. It validated and almost excused her own embarrassing unacceptable feelings. It meant she wasn't weak. Jarl was strong enough to fight the gods, and yet he, too, was possibly having difficulty fighting this. The longer he stayed the stronger his feelings must be.

Or was there another explanation? A dark terrible explanation. Something she had never allowed herself to consider before—something that filled her with a deep uneasiness as she considered it now. What if Jarl had truly been the gods' choice for her? What if she had denied them and was being punished? It would explain the discontent she felt with her life and her future. What if he had come now and still remained because the gods had sent him for her? The idea was ridiculous of course, but what if....

"Some women were just not meant to weave," Jalla's resigned voice startled her from her thoughts. "I thought it would come naturally to you, because of your mother..." Her voice trailed off as she stood frowning at Nena's haphazardly loose excuse for a carpet. "But clearly it does not. You should not waste any more time here. Your calling clearly lies somewhere else."

"A large force is coming from the northeast, sir," the breathless scout announced as he burst into Jarl's fire ring area.

"The northeast?" Jarl asked as he stood. The Teclan cliffs were due west. "How many?"

"I don't know for sure. Many. Their dust extends for miles."

"Dust—so they're traveling fast." Jarl thought out loud. Was this some trick of Meln's to try to take them unaware? Would he assume their focus was on the gates and they would leave their flank unguarded? But why would he go to the trouble to send a large force whose movement would alert them? Jarl's men were few. If Meln wanted to kill them in a sneak attack from the opposite direction, he would not need to bring so many. But if not Meln, then who? Jarl knew of no other force of size in the area.

"Eskil went closer to see if he could identify them," the scout continued. "He shouldn't be long behind me. We split up, and I came straight here. We thought you'd want to know right away."

"Good work," Jarl acknowledged.

Jarl didn't wait for the second scout to return before giving the command to douse the fires and ready the camp's defenses as best they could. Maybe it was an army on its way somewhere else and would pass unnoticed. With the Bloodcliffs and Teclan warriors at his back, there was no retreat to the west. Until he knew who they were, he wasn't about to run further south. He had to see for himself. Jarl grabbed his scope and went to saddle his stallion. Tryggr soon joined him, and the the two men mounted and headed northeast toward the plains.

"What the hell?" Jarl swore as he lowered the scope from his eye.

"What is it? Whose banners are they?" Tryggr asked.

"They're ours," Jarl muttered.

"Ours?" Tryggr asked bewildered. "How?"

"We're about to find out." Jarl kicked his stallion into a gallop.

As Jarl and Tryggr descended from the hillside, Gunnar's sorrel broke away from the front of the long line of dusty troops to meet them. His blond hair was unmistakable.

"We're not too late, are we?" Gunnar called out to them. "Haven't missed the battle yet, I hope?" His voice was cheerful, but the weariness of a long double-time march was evident on his face as he rode closer.

"What are you doing here?" Jarl asked. "I gave orders for you to proceed to the port. Did you not get the message?"

"Yes, I got it, but I focused more on the part where you put me in charge in your absence." Gunnar grinned.

"Where are the prisoners and who is guarding them?" Jarl demanded.

"Relax. Halvard was able to find new trading partners for everything at half again more than our original expected price. We are all rich men, and Piltor is probably standing with cock in hand at this very moment wondering what happened. It is done. The payment is loaded securely on the ships and a contingent of men left behind to guard it. When I learned you were in need of assistance, and there was sport to be had, I hastened the time frame a bit."

"I appreciate the gesture, but this is not a fight I would ask another man to bleed for."

Gunnar shook his head, suddenly serious. "We all know the prize, and there is no man here who did not volunteer. We have followed you into worse...." He glanced at the imposing red cliffs in the distance and raised his eyebrows. "Well, perhaps not worse situations before, but we are not about to change now. If you are willing to risk your own life, then so are we. The gods have always favored you. "

"Speaking of the gods, please tell me you brought some ale," Tryggr interrupted him. "I have prayed to them for some every day."

"Ale? Of course I brought ale—and wine and mead. What kind of party would it be without those?" Gunnar laughed and slapped Tryggr on the shoulder.

Nena was just leaving the bath hut with Exanthia when the messenger came running up. "More Northmen have arrived outside the canyon walls," the messenger panted. "Your father requests your presence right away."

Nena handed her bath supplies to Exanthia. "Take these back to the tent for me. I will come back as soon as I am finished. Everything is alright." Nena smiled to reassure her, then stroked the back of Exanthia's wet hair. As soon as the girl moved away, Nena turned back to the messenger and nodded, her expression serious. He picked up a jog, and Nena matched his pace back to the council tent. She slowed her breathing as she followed him inside.

"A large Northmen force has joined the small camp outside the gates. They are sending multiple groups to the northeast and southeast sides of the mountain," one of the cliff guards reported.

"Are they trying to breach?" her father asked.

"Occasionally, but they are easily turned back. These Northmen do not have the stomach to fight."

"They are reconnaissance scouts," Nena interrupted. "They are not trying to breach. They are probing our defenses and reporting our responses back to their leader," Nena said, her voice grim. "They do this before every battle; then he decides the best way to attack." She thought of the many times she had heard those reports relayed to Jarl.

"Attack? Why would they return to do that? They avoided our lands the first time and were well past us. Why do they come back now?" someone from the crowd asked. "I thought you said they would have to leave. Not only did they not leave, now there are more of them—many, many more of them."

Nena's mind was racing. From the sounds of it, Jarl had moved his full force to the gates. He would not have done that for her. He would not risk so many of his men for a woman—a slave. Then why?

The answer hit her like a blow to the stomach. She was a fool. He had not come for her at all. His spirit was not being choked. The gods had not sent him. He'd come for the Teclan treasure—the treasure she had told him about. All this time, she'd been so concerned with her feelings for him and his possible feelings for her, she'd been blinded to his true purpose. She had told him of the wealth they possessed to try to entice him to ransom her back to her people, and now he was here to claim it.

She thought back to that night in his tent. How he had speculated out loud that all a man would have to do was take the Teclan mountain and he'd be wealthy beyond his wildest dreams. He had never mentioned it again in her presence, but he must not have believed her when she said it was impossible. This was all her fault. She'd given information to the enemy, and now her people would suffer for it.

"It doesn't matter why there are more of them here," Lothor shouted. "They could bring thousands, and thousands would die. We have nothing to fear. We should be thankful. Now we can kill them all and finally have our vengeance." Lothor paused, then continued, his voice slightly quieter, but still tight with excitement. "I have prayed for this. It is a gift from the gods. Not only will we not have to wait to avenge Ruga's death, but those directly responsible have delivered themselves to us and prepare to attack on our terms. It could not be better. The gods truly smile upon us."

"Yes," Meln agreed, though not with the same conviction.

"Of what do you worry?" Lothor was clearly puzzled and concerned at his father's lack of enthusiasm. "Why do you not give the order to attack?" he demanded. "Now, before they change their mind and leave?"

The fact that Lothor was unable to keep his disapproval in check, and openly questioned their father, revealed the depth of the discord that still smoldered inside him. Nena knew from his heated words with her before, that even though he had the highest respect for their father's battle insight and authority, he was very troubled by the change in him since his injuries. The change she had also noticed on her first day back. When the flame of that doubt was fanned by his deep, almost desperate desire for revenge, Nena feared what Lothor might do. For him to challenge her father now to lead the tribe, would tear it apart and leave them all weak and vulnerable. He had to know that.

But her father wasn't the only one who had changed; Lothor wasn't the same either. He himself recognized he was dangerously consumed by his hatred. By his own admission, he was not thinking clearly because of it. And if he did challenge her father, what would she do? Or the others? Where would they stand? Lothor would be the next chief. All knew and accepted that. But not yet. And not by coup. That could not happen until her father relinquished the position to him.

Nena glanced around the council and saw the unease on some of the other warriors' faces as they also recognized the potential for disaster in Lothor's next words. She was disturbed, however, to see eagerness on the faces of some who appeared to relish a changing of the guard. They were those closest to Lothor— Baldor, not surprisingly, was among them.

"I wish only to understand their motive, as you should also," Meln admonished him, seemingly unaware of the precipice on which they stood. "To know how hard an enemy will fight, you need to understand what they fight for."

It was basic warrior training, and even the youngest warriors knew it well. A single man protecting his family, or a mother protecting her child might be a dangerous opponent, while an army fighting for another's cause was often easily defeated.

Nena wrestled with her conscience and guilt. She had the answer they sought. She knew what the Northmen would be fighting for, and she also knew how powerful an incentive it was to them. The same drive for riches and conquest that drove them far from their homes year after year. When combined with their lack of fear—nay, their desire to die in battle, she knew they would be the most formidable adversary her people had ever faced. They would be relentless and merciless once Jarl gave the order. Her gut twisted. She should reveal what she knew. To withhold the information of why the Northmen were here and what they were willing to die for was dangerous for everyone if they did not take the threat seriously. She stood mute. She couldn't do it—not when she was the cause of it all. She couldn't stand to see them look at her with shame and disgust, like she was a traitor.

"They are stupid Northmen," Baldor shouted.

"They have not been stupid in the past," Meln reminded him.

"We must do something. If they remain camped there, we cannot leave to raid," Baldor added.

"They have never overwintered in our lands before," an older warrior said, joining the debate. "I believe Nena's words before to be true. They won't be able to stay. They must return to the North before the rivers freeze, or they will be trapped and not be able to make it home. They will have to leave soon."

"Then that means they will have to attack soon," Lothor said quietly.

Murmurs filled the tent as the warriors took this in.

Meln waited for the tent to become quiet, then spoke. "We have the tactical advantage and our priorities must remain with protecting our people and this mountain," he announced, taking control like the Meln of old, his tone brooking no argument. "Vengeance is secondary, and we will not risk all by venturing beyond our protection to have it. Have the elderly, the children, and the pregnant women prepare to move to the safety of the winter caves on short notice. Everyone else needs to prepare to fight. Lothor, triple the guards on the walls and station warriors behind the stones in the canyon. If the Northmen decide to attack, we will be ready. And station our fastest messengers along the trails. If reinforcements are needed, we need to know when and where as soon as possible."

"I have a suggestion for that," Nena offered, finally finding her voice, thankful the tribe was preparing for the worst without her having to reveal her own accountability. She briefly explained the Northmen's use of horns and whistles.

"Yes. I like that," Meln agreed. "If three men with horns were set up along the trail, they could pass the signal in seconds." He turned to Lothor. "See that it is done."

Lothor nodded. "After that, I'm going to the Gates," he said. It was not a request. "If the Northmen do decide to attack, I will be among the first to greet them."

Word spread quickly of the growing size of the Northman camp. As preparations were made for emergency evacuation and battle, the strain began to tell on everyone, but none more than Exanthia.

"They are coming for us, aren't they?" She whispered her fear to Nena one night as they lay in the darkness. "It's because we escaped, and they've come to take us back. This is my fault. Everyone is in danger because of me."

"Shh, shh," Nena soothed. She reached for the girl and pulled her under her own furs, wrapping her in a tight embrace. She understood how Exanthia felt. Her own feelings of guilt had plagued her since the moment in the council when she realized why they were really here. "It is not your fault and they are not going to take us," she reassured her. "You know what to do if the alarm comes?"

"Yes, I will go with Shia to the caves. But what about you and Jalla?" Exanthia fretted.

"If the alarm is sounded, we will be needed to fight."

"But I can fight, too."

"Not yet," Nena disagreed. "I know you are willing, but you must go with the others. Everyone has an important job to do and yours will be to help those at the caves. Belda will be there and she could have her baby any day. She will need someone strong to look after her. And besides, it will not come to that. We are safe here. You remember the tall cliffs we rode through? No enemy has ever passed through those gates—ever, in all of time, and many have tried. The Northmen are not stupid. They will see that it is certain death and they will leave. You'll see."

"But Jalla says there have never been so many before," Exanthia whispered.

"It doesn't matter how many there are," Nena said.

Exanthia squirmed to peer at her face.

Nena continued. "This is a valuable lesson on the importance of strategy in battle. With the narrowness of the cliff walls and the placement of the boulders, only ten can pass at a time. Do you understand what that means? It doesn't matter if there are a thousand or more, they are no stronger than the number of warriors who can fight at one time—in this case, that is ten. Our warriors can easily defeat ten. Gentok alone could probably take ten. Don't you think?"

"Easily," Exanthia agreed.

Nena knew the girl idolized Gentok. His gift of the bow and attention to her training had already earned him a special place in her heart. "Whenever you fight, if you look for an advantage, one can often be found. Deficits in strength, or weapons, or numbers can be overcome. Never forget that. Always fight smart."

"I will," Exanthia promised.

"Good. Now get some rest," Nena murmured.

Long after Exanthia had fallen asleep, Nena lay awake, trying to reconcile her own anger, frustration, guilt and fear. How could Jarl do this? After all his kind deeds and words of affection, how could he betray her this way?

Because this is who he is and what he does. And he is not at all unlike you in this way. It would be no different than if a foolish prisoner had given valuable information to the Teclan. Of course you would use it. And you would scoff at the one who gave it up so readily. The blame lies only with you. Altene was right. You are a naive fool.

The true source of your anger stems not from his actions at all, but because you allowed yourself to become soft toward him. Even after everything—your escape, your return home, your decision to choose Gentok, deep down when you thought he might be there with the scouts, you maintained those soft thoughts about him. Now you know the truth. He may have enjoyed you in the furs— even your company as he professed, but it meant nothing to him compared to the wealth of your people.

Now you must put all that behind you, once and for all, and focus on the business at hand. While the words you said to Exanthia are true, these Northmen are unlike any force the tribe has ever faced, and you know it—and not just because of their numbers. They are skilled fighters and far more organized than any who have previously tried to attack the mountain. And they are far more motivated; while others may have suspected the riches the Teclan held, Jarl knows of it—thanks to you.

Nena pushed the berating of her guilty conscience from her mind. Even though the Northmen posed a more serious threat than she had let on to Exanthia, the huge tactical advantage provided by the canyon was also true. So would Jarl still attack? She had never seen him risk the lives of his men needlessly before, but she'd also never seen him avoid a fight—except when he'd considered the prize to be too small. That was certainly not the case here.

He always came up with a strategy to best get around his opponent's strengths and defenses. But there was no way around the cliffs. Surely he would see that. And knowing the casualties to his men would be staggering, would he actually attack them? And if he did, would she meet him on the battlefield? If so, could she kill him? She envisioned his handsome face as the target past the tip of her drawn arrow. Even fueled as she was by her anger and frustration, her imagination hesitated to loose her fingers from the bowstring. What was wrong with her?

Laughter filled the Northmen's camp at all hours of the day and night. The men were rested and spirits were high. They had been a force to be reckoned with for some time, and to a man, they were confident in Jarl to find a way.

"What's so funny?" Jarl was on the way to his own tent but stopped and asked several of the men who were still laughing.

"Bjorg snuck out there a ways and introduced those savages to his new long bow," one chuckled. "Some young buck was up there dancing around and thought he'd take a piss off the rock in our direction. Bjorg showed him he better piss somewhere else."

"Did you hit him?" Jarl asked Bjorg directly, impressed that an archer could have that kind of range.

"Nah, but I scared him bad enough; he probably has a little piss on his sandals," Bjorg answered.

They all laughed again.

Jarl stepped away and looked at the Teclan sentries on the cliffs above. He wondered if Nena was among them, watching him. With their ranks swelled to near full force, Jarl knew they were an impressive sight. Was she frightened? Was Meln? Surely they had to realize that even with their huge advantage of the natural barriers, Jarl's numbers were such now that he could quite possibly overrun their defenses—could quite possibly succeed where no one had before. There would be massive casualties among his men, though strategically for the future, he could justify it. With the Teclan in place, he and other vikings had to go far out of their way to avoid them, adding many miles to their trips. But if the Teclan were gone....

Jarl knew he could sell it—actually knew he didn't need to; there was always the compelling detail of the sizable wealth the Teclan had amassed over the years, though Jarl still kept that particular fact to himself. He couldn't risk greed splintering his group by driving some to challenge his authority or act on their own. He glanced back at his men. They were seasoned fighters. Even with death likely for some in the near future, every day they waited and rested, their eagerness grew. They were ready. They wanted to fight, to kill, and Jarl knew their easy laughter now would be nowhere to be seen when he gave the order.

But if he took the mountain, what would he achieve? He would be a richer man—richer beyond his dreams if what Nena had said was true. But he already had more wealth than he could ever spend. Assuming he was one of the survivors, and Nena was as well—which he knew was a long shot, since he fully expected her to be among the front line of fighters—what would he have won? He would never truly have her after that. Not after murdering her family, her people. Any feelings she did have for him would be lost, never to be regained. And contrary to what Tryggr said, she did have feelings for him; he knew it. He'd felt it.

And what would he do if he saw one of his men about to deliver a death blow to her? Would he kill him—his own man? Jarl had gone over this, along with all the other dilemmas he faced, from every angle a thousand times— as many times as he had gone over the Teclan defenses. There was much to consider, but really there wasn't. While he waited for the last scouting party to return, Jarl made up his mind. He knew what he had to do.

Even though his large tent had been set up after Gunnar's arrival, Jarl chose to have the scout leader present the latest report outside under the stars. He glanced at all of his higher ranking men, seated tonight around the fire ring, while Altene moved silently among them, keeping their cups filled with wine.

Jarl's full mug remained untouched beside him. With his fingertips steepled in front of his lips and nose, he stared into the flames as he absorbed the latest report. This scouting party had just returned from the longest expedition yet to the northwest, but the scout leader reported much of the same. They had probed the Teclan defenses for many miles, but anywhere the terrain was even remotely passable, the Teclan were ready.

"We thought we found a spot," the scout said. "Instead of sheer cliffs, the hillsides are steep with a few scattered boulders that could provide us some cover. But after further inspection, even though it can be climbed by men on foot, it would be slow going. The Teclan could pick us off at their leisure. It's not nearly as heavily guarded as the gates, but it doesn't have to be."

"We are running out of time," Jarl said. "With everything you have seen, what, in your opinion, is our best option?"

"I think the best bet for a successful breach is still here at the cliff gates, even though it's the most heavily guarded. The terrain is flatter, and while it's only wide enough for ten men abreast, we could at least move with speed. And I think we'd have the element of surprise. With the reputation of the area, no one will be expecting us to attack here," the scout said.

"I agree," Gunnar said. "We could charge in one bull rush and carry double shields."

"But double shields would leave us no hands free for weapons," Tryggr disagreed.

"We would have no need of weapons, initially," Gunnar explained. "There will be no one to fight—at least not in the first part of the canyon; we can see in that far. And it would be a waste of time for our archers to try to shoot straight up in the air. The first row of ten men would carry weapons and a single shield to deal with any Teclan warriors we come across in the canyon. The rest would keep their weapons sheathed and use double shields to maintain a shield wall over our heads. The casualties would still be high, but the Teclan wouldn't be able to kill all of us. Many should make it through. Once through the gates, we'll drop the extra shields, arm ourselves, and regroup to move on their village. We don't have maps of the area, but it should be easy enough to find."

"I don't know." Tryggr shook his head, his face reddened from the wine. "These gates have a reputation for a reason. Perhaps there is more beyond that we cannot see, some obstacle that would prevent such a charge—a blockade further inside to slow or even stop us. If that was the case we'd be sitting ducks. Their archers would wreak havoc on us, double shields or no.

"And say we made it past the first round of their defenses, then what?" Tryggr continued. "Do you think that's all they have? Do you think we'll just march in and take their village? We'll be advancing blind, and they'll most likely have traps. These Teclan are not to be underestimated. They've known we were here from the beginning. They'll be ready for us. And they don't fight like any of the other Dor we've encountered. Hell, look at what one woman did to my ear."

"I disagree." The scout interrupted, shaking his head. "There would be no reason for them to have significant reinforcements beyond the cliffs. No army has ever made it past them before. And while I'm not saying they won't fight, they'll be disorganized, and we'll have the advantage. They're set up to repel an attack coming from in front of them—from outside the cliff walls. Once we are inside, they lose that advantage. Everything becomes equal. And unlike Tryggr, I'm not afraid to fight a woman." He raised his cup to Tryggr while the other men laughed. Tryggr's encounter with Nena was still a sore spot they loved to poke, but only when Jarl was present for protection.

"Why you little fuck. I'll show you afraid," Tryggr roared.

"That's enough. Everyone settle down," Jarl intervened. He turned to the scout. "Gratitude for your report and your opinions on the matter. I agree with you and Tryggr both. No matter what area we choose, some would make it through, but for the rest it would be a slaughter." Jarl's voice was filled with resignation. He had come to the same conclusion many times. "You may go now. Get some rest. And there's no need to send out more scouts in the morning. I've seen enough."

Thankful that Jarl had finally come to his senses, Tryggr breathed a sigh of relief. He drained the last of the wine from his cup and waved Altene off from refilling it, as all of the other men, except for Gunnar, stood and filed away. Leaning back, he waited for Jarl's next words, fully expecting for them to be instructions to break camp in the morning and return to the ships.

Jarl picked up his own cup and took his first drink of the night, then looked up at the three of them.

"Tomorrow morning, I go in alone," he said.

Chapter 24

Altene gasped.

Tryggr and Gunnar both stared at Jarl dumbfounded for many seconds before Tryggr exploded. "Are you out of your fucking mind? That's madness! These Teclan are not to be trifled with, Jarl."

Gunnar nodded in agreement.

"I know," Jarl said.

"You know? You know?" Tryggr spluttered. "That's all you can say? You would risk your life for this woman? Hell—not risk, there would be no risk. You would throw away your life for her? It's suicide, Jarl. Do I need to remind you, you didn't fall for some peaceful river tribe lass—one that we could go take back without receiving so much as a scratch. These are Teclan—the most brutal fighters in the land. What is your plan? You'll just go in and ask them to hand her over?"

"I don't know. I don't have it all figured out yet, but I'll let you know when I get back." Jarl smiled a small smile.

"You won't get back," Tryggr countered. "And if you did, it would likely be without a tongue, so I'd still never hear your tale."

"She's carrying my child." Jarl attempted to justify his rash decision.

"Oh, fuck that. You don't even know that for sure. And even if it were true, do you have any idea how many red-haired bastards I've left in our camp's wake? You don't see me chasing after their mother's skirts, do you? If you want a child so badly, live and make another. And if it must be a part Dor child—make one with her," he thumbed his hand at Altene. "She pleased you for a long time."

"She doesn't please me now," Jarl said.

"Fuck that," Tryggr repeated, grumbling under his breath.

"If I don't make it back, you'll have the helm of The Huntress," Jarl said to Tryggr.

"I don't want the fucking helm, Jarl. I've actually been thinking for some time now, it may be time to retire—to enjoy my golden years. A man can only fight, fuck and loot for so long and I think I've finally reached that point—well, at least for the fighting and looting," he corrected himself. "I used to laugh at those old bastards we left at pretty places along the way, but now I see their point. It might not be so bad to settle down in one place, drink pints of mead and have a woman look after me." He darted a quick glance at Altene. "No more saddle sores. No more wounds to heal. The only reason I've kept at it this long is to keep your bloody ass safe, and now you want to piss it away?"

"What do you think, Gunnar?" Jarl asked.

"I don't like it, but I don't have a better plan."

"I thought you liked the bull rush plan?" Tryggr turned his attack on Gunnar. "I had my own doubts about it, but it beats the hell out of this."

"The bull rush is still the best plan to get the army, or as much of it as possible, through their defenses, but that does not achieve Jarl's goal." Gunnar had come to Jarl's earlier conclusion. "In accomplishing that and taking their village, we might very well kill her in the process, or at the very least, kill those she knows and loves. Either way, Jarl loses."

"And what exactly do you think he'll win when he's dead?" Tryggr demanded, hurling his empty cup into the fire, sending up a spray of sparks.

"Peace," Gunnar said. The word hung on the air for several seconds before Gunnar continued. "Jarl will either succeed and have his woman back, or be in Valhalla. One way or the other, he will have peace."

"Don't do this," Altene whispered feverishly to Jarl after Gunnar and Tryggr had left. She clutched his arm. "Nena was not pregnant. I only said that because I thought you would not follow her. I lied to you."

"Or are you lying now?" Jarl asked quietly. "Can you swear to me with certainty she is not carrying my child?" It was still the only thing that made sense to him. The only thing that could have spooked her and made her change so suddenly. His heart could not accept anything else. Tryggr was wrong about it being false. He had felt it. He had felt their bond.

Altene paused while she recounted her last conversation with Nena, how she had withheld the herb, and her flippant words about Nena's last night with Jarl being unprotected.

"I thought not," Jarl answered for her.

"Then take me with you," Altene said.

"No. It's too dangerous."

"You will need a translator."

"No," Jarl repeated. "Besides you already told me they understand my language, and you were right."

"That is true, but you will not understand theirs, and you might need someone to explain their beliefs and laws. That is why you brought me along, isn't it?" she asked.

"That all sounds good, but I'm not anticipating this being a civilized affair where they allow me to represent myself and consult my counsel. I think it's going to be pretty straightforward. Besides, if they killed me, they would kill you, too. Would they not?"

"Yes, but…"

"The answer is no. You have helped enough."

The next morning Gunnar and Tryggr watched Jarl strip off his armor and pile it next to his sleeping furs. "Want it to be quick death, do you?" Tryggr asked.

"I want them to know I don't come to fight," Jarl replied.

"Oh, that's rich, Jarl. I hardly think they'll care. One man—even one fighting his ass off, will hardly worry them. And even if they do wait long enough to ask you your intentions before they kill you—which I doubt, what will you say? I didn't come to fight, just to take your princess, who I already molested and planted with my illegitimate child? That will be sure to sway them."

"This is all your fault, you know." Jarl turned to him.

"My fault?" Tryggr was incredulous. "How is any of this my fault? I've been the only one with the voice of reason since we started out on this whole thing. Hell, since you took her in the first place. I knew she was trouble."

"If you hadn't fought like a girl and allowed her to take your dagger and cut off half your ear, she would be yours, and I wouldn't be in this position." Jarl smiled and placed his hand on Tryggr's shoulder.

"Aye." Tryggr nodded, beaten. "And then maybe it would be me going willingly to my own death. Maybe then I would understand it."

"Gunnar?" Jarl turned to the other man. "You've been quiet."

"There is nothing I can say. I understand you have no choice. If I thought taking all the men would make a difference, I would argue. But I agree. Your plan has the greatest chance of success."

"And what chance do you think that is?" Jarl asked.

"Slim," Gunnar admitted. "Very slim."

"The Dor wench gives you only a fifty-fifty chance of them even taking you to the village alive. I give you less than thirty," Tryggr interjected.

"You're confidence is inspiring, Tryggr. Gratitude," Jarl joked.

"I'm not trying to inspire you, you damn fool, I'm trying one last time to talk some sense into you and save your ass."

"You can save your breath. My mind is made up."

Jarl could still hear Tryggr muttering behind him as he exited the tent. Standing in the full sunlight, he felt naked without the hard leather plate over his chest and back. It had saved him in many a battle. How would the gods see his act? As reckless? Would they view it as a taunt? That he felt himself more powerful than they? Would he even make it to the cliffs? Or would a winged death pierce him as he drew near. Jarl forced himself to stop thinking about it. He had made his decision. It was the only way. He turned to Altene who was waiting outside. "Any last advice?" he asked.

"The Teclan respect bravery and courage above all else," she said. "Show no fear. It is your only hope."

Jarl smiled wryly. "I'll try to remember that when they're tearing off my toes."

Jarl debated taking another horse instead of his stallion. If they did kill him, which he accepted was highly likely, he didn't want them to be better mounted for it. With his stallion and the mare he'd given Nena, the Teclan could produce a breed of horse that would only further escalate their dominance. He saddled the bay anyway. Maybe she was on the cliffs and would recognize the horse. Maybe it would stay her hand. Or maybe he just wanted his last minutes to be on a great warhorse. He was already naked without his armor; not having his horse would be too much.

Jarl mounted and rode through the silent group of men who had assembled to see him off. Some nodded, some saluted, but no one spoke. Jarl was disturbed to realize that was probably exactly how they would watch his funeral procession. He pushed the thought from his mind and rode the short distance through the no-man's land—the area between the two forces where neither could reach with their archers, except perhaps Bjorg with his new longbow.

When he reached the edge of the Teclan bow range, Jarl dropped the reins around the horse's neck. Raising his hands out to both sides to show he was unarmed, he guided the stallion forward with his legs. The last distance to the cliffs was agony. His skin tingled with the expectation of piercing pain with every step. His ears strained to hear the whir of arrow fletching on the wind. He could see the warriors on the ridge clearly now. Some were moving quickly. Others remained poised with their bows drawn on him.

As he entered the shadows of the narrow canyon, the temperature dropped several degrees. Jarl appreciated the fact that he was alive to feel the coolness. His senses were stretched. Everything was amplified. The gurgling of the gentle stream to his left seemed a roar. His stallion's soft footfalls pounded in the dust.

Within minutes he was surrounded by mounted Teclan warriors shouting in the Dor tongue. Jarl could not understand them, but their meaning was clear enough. He recognized the Teclan star on all of their arms and tried to look for other symbols Altene had taught him. But unlike the women who bore only a few life-identifying marks, these warriors' arms were covered with tattoos, documenting their battle prowess. His stallion screamed in warning at the jostling from the other horses. The animal was unaccustomed to being restrained from attacking any who came close in combat, but he obeyed Jarl's command and remained steady.

Jarl quickly evaluated his opponents out of habit, though he knew he would not fight. One heavier-muscled warrior was clearly trouble. He seemed more agitated than the others and continued shouting in their guttural tongue as he circled him. Jarl hoped he wasn't in command. As he passed behind him, Jarl focused on those he could still see in front of him. His eyes lingered on one in particular. This one was calmer, though his eyes were possibly even more fierce. His tattoos were the most extensive. Both arms were completely filled well up onto his shoulders. He was still trying to focus on them when he saw the shadow of the club swinging through the air behind him. Too late, he ducked.

When Jarl awoke, his first thought was to be thankful he was still alive. The throbbing in the back of his head soon made him question that. He tried to gather his wits. He was still in the canyon, lying on his side where he must have fallen after being struck from his horse. A Teclan warrior held the bay stallion off to one side. Jarl tried to sit up, but his hands were tied behind his back. Seeing his movement, one of the warriors jerked him to his knees and held him facing the calmer warrior with the extensive tattoos.

The warrior eyed him in silence while the others continued to shout words in Dor. It was clear they wanted to kill him, but required the approval of this man. That was when Jarl saw the symbol below the Teclan star on his arm. The symbol he had seen many times and knew so well. The lightning bolt. This warrior was the blood of Meln. Then he had to be Nena's brother, Lothor. Now that he was looking for it, Jarl could see the family likeness in their cheekbones and the shape of their eyes. From Altene's accounts, Lothor's reputation as a fighter was known far and wide—a fact supported by the extensiveness of his tattoos. Lothor held up his hand for silence. When it was quiet, he spoke in Jarl's tongue, though his face remained ruthless. "We'll take him to my father. He will decide how he dies."

Jarl was sure the change in language was not done out of any favor to him. It was to make sure he understood he was to die and could be terrified. But Jarl focused only on the fact that he had avoided death yet again. By his count, that was three times so far since he had left his camp. No arrow had pierced him. Being clubbed from his horse hadn't killed him, and now Lothor had chosen not to kill him here. While part of him was thrilled, another part cautioned against being too excited. Lothor had said *"father."* So Meln yet lived. While Jarl had never heard of Lothor before meeting Nena and Altene, he'd heard plenty of Meln, and they were not stories of Meln The Merciful. When combined with the fact that the others readily accepted Lothor's decision, and seemed only mildly displeased with the delay, Jarl knew it did not bode well for him. The chief must have other, more spectacular ways to kill a man.

A length of rope was attached to his lashed-together hands and then handed off to the large loud warrior, who Jarl had mentally nicknamed, Club. Jarl stood and moved closer to Club's horse, so as not to be jerked off his feet when the animal moved. With his stallion being led somewhere behind him, Jarl began the trek to the Teclan village on foot. His head was ringing, and he concentrated on placing every step carefully so as not to stumble. He knew that if he fell, they would not stop.

A small crowd met them at the outskirts of the village. No one spoke or made a sound. Jarl expected to be pelted with rotten food and stones amidst catcalls and spitting, but they only stared at him. He searched every face, but Nena was not among them. The procession stopped outside a large tent. Club dismounted and shoved Jarl through the doorway. The air inside was thick with smoke, and Jarl struggled to focus in the darkness. The walls were lined with warriors. He was led to the center before being forced to his knees facing an older man on a dais.

By their extent and shape, Jarl recognized the hideous sunken scars across Meln's temple and right eye to be the work of a battle-axe. The fact that the scars were still reddened and fresh led him to assume the wounds had come from one of his men when Nena had been captured and her younger brother killed. Yet another thing not in his favor. Lothor stepped up and stood before his father, then began to speak in Dor, but the chief stopped him and ordered him to use the Northman's tongue. They were at least polite about their mock trials, Jarl acknowledged. It was more than he had expected.

"We have captured this Northman trying to pass through the cliff gates," Lothor reported.

"And the others?" Meln asked.

"At the time we left, they remained in their camp. I have increased the guard again, just in case," Lothor said.

"Good," Meln acknowledged.

"We brought him to you for you to decide how he is to be killed."

Meln nodded.

"I would speak with Nena," Jarl interrupted their interchange.

Angry shouts filled the room, and even Meln's face twitched with rage. A blow to the side of his head knocked Jarl to the dirt floor. It disoriented him for a moment, but he was thankful to discover it had missed the back of his head and the previous injury.

"You do not speak her name, northern dog," Club spat.

"I would speak with Nena," Jarl repeated as he slowly regained his kneeling position. "*Show no fear,*" Altene had warned.

The chief raised his hand for silence and studied him with his single shrewd eye. "Nena should be here for this," he said. "Someone find her."

"I will go." A tall warrior who had been in the group that met him in the canyon, volunteered, then left the tent.

"Until Nena arrives, I would hear suggestions on the manner of his death," Meln said and looked to the crowd.

The room came alive with suggestions as to what would be the most appropriate. As a viking, Jarl was no stranger to torturous deaths, but even he was surprised by their creativity on the subject. No mention was made as to whether or not he was guilty, or even what his crime actually was, but they were all more than ready to kill him.

Lothor asserted that no matter what method was decided, it should be delivered by his own hand. Others also requested the honor. Someone suggested that Nena be allowed to kill him to avenge her captivity. Then Club suggested that he not be killed at all—that he should be mutilated, then castrated and made to serve, the most severe form of punishment known to the Dor.

That seemed to appeal to Meln, who had spoken not a word since asking for suggestions. "To live a eunuch is far more shameful than to die a man," he concurred.

Word had spread like wildfire through the village that a Northman had been captured. There had been no alarm or report of an attack, so Nena was sure it was one of the many foot soldiers sent to probe their defenses—one who had gotten too close and would now pay heavily for it. She chose not to attend his questioning and certain death. She did not need to see it. She was still wounded from the realization of why Jarl was really there—still embarrassed by her foolishness to have ever thought he was there for her. She would not make that mistake again, and would distance herself from any further decisions pertaining to the Northmen.

Instead she sat today with several other women, preparing hides for tanning, her latest attempt to find her calling. Everyone was on edge, but work still needed to be done. It was a tedious chore, scraping off the inner layers of fat and sinewy tissue with a dull knife. And no matter how careful she was, the smelly tallow had a way of coating her dress and skin by the end of the day. But even that was better than weaving. At least here she could take her frustrations out on something. She felt one of the other women's eyes on her and looked down at the hide she was working on. In her fervor she had come dangerously close to scraping clear through it. She moved her blade to a fresh area.

Nena tried not to dwell on the fact that this was what she had to look forward to from now on. She had yet to see Gentok to give him the news. With the arrival of the main Northman army, and the increased guard at the cliffs, he had still not returned. So when he called her name now, it startled her.

"Nena. Your father requests that you come to the council immediately."

Nena stood at the urgency in his voice and nodded. Gentok led the way through the village in silence, his pace brisk. Her news would have to wait.

"Is it about the captured Northman?" she asked.

"Yes," Gentok replied without slowing.

Nena couldn't help but wonder what this Northman could have possibly said or done that would require her presence before he was killed. Did he bring a message from Jarl? It couldn't be that. Neither her father nor brother would have honored the request of an enemy to deliver a personal message. Had he mentioned coming for the treasure? Did her father wish to confront her about her shameful disclosure and force her to confess? But it couldn't be that either; Gentok had not looked at her with accusing eyes. She reined in her guilty thoughts. She would know soon enough.

They were just outside the council tent when she heard it, the scream that set every nerve in her body on edge. Her eyes whipped to the small group of warrior horses off to her right. There they discovered the young man attempting to hold the raging bay. Nena would have recognized the horse anywhere. The stallion screamed again.

Nena stumbled and stopped.

But that would mean….

The Northman in the tent had to be….

Her mind reeled. But how? There had been no battle for him to have been captured. And they had said a lone Northman, which implied a scout. Jarl was never a scout. Gentok shifted his weight impatiently at the entrance, a curious frown on his face. Nena struggled to regain her composure, thankful, at least, for the warning and the opportunity to do so before being blindsided by his presence in front of the council. With her insides a swirl of emotions, but her face once again as blank as she could manage, Nena nodded and followed Gentok inside.

Chapter 25

When the tent flap lifted and all eyes turned toward it, Jarl did the same. At first the bright sunlit backdrop only allowed him to make out that there were two figures. The first was male. He dismissed it. The second set his heart pounding. Her tall, lithe silhouette and the way she moved with supple athletic grace were unmistakable. Every step she took revealed more subtle details in the dim light. First, the hint of tan color in her leather dress. Then her hair, darker than the rest of her, that still remained in shadow. She was like a goddess stepping from the smoke. Finally he could see her. His eyes devoured her. If he was soon to die, which it appeared that he might, it would at least be with the fresh image of her in his mind to take to the afterlife. She was so breathtakingly beautiful.

Pain exploded in his head as another blow, this time closer to the original mark, slammed him face down to the dirt.

As Nena entered, she saw Jarl kneeling to her right with Baldor standing behind him. She did not acknowledge him, and walked to stand equidistant from her father only a few strides away. Using her peripheral vision, she first noted the blood trickling from the back of his neck, then his lack of armor.

How was he alone and wearing no armor? Why? Did he think he could negotiate for the treasure? No. He would know better than that. She had told him the Teclan did not negotiate. So what then? Why would he leave his army and offer himself up like a sacrifice? Unless....

But that couldn't be. She had spent the last days convincing herself of her foolishness for harboring such thoughts. She was loathe to go there again. But it was the only explanation. He had not come for the treasure. He had come for her. In a move as bold as fighting the gods for her when she was dying, he had come for her!

Knowing the why also made the how of his presence crystal clear to her. She knew him. He had probed their defenses and had run out of time as she had known he would. When he could find no acceptably safe way in, he had not risked the lives of his men. She felt his eyes on her—felt her body respond to his presence, even with the distance that separated them and the humbling position he was in. She reveled in the feel of the connection between them— until Baldor clubbed him to the floor.

It took all of Nena's training and self control to deny the sudden protective rage that engulfed her. To not scream and fly across the room and rip the club from Baldor's hands before using it to bash his head in. Jarl lay unmoving on the floor. Was he dead? Nena wanted to run to him, but knew she dare not. The rush of mixed emotions, so strong and unexpected, left her shaken and confused. But one thing she remained sure of. To every other soul in this room, Jarl was their enemy—possibly their worst enemy. To show anything but coldness toward him now would be unacceptable and dangerous for them both.

"That will teach you not to lay your lustful eyes on her, northern dog," Baldor gloated.

For many seconds, Jarl could not move. Altene's words echoed in his mind. *"The Teclan respect bravery and courage above all else. Show no fear."* He struggled to get back to his knees, the pain in his head having long since replaced any fear he might have had. Nena had turned from her father and was looking at Club now.

"And to which warrior goes the honor of such a bold capture?" she asked.

"It was I," crowed Club.

"It must be a great warrior's tale to have avoided all sentries in the dead of night and returned unscathed with a Northman prisoner. It had to have been in the dead of night, was it not? That is, of course, the only time he would have been without weapons and wearing no armor. Did you sneak past their guards and put a knife to his throat as he slept, or did you kill them first?" Nena challenged, knowing it was neither.

"No. The coward surrendered himself to me." Baldor turned to the crowd and tried to win them back. "He saw how fearful we were and surrendered without a fight."

"He left his camp and surrendered to you, with no weapons and wearing no armor? What a great feat. Hopefully it wasn't too difficult for you. You must be sure to mark that on your arm." Nena turned back to her father, satisfied she had discredited him and knowing that would hurt him as much as any physical blow she could have delivered. "What is it my father asks of me?" Nena asked, bowing her head slightly, while the crowd snickered and Baldor gurgled with rage.

"Perhaps his capture was not worthy of recording, but his death will be!" Baldor shouted.

Nena spun back in time to see Baldor raise his club for the final blow. Her words had so incited him, Baldor was going to kill Jarl!

"Stop, Baldor!" She heard her father command, but it was too late; Baldor's club had already begun its descent. Nena could only watch with helpless horrified dread as the club reached the back of Jarl's neck. A blur tackled Baldor in mid body. The club still struck, but was deflected and did not hit with full force. Jarl fell limp as Baldor and his attacker tumbled to the dirt floor.

The tent erupted in chaos. Jarl remained still.

"How dare you!" Lothor raged from on top of Baldor, his dagger blade held tight against Baldor's throat. "How dare you try to steal my rightful honor? I could kill you for the insult."

Nena prayed he would do it. Prayed he would do what she wanted so desperately to do, but could not.

"Enough!" Meln roared as he stood and pounded the dais with his staff. "You will cease this madness immediately!" His entire face was beet red, and his fresh scars now had a purplish hue. "Anyone who cannot conduct themselves with honor will lose the privilege to be here. Do I make myself clear?" Meln shouted.

The room grew eerily quiet as all faces turned to him. Lothor withdrew the blade from Baldor's neck and both men stood. Meln looked around the council tent, meeting the eyes of each member for emphasis, then took a deep breath to compose himself before resuming his seat. "Does the Northman yet live?" he asked.

Before anyone else could respond, Nena sprang to Jarl's side and felt his neck for a pulse. His heart still beat, even and strong.

"Yes, Father," she said, trying to disguise her relief.

"Take him to the cell and guard him closely," Meln commanded. "Not you," he said to Nena as he saw her preparing to ask others for aid. "Not any of you three." He waved to Lothor and Baldor.

Gentok stepped forward and knelt across from her, preparing to grip Jarl's shoulder. When Nena did not vacate his other side for someone else to do the same, their eyes met and locked over Jarl's prone body. Gentok's gaze was curious as he studied her. Nena stood and stepped aside, wondering what he had seen. Everything had happened so fast. Her feelings were so tumultuous and confused, she had no idea what her eyes had revealed to him. She watched as Jarl was lifted by his shoulders between the two men, then dragged from the tent, the toes of his boots leaving twin trails in the dust.

The trio stood before Meln with their heads bowed. "Your behavior and utter lack of restraint is a disgrace. You dishonor yourselves and you dishonor me." He turned his attention to Lothor. "You shame me with a brawl in my own council tent? I had thought to soon turn the mantle of chief over to you, but your rage so consumes you, I fear I can no longer trust your judgment. Your display here today only deepens my doubt."

"And you." Meln turned to Nena. "You are not without fault. You insult a fellow warrior in front of his brothers? In front of me?" His voice rose again at the thought of her ridiculing verbal assault on Baldor. Meln paused to take another deep breath. "Do you recognize the Northman?" he asked her.

Did she recognize him? In every way possible. By sight, by sound, by scent—by touch. She would know him anywhere. "Yes. His name is Jarl. He is the leader of the Northmen."

A murmur rippled through the council tent. "Their leader?" Meln said, and sat back as he contemplated the significance of her words.

Nena did not speak. She knew he was thinking that Jarl must have come to negotiate something important. She couldn't tell him, that like the Teclan, the Northmen negotiated with their swords, not their words. Thankfully her father didn't ask her what she thought it might be. Instead, he turned his attention to Baldor.

"Perhaps you can tell me why the leader of the Northmen is here, Baldor, since I can hardly question a man who is not conscious. Did he come here to negotiate? Did he come to make offer of something? You must know the answers, or you would not have dared to dispatch him. So tell me, why is he here?"

Baldor shook his head and remained staring at the floor.

"You respond to insult with rage, like some novice warrior with no training. Then you take it upon yourself to make sentence on my prisoner and execute it as if you were chief? Remove yourself from my sight. I will let you know your punishment later. You are fortunate the cell is occupied or you would find yourself there this night."

Meln leaned back and brought his fingertips together under his chin, then turned to address the other council warriors. "I will delay my decision on the manner of his death until I hear what the Northman has to say. Send word to me as soon as he awakens. In the meantime, I will consult the gods. This council is adjourned." He stood on the dais and dismissed the meeting.

Nena stood in the trees for many minutes, staring at the cell. The lone clay and thatch hut in the center of the clearing was a forbidden place for children, though she'd been in it twice as a child to satisfy a dare. Ruga and Lothor had each spent a night there in chains, on her father's orders, to show them what imprisonment would be like if they were ever captured. In an uncharacteristic soft decision, he had not ordered Nena to also experience it, but the looks on both of her brothers' faces when they returned had made a significant impression on her. Even now she felt the fingers of apprehension squeezing her stomach, though it was nothing compared to the apprehension she felt to face who was inside.

Nena took a deep breath and stepped out of the trees to walk the last distance. A guard stepped out of the shadows as she drew near. It was Gentok.

"I have brought water for the prisoner," she said, without meeting his eyes.

"Set it down. I will give it to him later."

"Is he awake?" she asked.

"I don't know. I've heard no sounds and have not looked inside since we brought him here."

"My father has expressed his wishes to be notified as soon as he awakens. I would check on him," Nena said.

Gentok did not move from in front of the door.

"My father did not order no access to the prisoner, Gentok," she asserted, and wondered if he would be so reluctant to allow anyone else to pass.

"He said 'guard carefully'. It was implied," Gentok responded.

"Do you think I would try to free him?"

"Of course not," he said as if the idea was ridiculous and had not crossed his mind. "He may try to harm you."

"I know him. I will come to no harm at his hands."

Gentok's expression hardened.

"Gentok, this man saved my life. I would have words with him."

His face grew hopeful. She knew he took her words as explanation for any feelings he had seen in her eyes before. Owing a life was an acceptable excuse. He took a deep breath, and Nena could see he was wavering.

"You'll be right here," she coaxed. "If I need any assistance, I will call you."

"Very well." He pushed open the door and stepped aside.

As Nena entered the cell, she was relieved to find Jarl sitting up, leaned against the center roof support pole that he was shackled to. She glanced around the room quickly to familiarize herself with it. There were no windows. The only furniture was a chair and small table near the doorway. She knew Jarl's chain would not allow him to reach either. They were not put there for the comfort of the prisoners, but for their interrogators. She moved forward with the waterskin to offer him a drink.

"You are the last person I expected to see," Jarl gasped, after he had drained half of the waterskin without taking a breath.

"No one else will tend you," she murmured.

"Are they afraid? You can assure them I am quite secure." Jarl held up his bonds. "So what happens to me now?" he asked.

"I don't know. My father consults the gods."

"Will you put in a good word for me?" he teased.

"It would not matter," she murmured. "You should not have followed me."

"You should not have run."

Nena did not respond, only offered him the waterskin again.

He took it, then chuckled when he had finished drinking the rest of it.

"What could you possibly find amusing?" she asked.

"I was just considering the irony of my being chained to a pole as your prisoner, much as you were mine."

"It is not at all the same. Both cases were brought about by your own actions. I did not capture you and bring you here."

"No, you did not," he agreed. "I came of my own free will, but make no mistake, you have captured me in other ways, and that makes it no less your fault."

She wondered how much of the exchange Gentok could overhear. The walls were thick with a solid wood cage frame underneath. The clay and grass plaster mixture between the bars should muffle most sounds, but the door was only made of thin slat wood.

She held up her finger to her lips and nodded toward the door, but Jarl shook his head. "Let him hear. Let them all hear, and know why I've come. If I have my way, they will all know soon enough." He paused. "You could release me, you know."

"I think not." Nena shook her head.

"I won't go anywhere. It's not like when I held you prisoner. I chose to be here."

"Except that now you know you will probably die."

"Do you think I did not know that before I came? I'm actually more than a little surprised to still be alive now," Jarl admitted.

"Then why are you here?" she whispered.

She seemed confused and more than a little miserable, or was that just his wishful thinking? Jarl couldn't be sure. "You know why," he said softly.

The intensity in his eyes trapped and held hers. She could not tear her gaze away. Her heart skipped a beat and then began to thump wildly in her chest.

"Or perhaps you don't, so I will speak plainly, to ensure there is no further misunderstanding between us. I came because I am in love with you. I think probably from the first moment I saw you holding that oversized sword against Tryggr and the other men, but confirmed when you chose me—and further cemented every time we lay together from that point on. Because you fill my thoughts every waking moment, and the thought of life without you is not a life I care to live. I love you."

Nena could not hear these things from his lips. It had been one thing to wonder about them, when he was camped far below, to make herself feel better about her own feelings and doubts, but not for them to be so real that he would sacrifice himself for her. She was desperate to change the subject. "The Teclan do not have this word," was all she could come up with.

"Surely the Teclan have a word for love."

She shook her head.

"If a Teclan woman does not always marry the man of her first choosing, or if she does and he dies, how does she choose her next husband? How does she choose one over another when it is not the gods' choice? Does she not base that decision on love or strong feelings?" Jarl asked.

Nena knew that should be an easy question for her; she had faced it so many times lately. But if the answer was simple, then why had choosing been so difficult? She shared none of this with Jarl and instead said, "She looks at many things and chooses a man who can best provide for her—one who is a good hunter or who is a great warrior and will return to her from battle. Or sometimes she chooses one who has status and will elevate the status of her children."

"I am all of those things," he whispered, his voice intense. "I have jewels and gold and I am the leader of my people. I am a great hunter, and I have returned from many, many battles. I will match myself against any Teclan warrior, right now, to show you."

"You are not Teclan."

"Neither were the men competing for you in the tournament on the plains."

"But they were Dor."

"In what way am I different? You gave me the criteria a Teclan woman would use to choose a man, and I meet all of them—and have offered to prove it to you."

"You are in no condition to fight. Let me look at your wounds. " Nena changed the subject again. Jarl surprised her by not declining, and she moved around to kneel behind him. He tipped his head forward as she parted his thick chestnut hair with her fingers to reveal the three swollen gashes. She took off her sash and shook the last drops of water on it from the waterskin, then began to clean away the dried blood, thankful for something other than his words to focus her spinning thoughts on.

Jarl held very still, reveling in her nearness. Her touch on the areas where he'd been clubbed was painful, but her being so close to him and not touching him anywhere else was excruciating. "You say you do not have a word for love, but when a warrior is killed, what does his wife do? Or if a wife dies, how does a Teclan man react?" Jarl asked.

"You speak of the spirit sickness."

Jarl smiled. "I suppose many would agree that love is an affliction. Tryggr certainly would. Has it never happened that a Teclan felt the spirit sickness so strongly they could not go on living?"

Nena knew he had worked her into this trap much as she had done Baldor in the council tent. "No one dies from spirit sickness. It's not a true illness." Even as she said it, she wondered if it were true. Lornel had refused to eat or drink when her husband was killed and soon joined him in the sky. And Pragdor, a great warrior, had allowed himself to be slain in battle, by a far lesser foe, after his wife died in childbirth. No one spoke of those things, but they all knew.

"That is what I feel for you," Jarl said. "That is why I will not escape. I have nowhere to go where the spirit sickness will not follow."

Nena finished and moved back around to face him. She knew she should leave, that her father was waiting for a report, but she couldn't go.

Jarl could see she was upset, but could not read her to know for sure why. He pressed her further. "If you do not believe my words, or they are not enough, remember one important thing. You chose me. And through that choice your gods revealed their will. Your gods chose me for you, Nena," he continued softly. "So how can you defy them now?"

Nena wanted nothing more than to flee the hut. He could not be right. Yet even she had once wondered the same. And if he was wrong and her choosing him had been only to allow her to escape, why had she balked at choosing a Teclan warrior once she was safely home? Why did her body, even now, yearn for his touch?

"I must go...to tell my father you are awake. He wishes to speak to you. He wants to hear why you are here from your own mouth."

"I will not lie," he warned, trying to gauge her response.

"I know." Nena nodded and turned to leave.

In a sudden move that set his shackles rattling, he grabbed her arm. "Will you return?"

She nodded. "Yes. I will bring food and some ointment for your wounds...." Her voice trailed off as something occurred to her.

"You mean if I am still alive?"

Nena nodded as she stumbled for the door, unable to trust her voice to answer him. Gentok was waiting for her.

"Nena," he said.

"Not now, Gentok," she said in Dor and pushed past him. "I must find my father and tell him the Northman is awake."

———————————•◆•———————————

Nena stood frozen outside her father's tent, unable to enter. Her steps there had been in a daze. Her father would have him killed. She knew that. She didn't know how, or when, but she was certain of that fact. Nothing Jarl could possibly say would change it. Certainly not the truth of why he was there—that he'd come for her and couldn't live without her.

Her mind drifted. He had come for her. Not the treasure. It had never been the treasure. She was shocked by his confession of love and what he was willing to risk for her. But that just made it all the worse. What did he think could possibly happen now?

Nena stared at the flap to her father's tent, trying to compose herself, then lifted it and stepped inside. The tent was empty. Her father must still be consulting the gods. She chastised herself for the flood of relief she felt at the delay in hearing Jarl's sentence.

Nena made her way to the bend in the creek in the Meadow of the Idols, where her father took his morning tea, but he was not where he normally sat. Perhaps he had already decided Jarl's fate and had returned to the council tent. She couldn't go there—not yet. She wasn't ready to hear her father's decree or face the joyous, raucous response of the tribe's warriors to his decision.

She wandered among the idols, trying to sort through her tortured jumbled thoughts, still reeling from Jarl's words and her own feelings. Her response to Jarl, first in the council and later in the cell, had been instantaneous and undeniable—as natural as when they had shared his tent after she had chosen him. There had been no trying, no searching for feelings or physical reactions that weren't there. Their connection had been immediate.

Her father would have him killed.

Jarl had offered up his life for her. He was willing to die because he loved her. He had saved her life. The gods had chosen him for her.

Her father would have him killed.

Her feelings didn't matter. Jarl's feelings didn't matter. None of it mattered. She was Teclan. He was the enemy. Her father would have him killed. Her mind raced in the same circles.

"Nena? Is that you?" Her father's voice startled her. She hadn't noticed him seated at the base of the large moss-covered monument to her left.

"Yes," she said.

"Come join me. The gods have not yet seen fit to give me an answer. Perhaps they have questions for you."

"Apologies, Father. I fear I have no answers, only questions as well."

"Have you been to see the Northman?" he asked.

"Yes."

"Is he awake then?"

"Yes."

"Did he speak to you?"

She nodded.

"Why is he here? Does he bring some offer?"

Nena hesitated. There was no sense withholding anything. Even if Gentok had not overheard them, Jarl had made it clear he would tell anyone who would listen. "He is here for me."

Her father rocked backwards and sat in stunned silence while he considered her words and their implications, then thought back through everything that had transpired. "A man, especially a leader, does not risk everything for a slave prisoner—even a very valuable one." He eyed her carefully. "So he is the one who held you captive?"

Nena nodded.

"And is he also the one the gods chose to be your first union?"

Nena could only nod again.

"That is irrelevant and changes nothing. The reasoning behind the gods' choice is often impossible for men to understand. It could have been something as simple as the gods intent to lure him here for us to kill him. Or it could have been..." His voice trailed off. He could clearly think of no other reason—at least none he was willing to voice. "You are Teclan and he is Northman. He is the enemy," he said with finality.

"I know. I told him that."

"And what did he say?"

"He asked me how a Teclan woman chooses a warrior to marry after the gods' choice. I explained to him that the man must be a good provider, a good hunter, a great warrior."

Her father nodded in agreement.

"He said he is all of those things," Nena murmured.

After a moment of consideration, her father shrugged. "I suppose he is right—in a way. But it is no different than if he was lion and you were wolf. Both are fierce powerful hunters, yet they are not compatible." He dismissed the idea without another thought. "What else did he say?"

Nena's troubled frown returned.

"He said he would match himself against any Teclan warrior to prove it."

"He would be killed, of course," her father said with no hesitation.

"Perhaps, but he is also a great warrior. His people say he is favored by their gods."

"Maybe that is the answer, then."

"What?" Nena felt sick.

"If his gods truly favor him, and he is willing to fight to prove it, then fight he shall."

"Who?" Nena whispered. She prayed her father would say Baldor. Baldor had taken credit for Jarl's capture. Baldor was their largest warrior and an impressive fighter, but Nena knew Jarl could defeat him. Jarl had defeated Tryggr, who would make even Baldor look small. She willed the name Baldor to be the next word that passed through her father's lips.

"Lothor, of course," he said. "He is your only remaining brother, and he longs for such an opportunity to avenge Ruga. Perhaps this will finally satisfy the blood-lust that fills him."

Her father never considered, even briefly, that Lothor could lose. He was undefeated. But so was Jarl, as far as she knew. Not that any of that mattered now. Only one would remain undefeated after this match because only one would still be alive. It would be a fight to the death.

Chapter 26

Nena left the Meadow of the Idols and made her way to the horses, seeking solace from her tormented thoughts in the mare's warm energy. She buried her face in the horse's thick mane, inhaling the warm earthy horse scent. She could feel the animal's steady strength, but it was not enough this time to calm her.

She needed to force the chaotic thoughts from her mind. She didn't have time to sort through them now or to try to determine the true root of her feelings. She had to focus on saving his life. The answers to all of her questions were irrelevant anyway, as her father had pointed out. She was Teclan. Jarl was Northman. Lion and wolf. Equals but enemies. They could never be together. She had to accept that and instead address the impending predicament that faced them.

She could not allow Jarl to be killed. And she could not allow him to kill her brother. This trial by combat could not happen. She must find a way to free him and spirit him away back to his troops. The Northmen had not been able to find a way in, but Nena knew where the weaknesses in the Teclan defenses lay. She knew every hidden game trail—where every sentry was located. She could get him out safely.

There would be punishment of course. Anyone so blatantly defying the chief's direct order, even his daughter, would be punished, but she could take it. She was strong. She was the daughter of Meln. There would be a physical penalty, and then most likely a period of shaming, but that would pass. She would survive. If Jarl remained here—either he, or her brother, would not.

The one glaring flaw in her plan soon became apparent. Assuming she could convince Jarl to escape in the first place, something that was far from guaranteed, what good would it do? He had made it clear he was here by choice. He would not stay away. After she was punished, she would never be allowed in a position to help him a second time. They would end up right back here where they started. It would all be for naught.

She had to find another way.

"Nena, I would have words." Gentok's voice surprised her. It was the second time in one afternoon that her thoughts had so consumed her, she had allowed herself to be approached unaware.

"Apologies, Gentok, but I do not have time right now."

"You seem to have nothing but time—and I insist."

She was about to protest, but then nodded and waited for him to proceed. His face was agonized as he sought for the right words. She could see how difficult he was struggling to reconcile what he had always known and felt for her, with what he had overheard.

"Just say what you have come to say, Gentok," she said, resigned.

"You told me you wished to see him, and that he would not harm you because he had saved your life. I assumed he was the one who helped you to escape. I even went so far as to think that maybe that was why he was sent here unarmed—as punishment for helping you. I thought all kinds of things a normal person would think. Then I hear that he is actually the one who held you prisoner? That he is the one the gods chose to be your first? I was just about to step inside the cell to stop you from killing him, but I hesitated—torn between whether to obey your father's command, or to allow you to have your well-deserved revenge. I was sure that had to be why you had come...until I heard the last part... that you...you...chose him? ...and then continued to lay with him willingly?" The idea of it was clearly so shocking and unbelievable that he still had great difficulty accepting it.

"You listened to us?"

"You made no attempt to lower your voices," he defended himself. "And trust me, I would prefer not to have heard."

"Who have you told?"

"I would never betray you," he said, his voice pained. "I have not shared your words with anyone, nor will I. Not even your father, if you do not wish it. But everyone will know soon enough. The Northman will make sure of it. The only way to keep that from happening is if he is forever silenced. I will kill him for you and make it look like he died of his injuries from Baldor—that his wounds were more severe than first thought."

"No! You must not. Swear to me now, you will not harm him," Nena insisted.

"Nena?"

"Swear it to me."

"I will swear it only if you will swear to me that you will not do something stupid—not try to help him escape or whatever other ideas you are thinking."

She looked at him blankly. *Could he read her mind now?* "You heard his words," she murmured without agreeing. "Aiding his escape would do no good; he would only return."

"That is my price, Nena. Agree to it, or I will go back and finish him now," Gentok threatened.

Nena hesitated, then nodded. "I swear."

"As do I." He took a deep breath and then let out a long slow exhale. "But if he remains and speaks as he says he will, the others will not understand. You must know that. I, who care for you—who have only ever wanted to be with you, am struggling to do so and cannot. They will shun you. He is a Northman," he spat, his voice thick with disgust, unable to see Jarl as anything other than a man-beast.

Nena knew he was right about the tribe's response. She thought of Lothor's reaction—her own blood, and he had only suspected she had willingly lain with the enemy. When Jarl was given the opportunity to speak, they all would know.

"But there is another solution," Gentok continued. "Choose me now. Our union will protect you from any doubts the Northman's words will raise with the tribe. If we are married, his words will fall on deaf ears; no one will believe him. Your reputation will remain intact." His voice softened. "And knowing the truth changes nothing for me. I said I would be waiting for you, and I meant it."

When she did not agree right away, he stared at her, incredulous. "You cannot possibly be swayed by his honeyed words," he said, his voice laced with disgust again. "Even if he speaks the truth—you are Teclan. He is Northman. There is no possible future for you together." He echoed her father's words. "You know that. Deep down you knew it all along, and that's why you escaped him to return home. Your life and your future are here with your people. With me."

He was right. About everything. No one would listen to Jarl or doubt her if she and Gentok were married. And Gentok was a good man. She should just say the words that she had been prepared to say that very morning. The words she knew he had always longed to hear and desperately awaited now.

"Gentok, your understanding and concern is more than I deserve, and means more to me than I can express, but I will not choose until this is over."

Gentok leaned back on the balls of his feet and exhaled sharply, responding to her words as if they had come in the form of a physical slap.

"But that will not be long, now," she continued quietly. "My father will announce tomorrow that the Northman is to face Lothor in single combat. Many things will be settled then, for good."

After taking a moment to process the significance of her words, Gentok nodded and seemed satisfied. It was clear he also had no doubt of Lothor's victory.

———————————◆———————————

Nena returned to Jalla's tent and was thrilled to find it empty. Jalla and Exanthia must be at the baths; she wouldn't have to explain her actions, but she knew she didn't have much time before they returned to cook the evening meal. She went straight to Jalla's shelves and began rifling through the vials and small crocks. She opened a few to smell them, even tasted one with the tip of her finger, before she found the one she was looking for. She grabbed a fresh waterskin, a hunk of leftover bread and a handful of dried salted meat from a net bag hanging in the corner. Throwing everything onto a tray, she took a deep breath and headed back to the cell.

She nodded at the guard who had replaced Gentok outside the door.

"I have brought food for the prisoner," Nena said and waited, fully prepared to argue with him when he refused her, but the guard only nodded her through. Unlike with Gentok, she doubted she had needed to provide him any explanation at all.

"Are you taking me to see your father now?" Jarl asked as she stepped inside.

"No, he doesn't need to speak with you after all."

"Because you told him why I am here?"

"Yes."

"Was he alone?"

Nena nodded and wondered why he would ask that.

"So he doesn't want anyone else to hear it and know," he concluded.

Nena pondered that for a moment. "Perhaps," she agreed. "My father has decided you will face Lothor in a combat trial."

"Are there rules?"

"Only to survive."

He nodded and seemed satisfied. "When?"

"I don't know. It will be soon."

He shrugged and seemed unconcerned. "Good."

Good? How in any way was that good? "If there was a way for you to escape and return to your men, would you take it?" Nena asked him quietly.

"You know I would not."

"But you are soon to face mortal combat."

"And consider myself lucky for the opportunity. To be allowed to fight for what I want—to determine my own destiny with a sword in my hand against a single opponent...it is far more than I had dared hope for. You know I would never leave. This is why I came. Perhaps now, I can prove to you, and any who would question it, that I am as worthy—nay, more worthy of you than any Teclan warrior." He paused. "What did your father say when you told him why I was here?"

"That we are lion and wolf."

Jarl's forehead furrowed.

Nena recognized the look and knew he was puzzled. "Both are fierce and strong, but they are not compatible," she explained, then changed the subject. "I brought ointment. It will ease the pain and swelling in your head."

He nodded and she picked up the jar from the tray and returned to her position behind him. She knelt and parted his hair, then began to apply the salve.

"He's wrong you know," Jarl said. "We are not so different."

Nena didn't respond, just finished dressing his wounds before taking the jar to the tray and returning with the waterskin.

"Why did you run?" he asked, his voice low.

"I had to."

"Do you carry our child?"

Nena looked at him, surprised he would ask that. "No."

"Did you...ever?" He seemed almost afraid to ask the last part.

"No."

He seemed both disappointed and relieved at the same time. She offered him a sip of water.

"Why did you think that I might be with child?" she asked.

"Besides the obvious reasons?" He smiled. He wanted so badly to touch her. "Altene said you asked for herb to shed the baby."

Nena frowned.

"Is that not true?" he asked.

"No."

Jarl swore under his breath.

"It is not without all truth," Nena admitted. "It was Altene's idea for me to choose you to facilitate my escape. If I would do it, she agreed to give me the herb to keep your seed from taking. But when I ran out the day before the battle, she refused to give me any more. She was worried I had changed my mind and would not leave you."

"Is that why you ran?"

"No. I had already made plans to escape during that battle. You were taking so many of the men, I knew the camp would be poorly guarded."

"Well, I must thank Altene—if I see her again, at least for giving you that initial suggestion." He paused and looked deep into her eyes. "Though if I had it to do over again, upon receipt of that gift, I would cancel all further raids and return immediately to the ships."

"Does Altene await you then, in the camp outside the cliff gates?" Nena asked.

The question seemed straightforward, but something in her tone made Jarl careful with his reply. "Altene travels with the group, but she is not with me." He could see Nena was unconvinced. Like Tryggr, Nena did not believe a man would travel with a woman, especially a woman like Altene, if not for his comfort. "Even during the great storm that battered us while we tracked you, she took shelter in Tryggr's tent, not mine."

Nena looked at him, her eyes searching his face for the truth.

They were interrupted by heated voices outside. The door swung open. A warrior who Jarl recognized as the one who had volunteered to go find Nena when he was first brought to the council tent, stepped inside. He glanced around the room, his eyes first taking in the tray on the table, then the two of them. He stood in the open doorway, not saying a word.

Nena looked up at him slowly, her gaze hard. She didn't seem at all surprised to see him, in fact seemed very annoyed. They exchanged a long hard stare. Jarl wondered if he was some personal bodyguard to her father who had been sent to watch them. It would explain their familiarity and her annoyance.

"You have given him word of his fate?" Gentok asked.

"Yes," Nena replied.

He glanced at the jar. "And dressed his wounds?" he noted, his jaw tightening.

"Yes."

"Then you should give him the food and leave."

Nena glowered at him, but he crossed his arms over his chest, clearly not leaving until she did. She moved to the table, picked up the tray of food and set it next to Jarl. "I will return in the morning with more food and water," she said, then stood and left, brushing past the warrior without acknowledging him.

With a final disgusted glare at Jarl, the warrior turned and followed her.

After a night of fitful dozing, Nena arose early and began preparing another tray for Jarl. She wondered if Gentok would be waiting for her at the cell. Well, if he wanted to sit and listen to them, then so be it; she would not let him run her off again. She pushed the galling memory from her mind and returned her focus back to the tray. She took more care this time to add things Jarl would like: two fresh plums, a pear, and her portion of the venison strips sauteed with mushrooms and onions that Jalla had made the night before—normally one of her favorites, but she'd been unable to eat a single bite.

A courier arrived with the message that her father had called a council to announce his decision on the Northman's fate. Nena thanked him but didn't follow. He had not said her father requested her, and she already knew what his announcement would be. Instead she looked around for anything else she might add to the tray.

"What are you doing?" Jalla asked, sleepily. The arrival of the messenger had awakened her, but Exanthia still slept.

"Taking food to the Northman," Nena replied.

"Why?"

"Because he needs to eat. Or do we not feed prisoners now?" Nena snapped at what she perceived to be Jalla's criticism—still fuming at Gentok ordering her from the cell the night before, like she was an errant child.

Jalla cocked her head and raised her eyebrows, clearly taken aback by Nena's hostile response. "I only meant, why you?"

"Who else would do it? I am the most appropriate."

"Given your history, I would disagree and say you are the least appropriate."

"It is something I must do."

Jalla considered that, then nodded. Nena knew Jalla mistook her words to mean she was doing it to face her fears, but she did not correct her. Facing her captor to show she was unafraid and fully recovered from anything that had happened to her was acceptable—even worthy of admiration.

"Will you not attend the council to hear his fate?" Jalla asked.

"I already know his fate. I was with Father last night when he decided."

"And?"

"He is to face Lothor in trial by combat."

Jalla nodded. "When?"

Nena frowned. "I don't know."

"Then you should go and hear."

Nena hesitated. She didn't want to know, but knew that Jarl would. She nodded and draped a thin rabbit hide over the tray to keep the flies from the food while she was gone. Without another word to Jalla, she left the tent. Dread dogged her every step to the council. What if her father announced it was to be today?

By the time she arrived, her father had already made his announcement, and though Lothor was eager to avenge Ruga's death, he stood on the dais and insisted the fight be postponed until the Northman was healthy. When he killed him, and Lothor was sure of that result, he wanted no smirch on his victory, no whisper, no doubt. The cloud of bitter rage seemed to have lifted from him completely, and he appeared to have regained the restraint that would make him a great chief one day. The fight was scheduled for the next new moon, one week hence.

Nena left without hearing anything more and returned to Jalla's tent to finish packing the tray. She was ecstatic with the decision, though she told herself it was only because it gave her more time to figure out some other way to prevent the trial completely.

Her step light, she made her way back to the cell. She was surprised to find two guards stationed outside the door now. She took a deep breath, fully expecting trouble, but both nodded at her, and one even moved to hold open the door. Pleasantly surprised at not having to do battle, she nodded back and stepped inside. She was shocked to find a third guard inside seated at the table.

"I will watch him now. You may go and have a break." Nena said to him in Dor as she set the tray on the table.

He shook his head. "My orders are to remain."

"I'm sure your orders were to make sure the prisoner was watched at all times. I am here and will do that now. You may go." She used her most imperious tone.

The guard looked uncomfortable but again shook his head. "My orders were clear," he said with stubborn determination. "I am to remain inside at all times, even when someone else comes to speak with the prisoner or to care for him. Though why we waste valuable food on him is beyond me," he muttered. "If anyone insists on anything different, I am to send word to Meln and hear back from him before leaving my post. The only one able to rescind the order is Chief Meln himself."

"Did my father give you those orders?" Nena asked, curious.

"No."

"Then who?" she asked, though she knew.

"Gentok."

"So you mean only my father and Gentok can rescind it."

"No, Gentok was very clear on that. No one, not even he, himself, is to be allowed time alone with the prisoner.

Nena scowled and turned away.

"What did he say?" Jarl asked as Nena brought him the waterskin, and the guard resumed his seat.

"He said that his orders are to allow no one private access to you."

"Concern for my safety, I'm sure."

Nena looked up to correct him, but saw the indents in his cheeks and the hint of a smile on his lips. He was teasing her, something she had never quite grown used to—the Northman way of saying one thing but meaning another. "Yes, I'm sure that's it," she agreed instead, hiding her own smile and relishing the comfortable feel of their secret communication.

"You just missed your brother," Jarl said.

"Lothor was here?"

Jarl nodded.

"What did he want?"

"To tell me personally that he is delaying the trial to make sure that I am healthy and fully returned to form when he kills me. He wants to make sure there are no rumors later that he defeated an injured man. He also said there are Northern swords I will be allowed to choose from—left behind by your previous captives, apparently—or I can choose a Teclan sword. And that there is no Northern armor that will fit me, so that will have to be Teclan, but he will make sure suitable armor is provided. He doesn't want me to die too quickly." Jarl smiled. "He's very serious, isn't he?"

"As you should be, too."

"Don't worry, when the time comes, I will be sure of purpose," he said darkly. "Though I see no reason to wait so long."

Nena was exasperated. Her brother's eagerness she understood, but Jarl could barely sit up without becoming dizzy. And what did he think would happen if he won? Did he think that his past transgressions would be wiped clean, and he would suddenly be accepted and welcomed by the tribe? Nena didn't even know what would happen. There was no precedent, and if there had been, there was never a captive who wanted anything more than their life and their freedom. Upon victory, they would not have hesitated to leave. Jarl did not want that, nor would he accept it. Her father had given no specifics on that count. She was sure it was because he had no doubt of Lothor's triumph. But what if Jarl won? What if he killed her brother? Jarl's life would be spared, that much was certain, but what would happen after that when he refused to go?

"Do not fear for me, Princess," Jarl said, misunderstanding her troubled pondering. "I have fought the gods for you and pulled you back from the afterlife. I do not fear one man."

Nena did not respond. If it were only one man, she might agree with him, but it was Lothor.

"And I told you before, there has never been anything in my life that I wanted that I could not win. I only wish there was some way to do so now that did not come at the expense of your brother's life."

Even as he said it, Nena could see he was glad for the opportunity to prove himself—to her people, to her, to himself. He had no reservations and seemed to welcome the test of himself as a man. He was clearly confident he would pass it.

"But with this delay, I must get word back to Tryggr and my men. They will be worried about what has happened to me, and I cannot have Tryggr screwing things up now by storming the cliff gates. Even though I gave express orders for that not to happen, I can very well see him doing just that if I do not return."

"My father will not release you to speak with them, nor will he risk them killing an emissary."

"There must be some way. If they have no word, I cannot guarantee what he will do," Jarl warned.

Nena thought briefly about the wild tempered, flame-haired giant and secretly agreed with him. "You said Altene is there?" she asked.

"Yes."

"Then I have an idea."

Nena went immediately to share Jarl's concern and express her plan to her father. She was disappointed to find Lothor there.

"It is madness," Lothor voiced his disapproval when she was finished. "They will kill her, or capture her and demand an exchange. Maybe that was his plan all along."

Nena seethed at her brother's presumption that it was up to him to decide, but controlled herself. She could not allow his words to goad her into an imprudent response. Lashing out at him now would only ensure that her father declined her request. When she spoke her voice was even and steady. "The Northman's second in command is hotheaded and impulsive, driven by emotion and rash thoughts of revenge." She looked pointedly at Lothor. "He will not hesitate to endanger his people without thinking beyond that. They have a Dor woman. I will present the banner. She will explain to them what it means," Nena added.

"The Northmen have no honor. They will not respect the banner," Lothor exclaimed. "They attacked the Eastern Plains tribe during a tournament

The protection banners were flying then. They are savages," he said, his nose wrinkling with contempt.

"They did not know our ways. They have learned much since then," Nena countered.

"Do you think they will care if it means getting their leader back? No. I will not allow it," Lothor said.

Nena turned on him then, her voice icy. "You are not yet chief, Lothor, and I do not require your approval, nor your assent in this matter." She looked back to her father who had watched their interchange closely. He gave a small nod as he made his decision.

"I think you both allow feelings to taint your judgment where the Northmen are concerned. Your brother has made valid points, but I agree that a messenger bearing the banner should be sent." He studied Nena for a long moment. "I do not think it should be you—but I will not forbid it. You understand what is at stake, but you also know them better than anyone else, so I will leave that decision up to you."

"It's been three days," Tryggr muttered as he paced in front of the fire. "I say we go in. Even with high casualties, some will make it. We'll get Jarl—assuming he's not dead, maybe even get the damn woman for him and get the fuck out of here."

"That was not Jarl's wish," Gunnar said. "To go now would be nullifying his own risk, and defying his direct order. For all we know, things are going according to plan."

"You're one to be talking about following orders," Tryggr snapped. "He ordered you to take the army to port and yet here you stand. And Jarl hasn't exactly been himself lately, now has he?"

"I think he's seeing things more clearly than he ever has," Gunnar said.

"Oh, you and that 'woman in your blood' crap. You're as much to blame in this as anyone. Filling Jarl's head with that nonsense. Does a clear-thinking man take off his armor and ride straight into the hands of the enemy?"

"A clear-thinking man evaluates all his options and chooses the best. That was the best option Jarl had. If you had a better one, I sure didn't hear it." Gunnar spoke calmly, refusing to be drawn into a heated debate.

"The best option was to pack up and leave this gods-forsaken place and go home. How's that for an option?"

"I can tell you from my own experience, for Jarl that was never an option at all," Gunnar said.

"So how long do you think we should wait?" Tryggr grumbled. "If it's too much longer, we might as well make plans for it to be a long time. The rivers in Rusland will be frozen, and we'll be far better off being stuck here for the winter than somewhere along the way."

"I don't know. They haven't produced his body, or his head on a spike. I haven't seen any smoke from a great fire like they had burned him or were celebrating. But I'm not really sure what they would do with him if they killed him. One thing I do know, with us camped here, it will be difficult for them to move their own forces to go raiding, and even if they have other ways out, they won't want to leave their village unprotected. I would think they would want us to move on as soon as possible. Surely they will give us some sign if he is dead."

Nena stopped at the base of the great cliffs, just outside the entrance to the canyon and reined in the mare. Though the temperature was warmer here in the full sun, she shivered. The Northmen camp sprawled before her in all directions. She'd seen it many times before, but here, so close to her home, their numbers were even more intimidating. She felt exposed, even though she hadn't yet ventured far enough beyond the canyon that she could not easily retreat back to the safety of its walls. From here she was still protected by Teclan warriors above, but that would not be for long.

She pushed the mare forward and did not stop again until she was well outside the Teclan bow range. She halted the mare once more and sat perfectly still, holding the tall three-split, white banner. The blanched fabric rippled and flowed above her on the breeze. It was the only movement. The only sound.

Nena doubted the Northmen would know its significance, but she was counting on them to consult Altene. She prayed Altene had not been taken from her tribe too young to know what it meant. She would know. She had to. Altene seemed to know everything, Nena reassured herself as she stood alone in the open.

Tryggr handed the scope to Gunnar and waited for him to focus before asking, "That's her, isn't it? Jarl's woman? What does she want? Why is she just sitting there? Do you see any sign of Jarl?"

"No," Gunnar replied, his voice grim.

They'd been watching her ever since a scout had first reported her exit from the canyon. It had been ten minutes with no change. "What do you think that flag means? Do you think he's dead?" Tryggr wondered out loud.

"I don't know," Gunnar replied.

"Have you ever seen a flag like that?" Tryggr asked.

"No."

"It could be some sort of trap to lure us closer."

"I might agree, but she has stopped well outside her archers' range. They couldn't reach us there."

"I'll go get Altene; maybe she'll know." Tryggr left and returned with her shortly.

Gunnar handed her the scope and the two men waited impatiently as Altene struggled to familiarize herself with the strange tube. As her untrained eye bounced up and down over the target, bit by bit, she was able to take in her rival and the three-layered split white flag. Her next words were cryptic. "She has a message."

"About what?" Tryggr asked.

"I don't know, but that's a safety banner, to exchange messages unharmed, even in battle," Altene explained.

"It could be a trick," Tryggr muttered.

"I will go. I'm not afraid," Altene offered, her voice flat. "It will be a message about Jarl." Her lack of enthusiasm and the fact that Jarl wasn't bringing it himself, told both men what she feared the message was.

"Bullshit. I'm not afraid. I'll go," Tryggr said. He paused and looked at Altene before adding, "and I guess it might be good if you came, too." He lowered his voice to a menace. "But I can tell you right now, safety flag or no safety flag, if Jarl is dead—so is she."

Chapter 27

After Jalla watched Nena ride out with the white banner, she returned to her tent and dragged a stool over in front of her shelves. Climbing up on it, she retrieved the heavy wooden box from the back of the top shelf. She knew what had to be done. She understood the reasoning behind Lothor's delaying the fight, but only Jalla could see what it was doing to Nena. Her niece was clearly tortured by the Northman's presence. Since his arrival, she had barely eaten and her sleep was wracked by nightmares. It had to be the constant reminder of what she had endured at their hands. Though she had never spoken of it, Nena's reaction now told Jalla how terrible it must have been. To make matters worse, Nena insisted on tending to the prisoner herself. Jalla respected that Nena was following her warrior training and confronting her fears head on, but the toll it was taking on her was too high.

When the Northman was dead, it would no longer be an issue. Lothor would most likely take care of it, but Jalla was old enough and had seen enough, to know not to believe in certainties. Especially after seeing what the Northman was doing to Nena—a female equivalent to Lothor in strength as far as Jalla was concerned. What if, by some fluke, Lothor failed and was killed? Meln would be destroyed. The tribal leadership would be in disarray. And Nena? What would it do to her? Jalla could not allow that to happen. This needed to be over once and for all.

How and when she was going to accomplish the feat of dispatching the Northman had proven to be quite problematic. That was, until Nena had announced her decision to personally deliver the message that morning. She had actually requested that Jalla take over providing for him. Everything had fallen into place. Jalla was certain the gods were behind it; they were happy with her plan.

She lifted the heavy wooden lid and gently sorted through the tiny vials inside. Smiling, she withdrew one from the box and stepped down off of the stool. She pulled the cork stopper and carefully tipped it over the tray of food, watching with satisfaction as the clear droplets fell, one by one, and disappeared as they made contact. Invisible. Odorless. Tasteless. She replaced the cork and washed her hands thoroughly, careful not to touch any part of her body or face with her fingertips before they were rinsed, even though she was sure none of the liquid had touched her. One could not be too careful; it was not worth the risk.

By the time Nena returned, it would be too late. The Northman would be dead—or perhaps still dying. The poison she had chosen was not overly quick, but there would be no saving him. He would die painfully—as he should. Lothor and Meln would both be furious with her, and there would be punishment, of course. For anyone, even the chief's sister, to go against his direct order would mandate that, but Jalla knew she would survive it. It was for the good of the family and the good of the tribe.

Jarl tried to remain calm. His strength was returning rapidly, and he chafed at the restraints now more than ever. Nena would be delivering the message to his men. He could only pray that Tryggr would seek Altene's counsel and not do something stupid. Over and over he played out different scenarios in his mind. In many of them, Nena ended up dead at Tryggr's hand. He berated himself for ever suggesting that a message be taken in the first place—but he had never dreamed it would be her who went. And once she had it in her head, there had been no changing her mind. He'd expressed his concerns repeatedly, but she'd dismissed them. She was going, regardless of anything he said, and he was powerless to stop her. Being in such a subordinate and helpless position when it came to making decisions was unfamiliar to him, and it was harder in many ways than the physical shackles.

The creak of the door and the sudden shaft of bright light from outside surprised him. He'd heard no footfalls approaching and no words exchanged with the outside guards. With Nena gone, he expected to do without anything until she returned. He'd been surprised her father had ever agreed for her to be the one to go, and suddenly realized he may have done so to take her away. He squinted, trying to identify the threat, now somehow sure in his gut that there was one. Relief flooded through him to see the form in the doorway was female and she was alone.

She said something to the guard who was seated inside. Jarl could not understand their words, but the guard shook his head declining her request, though he looked away uncomfortably as he did so. The woman said something else, her tone low and even. The guard looked backed at her, his eyes widened slightly with fear. He hesitated, then gave a brief nod and hurried for the door. Jarl's inner alarms clamored. Who was this woman who was able to do in a few words what Nena, daughter of the chief, had been unable to? And Nena had said only Meln could be alone with him. So had he sent this woman? Is that what she had told the guard? She carried no weapon that he could see, only a tray of food and a small blue jar of ointment. He eyed the container warily; the jar Nena always brought with her was brown.

From everything Nena had told him, her brother longed for this match, and Lothor himself had insisted that it be fair, but Jarl realized Meln might not share in that desire. But would he actually send someone to kill him? If he did, both he and Lothor would lose face. Jarl discounted it. Far more likely was that Meln would have someone wound him in some small way, or poison him with something that would hinder him. He would still be able to fight, but the outcome would be assured. Lothor's victory could be guaranteed without the tribe ever being the wiser.

With that in mind, Jarl realized, the order could just as easily have come from Lothor himself. Perhaps he was not as confident as he professed. Perhaps that was why he had insisted on the delay, to make sure there was time for this to happen. It was genius really. Lothor would win on two fronts. The first for being honorable and fearless by insisting on the delay. The second for being victorious against a powerful enemy. Jarl wondered if the other Northmen prisoners had met their fates in a similar manner.

But why would whoever was behind it, choose a woman? Was that also part of the plan—to allay any suspicions he might have? Though his guard was up, Jarl was still curious about her. Had she volunteered? Had she been hand-picked by Meln or Lothor? Like Nena, she was tall, but her face was wider and her features flatter. She set down the tray and looked him over with distrustful eyes.

"Who are you?" he asked.

"I am Jalla, Nena's aunt. I have brought ointment for your wounds." She picked up the unfamiliar blue jar.

"No offense, Jalla, but that would make you Lothor's aunt, too, so I think I'll skip the ointment today."

She set the container back on the tray. "Then I suppose you'll not want any of the food I brought either?"

"Probably not," he said.

"As you wish," she said but did not leave.

"Why are you really here, Jalla?" Jarl asked. "Have you come to kill me?"

She examined him for a long moment, seeming to be debating whether or not to answer him. "I haven't decided yet," she answered truthfully. "Nena asked me to come. I accepted her request to finally see the man who so tortured my warrior niece that she still has nightmares every night like a child. I have come to ask with what methods you tortured her, to better help her overcome it. Not knowing what she endured at your hands makes it difficult for me to aid her."

"Did she tell you I tortured her?" Jarl asked, his tone curious and hurt.

"No. She does not speak of it. A warrior would never speak of such things. Clearly with her circle filled in, you raped her. Did you share her with other Northmen? Were there many?" she asked, and gave him a withering look.

"No. Nothing like that ever happened—I swear to you. I never harmed her, and would never harm her. In fact, I would kill anyone who dared try. It is true she was my captive, but she was never mistreated."

"Then of what does she dream that makes her cry out in the night?" Jalla accused.

"I don't know," Jarl said and frowned, truly disturbed. "Perhaps you should ask her. I care deeply for her. It is why I am here."

"You cannot possibly think she returns your affection," Jalla snorted. The idea was clearly ludicrous to her.

"Yes, I do," Jarl said quietly. "But you should ask her that, too."

Jalla sat evaluating him as she absorbed his words in silence. "I did come to kill you today," she admitted. "I was expecting to find a brutish savage monster. You are not what I was expecting," she conceded. "I will speak to Nena when she returns from delivering the message to your men. But know this, Northman, if I find out you are lying, you will have no need to fear Lothor's sword."

"Understood," Jarl said.

She picked up the tray. "I will take this with me. I don't think you'd have found the food to your liking."

Jarl nodded and watched her leave. He prayed for Nena to return unharmed, and soon.

The two riders halted facing Nena under the rippling triple white banner. Altene's eyes were swollen and red from crying. Tryggr looked little better. Deep lines creased his haggard face, and his red hair was even more tangled than usual.

"Does he yet live?" Altene whispered.

"Yes," Nena replied.

"Is he still…" Altene could hardly say the words, "…whole?"

"Yes. Jarl has sent me to bring you a message. He is recuperating and will fight my brother in trial by combat on the next new moon. The battle shall decide his fate."

"Which brother?" Altene paused. "Not Lothor?"

"Yes, Lothor."

Altene paled.

"Jarl can take any man so long as there's no trickery involved," Tryggr snapped and eyed her suspiciously.

"My brother insists Jarl be healthy and strong for the trial. That is the reason for the delay. He wants there to be no question of his victory." Her voice trailed off.

"How is he injured? You said he's recuperating," Tryggr asked, still suspicious.

"He took several blows to the back of his head when he was first brought to the village."

"The head, you say?" Tryggr smiled with relief. "I've never known a man more hardheaded than Jarl. I was worried it would be something that might slow him down, like his leg or his sword arm." Tryggr nodded and seemed satisfied. "He will win. I have seen him fight too many battles to think otherwise. The gods favor him. Prepare to lose a brother, woman."

"I came only to deliver that message. I must return now." Nena turned the mare around and ended the meeting. She tried not to show how Tryggr's words had upset her. She'd been over the same thoughts too many times. The gods favor Jarl. Was it true? And prepare to lose a brother? Could she do that? For all their recent differences, Lothor was still her blood. They had been close once, and Lothor was an honorable man. And what would it do to her father? To lose Lothor so soon after losing Ruga would kill him. But even knowing that, and how devastating Lothor's death would be to the tribe, she could not bear the thought of Jarl being killed.

Nena rode directly to her father's tent to inform him that the message was delivered, and that she had returned safely.

"Good." He nodded, satisfied.

She turned to leave.

"You are to report to the cliffs tonight to begin your shift there," he said.

"What?" Nena asked, incredulous.

"With the increased guard for such an extended period of time, we are rotating warriors at the cliffs in four day shifts now."

"But..." *Four days would be until the day of the trial!*

"You've had enough time to recover from your journey home. There is no reason for you not to resume your responsibilities as a warrior. At least until you choose...."

Was this his way to strong arm her into choosing? Or was it something else? "But who will attend to the Northman? Lothor wishes for this to be a fair fight," she reminded him, trying to make it seem like her concern was based on Lothor's request and not her own desires.

"Someone else," he said with finality.

She opened her mouth to plead her case further, then closed it and bowed her head. "Yes, Father," she said and left the tent, stunned by his command. Jalla was waiting for her when she stepped outside. Nena groaned inwardly.

"Nena, come straight to my tent when you have put your horse away."

"I must give message to J..., the Northman," she corrected herself.

"I have already sent word to his guard that you have returned. Your full accounting can wait until you take his next meal. I would have important words with you."

Nena wanted to refuse, but her aunt stood waiting with a stubborn look that indicated she was not going to accept no for an answer. "Very well," Nena acquiesced. "I will join you shortly."

As she fed and watered the mare, Nena wondered what Jalla had to say that was so important. Perhaps she had information about her father's sudden decision to send her to the cliffs. After a quick, cursory brushing to remove the mare's sweat marks, Nena hurried back to Jalla's tent. She found her aunt sitting inside alone.

"Where is Exanthia?" Nena asked.

"She is off with her new friend. Sit down and I will redo your braid for you. It's a mess. I can see you're in a hurry, so I won't keep you for long."

Nena sat and Jalla removed her hair tie, then began to comb out her long tresses. Once the tangles were removed, she separated the hair into sections and began to plait it back into a single thick braid.

"Nena, I am going to ask you something important, and I need for you to tell me the truth," Jalla began.

Nena was surprised by her aunt's strange request. She would never lie to her—evade telling her the whole truth perhaps, but not lie. "Of course," she agreed.

"Of what is it you dream at night when you cannot sleep?" Jalla felt Nena tense, and tightened her fingers in her hair.

"I cannot," Nena whispered.

"I never asked before because I assumed you were reliving the suffering you endured while being held prisoner. There was no reason for me to hear the details of that. But now I have come to doubt that is the true source of your pain. Is that what haunts your dreams?"

"No," Nena murmured.

Jalla exhaled slowly. Nena's reaction told her there was at least some truth to the Northman's words. "So he did not harm you?"

"No."

"Did someone else?"

Nena shook her head.

"Then what?" Jalla probed gently. "It is of him you dream, yes?"

Nena's stiff silence was the only answer.

"If he does not harm you, what does he do that so troubles you?"

Jalla's question hung in the air, but Nena couldn't answer. Even though she wanted to share this secret, this burden with someone else, she was terrified. She knew what her aunt's reaction would be. What it should be. Her feelings were absurd. No, they were beyond absurd; they approached madness. But she had agreed to tell the truth, and truthfully, she no longer wanted to keep it inside. "He forsakes me," she whispered. Nena held her breath, waiting for her aunt's outraged rebuke. Waiting to hear how she was stupid and weak. Waiting to hear the scathing disappointment in Jalla's voice, as she had in Lothor's, or the shock and disgust, as she had in Gentok's.

"I see," Jalla said, and resumed braiding as she struggled to process the enormity of what had been revealed to her, first by Jarl, then confirmed by Nena. Her niece's predicament was suddenly crystal clear, and though everything made sense now, it only made the situation that much more impossible.

"You have no answer for me?" Nena asked.

"I do not, but I am only a woman, Nena. You must trust that the gods have a plan."

"That is my deepest fear," Nena admitted with a whisper. "I fear the gods had a plan when they chose him to be my first union, but in my arrogance and blindness, I thwarted their wishes. Now others will suffer the consequences of my actions." Both women sat in silence while Jalla finished the braid and tied it off. "Did you know Father is sending me to the cliffs?"

"No," Jalla said quietly.

"For four days."

"Did he say why?" Jalla asked.

"He said because it is my warrior duty," Nena said cynically.

"Do you think he knows of your feelings for the Northman?"

"I don't know. But he does know why Jarl is here."

"Your father never acts without purpose," Jalla contemplated out loud.

"I know, which is why I have a favor to ask of you," Nena said. "I need you to look after Jarl while I am gone."

Jalla shook her head. "Nena, you put me in a difficult position. I am Lothor's blood, too. And surely your father has no intent to harm him before the trial." Even as she said the words, Jalla wondered if they were true. Desperation made people unpredictable. She thought of her own plan to kill the Northman earlier that day. But Meln? And if it were true, maybe it would be for the best. Why prolong Nena's heartache when she could never be happy? And why risk Lothor's life? If Meln did plan to kill him, both her niece and nephew would benefit. The tribe would benefit. Jalla knew she had to decide quickly. Once she gave her word to Nena....

"It is at Lothor's request that Jarl requires care for these days," Nena added. "You can look at it that way—that you are doing it for him. Just promise me you will tend to him." Nena waited for her response.

"Very well. I will care for the Northman in your absence. Little did I know the answers to my questions today would come at such a price," Jalla said and shook her head.

"You are the only one I trust." Nena stood and hugged her briefly before leaving to tell Jarl.

Jarl's eyes covered every inch of her as she passed through the doorway. "It is late. But you are safe," he said, relief evident in his voice.

Nena ignored the guard seated at the table. "Apologies for worrying you with my delay. My aunt said she sent word to you of my safe return." Nena spoke quietly and quickly under her breath. She knew the guard understood the Northman tongue, as all the Teclan did, but they were not as fluent in it as she was, thanks to her time with them. If she spoke rapidly and low, he would probably not understand much of what she said.

"She did, but I did not believe it. I could see no reason, if it were true, why you would not have come to tell me yourself."

"My father has ordered me to the cliffs to stand guard until the trial."

"Why?" Jarl asked.

"He said because we have increased the guard for so long there, we all need to take shifts."

"But you do not believe him."

"I don't know. I think he suspects I would try to free you or do something else foolish."

"Why would he think that?"

"I fear someone has put that idea in his mind."

"Who?"

"The guard who interrupted us that first night." She confessed her suspicion. She could not accept the idea that her father had foul play in mind. Gentok was the only one that made sense to her.

"Why would you think him? He seemed alright to me. He even assigned my safety detail." He smiled and nodded to the guard at the table.

"Gentok heard us the first night. And...he wants the same from me as you do."

Jarl took a moment to comprehend what she was saying. He looked at her, his eyes sober. "Does he have cause to feel that way?"

Nena sighed. "When it was the gods' choice, Gentok professed his willingness to be chosen only to me. There were whispers about it at the time, but then that passed. When I returned and my father made it clear I was expected to make my second choice quickly, Gentok again expressed his desire and renewed his willingness. I would have chosen him, had you not come," Nena admitted bluntly.

"Do you have feelings for him?" Jarl asked.

"No." She paused. "But I would have chosen him anyway." She looked up at him, her eyes haunted.

"If he heard us, why would he think I would escape?"

"He came to me that night after I left you, and warned me against doing anything shameful. He mentioned helping you to escape, specifically. He also asked me to choose him then, to insure that your words of our...being together, would not make the tribe look upon me with shame."

"What did you say?"

"I told him I would not be making a decision until after the trial."

"And I suppose if I were to fall, he is expecting to be chosen?" Jarl asked, his jaw tight.

She nodded.

"When do you leave?" he asked.

"Tonight. Now."

"I will miss not seeing you, but at least you will be away from this Gentok, too. Will you return for the trial?"

"Yes."

"What if your father commands you somewhere else?"

Defiance flashed in her eyes. "I will be there."

He nodded. "Good. Do you anticipate any treachery while you are gone?"

"No, but just in case, Jalla will be caring for you. Eat or drink nothing that she does not provide."

"Jalla?" Jarl exhaled and screwed his face into a grimace. "Are you sure?"

Nena smiled at his reaction, not knowing its true cause. "She may seem unyielding, but she knows the truth about us now. No harm will come to you at her hand."

"I guess I'll have to trust you in this—it appears I have no choice."

"Nena." Gentok was the first to greet her when she arrived at the cliffs in the dark.

Nena stared at him for a long moment before she slid from the mare's back and held up her hand. "Do not speak to me unless it relates to guard duty," she said, and turned to walk away.

"Nena, what's wrong?" he asked. "Has something happened?"

She whirled to face him. "Do you think I am stupid? Did you think I would not know you betrayed me when I was suddenly sent here?"

"What are you talking about? And lower your voice," he cautioned.

"There will be no need to lower my voice. We will not be speaking." She turned away again.

"Yes, we will, but in private." He grabbed her by the arm and dragged her toward the trees. "Now, what is the meaning of this attack on me?" he demanded when he stopped out of earshot of the others.

Nena jerked her arm away from him. "Did you really think I would find it coincidence that my father suddenly sends me away until the day of the trial? And that you are also conveniently here?" she seethed.

"You are needed here," he responded. "As am I. As are all the warriors here. You would never have questioned that, had that Northman not twisted your thoughts. Of what is it you accuse me, Nena?"

"You told my father what you heard that night, to manipulate him to send me here with you."

"Listen to what you are saying! First you rant at having to do your warrior's duty like a spoiled child, and then you make accusations—all because it takes you away from the Northman! He is the enemy, Nena, or have you forgotten that? In less than a week, he will try to kill your brother—your only remaining brother—as he killed Ruga, or have you so easily forgotten that, too? What has happened to you? I told you before, neither of you were quiet with your voices that night. Someone else could have heard you. The Northman even bragged he would tell anyone who would listen. Perhaps he told someone else."

"But 'someone else' was not waiting to be chosen by me, Gentok. 'Someone else' did not have so much to gain."

"What is wrong with you? Why do you defend him over me? You shame yourself!" Gentok took her by the shoulders, his fingers biting into her skin. She expected him to start shaking her. "I did not betray you, Nena, no matter what you might think. But seeing how you act, I am grateful to whoever did. It is clearly for the best that you are here, away from him, to prevent you from shaming yourself even more. He has some spell over you. Somehow he has trapped the honorable woman I know inside an unrecognizable shell." His face was contorted with emotion.

But if Gentok was telling the truth, then who? Nena was suddenly terrified. *Jalla?* She had told Jarl to trust her, and now there was nothing she could do about it. She could not leave her post and race back to the village on a suspicion. Everyone would think she was mad. Was she?

Gentok was still staring at her, breathing hard from their explosive confrontation. That he cared for her deeply was clear, but that did not necessarily make him innocent. She took a deep wavering breath.

"Apologies, Gentok. You are correct. I am not myself. Please forgive me."

"Nena, I worry for you," he began.

"I know. I will be alright. This will all be over soon."

"Why don't you rest. I will cover your shift tonight," he offered.

"Gratitude, Gentok, but sleep will not come to me. It will be better for me if I am useful."

"As you wish." He nodded. "Since you are the most familiar with them, you have been assigned the post with the clearest view of their camp. You will be best able to recognize any changes in their routine, and know if they are planning anything out of the ordinary."

The next four days were an unending hell. As she watched the relaxed activities of the Northman camp below, Nena knew Gentok was right; she would have easily recognized the battle preparations that always preceded their attacks. There were none. They clearly posed no threat, and it made her presence there even more useless and frustrating. But she could not say a word. Gentok would assume she was only looking for some excuse to return to the village. He hadn't approached her again after the first night, but his eyes always followed her with concern.

Nena regretted her outburst, but did not apologize. She was consumed with far bigger worries. She looked to every messenger or replacement warrior arriving from the village with trepidation, more than half expecting one to bring word of Jarl's death. The more thought she gave it, she could not believe Jalla would lie to her and then betray her. She would not have promised to care for him. And if she believed Gentok, which she was inclined to do, that only left her father.

She had assumed someone had told him, but her father was not a fool. He knew why Jarl was there, and he had witnessed her uncharacteristic response to Baldor that night in the council. Most importantly, he would have noticed that she had never once demanded revenge. She had assumed Gentok had positioned himself to be at the cliffs at the same time, but even that could have been her father's doing. He had not disguised the fact that he wanted her to choose, and he would know of her leanings toward Gentok.

Or—and she hated to admit this, her being sent here could just have been a coincidence. Gentok was right about that, too; she never would have questioned it, had she not wanted to be near Jarl. Guarding the cliffs was a normal expected duty. And the other warriors were, in fact, taking four day shifts. Had she just overreacted? Gentok's other words burned in her mind. Did she shame herself? The concept was so foreign, it was difficult to even imagine. She had always been the one others emulated. Successful. Strong. Never before would the word shame have even been breathed in the same sentence as her name. But now?

She tried to imagine the situation through their eyes, as if she'd never left the village, as if it were some other female warrior who'd been captured and returned acting as she did. Some other woman who now cared for an enemy prisoner—a Worick perhaps. Woricks were the only enemy she could think of that her people despised as much as Northmen. She imagined this other woman caring for a bulging-skulled, jewelry-pierced Worick—bringing him food, thinking of him, pining for him. It made her sick. Nena had no doubt she would have looked at such a woman with pure and utter disdain. As Lothor had looked at her.

And, she would have believed, beyond a shadow of a doubt, that for Lothor to kill such an enemy was the best thing for the woman. The certainty of her conviction left Nena shaken. If she would have felt that way about someone else, then was it right? Was she under some spell that she needed to break free from? The thought made her heart ache even more because now it added guilt to the existing pain.

How had she come to this? How had she turned into someone who had to restrain herself from attacking one of her own people to protect an enemy?

And Jarl was the enemy; why did it not feel that way? Baldor had never been a favorite of hers. His heavy-handed, brutish ways had eliminated him from ever being chosen by her, but to want to kill him? And in that moment when he had clubbed Jarl to the ground, she had wanted to kill him—had wanted to fly across that space and beat him to death with his own club. How had her loyalties become so skewed?

Was it because she owed Jarl her life? Because he had fought the gods to keep her alive? Or because the gods had chosen him to be her first? Could Jarl be right? Had the gods been trying to show her their choice all along, but she'd been too stubborn to see it? Had she defied them? What she felt now—was it the spirit sickness Jarl called love? Or her spirit being strangled as her father had predicted?

Her mind felt like it was shattering into a million pieces. Trying to balance what she felt with what she knew, was tearing her apart. How could she do what was right, when she couldn't even tell what was right anymore? How could everything and everyone she cared for, push and pull her in such opposite directions all at once?

But even if she had the answers, it would not solve her most pressing problem. She had to find some way to keep the trial from taking place. To do so, she needed to clear her mind of everything else and focus on that. This was all her fault, and she had to find some way to put it right. There had to be some other option—something else she could do. She couldn't just sit there and do nothing.

Jarl would not leave without her—he had made that clear. But what if he had his prize? Would he agree to go then? Nena wasn't sure. There was more at stake for him now. Pride. Honor. A desire to prove himself up to the challenge—to prove he was worthy. He had not requested this trial, but he had embraced it.

And if he would agree to run, could she do it? Could she skulk off with him in the night? Jarl had risked all for her—could she do the same? Assuming she could find some way around the increased guard on the cell, could she forsake her people and leave with him? It would ensure her father did not lose Lothor, but he would lose another child. Would that be any easier for him—especially to lose one in such a shameful way? Nena wasn't sure.

And if she were to go through with it, it would affect far more than just her father. There was Exanthia. She would forever be known as the ward of the shamed one. Her life would be destroyed. No man would ever profess to be chosen by her when she came of age.

There was also Lothor. Losing the opportunity for revenge could quite possibly send him so deep into his pit of rage that he would never recover. Even if it did not, the smear to their family name quite possibly would. It would be the legacy left to his unborn child and all who came after. Whispers of weak blood would plague them. Some would perhaps even blame it on their mother for coming from the Southern Plains tribe. Forever forward her family would be known, not as the fierce or the strong, but as the weak, the shamed, the undisciplined.

Nena knew she could not do it. If it were only to reflect badly on her, perhaps, but such an act would have immediate harsh consequences for all who were close to her. Ultimately the whole tribe would suffer—when her brother dragged them into his relentless quest for revenge.

❖

As she sat on the cliff edge staring out over the Northmen camp on her final day, only one answer had become clear to her. She could affect the outcome of the trial, but nothing she could do was going to prevent it. What Jarl wanted, what Lothor wanted, what her father wanted, and her own responsibilities and obligations outweighed what she wanted—especially when she couldn't even pinpoint what that was. What did she want? To be with Jarl? How could she want that? It was impossible. They were lion and wolf.

She had promised Jarl she would return for the trial but wasn't sure now that she could do it. How could she watch two men she loved trying to kill each other without doing something she would regret? But she had given him her word. She had to be there.

If she was not of clear mind and purpose, which Nena accepted that she was not, the only way to successfully get through it, would be to steel herself against her swirling emotions and bury them deep inside until it was over. She'd been tested so many times before and had always passed; she could not be weak now, and she could not act in a manner that would shame her family. She was the daughter of Meln. She would attend the trial and accept her fate with dignity. She had no choice. She had to trust that the gods had a plan—and that it was more than just to punish her for defying them.

Just before dawn, without a word to her replacement or Gentok, Nena grabbed a handful of gray mane and swung aboard the mare, kicking her into a gallop for home.

Chapter 28

After putting the mare away, Nena went to the baths. She fought the urge to go straight to the cell, reminding herself she would not have done so if she were normal. Since she could not trust her own judgment, the only reliable way she had come up with to ensure she did nothing regrettable, was to measure her every action through the eyes of someone who had never left the village. After days of mental searching, she was no closer to understanding or resolution. What she felt was still in clear conflict with what she knew was right.

She returned to Jalla's tent and asked her to prepare her hair, as she would have before any other trial. Jalla looked at her curiously, then pulled up a stool beside her and began to separate her long dark hair into sections. Today she chose not the single utilitarian braid of a warrior, but a more feminine style with multiple smaller braids. Normally Nena found her touch relaxing, but this morning the quill brush raked across her scalp. Sitting still while the tension inside her continued to build became nearly unbearable. She felt as if she would explode. As the minutes ticked by, Nena couldn't help but think of the upcoming battle, despite her strong earlier resolutions not to do so.

Her brother would have no mercy when it came to killing Jarl. And even if she could convince Jarl to be merciful—to offer her brother the chance to submit if it came to that, Lothor would never take it. He would not submit to the enemy. He couldn't submit to the enemy without losing the respect of his people. And Jarl was the enemy.

"Did you know your father was not chosen by your mother the first time he competed for her?" Jalla interrupted her thoughts. "Even though he won the Southern Plains tournament, she did not choose him."

"Then how did they come to be together?" Nena asked.

"Have I never told you this story?" Jalla paused. "It is a good story. The word of your mother's beauty and bravery on the battlefield was legend. She and her brother's raiding achievements were elevating the Southern Plains tribe to one to be reckoned with. You take after her, you know. I see it in you, and I'm sure your father does, too.

"Your grandfather was hoping for a match between his son, your father, and a daughter of the Sea Tribe to the North. Which as you know, was later satisfied when the gods revealed their match there for my sister, Darna. But the legend of your mother and the upcoming Southern Plains tournament beckoned your father like a flame calls to the moth. One night he sneaked off in disguise to steal a look at your mother and judge for himself. And even though he did not meet her then, he decided she was the one for him."

"But he does not decide," Nena protested.

Jalla chuckled, glad she had at least temporarily diverted Nena's attention. "As he was soon to discover. He persuaded your grandfather to allow him to compete in their tournament and upon his arrival was soon the favorite. His gift to her was some poorly thought out thing; I do not even recall now what it was. He was sure all he needed to do was offer himself and win the tournament, and of course the gods would choose him for her. He was Teclan, after all, and next in line to be chief. He was cocky back then, your father." Her aunt smiled. "I can still see it so clearly.

"But his gift left your mother and the gods cold, or perhaps it was his attitude. When he vanquished his last foe and looked to the dais for the words he so expected to hear, your mother stood and left, leaving her father to announce that the gods had chosen none for her that day.

"Your father was in shock, I think, but he was stubborn. After he returned home, he petitioned your grandfather to have a tournament here, and to invite her, much as you were invited to the Eastern Plains village. But this time was different. Victory in the tournament for him was a given, inasmuch as such things can be, so this time he prepared for the gift more than the events. He carved her a bow from mountain black cedar. And when he presented it to her, he knelt with the greatest respect and vowed to win the tournament, not for himself, but for her, to show the gods his worthiness of her and their union. That she was meant to be Teclan and should have the finest Teclan bow." Her aunt paused and smiled at the memory. "He had quite a speech, which as you know, for your father and his normal shortness of words, was no small wonder in itself.

"The gods must have liked this gift better, or his words—or perhaps it was only then the right time. Who knows with the gods?" Jalla shrugged. "The final round was between your father and your mother's brother, your uncle. They had not met in the previous tournament, because her brother had been recovering from a battle wound. But now he was fully returned to form and gave your father fierce competition.

"Ultimately your father got the upper hand. While he was still crouched over your uncle's prone body in the tournament arena, your mother stood on the dais. She was in such a hurry, she did not even wait for her brother to signal yield before she announced that she had chosen your father. It is a good story, no? It is hard to imagine your father, so young and full of folly."

"Yes. It is a good story." But Nena's thoughts were again back to her own plight. Someone she cared deeply for would die this day. She had no more time for childish stories now.

"You are finished. Go to your Northman, Nena. May the gods have mercy on us all today."

Nena stepped past the four armed guards outside the cell door. When she entered, she understood their increased presence. Jarl was standing alone, unshackled and half-dressed in Dor armor.

"You are well," Nena murmured as she took in his tall frame and the wave of energy she felt from him.

"You seem relieved. Did you not have the confidence in your aunt that you professed?" Jarl asked.

"I did at the time, but when I arrived at the cliffs, Gentok swore he did not have anything to do with it. Then I wasn't sure."

"He was there?" Jarl's jaw tightened, and a small muscle in his cheek ticked. "And you spent the four days with him?"

"Yes." Nena recognized his anger and jealousy. "Though we did not speak after my initial arrival."

"But you believed him?"

Nena hesitated. "I think so. Gentok has never lied to me, but honestly, I don't know who to believe anymore." *Not even myself.* She stepped toward him and adjusted the laces on the sides of the Dor armor. She watched as Jarl flexed and twisted inside the plates of hardened leather, testing the fit and range of motion. He nodded, seeming satisfied. "Why do you help me and not your brother?" he asked.

"No one else will help you."

"That doesn't answer my question. Why do you help me? Do you want me to win?" He smiled at her, his battle fever already spiking in anticipation of the upcoming fight. There was no fear, no hesitation, no consideration for loss on his handsome face.

"My brother wants this to be a fair fight," she murmured.

"So you do it for your brother? Is that the only reason?" he pressed.

Nena did not answer, but her eyes were troubled.

Jarl's expression grew suddenly serious. "I was worried you would not return."

"I told you I would."

"I know, but being here among your family, your people, I realize this must be very hard for you."

How did he always know what to say? How did he always know what she felt, when people she had known her whole life did not?

"Nena, why did you leave me before? If you weren't pregnant, why did you run? Your aunt said you dream of terrible pain. Did something happen to you that I don't know of? Did someone hurt you while I was away?" The fury he felt at the thought was unmistakable in his clenched jaw.

"It doesn't matter now," she said.

"It does to me, and I have risked my life to be here. Doesn't that qualify me to know the truth? If everyone else is correct and I am soon to die...."

Nena took a deep breath. He was right. He did deserve to know the truth. And being so close to him now—feeling their connection, she knew what the truth was. After so many hours and days of soul searching, she knew. She hadn't escaped to return to her family, to her people. She hadn't escaped to return home to the mountain. While all of those things had factored into her decision, what had truly driven her away was clear. It was what her dream had showed her almost every night—what she had admitted to Jalla. "I could not bear to become to you as Altene was. For you to one day tire of me and hand me off to another as you did her."

"Altene," Jarl exhaled with a whistle. "Altene is nothing to me—was never anything more to me than a companion. You, on the other hand, are everything. Can you not see that? I don't understand how or why, but you have become such a part of me, that without you I am no longer whole. I could no more leave you than I could leave my leg or my hand. I cannot explain what I feel for you—how complete I am when we are together, how empty I feel when we are apart. When I returned from battle and you were gone..." He shook his head. "Words cannot describe the depth of what I felt," he repeated. "I never knew it was even possible to feel that way."

They were close now. He could smell the floral-imbued oil in her braids. "I like your hair like this," he said as he ran his fingers through the multiple smaller braids. "But I like it better loose around you, spread out over my furs." He grinned.

How could he joke? He could be about to die. How could he not take it seriously? Her brother had never been defeated, and today would fight with their younger brother's death spirit behind him. He was sure to be a formidable adversary.

Jarl reached his hand up to the back of her neck beneath her braids and pulled her closer. "Kiss me," he said.

"No," she said, but she did not pull away.

"Would you be so stingy as to withhold the one thing a man is willing to die for? A kiss, so that if I go to the afterlife now, it will be satisfied?"

Nena leaned into him and pulled his head down toward her. She felt him groan with pleasure as their lips met. His arms were around her waist, pulling her tight against him. She pressed herself against his armor, her body answering his desire. She would have lain with him at that moment if he had asked—would have given him more than a kiss to take to the afterlife. But he pulled away.

His eyes blazed and his handsome face bore a confident smile. "I will come back for the rest of that when I am victorious. With the taste of you on my lips, I cannot be defeated. The gods will wield my sword."

Breathless, Nena did not doubt him. How could she have been so foolish to not see it before? There was no more question. No more doubt. The gods truly had chosen him for her. She felt it now with every fiber of her being.

But now it was too late.

Chapter 29

The contest area was a cleared circle of flat ground on the edge of the village. Surrounded by open land, there were no trees or brush to offer the contestants or the spectators any shade. Only the dais and the chief's lone banner threw any shadow. The area had been used for tournaments, to settle differences and dispense punishment for more years than anyone, even the eldest in the village, could remember. Though it had not been used in many months, the bare ground remained devoid of even a sprig of foliage. The dry earth was so hard packed from countless feet and bodies and blood, that even after months of rest, seedlings could not break its unforgiving surface. Unforgiving. In more ways than one. Not only would the thin surface layer of dust offer no cushion to a fallen competitor, the tribe would offer no mercy.

For a tournament the dais would have been covered with a brightly colored shade, and gay banners would have been set up around the entire area. But not today. Today was no celebration. The crowd would suffer along with the combatants. There would be celebrating when Lothor won, but even that would be subdued in recognition of the avenging of Ruga's death. It would be more of a putting right of the world than a festival.

After today, Nena's world would never be put right. She knew that now. The death of Lothor would not only be her loss, it would be the entire tribe's loss, and what it would do to her father would be irreparable. It would break the strength left in Meln. Nena knew it—and knew it was all her fault.

But if Jarl were killed today, part of her would die with him, and she feared the rest of her would soon follow. She knew now she could not go on—could never marry Gentok and have a normal life. The spirit sickness would overcome her. How had Jarl worded it—that she had become a part of him, and without her he was no longer whole? She understood it now, and knew that it was the same for her.

That thought brought her even more anguish. Not the fact that she would die, but what would happen when she did. Could they be together in the afterlife? If so, would it be in the sky with her ancestors, or in Jarl's Valhalla? Or would their separation extend beyond this life into the next? Was her father right about them? Were they lion and wolf? Would they be denied being together for eternity?

Nena took her seat on the end of the dais and waited for the gods to reveal her fate.

Jarl was offered his choice of the previously captured Northmen's swords. After testing them both in the air, he chose one and nodded, seeming satisfied.

The two men circled each other, balancing lightly on the balls of their feet. With intense concentration and focus, they sparred, each measuring their opponent's responses. Lothor's moves were very familiar to Nena. She had practiced with him or watched him fight with others from as early as she could remember. She knew all of his strengths. His ability to switch hands with his sword and fight almost equally as well was his most effective. That threw many an opponent off their stride. Even if it was only for a second, that was often all Lothor needed to deliver a decisive final blow. She had wanted to warn Jarl of that, but could not. Could not betray her brother, could not interfere with the gods' will again.

Other than when he had captured her, Nena had never seen Jarl fight, and even then he had only briefly handled a weapon against her. Watching him now, she realized he possessed a mastery of the sword she had never seen before. After not falling for Lothor's tricks, Jarl instead drew him in to two near misses. Only Lothor's catlike reflexes managed to save him from Jarl's blade. The crowd drew in a collective sharp gasp each time Jarl's sword sliced through the air. They cheered every blow Lothor was able to land, and groaned at every one he received.

At one point when they stood close, their swords locked at the hilts in a battle of sheer strength, Jarl dove between the crossed blades in an attempt to headbutt Lothor and knock him unconscious. Lothor feinted to the side at the last second, and the blow glanced off the side of his forehead just above his left eyebrow. It was still enough to split the skin, and blood began to trickle down his left cheek.

Nena could see the grim determination in the set of Lothor's jaw as he realized this would not be the quick decisive victory he had expected. But there was still no fear in him—no doubt of the outcome. Jarl's handsome face was a stony mask of cold hard savagery. Nena had never seen this side of him, but now she understood what his men said about him. Why they feared him, and felt the gods favored him. He fought like a man possessed by a god. Neither man allowed his opponent to rest, keeping the other hard pressed. Each so proficient, so dexterous, and so calculating in their movements. Each so confident in their ability to win.

Nena flinched, feeling every blow, no matter who sustained it, as if they fell upon her own flesh. The two men were equally matched in strength and skill, and it was soon to become apparent, matched in determination as well. After an hour of fighting, neither showed any hint of weakening resolve. Never had a contest been known to go on for so long, and never in the blazing midday sun. The pace was slower now as their bodies labored in the heat, but still they battled on. She knew them both so well, knew what they were feeling, knew the fire that burned in their muscles from the exertion—knew the fire that burned in their hearts that overcame it.

Nena wondered if her mother had sat in this very spot and watched the young Meln fighting her own brother. How had she done it? Had she sat in silence as Nena herself did, unable to cheer for either competitor? Had fear for two men she loved tore at her heart while it left her mute? But her mother had only to fear injury to pride, not mortal injury. Tournament weapons were blunted to prevent that. Not like today, where the steel was sharpened to a razor's edge.

A sudden clashing of swords, louder than before, jolted Nena back to the present and the two men before her. Jarl had gone on the offensive, pressing her brother much harder now, drawing on a reserve of strength from deep within. Lothor blocked, parried and stepped away, but Jarl's blade flashed in the sunlight, each strike coming faster and harder—keeping Lothor off balance and on the defensive. Lothor continued to fall back, struggling to match and block each deadly blow.

He stumbled.

The crowd gasped.

Jarl's sword struck just above the hilt of Lothor's, ripping it from his grasp and sending it flying through the air. In the same second, Jarl reared back and kicked Lothor hard in the center of his chest plate. Lothor staggered, his arms flailing before he slammed to the ground on his back. Before he could roll away, Jarl was on him. Straddling his chest and pinning him to the ground, Jarl leveled his sword on Lothor's neck.

A hush fell over the stunned tribe. Only the sounds of the two men's harsh labored breathing could be heard. Nena wondered how many in the crowd were holding their breath, as she was. Her father's banner flapped gently in the breeze above the dais.

"Yield," Jarl commanded, as he pressed the blade tighter against Lothor's throat.

Lothor looked up at him with acceptance of his fate, but no defeat in his stubborn eyes.

"I have no wish to kill you," Jarl said. "Yield, damn you."

Lothor remained stoically silent.

Jarl looked to Meln for an alternative to this end, but the chief only looked on, his face an impassive mask.

Jarl was in an impossible position. He knew he could not release Lothor. If he stood and allowed Lothor to rise, the battle would continue until one of them was dead—meaning it would either be him on the ground, or they would be back in this position again. Yet how could he kill him and expect to gain Nena's hand? But that concern would no longer be valid if he himself were dead. He had to do it. He had to kill him. Teclan respected strength and bravery. It was the only way. He had known it would come down to this before he ever entered the arena, so why was it difficult? Why did he hesitate?

Nena's heart pounded in her chest, but she was thankful for the momentary reprieve in the blows. She had longed for it to be at an end, not sure how much more she could take, but now that the end was imminent, she knew she could not take this either. Yield, she prayed silently to her brother, though she knew he would not. Not ever.

Jarl looked first to her father, then to her. Was he asking for an answer, or forgiveness—or both? He had waited to deliver the final blow, was still waiting for mercy to be ordered from her father, but that was not their way. Nena saw Jarl's face change as he recognized it. She read the disappointment, then determination as they spread across his features as clearly as if he had spoken words out loud. He looked back to her brother, and tightened his grip on the hilt of his sword.

Flashes of her aunt's story blurred with the scene before her—her youthful father crouched over her uncle in a death blow stance, while Jarl's words echoed in her mind. "*In what ways am I not Teclan?*" Years ago, it had been her mother's brother; now it was her own. But unlike years ago, her mother's brother would yield—could yield with no shame, because he was yielding to another Dor. Lothor didn't have that option, even though Jarl had offered it to him. Because Jarl was not Dor. "*In what ways am I not Teclan?*" Jarl's question echoed again in her mind, followed by his claim that he embodied every aspect of a Teclan warrior that a woman would use to choose. If he truly possessed all the qualities the Teclan respected, and he did, then why couldn't he be one?

He could be! In the same way her mother and Exanthia had been inducted to the Teclan tribe, Jarl could be. They were not lion and wolf. They were only wolves from different packs. Man and woman from different tribes—as Altene and the other women prisoners in the camp had tried to tell her—as the gods had tried to show her.

"Wait!" Nena shouted as she leapt to her feet.

Jarl paused and looked up at her, though thankfully he did not release his grip at her distraction.

The crowd looked at her in shock, and an uneasy murmur rippled through them. What was she doing? No one interrupted a trial—not a loved one, not even the chief. Her father knew that, which is why he had not intervened, even when Jarl had so clearly requested it with his eyes.

"I, Nena, daughter of Meln, chief of the Teclan tribe, accept the gods choice of Jarl as my first union and choose him as my husband, if he accepts my choosing?"

Jarl recognized the significance of the timing of her words. "He does."

"Then by our union, he is eligible to become Teclan." She paused and looked to her father. "If my father permits?" She waited with bated breath as did everyone in the crowd, praying he would agree. Her father nodded, and Nena breathed a sigh of relief, but she was not yet finished. "From this day forward you shall be known as Jarl of the Teclan, Husband of Nena, Daughter of Meln, Chief of the Teclan tribe. Your previous life is forgotten. Your blood is now as true Teclan as any born to the mountain. You are one of the Teclan people, deserving and entitled to all rights, equal in every way." Nena continued in a softer tone, her words directed now at the recumbent Lothor. "As Teclan and as my husband, Jarl becomes my brother's brother. My brother would yield to a brother."

The crowd was nodding in agreement, but Lothor remained unmoved. Nena held her breath as she waited for his response. He was proud, perhaps too proud, and she knew how deeply he was still wounded from their younger brother's death. How deeply he considered Jarl to be his worst enemy. How deeply he had longed to kill him. This was to have been Ruga's avenging and he had failed. In his shame, would he refuse the reprieve she had given him? With her father's support thrown behind it, he should accept it. Yet he remained motionless and silent. Whispers began to spread through the crowd. At first Nena was unsure of what they were saying. Then she heard someone close to her picking up the word.

"Yield. Yield. Yield," they chanted.

The words must have reached her brother at the same time. She saw his hand clench into a fist at his side before he extended his two fingers in the symbol of submission. He was still too proud to speak the words, but it didn't matter. The gesture meant the same.

Jarl stood and grasped Lothor's wrist before hauling him to his feet. They stood facing each other, bloody, battered and exhausted.

"My sister has chosen a great warrior," Lothor said quietly. The words were stilted and forced, but they were spoken. For whatever else her brother was feeling at that moment, he did what was expected of him. And whether he wanted to admit it or not, there was an obvious respect there. He had never been bested since he was a boy.

Nena leapt from the dais and went to stand beside Jarl, but he pulled her into his arms and kissed her passionately on the lips. He felt her stiffen, but didn't stop, refusing to release her. In that moment he had no care for Dor customs or rules on public displays of affection. He had won. He had won the greatest battle of his life, and he had won her. He felt her melt against him and return his kiss.

For an instant Nena was embarrassed for him as a man, to be so expressive of his emotions in front of other men. But he had just defeated Lothor, the greatest warrior among them! No man would dare to consider him soft— bizarre perhaps, but never soft. Caught up in his passion, she returned his kiss, suddenly unaware of anyone or anything around them. When he lifted his head and pulled away, Nena's senses returned. She stood flushed and embarrassed to have been so touched in front of the entire tribe, and to have reacted to it. She glanced at the crowd out of the corner of her eye, expecting to see indignant disapproval, but was surprised to find her aunt and several of the other women smiling, whispering, and nodding.

Jarl kept his arm possessively around her waist and turned to the chief. "I would have my horse, to report my victory to my men."

Meln nodded.

"Come. I'll show you where the horses are kept," Nena said and took his hand.

"You're coming with me," he said. It was a statement, not a question.

Nena smiled and nodded. There was no way she could have tolerated being separated from him.

Nena handed Jarl the bridle and watched as he slipped the bit into the stallion's mouth. He didn't wait for her to retrieve the saddle before vaulting onto the horse's bare back. "No saddle," he said. He slid back and patted the horse's back in front of him. "I want you here, to be able to see you, to feel you, to smell you." He reached down and pulled her up in front of him. She leaned back against him, but his rigid leather chest plate jabbed against her spine.

"Hand me your dagger," he said. "I want nothing between us."

She did and heard him cutting the laces on the armor behind her. He threw both front and back plates to the ground, returned her knife to her, then put his arm around her waist and pulled her back against the hard rippling muscles of his chest.

"Much better," he whispered.

Nena settled in close to him. With his cheek pressed against her ear and his arm tight around her waist, she reveled in the warm strength of the man behind her and the energy of the horse beneath her. She sighed deeply, surprised at how, when her future was still so uncertain, she could feel so utterly content. "Where will we go? Where will we live?" she murmured, not really caring what his answer would be, wondering if he even had one.

"As long as we're together, we are home, and I intend for us never to be apart again." He paused. "That being said, I have an idea, and I think you'll like it." Jarl turned the stallion down the trail toward the cliff gates.

Chapter 30

Cheering men raced out to meet them, converging on them and surrounding the horse in the middle of the no man's land. "Jarl, you are alive," Tryggr exclaimed.

"And properly accompanied," Gunnar noted with a huge smile on his face.

"Did you kill the bastard then?" Tryggr asked, then continued without waiting for a reply. "I knew you would. When she said you were injured, I was worried, but then she said the injury was to your head and I knew you'd be fine. No one is more hardheaded than Jarl, I said."

"I did not kill anyone." Jarl smiled. "But all is well. Let's go have a drink and I'll tell you about it briefly. Then you'll need to have the men start breaking camp. If you march straight back to port, you should still have plenty of time to make it home before the rivers freeze."

"What about you? You're not coming?" Tryggr asked.

"Nena and I have a few things to take care of here. Then we'll meet you at the ships. As you know from our trip down here, she can travel quite a bit faster," he said ruefully. "So we should arrive at about the same time."

"Where will we sleep? Or not sleep?" Jarl asked, and nuzzled the side of her neck as they arrived back at the outskirts of the Teclan village. "I would offer to share my hut with you, but the accommodations there are fairly sparse," he teased.

"I don't know for sure," Nena said. "Exanthia and I have been staying with Jalla."

"Well, that won't do," he said.

"No, it won't," she murmured in agreement.

"The weather is fair; we could sleep outside, but I would prefer for your people not to see what I have planned for you," Jarl said.

Nena flushed and felt her stomach flip as she imagined what that was going to be. "No. That won't work either. I'll come up with something."

"Make it fast."

"I will."

Nena directed him to her aunt's tent. After handing him back the bag of his belongings and weapons she had held balanced on the horse in front of her, she threw one leg over the stallion's neck and dropped to the ground. Exanthia came out at that moment carrying Nena's sleeping furs. She looked nervously at Jarl, then at Nena.

"You do not need to fear him, Exanthia," Nena reassured the girl. "Jarl is Teclan now—as you are."

Exanthia nodded. "Jalla has set up a tent for you, this way. All of your things are already there. It is her gift to Jarl for becoming Teclan. I do not have a gift yet," she confessed in Dor.

"Don't worry about that. This was all very unexpected." Nena turned to Jarl.

"My aunt has a gift for you."

"I have another gift in mind right now, and it does not in any way involve your aunt."

Nena smiled. "It is your own tent."

"Then lead the way." Jarl returned her smile and slid from from the horse's back. As his feet hit the ground, he stumbled. He grimaced and paused, holding on to the horse to steady himself for a moment.

"Are you alright?" Nena asked, worried.

"Yes." He nodded. "Just a little stiff and sore. I'm fine. I'll follow."

<hr />

"It is not yet ready," Jalla informed them as she looked them both over. The insides of both of their legs were covered with dried sweat from the horse. Jarl was covered from head to toe in blood and dirt. "You have just enough time to go to the baths while I finish," she offered, though her tone let them know it was more than a suggestion. "Exanthia has already placed a clean dress for you in the women's bath, Nena. Apologies, Jarl, I had no Northman clothes, so there are Teclan clothes for you in the men's bath."

"Gratitude for the thought and effort, but I brought a clean change of clothes back with me," Jarl said. He turned away so the women could not see his face as he dug into his bag, his teeth gritted against the pain.

"Come," Nena said to Jarl. "I'll show you where the men bathe." She led him to a large clay and thatch structure, similar to the cell, but larger, then stopped at the doorway, pointing inside.

"Will you not join me?" he asked.

"No," she replied with a smile and a small shake of her head.

"Why not? We're married now."

"That doesn't matter." She glanced around, thankful to find no one close enough to overhear them. "Men and women do not bathe together."

"Never?" he asked, incredulous.

"No, it is forbidden," she whispered.

Jarl smiled and shook his head. "That is something we will have to remedy one day. I will take great pleasure in introducing you to a shared man and woman bath."

Nena flushed and lowered her voice. "You must not say such things where others can hear. I will meet you back at the tent," she said as she turned away.

"Don't be long," he called to her retreating back.

She turned and smiled. "I won't."

Nena entered the women's bath, surprised, but happy to find it empty. She found the dress Jalla had mentioned, carefully folded on a bench. Nena picked it up and held it to her body. No doeskin warrior dress for her now. The soft pale peach-colored fabric felt like a cloud as it swirled against her. The color complimented her dark hair and skin. Jarl would like it.

As she slipped into the warm water and untied her braids, she couldn't help but imagine bathing with Jarl. Her stomach fluttered. She hurried through the rest of the process, anxious to get back to him. Back to.... She squeezed the excess water from her hair and quickly fingered one of her favorite scented oils through the damp tresses. She picked up a quill brush and combed out the remaining tangles but did not braid it. It was still too wet—and Jarl liked her hair down. She smiled, realizing this was the first time she had ever prepared herself to try to appeal to him. She grew warm at the thought of his eyes when he saw her.

This would be the first time they would lie together with no secrets, no hidden agendas. The first time that she would give herself to him completely, body and spirit, with no questions, no doubts, no fears. Their first time as man and wife. Nena slipped into the new dress and ran the brush through her hair one last time, surprised at how nervous she had suddenly become.

Jarl entered the tent, glad to find Jalla gone, but disappointed Nena was not yet there. He glanced around the unfamiliar space. Brightly colored woven carpets covered the walls and floors and a substantial pile of sleeping furs dominated the area, taking up almost half. He smiled. On the other side was his bag of possessions, a few items he recognized as Nena's, and a small wooden table with two chairs. The table was heavily laden with food: a carved bowl filled with various fruits, a platter of smoked meats, a loaf of bread, and four waterskins, two on either side. He opened one from the left side and sniffed, then took a sip. It was wine. He opened the second. It was the same. He moved to the right side of the table, picked up one of the waterskins there and checked it. Water. Jarl smiled again and nodded to himself. Jalla had made sure they were well provisioned. There would be no reason for them to leave the tent for anything.

The soft sound of the tent flap lifting pulled Jarl's attention to the entrance. Nena ducked through the opening and stood once inside. She remained there for a brief moment, seeming almost unsure. Though most of her damp hair still flowed down her back, sections on either side had fallen forward when she bent over to enter the tent. They now lay dark against the pale orange of her dress. The dress took him by surprise. Only once had he ever seen her in anything other than a leather warrior dress, and that had been only briefly. Jarl took a deep breath and exhaled slowly.

"You are truly the most beautiful woman I have ever seen," he murmured and shook his head. "I still cannot believe how lucky I am. Cannot believe that you are truly mine."

Nena smiled at that and moved toward him. He pushed one side of her hair over her shoulder with the back of his hand, while his fingertips caressed along her jaw, over her cheek and ear, to the back of her neck. Cradling her head, he leaned down and kissed her tenderly on the lips.

Nena returned his slow sensual kiss and pressed the full length of her body against his. She reached her arms around him and squeezed him tightly. He tensed and groaned, but not with pleasure.

"You are hurt," she said, and pulled away to look into his eyes.

"I'm alright," he said, but she could still see the traces of the grimace on his face.

"Where are you hurt?" she asked.

He smiled a rueful smile. "Apparently everywhere. I felt fine before, but as the battle fever subsides, there is no part of me that does not strongly complain."

"I have never known you to be so after a battle."

"Nor have I been, but I have never before faced such an opponent."

Nena nodded. "Are you too sore to...?"

Before she could finish, he cut her off. "Not so long as I draw breath," he said with a determined grin. "Come." He took her hand and led her the last few steps to the furs. As he knelt and began to pull her with him, he caught his breath and froze.

"Jarl?"

"I'm alright. Truly. Just give me a moment." He flopped clumsily into the furs, moaned with pain, and then rolled over to face her, breathing hard. He smiled and shook his head. "This is embarrassing, and not at all how I planned our first night together as man and wife to be," he admitted.

Nena had to laugh at the situation. How helpless he was. How hard he was trying to fight it. How strange it was to see him in that condition. Even more humorous was the pressure they both clearly felt about their first time together after so long being special.

"Laughing really doesn't help," he grunted, then he chuckled, too.

"Well, fortunately for you, you have a wife to take care of you now." Nena knelt beside him. "You must lie still and let me make you more comfortable," she said as she rearranged the furs behind his back. "Better?" she asked when she was through.

"Yes," he said and nodded.

"No, something still doesn't look right," Nena murmured and looked him over with a mischievous glint in her eyes. "It's your tunic. It looks very uncomfortable to me." She leaned over him, her breasts pressing through the soft material of her dress tantalizingly close to his face, and untied the laces at the front of his tunic. One at a time she pulled each of his arms out of the sleeves and then pulled it over his head. She threw it to one side and ran her fingers through the hair on his chest. "That looks a little better. But still..."

She glanced lower and allowed her fingers to trace the hair along the center of his rippled stomach down to the top of his trousers. Jarl exhaled when her fingers stopped at the laces there. "These trousers look very binding to me." Scooting her body lower, but still sitting beside him on the furs, she unlaced the ties of his trousers with excruciating slowness. Before she had finished, the front of his trousers were, in fact, very binding.

She glanced up at him and smiled. His eyes were the green she had imagined so many times since her escape, but the intensity within them now was even more than she remembered. She caught her breath. He said nothing, only watched her. "I'm sorry, but the trousers have to go, too," she said with a smile. She turned back to her task, peeling both sides of his trousers open and down. His erection sprang up at the sudden release. She did not touch it. Instead, she stood and moved to his feet, lifting each leg and pulling the trousers off of him one leg at a time.

Still standing at the base of the furs, she allowed her eyes to feast on her handiwork, taking in every detail of his lean naked masculine form. "You still don't look comfortable," she murmured.

"Imagine that," he said, his voice tight.

"I know what you need," she murmured.

"Not that hard to guess from your vantage point, I'm sure."

Nena reached up behind her neck under her hair and untied her dress. She held onto the ties with both hands and only slowly let it slide down her body.

"Nena," Jarl groaned. The depth of his need and desire for her in his tone were more stimulating than she could have imagined. He had yet to touch her, but her body was on fire for him. She let the dress fall to the floor, tired of her game—having become as much the victim of it as he was. Stepping toward him, she knelt and straddled him above his waist. She leaned forward and kissed him, her hair fanning softly around them. Jarl grabbed her by her upper arms and pulled her tighter, returning her kiss. Holding her there, he pulled his lips away and ducked his head, securing one of her nipples with his mouth, then the other.

Nena moaned with pleasure. She pushed his shoulders back into the furs and pulled away from him, sliding her body down until she felt his shaft between her thighs. She squeezed and pressed her pelvis lower taking him inside her, not stopping until the full length of him was buried deep within.

Jarl grabbed her wrists and pulled her hands from his shoulders. Taking control, he sat up and suckled her breasts again as he thrust within her. It was too much—Nena felt her climax coming already and clutched at him, her fingers twisting in the hair on the back of his head as she gave into it. As she let out a long gasping moan, Jarl gave two hard final thrusts inside her. His fingers dug into her shoulder blades pulling her down onto him even tighter, his face buried in her neck. They sat suspended that way for a moment until Jarl fell backward into the furs with a groan, pulling her with him.

"You are going to be the death of me. I swear it," he said with a smile.

Nena smiled and snuggled in against the chest she had so missed.

"I have brought ink for you. For us both," Nena said as she entered their tent the next day.

"For what?" Jarl asked.

"You were so worried before about having your name on my arm for the world to see, and now it will be so—though what symbol to use for you has given the council cause to consult the gods."

"And what have they decided?" he asked. "Hopefully it will be something bold," Jarl said, though he was fully expecting something degrading. Nena frowned which only deepened his concern.

"I don't like it, but it's already been decided. It is the curved head and neck of a serpent. They say it represents your ships, but I do not understand a ship formed in such a manner. And I don't care for serpents," she added. "My mother died from the bite of a serpent. I do not remember it, but they say it took several days to kill her, and her death was very painful."

"I didn't know that."

"It was long ago." She changed the subject. "I can draw it for you if you'd like?"

"Yes."

Nena picked up a stick, and drew the figure from memory, in the soft exposed dirt near the fire ring, the only place on the floor that wasn't covered with carpet.

Jarl smiled and nodded. "It is a good symbol," he said, satisfied.

Nena looked to him to explain.

"It's not a serpent, well, maybe a serpent of sorts; it is the head and neck of a dragon."

"A dragon." Nena repeated the word, the "r" rolling off her tongue with the guttural undertones he found so appealing. "I do not know this word. Describe the animal."

"The dragon is the most powerful beast that has ever lived. It has a serpent's head, but legs like a lizard, and a body so large it can carry multiple men on its back. It's covered with thick heavy scales that can rarely be pierced by arrow or sword, and it has a long tail and great wings that enable it to fly like a bird."

"A giant flying serpent?" Nena was incredulous.

"Yes," Jarl nodded. "And it has huge teeth and claws, easily capable of ripping a man to shreds." He paused. "But its most powerful weapon, by far, is the ability to throw a stream of fire from its mouth—enough to burn a man alive."

Nena sat back annoyed that he had fooled her for as long as he had.

"It is true," he said, responding to her skepticism. "You can ask Gunnar or Tryggr, or any of the men when we next see them."

Nena shook her head, refusing to be more gullible. "And you have seen such a beast?" she asked, her eyebrows raised.

"No," Jarl admitted. "The last dragon was killed in the time of my great grandfather. They were so dangerous and so deadly, men launched long campaigns to hunt them down in their caves in the mountains where they slept and kill them. Even then, many men were lost." He could see he had her interest again. "To this day many of our ships carry the image of the dragon on their bow. We believe it imparts some of the dragon's power. It is a good symbol to represent me."

"If it so powerful, why would all of your ships not have it?"

"The dragon is reserved for drakkar—lead warships," Jarl explained, then went back to something she had said earlier. "You said you had ink for both of us. Why would I need it?"

"You are Teclan now. You will bear the mark of the tribe, and since you have been chosen, you will also bear my mark."

"I will have a star?" he asked with a grin.

"And a lightning bolt," she said, smiling at his boyish enthusiasm.

"Who will do it? I have no qualms with you doing mine, but I would not be responsible for putting anything less than perfect on your skin."

"Jalla is skilled with the needle. She can do both of us, so they will be the same."

"We could stay here, if you want," he offered, his eyes suddenly serious. "I would stay here for you."

"No." Nena shook her head. "My people have accepted you for me, but you could never truly be one of us. Unlike Exanthia, you will never look Dor, and while that doesn't really matter, our history of being enemies will be difficult for many to overcome. Besides, I can't see you raiding with the other Teclan warriors while taking orders from my brother." She paused. "And it would be very difficult for him to look upon you every day, and to have the other people of the tribe look upon you, knowing you had bested him, when he is to be chief. Your plan is for the best," she said.

"But if we stayed," Jarl pondered out loud. "What would our life be like? What would my responsibilities be? Hunting to provide food for you and Jalla, and Exanthia until she chooses? An occasional raid that I would not have to organize or be responsible for? And you would tend to all my daily needs, cooking, and weaving these nice carpets and waiting at home for me, while I was away? You told me once that was all a Teclan woman longs for after she chooses. You probably have already lost all desire to even ride a horse again, now that your choice is behind you." He smiled a mischievous smile.

"You are a wicked man, Jarl. I know that you only pretend to be enamored with the idea of an easy life here to tease me, when you know you would not like it. While you would not have the responsibilities of a raid, neither would you have any decision. You would be allowed to do only what my brother commanded you. That would not suit you," she said, smug and confident she had turned the tables on him.

Jarl heaved a great sigh, "It would be an adjustment at first, but one that might be worth the sacrifice to see you as a contented and dutiful demure wife."

Nena pursed her lips, even though she knew he was not serious. "You would not like that."

"I might," he disagreed. He laid back and locked his fingers behind his head. "Let's try it and see. Wife, fetch me a cup of water." He was grinning now. He was surprised when Nena stood to do as he asked. Although he was instantly wary when she returned with the full cup of icy mountain water and did not hand it to him. Instead, she stood over him, the cup suspended over his naked chest. Now it was she who smiled.

"Yes, my lord. Was this what you had in mind?" she asked sweetly. "Oh, apologies," she said before he could answer, and tipped the cup so that a few drops fell on him.

Jarl lunged and grabbed her ankles, pulling her off balance and down onto the furs with him. She shrieked as the water flew in the air, soaking them both. "What a naughty wife I have. One who would probably need to be punished frequently for her disobedience if we stayed here. So, I suppose it is for the best that we leave, but only if you first admit that you are the one who would have more difficulty adjusting if we stayed."

Nena clamped her lips together.

"Admit it," he repeated, moving his hands along her ribs, as if he were going to tickle her.

"It is true," she gasped. "It is not only you who wouldn't fit in here. Though these are the only people I have ever known, I feel I no longer belong. I would be bored with that life. You have shown me too much of the world for me to be that woman now, though perhaps I was never that woman before," she confessed.

"I don't want that woman. I never wanted that woman." He pulled her close and looked into her eyes. "Then it is settled? We both agree? We will meet my men at the port?" he asked.

"Yes." She nodded. "I will tell my father."

"Later," he said. "With all that squealing and carrying on, everyone is probably imagining what we are doing. I would not have them think such things, absent cause," he murmured as he pulled her into his arms and kissed her.

Jarl watched in disbelief as Nena divided large handfuls of gold and jewels among the horses' packs to better distribute the weight. "In case we are set upon by bandits on the way and have to run," she explained as she saw him watching. "They must be evenly weighted or they will slow us down."

"To this day I thought you exaggerated about having a huge collection of wealth," he said.

"Why would I have done that?" she asked.

"I don't know," he shrugged. "Perhaps to convince me to ransom you."

"But if the jewels were not really here, arranging a ransom no one could pay would have done me no good."

"I suppose not," he agreed. "Still. I never guessed there would be so much. And this is all your share? You haven't accidentally taken someone else's?"

"Of course not," she said, indignant. "And this is only a portion of my share, but you said we needed to travel fast, so I didn't want to weigh down the horses. We can come back later for the rest. And I thought with what you had also accumulated in your raids, it would be enough. Do you think we'll need more?"

Jarl looked at her, his mouth agape. "This will be plenty, but there is more?"

"Would you like me to show you?" Nena asked.

He nodded.

She smiled and took his hand. "Then come, Husband. Let me show you how large your wife's fortune is."

After an hour of meandering through the cave system, Jarl had seen more treasure than he thought existed. Every time he thought they had come to the end, another tunnel branched off, lined with alcoves filled with jewels, silver and gold. The gems and precious metals glimmered and sparkled in the light cast by the flame of their flickering pitch torch.

"Who guards it all?" he asked. He had yet to see another soul.

"We do," Nena replied.

"I mean, from each other," he clarified.

"There is no need. Some may have more than others, but as you can see there is plenty to go around."

"When we are back among my people, you should never speak of this to anyone but me," he cautioned.

"It is safe here."

"Yes, but it would be better not to provide temptation."

"When I saw you had brought your whole army, I thought you had come for it," she murmured, frowning.

"I didn't bring the army," he said and pulled her into an embrace. He could see the memory still pained her. "I sent the army with Gunnar to the port, while I tracked you. They were to head for home if I did not return and leave behind only four ships. You were the only treasure I was after."

"I realized that when you came in alone. That was very foolish. It all worked out, but you could have just as easily been killed."

"I had no choice. And only with great risk comes great reward. You are my greatest reward."

They had made their way back to the entrance and Nena's personal alcove of treasure, still over half full. She grabbed another small bag full of gems and smiled. "For an emergency," she said.

Jarl reached down and picked up a net of fine gold chains and gold filigree. He held it up for her to see. "You need to take this with us, too. When we get settled, I want to see you wearing only this, lying on a pile of furs surrounded by jewels." He closed his eyes and smiled, imagining the sight of the delicate gold against her dark skin, her body surrounded by rubies and sapphires winking in candlelight.

"As you wish, Husband." Nena took the gold netting from his hands and added it to the pouch, before dousing the flaming pitch torch in a bucket of water by the entrance.

They returned to the horses, and Jarl watched as Nena decided which pack horse to add the extra weight to, then rearranged the load again for it to be the most comfortable for the animal. He looked around, surprised to not find any other Teclan. Were they angry? Was this some sort of shunning to punish her for leaving? Everyone had seemed to accept the announcement. He had seen no sign of resentment or animosity in the past few days as they had made their preparations to leave. He looked to Nena, but she seemed not to have noticed.

"Where is everyone?" he asked.

"They will not come to see us off," Nena said. "We do not say good-bye. It is not our way."

"Why not?"

"We do not want our last memories to be sad ones."

"Are there none you would share special last words with?" Jarl probed.

Nena stopped adjusting the horses' packs and bit her lower lip. "Yes," she murmured.

"Then do it."

She hesitated.

"You are more than Teclan now, Nena. You are your own woman, free to do as she wants. If it will ease your spirit to share last words, then do it. I will wait for you here."

Nena found Exanthia by the creek and sat beside her. "Did you know this was my special place?" she said as she stroked the girl's hair. "When you reach the point in your training where you must learn to endure, you will need a special place to go to in your mind when things are hard. This was my place and it is a good one. Perhaps it will be yours as well."

Exanthia nodded.

"You can still come with us, if you have changed your mind," Nena coaxed.

Exanthia shook her head. "Why can't you stay here?"she whispered.

"Jarl could never be happy here."

"But these are your people, and he is not." Her tone was both bitter and confused.

"Jarl is my people now. The gods chose him for me, and I accepted their choice. It was the right choice for me. You will understand when you are older." Nena put her arm around Exanthia and pulled her close. "But I will miss you. There are so many things I wanted to show you, to teach you. Like this place, for one. And to help you practice your warrior skills. Jalla and Gentok will help you now."

"Jalla?" Exanthia asked in disbelief, the hint of a smile coming to her face at the idea of it.

"Yes, Jalla." Nena smiled. "Do not let her fool you. Jalla tries to act old and motherly, but never forget she is Meln's sister. She not only possesses knowledge of important things about herbs for healing and for poison, but she also possesses great warrior skills. It would be good for her to get out with you and clash the sticks. She would not just be helping you, you would also be helping her to not grow old too fast."

Exanthia giggled. "Jalla with the sticks?"

"You laugh, but she will surprise you. And I want you to promise me you will ask Lothor to take you to the waterfall. It is a secret place we found when were children."

"Lothor?"

"Yes. He is not as gruff as he seems. You are his niece now, and should build that bond. The waterfall is a full day's ride from here, but if you ask him, I know he will take you. It would be good for you both. Do you promise?"

"Yes," Exanthia agreed. "I will ask him."

"And Gentok," Nena paused, her heart heavy. She hadn't seen nor spoken with Gentok since the trial and her choosing. She knew it would have brought him pain and that saddened her. "He is a great warrior. Listen carefully to all he has to teach you."

"I will."

"Jarl is waiting. I must go." Nena stood and placed her hand on Exanthia's head. "You will be a great warrior one day, Exanthia of the Teclan. Always know that I am very proud of you."

Nena went next to Jalla's tent but found it empty. Disappointed, she returned to Jarl and the horses. They were just about to mount when Jalla approached them. "I just found this extra travel hide and have no need for it. I thought perhaps it might come in useful on your journey," Jalla said.

"Gratitude," Nena said as she took the hide and tied it on top of one of the horse's packs, even though they already had plenty. She knew it was just an excuse for Jalla to see her one last time. After the last knot was tied, she turned to the older woman and hugged her. "Take care, Jalla. May the gods smile upon you until we see each other again."

"And you, Nena," Jalla whispered as they separated from their embrace. "And Jarl." She nodded at him. "Travel safe."

"We will," he said. "And I swear to you I will protect her until my last breath."

She studied him and nodded. "You have proven that to me already." With that she turned and walked away, leaving Nena and Jarl alone.

"Are you ready?" he asked.

Nena nodded and mounted the gray mare, settling into the sheepskin Dor saddle for the long ride ahead. She waited for Jarl to mount his stallion and gather his two pack horses, then did the same with her pair before she followed him down the trail she knew so well.

Chapter 31

N ena leaned from the platform to touch the smooth carved wood. She traced the outline of each animal design with the tips of her fingers. From a distance they appeared to be only the scales of the great dragon's neck, but up close she could see the intricate detail. Her gaze moved up to the golden head of the dragon. Its eye looked down at her—and saw her. She could not shake the impression that the great beast was measuring her.

"It is beautiful," she murmured. And it was, though she'd been afraid at first and had approached the boat with considerable trepidation. Now that she was close and could see the loving craftsmanship that had gone into its creation, she was reassured.

"Yes, she is," Jarl said as he ran his own hand over the neck.

"She?" Nena asked with a smile.

"Of course. She was the most beautiful woman I had ever seen until you."

Nena looked back to the dragon's eye, sure now that this great ship had a spirit. She wondered how it would respond to his words. Would it be jealous as Altene had been? If so, she would never dare step aboard, sure that some mishap would befall her. But the great beast's eye seemed not fierce, but satisfied. "And do you have a name for her?" Nena asked.

Jarl smiled. "She is The Treasure Huntress. And she has lived up to her name on every voyage, though none have made me so rich as this one." He pulled her to him and kissed her.

Nena resumed her scrutiny of the tiny characters carved into the scales. "And who are these two lovers?" she asked, her fingers tracing over the two small forms locked in a lovers' embrace.

Jarl laughed. "There are no lovers there," he said without looking.

"There surely are." She looked at him but kept her fingers near the carving so as not to lose her place in all the intricate detail.

Jarl leaned closer and peered next to her fingertips. The male and female entwined bodies were unmistakable. "I never noticed that before," he murmured as he examined it closer. "That is very odd. I have never known of a ship to have such a symbol. She has kept secrets from me all this time. That had to be Leila's doing." Jarl was quiet for a moment lost in thought. "Sigurd said his wife, Leila, wanted me to get more than I bargained for, and he said it very strangely. I assumed at the time, he meant the reduction in the price, but now, looking back—I'm not so sure. I will tell you about them one day."

"So that is not you and some Northwoman?" Nena teased.

"No. There is no Northwoman." He stepped closer and squinted at the figures. "In fact, I think I see a Teclan star on her arm."

"You do not."

But Jarl saw her glance back at the carving again, still not always able to recognize his ways of saying one thing and meaning another. He pulled her into a brief hug, then keeping his arm around her shoulders, led her toward the back of the boat. "Come. Let me show you the rest." They walked further down the boardwalk to the middle of the ship. Jarl leapt across the short expanse of open water to the deck of the boat, but Nena's feet remained planted on the planks.

"It's alright. It's not far," Jarl encouraged.

"It's not the distance," she said, as she watched Jarl's body unconsciously compensating for the rolling motion of the boat beneath him.

"I will catch you," he said.

Nena chose a spot near him and leaped across, sure that she could do something as simple as stand on her own. She landed with both feet solid and flat on the boat's floor, but then it shifted, and she staggered. Jarl grabbed her flailing arm and supported her. She looked up embarrassed. "I'm sorry. I wobble about like a newborn fawn."

"Your body will soon learn to adjust to the motion. You won't even notice it—like riding a horse."

She looked out over the still surface of the water. "It looks so calm, but I feel its power even now, from below. I cannot imagine how it must feel when it is angry."

Jarl shook his head. "No, you cannot. It is a fierce and terrifying thing. Even knowing the ship is blessed by the gods, it is a trying experience for the bravest man. But it will not be rough for our voyage."

"How do you know that?"

He glanced at the brilliant red sunset with satisfaction. "A red sky at night means fair weather, and when a storm is coming, I feel it. Here." He placed his hand on his chest. "I'm surprised you Teclan are not masters of that. Your senses with other things seem so much keener than normal."

"We learn those other things. They are not natural abilities."

"So is predicting a storm. Though not all are able to learn it well. I will teach you someday." He stepped further toward the stern, pulling her with him. "Here is where the horses will ride. And here is where we will sleep. If the weather is wet or the sun too fierce, we pull this canopy over us. And this." He touched the huge roll of bound canvas. "We lift up to catch the wind. Often it will take us to our destination with little effort. But if the wind is still, then we row." He pointed to the oars on either side.

"How long will it take us?" she asked.

"Not long. It will only be a three day journey to the northwest shore."

"Three whole days on the Great Sea." Nena shivered.

Jarl pulled her closer, knowing her family's fear of going out on the water. "You will be safe with me. I am from a sea tribe. And though mine is a sea far from here, this sea also recognizes me. And now it recognizes you, too."

She nodded, unconvinced but determined. If he had told her it would be dangerous and they might very well die, she would still go with him. As he had been willing to die rather than live without her, she, too, felt the same.

Sensing that her uneasiness remained, Jarl changed the subject. "The northwest shore is a beautiful place at the base of a great mountain. It is not so tall as the Teclan mountain, but still large. We can go there if the summers are too hot, or anytime we want to hunt. The coastline has rich grasslands and fertile soil for growing food. And there are great rocks jutting out into the sea to protect the port we will build. They shall provide safe harbor for the ships even in bad weather."

"It sounds wonderful," she said.

"It will be," he agreed. "We should return to camp and get some sleep. We will need to be up and ready at first light."

"I thought your men who were retiring were going to settle on the northeast shore?" she asked, after his guard had taken away the plates of their evening meal.

"They were." He looked at her curiously "But the storms come from the south and west and they will be much worse coming off the Great Sea than the land."

"But the men say the northeast shore is closer for the trader's coming from the far, far east, and more direct for the other Northman boats coming off the river."

"Do they now?" He smiled. "How is it you know so much?"

"I listen."

"And I do not?" he asked.

She shrugged, and he pulled her in close, reaching for a spot where he knew she was ticklish. "And what else do my men say?" he asked.

"They say," she said, as she squirmed away from his fingers, "they say the far, far easterners will not be able to trade with you because they will not be able to cross the Great Sea." His fingers found her ticklish spot, despite her evasive maneuvers. She could not control her giggles. "Jarl, stop, please," she gasped.

He knew she hated it when he did that. Apparently for Teclan, it was unthinkable for an adult to be tickled, but it was his one weapon against her when she sassed him.

"You can tell my loose-mouthed men, since you seem to be so in touch with them, that if our settlement was destroyed by a sea storm, we would not have to worry about trading with the far, far easterners. There would be nothing left to trade with. And for their peace of mind, we will be settling where the Volga River joins the Great Sea. The other Northman boats will find us easily and the far, far easterners will not have to cross the sea, only the neck of the river, which they will do by the simple ferry that we will build.

"Though I do have a confession." He paused. "I chose the spot on the northwest shore for three reasons. The first is the weather, which I already explained. The second was to have wood from the mountain for building homes, fortifications and docks. And the third...I would not have you so far removed from all that is familiar to you. It is not the Teclan mountain, but I thought you would gain some comfort by its presence." He finished quietly, seeming almost embarrassed. "Though that is not something I would have shared with my men," he added ruefully.

Nena's heart swelled. He was always so considerate of her feelings and her comfort.

"With you, all new things will become familiar to me," she said as she snuggled against his bare chest. "But are you sure we cannot ride there? Must we take the ships?"

"We could ride, but what will take only three days now would take three weeks. You must trust me."

"I do. Now tell me the story of Sigurd and his wife, Leila—the ones who built The Treasure Huntress."

Chapter 32

It was dawn, when Gunnar stepped off the deck of the ship and found Jarl on the dock staring at The Treasure Huntress in the fog. "I don't have to take her, you know. I can still take the Sea Wolf," Gunnar said.

"No, the Sea Wolf is long past due to retire," Jarl said. "She's the perfect boat to leave behind, and more than I expected to have. Besides," he placed his hand on the graceful dragon's neck that made the bow of the ship, "I gave my word to Sigurd. The Huntress is young and was made for adventure. She will be far better off seeking treasure than stagnating here as a transport shuttle." He turned to Gunnar. "And I know she will be in good hands."

"As will you, I suspect," Gunnar said, and nodded toward the woman approaching them in the morning mist.

Jarl smiled and nodded in agreement. "Yes. As will I."

"You know I would like to stay and help more, but we must go now or we won't make it before the rivers freeze. We'll be cutting it very close now, I'm afraid. As much as I hate the heat here, a frozen Rusland winter sounds even less appealing," Gunnar said and shook his head. "And even with fair weather, I expect all the land portages to be even lengthier. Since you decided to stay, half the men have suddenly decided to stay with you. I have made up for much of the lost labor with extra slaves, but you know even the strongest equals half a Viking. The loss of Tryggr's brute strength alone required three slaves to replace."

"I fully understand," Jarl said. "Your help here in these past days has been an unexpected bonus, and very well received, my friend. We are far ahead of where I expected to be even months from now. Gratitude."

"None required." Gunnar dismissed it. "I look forward to seeing your progress when I return next year. I expect it will be much changed. And as much as I will miss not having the extra men for their labor, I am more optimistic about your survival here with the larger force. Though I would feel even better if you had more of them."

"More will come."

"Yes, that's what I'm worried about. I do not expect them all to be friendly."

"Thanks to you we are at least starting out with some defenses."

Gunnar glanced around at the rough, quickly constructed fortifications: ramparts, sharp poles, trenches, a watch tower. They were meager, but better than nothing. "I shall do as you requested with your possessions at home, and bring the equivalent of their worth on my next expedition."

"And mine. Don't forget mine," Tryggr said, as he heaved the last crate to be stowed on board, then joined them, overhearing Gunnar's last words.

"And yours Tryggr," Gunnar agreed. "Though it should be you now taking the helm of The Treasure Huntress, not me."

"Bah. Captaining is for the young. Raiding is for the young." Tryggr shook his head. "Besides, someone needs to watch out for Jarl, here. He's reckless, you know. Without someone to look after him, he'd end up dead for sure."

"Then I leave you to it." Gunnar nodded. "May Odin and Thor continue to smile upon you until we see each other again."

"And to you," Jarl said.

Gunnar leapt easily onto the deck and made his way to the helm. At his command all oars splashed into the water in one synchronized movement, and the ship slowly backed away from the makeshift dock.

Nena came to stand beside Jarl as he watched the ship row away. He put his arm around her waist and pulled her close. Neither spoke until the ship was but a speck on the horizon.

"Do you wish you were going?" she asked him.

He turned and looked deep into her eyes. "I am exactly where I want to be."

She smiled. "As am I."

Epilogue

Sigurd stepped up onto the low granite slab that jutted out over the fjord and glanced up at the sun. The muted orange fireball was just beginning its descent toward the horizon. His timing was perfect. He dropped the soft white rabbit pelt near the water's edge and carefully laid the two oxhorn cups on top of it before lowering the small cask from his shoulder. After filling both cups with the amber honey mead, he leaned them against the cask, then eased his stiff body down to sit next to them. He adjusted his position to avoid a sharp piece of ice jabbing him in the back and then settled in against the stone.

He exhaled a long slow exhale and watched his breath billow white in the crisp air before slowly dissipating. There was not a hint of wind. Just the way she liked it. He looked out over the smooth still water with satisfaction. The tide was full high and the calm water lapped gently at the edge of the rock slab. Picking up both cups, he touched them together, then leaned forward to pour the contents of the ornate silver rimmed one into the water, before taking a deep swallow from the other.

"He's done it, Leila," Sigurd said, looking to the place where her burning burial ship had finally slipped beneath the surface. "Jarl has given The Treasure

Huntress away, as promised." He smiled at the water. "I was in town today and heard it from a merchant ship at the dock. But that's only half of the story. According to the captain, Jarl has not only given up the ship, he's settled on the shores of the Caspian Sea with a native barbarian princess."

Sigurd recounted the passionate whirlwind love affair—the capture, the escape, the trial, as the man had described it to him, refilling his own cup twice in the process. "And I know you think I'm exaggerating, but as Odin is my witness, I swear I am not. The merchant said Jarl was so enamored with this woman, he offered up his own life to the gods to get her back. It's exactly as you said, love truly is more powerful than a man's sword—or his mind, and, once experienced, it's the most precious treasure of all. Jarl has discovered it as you had hoped. Along with great fortune," he added, nodding with satisfaction.

Sigurd looked out over the water. The bottom edge of the sun was already lost. "I miss you, you know. So much. Every day." He shook his head to fight back the tears that welled in his eyes. "I know. I know. I promised you I'd not be sad, but sometimes it's too hard. I still feel you with me, but it's not enough. I long so desperately to touch you, to hold you—to hear you laugh and see you smile. Hearing that man describe the ship to me today as if I didn't know it, for he knew not who I was, brought everything back so clearly. As he described the golden dragon's head and the animals on the dragon's scales, I could see you holding each one of the sketches." His voice quavered. He paused and closed his eyes. "Apologies. This was to be a happy conversation. A celebration of our success. And even though I miss you so much, I am happy you are free."

The sun was now a quarter gone.

"The ship is becoming a legend. They say she is everything we dreamed— fast, nimble, strong. Blessed by the gods they say." He took another deep swallow of his mead. "They also say Jarl gave her to his third in command not his second, a man named Gunnar Frederiksen. I thought that strange, but you probably already knew that, didn't you? You probably already knew everything I told you today. Hell, you probably even chose her next captain.

There was something about his second that you didn't like, so you swayed Jarl's decision." Sigurd nodded as he considered it. "Of course you did. I must admit the thought of you measuring and choosing another man makes me jealous, though in some ways I pity him for what you'll put him through." He smiled. "He doesn't stand a chance against you. And though the reward in the end will be more than worth it, that poor bastard is about to have his life turned upside down."

Sigurd smiled again and took another long swallow. "I think I shall become a regular at the port to hear of your next adventures—and as I hear them, I'll come here to share them with you. As much as I dislike going to town and being amongst people, I'll do it. I can see the huge smile on your face at the thought of me mingling with strangers, making small talk, pressing any who come for information of your travels." He frowned. "That was also probably your intent, guiding me even from the afterlife. I can hear you right now claiming it's for my own good. And I'm not saying I agree with you, because I don't, but I'll do it anyway. I wonder where you'll go, what you'll see...." His voice trailed away.

Sigurd raised his glass as the last glowing red rim of the sun prepared to dip below the horizon. "To your success with this next captain of The Treasure Huntress, Leila. I look forward to hearing all about it."

Can't wait to know what happens with the next captain of
The Treasure Huntress?

Keep reading for a special preview of

FIONA
Book Two of *The Treasure Huntress* Series

By ANN BOELTER

A s Gunnar slogged through the mud, he was at least thankful for the lull in the driving rain that had plagued them since leaving the Dublin slave merchant's estate earlier that night. He tried to imagine the hot dry days ahead when he returned to the East—the incessant red dust clogging his nostrils, the sweat chafing under his armor. He would long for this cool Irish damp then. He glanced up at the nearly full moon about to be overtaken by a smaller cloud, then at the more threatening clouds looming behind. The rain may have let up for the moment, but it appeared it was not to last.

"Run!" The unexpected shout and jangle of chains from one of the prisoners behind him jolted Gunnar from his musings. His hand closed on the golden hilt of his sword, just as the small cloud that had previously only flirted with the moon's perimeter plunged them into total darkness.

Gunnar turned and took a quick assessment of the group of slaves. None were moving. None seemed poised for escape. All remained securely tethered together with their iron neck collars and chains. He glanced at his men who were also trying to identify the recipient of the slave's sudden warning. Some had weapons drawn. Others had their hands ready on the hilts of their swords. All eyes and ears strained in the darkness, trying to detect any signs of an impending attack.

Gunnar cursed the cloud that prevented him from seeing for whom the warning had been intended. His decision to travel at night, to slip unseen by local raiders, if the rumors about them were true, was working against him. Now it was he and his men who couldn't see, and they had the added disadvantage of not knowing the terrain.

Lightning flashed overhead, giving a split second of vision before submersing them once again in blackness. Another flash. Then another. The unpredictable bursts bathed the countryside in an otherworldly light, creating unnerving mysterious shadows without providing enough time to discern what was real. Nerves stretched taut, Gunnar awaited the next flash, half expecting it to reveal a hard charging assailant closing in on him. He pulled Maid's Dream from its sheath.

The suspense was excruciating. If an attack was coming, Gunnar wished they would just bring it. Here, they were in an open spot in the road, easily defended. His men lived to fight, and could readily handle most adversaries, of that he was confident. Anyone who was unfortunate enough to get close to them would soon find that out—and, in doing so, would have lost their advantage of knowing the terrain. Up close, fighting hand-to-hand, they would fight on equal terms, and unless their numbers were so substantial that they could overrun his group, Gunnar was sure of the outcome.

Unless they had archers. If that were the case, this open position, so ideal to take on a foe armed with sword or battle-axe, would provide little protection. Gunnar's gut tightened at the thought of being showered with clouds of winged death from a faceless opponent, before realizing such a form of attack was unlikely. The rumors at the port had been that the slaves were being stolen. A blanket attack by archers in the darkness could not differentiate between captor and captive; it would kill Northman and Irish slave alike. Still, he found himself listening for the distinctive whir of feather fletching in flight, in time to raise his shield. He hated archers.

He glanced at Rorick who had moved up beside him. His tall, young second's sword was drawn, and his eyes were wary, but a hint of a smile played at the corners of his lips. Gunnar shook his head. Rorick would get his fill of blood soon enough in the rich East, and learn he did not need to seek it out in unnecessary places.

Gunnar returned his full focus to their surroundings, waiting for the cloud to pass. The wind picked up, and he felt several drops of rain, though the most ominous clouds still held off. Ever so slowly, the smaller cloud moved on, and moonlight turned the impenetrable darkness to near day. He could see the form of a woman on the mired road ahead of them, now. She did not appear to be aware of them—must not have heard the slave's warning for the wind. She stood, slightly stooped over with her back to them, holding up her horse's left front leg, while she inspected its hoof. The animal was a common farm steed, thick-legged and coarse, and the woman's hooded cloak was one of simple wool.

The men looked to him for orders, but Gunnar shook his head for them to wait. Had this been an ambush, he would have expected it to be set up in the dark woods ahead. Still, his gut told him something wasn't right. You didn't just come across young women alone on the road at night.

"Run, lass!" One of the prisoners screeched his warning again. This time his men were ready, and the man was quickly silenced with a club to the jaw.

The woman released the horse's foot, straightening as she turned to face them. At first she appeared to be relieved at the prospect of aid, and even took a half step toward them. But as her eyes took in the group of armed men, their round Norse shields unmistakable, then the smaller group of men huddled and chained together between them, she faltered, then stopped. Her body stiffened with alarm. She spun away, yanking on the horse's reins in a frantic attempt to flee down the road ahead of them.

The horse trailed gamely behind her, but was limping severely on his left front leg; Gunnar knew the animal would not make it far. One of his men chuckled. Another whistled. Then all looked to him for the order to proceed. Gunnar held up his hand, silently signaling them again to hold their position while he scoured the surroundings once more for signs of anything out of the ordinary. After one last hard long look at the empty countryside around them, Gunnar sheathed his sword and retook the lead. The group advanced slowly.

The darkest clouds had still yet to reach them, but the rain fell harder now, and the wind whipped with occasional stronger gusts. Though his men maintained only a slow march, they were steadily gaining on the woman. Every few strides she darted a glance over her shoulder. Each time she saw they were closer, she would tug on the horse's reins with renewed terror. Mud now caked the bottom of her skirt and her shoes, and the extra bulk and weight began to slow her even more. Gunnar was surprised she hadn't abandoned the injured animal by now, but people did foolish things when they panicked. He had seen it so many times before.

The road disappeared into a section of dark forest ahead, and for a moment she was lost from view. After another signal to his men to remain vigilant, they followed her. Gunnar's keenly trained senses took in everything as they entered the trees, his eyes quickly adjusting to the decreased light. Leaves from the taller trees rippled overhead and smaller saplings bent and swayed beside them. Nothing else moved. All animal life, other than them and the woman, was bedded down waiting out the foul weather.

Gunnar cast quick repeated glances at the woman, just long enough to verify she was still there and still frantically pulling at her steed, before returning to scouring the underbrush on either side of the road. After trudging on high alert for what seemed like an eternity, he finally saw signs of the next clearing ahead; the brighter light from the open area was like a beacon. Gunnar began to relax. Their path forward was clear. No blockade, no down or felled tree had appeared to block them. The woman's behavior hadn't changed; she was still desperately laboring in front of them in a futile bid for freedom.

As he watched, she slipped and stumbled to her knees. Only her grip on the horse's reins prevented her from falling headlong into the mud. Using the animal's front leg to steady herself, she clambered back to her feet, then whirled to face them.

FIONA

"Stay back!" she shouted as she backed away, floundering in the mire, the horse bobbing obediently beside her.

A great gust of wind blew the hood of her cloak from her head and, for the first time Gunnar could see her face. Pale Irish skin, huge eyes dark with fear and defiance. She was stunning. Without the protection of the hood, the wind soon freed her long dark wavy hair from its restraint. Red highlights glinted in the moonlight—not the fiery red of so many of the Irish, only hints of red like a prized sable fur. Gunnar, shocked by his visceral reaction to her, took a deep steadying breath.

"I mean it! You stay away from me!" she screamed again. Another gust of wind threatened to tear the cloak from her completely. She spun away from them, her arms flailing in an effort to pull the errant cloth back around her body.

Gunnar signaled his men to stop. The excitement that had been building in them as they stalked her was physically palpable now. The chase was at an end. Their prey was at hand. All could feel it. Gunnar waited for her to turn back to them. Waited to see her reaction when she realized it, too. He was close enough now, he would be able to see it in her eyes. She began to turn.

His eagerness to see her face as she recognized escape was lost, made her movements seem in slow motion. His eyes hungrily took in every detail of her as it was revealed—first, the soft curve of her jaw, then her high cheekbone, then the edges of her thick dark eyelashes. Finally, her eyes—the centers so dilated and dark he was unsure of their true color. So fully expecting was he to see her cowed expression, it took several seconds for Gunnar to comprehend what he actually saw. There was no fear, no resignation, no defeat in her eyes. They were, in fact, the opposite—hard and bright with triumph.

Gunnar frowned, confused. The wind whipped at her cloak again, but this time she made no attempt to stop it. As it lifted away from her body and blew back over her shoulders, she raised the loaded crossbow and aimed it directly at the center of his chest.

"You'll be releasin' those prisoners now," she called out, her voice steady and calm. Gone was any trace of the terror that had seemed to grip her only seconds before. In that instant, Gunnar felt, as much as heard, the forest around them come alive with men. He glanced over his right shoulder at the wall of drawn bows and swords, and swore under his breath. At the same time, he couldn't help but think how his previous commander, Jarl, would laugh at the predicament he'd gotten himself into over a beautiful woman. He had not only forsaken an easily defended position, he had allowed their guard to completely fall away after she lured them into the forest.

"Perhaps you Norse are as hard of hearing as you are ugly," she said. "I said release the prisoners. Now," she repeated menacingly.

Her lilting accent was like water running over smooth stones—pleasing to his ears. He watched as the wind pulled a wild lock of her hair and blew it across her neck. It landed at the base of her wet throat and stuck there. Gunnar stared, mesmerized, as a tiny rivulet of water ran from the soaked tress and disappeared under her dress. His eyes continued to follow its imagined journey downwards until his gaze landed once again on the crossbow. The sight of the loaded bolt aimed at his heart snapped him back to reality.

"Rorick, release the prisoners," Gunnar commanded under his breath, not taking his eyes from the woman.

"But, Sir," Rorick balked. "We can take them. Look at them. They're nothing more than a bunch of armed peasants. They'll be no match for us. We may not even lose a single man."

"Rorick!" This time Gunnar did tear his eyes from the woman, furious at the interruption and lost seconds of appraisal his second's insubordination had cost. "Release the prisoners—now," Gunnar seethed through gritted teeth.

Rorick opened his mouth as if to argue further, then snapped it closed at the look in Gunnar's eyes. He turned and relayed the order to the other men. Gunnar heard their grumbles as the order was received, then heard the clinking as the collar chains on the slaves were removed.

FIONA

"Send them forward," the woman commanded. His men held their ground until Gunnar nodded. The Irish prisoners rushed forward in a wave. Gunnar noted that even as she greeted them and accepted their gratitude, her crossbow never wavered a fraction from its target on his chest. She did not appear to be new to this.

A man appeared on the road behind her, pushing a rickety hand cart. No one moved as he labored toward them, forcing the cart through the mud. Finally he reached them and parked it beside her. She did not acknowledge the man's arrival, was clearly expecting it. Instead, she kept her eyes trained on Gunnar and his men.

"Now, one at a time, come forward and put your weapons on the cart," she demanded.

Amidst more grumbling from his men, Gunnar stepped forward and unbuckled the golden sheath that held his sword, Maid's Dream, from his waist. The bejeweled sword was his most prized possession—an incredible, unique trophy from his most recent Middle Eastern raids. As he laid it on the rough boards, he never took his eyes from her. "This is a valuable and honored family heirloom," he lied. "I would have it back."

She smiled a cold hard smile. "Aye, I'm sure that it is. Perhaps one day, we'll even be lucky enough to return it to the family you stole it from."

"I think I've been most obliging in this negotiation," Gunnar said, ignoring her barb. "You could at least tell me your name."

She looked at him with such utter disdain, it made Gunnar almost smile. Her haughtiness was certainly like no peasant girl he'd ever met before. But then again, he'd never met a peasant so bold who would dare to take up arms to attack Northmen—in feeble attempts to defend themselves perhaps, but never to attack.

"You'll be havin' no need of my name," she said. "You will never see me again."

He wanted her to say more—to say anything, so he could hear her voice and watch her eyes flash, but she only waved him off with the crossbow. After he and his men were herded back into a group in the center of the road, and the handcart was pulled away, she bent down and removed something from her horse's left front leg. Tossing it aside, she led the now-sound animal forward a few steps before climbing onto its back and galloping away.

As the armed men surrounding them melted back into the forest, Gunnar went to search for what she had discarded. He found it just off the side of the road in the underbrush. It was a simple device made from two leather straps and a small blunt piece of wood. When attached to the inside of the animal's leg, it had been unnoticeable, but every time the horse had taken a step, the wood had harmlessly jabbed it, causing it to limp.

Rorick appeared at his side. "Well, I guess that answers the question if the rumors of raiders are true. What now?" he asked.

"Send a small party to retrieve our weapons. Men pulling a loaded handcart in this weather will be easy enough to overtake—if they haven't abandoned it already. The rest of us will return to The Huntress. Tomorrow we'll pay a visit to the slave trader to replace the slaves."

"But we just paid good coin for this lot," Rorick fumed.

"Who said anything about paying for the next ones?" Gunnar said, his voice grim. "Only one man knew we were moving those slaves tonight. And only one man has much to gain by selling twice their number. I shall have a serious discussion with our Dublin friend and show him what happens to those who double cross us."

And discover the identity of his beautiful accomplice in the process.

Acknowledgments

I would like to take this opportunity to thank special people who have made this book and all the ones to follow possible. First I want to thank my mother for instilling in me a passion for reading at a very early age. It opened my mind to the endless possibilities of the world and beyond, and fueled a wild imagination that persists today.

Thanks to my father and stepfather, who provided me with an extraordinarily diverse life. From slicing through pristine snow on top of Independence Pass, to being part of the passionate celebration of freedom at the Brandenburg Tor, from leaping like gazelles in Panama City, to meeting the children of the Eel Clan in Pohnpei, from pulling crab traps and shrimp nets in the deep South, to opera in Hamburg. Looking back, the spectrum of my life experiences is breathtaking. Those experiences not only shaped who I am, they provided me with an immeasurably vast pool of memories to draw from for my characters and settings.

To my husband, I thank you for being a real man in an era where that is so increasingly rare. You are my inspiration, my rock, and my soulmate. It still amazes me every day that two people can be so right for each other. Not that we always agree on everything, (yes, there is a smile in there), but absolutely right for each other.

For my actual writing I thank my fellow Gourmet Writers, Janet and Maryann. I thank you for your candor in telling me when something didn't work, and I thank you for your truly invaluable expert editing. I thank you for all the good food and good times, even when times weren't good. Our meetings and lively discussions were always a bright spot, and I miss them. But it was your unwavering enthusiasm for my stories, week after week, year after year, that encouraged me to persist to publication. Without you, I would still be writing, but it would be unfinished stories and scenes that no one else would ever see.

Thank you, thank you, thank you...Or as Nena would say, *Gratitude.*

For information about the author and other books by Ann Boelter
go to her website:
www.annboelter.com

Printed in Great Britain
by Amazon